Fannie N Smith

Shiftless Folks

An undiluted love story

Fannie N Smith

Shiftless Folks
An undiluted love story

ISBN/EAN: 9783744748186

Printed in Europe, USA, Canada, Australia, Japan

Cover: Foto ©Andreas Hilbeck / pixelio.de

More available books at **www.hansebooks.com**

SHIFTLESS FOLKS.

AN UNDILUTED LOVE STORY.

BY

CHRISTABEL GOLDSMITH.

"My mother chides me when she asks me
Why those tears in silence move.
I could tell her, but I dare not,
All those tears are for my love."
GARDENER'S MUSIC IN NATURE.

NEW YORK:

G. W. Carleton & Co., Publishers.

LONDON: S. LOW, SON & CO.,

MDCCCLXXV.

TO

Her Dear Woman Friend,

JENNIE OWEN KEIM,

IN MEMORY OF

SEVEN LONG YEARS OF COMPANIONSHIP IN LOVE AND LABOR,

THE AUTHOR OFFERS THIS GOD-CHILD.

CONTENTS.

SHIFTLESS FOLKS:

AN UNDILUTED LOVE STORY.

CHAPTER I.

"Rub-a-dub, dub; three maids in a tub."

HIS narration is the tub: and I purpose to have three heroines, and three heroes. Their names are:

MARY McCROSS,	Spinster.
PEACE PELICAN,	"
DOROTHEA MULLIGAN,	"
CYMBALINUS ADOLPHUS BROWN, Bachelor.	
FRANCIS HAYTHORNE,	"
LOUIS ALLWOOD,	"
AMOS DALEY,	"

Besides these there are Mr. and Mrs. McCross, and Mr. and Mrs. Pelican: moreover, as Shakespeare would have it, other knights and attendant spirits, who, being for the most part married and settled, cannot be supposed capable of engrossing the attention of the novel-reading world. If Mr. Hale should look over my list, he would probably think I didn't know "how to do it,"—as well as himself, for I have set down more than my pair of trigemini. But I did it on purpose. Do you suppose

I am going to tell which is which on the first page, and
then roar gently as a suckling dove forever after? Heaven forbid! I have a higher ideal of a novel.

In this day of exact knowledge, when Agassiz clamors
of bones and Huxley of protoplasm, who that studies the
millions in the stars, and the millionths in the globule,
will be unfair enough to drop from the catalogue of
sciences the most profoundly important of all—human-
soul life?

How awful is the task of the heart of the historian,
poet or novelist! and the two gifts are so twin to each
other, that few profess the one without dabbling in its
complement.

To understand their fellows, is the pursuit of all men.
To know life, feel its experiences, see its sights, is the
dominant longing of the young. What reverence did not
our ten years of humanity give us for Pa's silly cousin,
who had been disappointed in love!

The novelist endeavors to make life's mysteries plain.
He it is who delineates the passion, the sorrow, the
strength; who photographs the pangs of mankind; who
teaches people to know and love each other through the
sympathy of a kindred, now revealed, humanity. It is
to the novel that we go for our life pictures. In our
favorite characters we are unconsciously fashioned. National taste, politics, religion, are more moulded in the
masses by the novel, than any other one means of education.

There is no sorrow so deep, no terror so ominous,
that the novelist dare not depict it.

To lodge a true principle in the hard heads of mankind through the unsuspicious sympathy of their hearts,
to help us avoid or bear misery, is the noblest sphere
of novelist or poet; and the trifler who mangles or dis-

torts truth must e'en see his work in human souls burnt out in fire of repentance and agony when he might have given the world a torch to light it on to good.

There is no calling which does not in its complete development touch infinity—and therefore God;—or his opposite.

Nor need the artist, who cares rather for art than humanity, beauty than moral beauty, be outraged hereby. For to present a just type of beauty is to show forth God; who, however, knew no better way to reveal Himself to us than to become man.

So from these poles of dissent we travel around the same circle. Who best shows man reveals God; to reveal God is to instruct man. It is all one. All good things tend to one end. But the poet and novelist are nothing more than professors of the science to whose province belong three eras—passion or motive; action; and condition or result, as you please to call it. Which after all are but three stages of one thing—the fretting of the divinity in man against his carnal limitations.

People can never judge of the worth of a novel to any one but themselves, because its value to a man is always exactly measured by the points where instinct, or instinct worked into experience, touches the thing in hand.

"O dear," said Peace Pelican, settling herself to "Barbara's History;" "one can never properly appreciate a novel till one's been in love and travelled in Europe, and I haven't done either!"

I am, as you know, Christabel Goldsmith. I tell the story. I'm not in it, because Serena, as the saying is, nabbed me in my innocent youth, and put me in hers; so, when long reflection on the above thoughts set me to writing, my best resource was gone, and I had to fall back on *my* friends.

1*

The people in this book are "Real Folks," and to my mind shiftless withal. But I like them on that account. There was a time when I was shiftless myself. That is one reason why I refused the offers of sittings from my present dear half dozen, and chose my characters from the companions of my early youth, who, thank God, have not failed me in my maturer age.

I have no objection to telling you how I became acquainted with them.

Mary McCross is my own cousin. Her mother and mine were Miranda and Hannah Price respectively. I was very young when they quarrelled, but I remember dining at Fir Covert, and seeing Mollie, a little girl about my own age, with childish flaxen curls and blue eyes. She stood up in a state of open mutiny on the step of her high chair, and called for chicken pie, and rejoined, "Keep 'em up, Pop," with immovable resolution, when her father commanded her to be seated. Her will was like iron, and is to this day. People with soft brown hair and blue eyes frequently have such—especially when they possess a pleasant smile, a tolerably even cut forehead, not over, nor under, common breadth and height, and what we call English complexion. Mollie's infant features gradually took on these peculiarities, or perhaps lacks of peculiarity, with womanhood. And when I met her again in after life, I knew her just as well as you do, now I have introduced her to your notice.

There was a little boy, a ward of Uncle McCross, in the house the day we dined there. He lay flat on the ground reading, with his fingers stuffed in his ears most of the time. After dinner he brought me some bumble-bees he caught fearlessly in his hands, and entertained me with the Pedler's Quickstep, performed on the black keys of the piano, by means of both forefingers. Mollie, who had not mastered this scientific performance, stood meanwhile at his elbow, in hearty admiration.

I met Peace Pelican at Herr Groenveldt's school, which we both attended. She was a general favorite, and foremost in all matters of fun—took a prize in mathematics.

I don't know anything first hand about Francis Haythorne's youth. It has been whispered that his mother, a devoted house-keeper, brought him up on "Helen Morris," "Mamma's Bible Stories," and "Tender Truths for Tender Minds." He wore blue and white calico aprons till he was nine years old, roundabouts and slippers till he was turned fifteen, had a tutor, and a pony, whose legs were so short that he used to take his feet from the stirrups and walk up the steep places. His mother, too, entertained a horror of subjecting him to contamination from plebeians and boys, and was a shining light in the mothers' meeting.

It was some years after the Fir Covert visit that I first saw Little Doppy—more correctly, Miss Dorothea Mulligan. The rain had fallen heavily all day, but, clearing at night, papa and I ventured a walk down through Syllabub. Before a puddle of lovely mud, black as jet and thick as pudding, stood this heroine—eying it with longing. Her cheeks were very red, her short hair stood in ringlets all over her pretty head, her pink gingham dress wasn't buttoned up behind, and disclosed white plump shoulders. She swung her fat little arms, said "one! two! three!" and plumped straight into the beautiful gutter. Then she waded out, and, pointing to the adhering soil with exulting glee, cried, "See my new shoes!" Thereupon a rough, black-bearded man, with a pipe in his mouth, took her into the "Solomon Rodgers," kicking and screaming, and shut the door.

Miss Almira Petingil has always been the village tailoress. The other folks came into my knowledge precisely as they will into yours.

CHAPTER II.

"And will you have her, Robin, to be your wedded wife?"
"Yes, I will," says Robin, "and love her all my life."
"And will you have him, Jennie, your husband now to be?"
"Yes, I will," says Jennie, "and love him heartily."

IT had all come about as herein stated, and now the pair were beginning to weave plans and promises, and hopes and reminiscences, in that happy, inextricable tangle that lovers always will weave, and I for one rejoice to have them.

Throughout my tolerably eventful career, I have been the chosen repository of my friends' love affairs, whether because I have happily settled my own, or because my vivid interest in such matters paves the way.

Of all the young folks who have rested their joys and sorrows in my intact (of course!) confidence, these two come nearest to my heart. But they never gave me more than the shell of their affairs—the kernel seemed too sacred in their eyes, even for speech. I have seen trembling lovers and exultant lovers, proud lovers and humble lovers, lovers who said their future spouses' goodness was a constant reproach to them, lovers whose conduct was sure to be a reproach to their spouses. The two people before us do not come into this list. Indeed, while I am on the subject, let me say that I am critical in love. I have no faith in the "woful sonnet to his mis-

tress' eyebrow" class.   I abominate lovers' pains, and
darts and follies.   True love, to me, means perfect
strength, and is therefore perfect peace.   Whether Louis
and Mollie realized it, is a different matter.   Further,
perhaps, I doubted their wisdom in loving at all.   What
right had two gentle, modest, retiring people, who neither
of them knew more of the world than could be gathered
from the simplest of village lives, thus to set out to battle the storms of life together ?   One is reminded of the
" children in the wood : "

> " These pretty babes, with hand in hand,
>   Went wandering up and down."

And so on to a finale of starvation on huckleberries, and
covering of oak leaves, which last about Roaring River
are apt to be a little worm-eaten.

Yet, after all, why should I trouble for them ?   In
love's sweet old story, which every one lives (or dreams of
living) just once in a lifetime, there is a mighty quality
of hope and God-so-orders-it-ness.

Touching the place where all this moralizing has gone
on, it is as homely as tradition paints the cradle of true
love—being nowhere else than Mrs. McCross' kitchen.
And the actors, who are too much absorbed in each other
to heed our scrutiny, are your old childish friends, Louis
Allwood and Mary McCross—both at your service.   The
concomitants are fit enough—a tabby cat purring contentedly in the window, a tall clock ticking behind the door,
a great pan of flour set near the moulding-board and
rolling-pins on the snowy table, a maple-wood fire crackling in the open stove.

I confess, however, that my interest is chiefly in the occupants of the unpoetic, feather-pillowed, chintz-covered
settle—one head laid so close to the other that the short

rings of his nut-brown hair swept her smooth braids scarcely a shade lighter.

"So you take me for better and for worse?" in a half-proud, half-anxious whisper.

"Yes, Louis," laying the face she raised to look into her lover's eyes back on his shoulder composedly.

"Through good report and evil report?" with a smile at the possibility that he would ever bear any repute but good.

Mary straightened herself, took both his hands in hers, and looking right into his soul answered solemnly: "Through good report and evil report, and sickness and sorrow, and death." She was putting her whole purpose into the compact he was too much a boy to fully comprehend. You could see it in every gesture, every expression of her earnest face. Even when she broke the pause that followed her declaration, by archly humming the old song,

"But my heart will be with you wherever you may go ;
Can you look me in the face and say the same, Jeannot?"

it was a mere surface ripple in the steadfast current of a resolve that carried with it all the forces of her life.

But he was earnest too—as far as life had knit him into capacity for it. He was truthful, and sweet in his boyish affection, and enthusiastic—with the easy springing into being of purposes that he had not followed into action enough even to tell their nature.

Boy or man, the young girl was satisfied; and, when he drew her pretty head before him, and gazed a long time into her pleasant eyes—so intent now in their outlook at vowed and faithful love, he saw a depth of something behind their blue, that made him strong for good, though he only knew of it that it was there for him.

Fidus Achates told me, the other day, that civil contracts and weddings had little to do with true marriage.

"That," said he, "is the simple yielding of two souls to each other, so that they are henceforth one ; the rest is only a blessing upon this deed."

Perhaps our pair felt it. They were silent a long while, each thinking his own thoughts. By and by the door opened and admitted Deacon McCross.

"What are you doing?" asked he, in rather short tones for so long a man.

The girl looked up with a strong glad light in her face. "Making love, father," said she quietly.

Louis rose with timid respect. "I have been asking your daughter to be my wife;" and the delicate color which had faded from his cheeks flushed and paled more than once before he finished his explanation. "We have been like brother and sister all our lives. We want to be something more. You will not refuse us?" -

The Deacon twisted uneasily under his daughter's glance. "Not as I know of," said he, looking very uncomfortable. "Her mother 'll make an awful time."

The trio gazed at each other in silence. His words were too true for prophecy. Louis was hurt. Mollie resolved, her father weak and hesitating.

The girl spoke first. "Perhaps she won't mind so much if you don't, dear," said she, hopefully.

"Perhaps she won't," answered the Deacon in a blank tone.

"Mrs. McCross may be more reconciled when she knows how my prospects have improved," began the stripling, in eager longing that an impossible joy should occur. As the Deacon's meek, wrinkled face, and pale blue eyes persisted in their expression of stolid disbelief, he stopped nervously. Mollie thereupon slipped her hand into his to reassure him, and he proceeded with more confidence: "I have accepted a position in the Pelicans' store in Top

Town, and Charley's father offers me a partnership at the end of three years—if I like the position and seem fitted for it."

"Liquor trade is money-makin' business," said Mr. McCross, relaxing. "Them Pelicans knows what's what. But my wife ain't agoin' to be satisfied with no expectations!"

"I shall do my best," answered Louis. "I *will* succeed—only give me time."

Did you ever see a young rooster try to crow when the old one was present? What a disagreement arose directly, and how, sans tail feathers and comb, did the poor little fowl limp away, followed by the exultant clarion of his conqueror. I have noticed something of the same instinct in the dealings of older toward young men. They snub them, criticise them, put them down in the presence of the people they admire most, and rejoice in it. In my day I have seen a great many boys started in stores. I like boys. They are energetic, honest, and free-spoken. A great deal of unpleasant work can be, and always is, got out of them. Yet I never asked after one of these earnest beginners in life, but his employer answered—not, "He does his best; he'll learn;" but, "Oh, he does tolerably; he makes mistakes; it takes a great deal of time to teach him; he'll know more when he's older;" or, meanest of all, "*I* may make a man of him some day; one never gets to the end of a business education."

You contemptible old humbug. Don't he run your errands, handle your goods, stand your ill-temper, fill all the gaps in everything, keep good-humored, and worship "our store"? What more could he do if you asked him?

Even Deacon McCross, whose long discipline in life

ought to have taught him better, turned combative, when Louis tried to talk business with the air of a man who knew about it.

" Young man," said he, putting on a pair of large, silver-bowed spectacles, and bestowing a look of superior wisdom on his wretched victim, " ef there's one thing I hate and despise, its shiftlessness, an' Mirandy sez you ain't nowise free from it."

Meanwhile Mollie sets the table—the McCrosses are as usual without servants—and turns her attention to the neglected biscuits, which go into the oven in no time and come out the perfection of that indigestible dainty.

Mollie was not small nor large, neither slender nor stout, neither beautiful nor homely. She was refined, perfectly free from self-consciousness, and had never had a week's illness in her life. She was therefore graceful. Perhaps the one adjective that describes her is "pleasant." She was pleasant to look upon, pleasant to hear, pleasant as a companion, and like any other pleasant thing, had nothing intrusive about her. She might have been an indigo bird, or a Java sparrow—bating the melancholy creak, or a forget-'me-not. Ah! now we have it !—a personified, modest, honest, stout-hearted, blue-eyed forget-me-not, describes her exactly.

She glided about the place in a deft, easy way—from dining-room to kitchen, from closet to cupboard—setting down the dishes one by one, just where they belonged, and where they stayed with a contented appearance, as if it was a real pleasure to be where she put them. Her father watched her—a fond, proud look glorifying his wrinkled old face. She was the one love of his heart.

Mrs. McCross had gone to tea and a social prayer-meeting at Squire Hitchcock's, so Mollie's table was only laid for three, and, in spite of the business ordeal poor Louis

was passing, they had a cosy supper. Mrs. McCross
said her husband drank his tea strong enough to bear up
an egg. To-night his daughter had brewed it green as an
emerald, and fragrant as a clover-field in full bloom. If
Mollie had a weakness, it was for genuine gunpowder
without sugar. Her father and she found immense com
fort in their kindred dissipation—the maternal head taking frequent occasion to stigmatize their decoction as
"Devil's broth," and generally assuming her seat at
breakfast with the remark :

" Well, Teapot, I suppose you've got to fill up your
stomach and addle your brains as usual."

Under the exhilarating influence of his draught, the
old gentleman waxed eloquent upon his favorite theme.
"There is two kinds of shiftlessness," quoth he, dangling
his tea-cup upon his thumb and forefinger in the characteristic attitude taken by a lover of the drug—just at
such a slant that the contents remained inside by sheer
defiance to the laws of gravitation; "leastwise there's
more, but two especially. It's my belief that the raft of
folks is shiftless in something. Ef they ain't in one they
be in another. There's shiftlessness in business *an'* shiftlessness in piety. It's darned shiftless of a man to waste
the opportunities of the gospel." Here Louis looked uncomfortable, but the Deacon didn't intend to be personal,
and ambled on thoughtfully, " Yes, throw them by year
in an' year out, an' not get religion ; an' its wuss'n that
not to meet a sixty-day note. Ef you bear this well in
mind, children, your firm 'll always have a good name on
'Change Street an' Church Street ; an' them two is all anybody needs."

Here the tea-cup, which Mollie had been sometime
eying with painful fascination, turned clear over, and in-
flicted a beauty spot on Mrs. McCross' beloved table-

cloth, but the originator only sighed sorrowfully, and, obtaining a fresh supply of the treacherous mixture, reinstated it in its former position, where it wiggled and wavered as before.

During his discourse the lovers held a kind of mute conversation, in which every simple action was made eloquent of their happiness. In a true wooing all things become conductors to the electric fluid of love.

"Louis," said Mr. McCross, dismounting from his hobby, "where are you going to board?"

"With Charley, at the Pelicans'. They offered to take me."

The Deacon, who had a belief common to the old that a dish of bread and water and the soft side of a stone is proper fare for the rising generation of his own sex, looked as forbidding as his lank and meek benevolence could compass.

"Is that economy?" he began; "when I was a farmer's boy, and went to New York to make my living, I owned just one suit of clothes and slept under the counter. For three months all I had to eat was beans; and I put my first wages at interest and began my fortune."

Louis had been very proud of his arrangements, and, boy like, looked forward to relating them to Mollie with eager enthusiasm. But now his face fell and he began to think it was all a mistake, and himself not fit to make plans. In short, the golden clouds about his sun of success had faded into dismal gray. He hadn't even courage to defend the course he had taken, and sat nibbling a biscuit he had forgotten to butter, with downcast glances, and bright, evanescent color.

Mollie had appeared far from happy when the Pelican partnership obtruded itself into the conversation; but she would not have him put down. If she disagreed in private, it was all the more reason why he should show a bold front in face of the adversary. She therefore offered him peach preserves with her brightest smile, and proceeded to ask every imaginable question about the Pelican household, and the business, and Top Town, and his ideas of a proper financial basis of operation; under which deferential treatment he once more recovered his equanimity, and answered with cheerful resolution.

Even Deacon McCross relaxed his disparaging expression, and joined in the talk with an air of interest and approval.

" I remember Charley Pelican," said he, setting down his tea-cup for freedom of gesture ; " he was a great boy, up to anything ! "

It is a curious fact that the very traits which bring a lad into an old man's detestation, reflect a kind of savage credit on him when he becomes of age.

" They used to call him Seed Pelican," went on the Deacon, rubbing his wrinkled forehead thoughtfully ; " he put apple-seeds on the stove at protracted meeting. I recollect it well. Miss Goldsmith was there, and her husband, young Fred. Deacon Williams had took a notion to repeat the genealogy of Christ, to show off his memory, and the seeds kept poppin' like a chorus at the end of every line. Then Deacon Proddy rose to pray, an' all the while the seeds kep' on explodin', till, after he'd ben laborin' full fifteen minutes by the clock, he said he'd be brief, as some evil-minded person was disturbin' the meetin'. You see he'd been licensed to preach once, an' was always itchin' to knock his elbows agin the pulpit."

The narrator picked his teeth reflectively, a few minutes, while Mollie entered upon a disagreeable train of thought relative to Louis' probable treatment at the

hands of this incorrigible, and the object of her solicitude recollected how Charley was the best hand to skitter
stones in his whole knowledge, and how no one could begin to match him at marbles, or base ball, or wrestling;
the old man finally relaxing into a chuckle as he bethought him of a certain day, when the thin, lean fish-
monger of the village, John Smith by name, found his
too generalistic door-plate reduced to more particularity
by addition of " Lamprey-eel " in red letters, the reflective
Charley being the author of the amendment. Supper
having been now concluded, Deacon McCross stretched
out his now not over stout legs, shaped indeed a good
deal like riding whips, with the tassel for the foot, and
throwing a red-and-yellow handkerchief over his head,
prepared for a nap. Suddenly an idea struck him.
"Daughter," said he, sitting up straight, still covered
with his brilliant head-gear, "let's sing a hymn."

" Do," answered she gayly, and came near to give him
a loving little pat. " Shall it be China, or Windham? "
Mollie always aided and abetted her father in his bursts
of gayety, never failing to look at him fondly when he
thus took courage, of a tremulous order at best, to assert his right to be jovial, and she frequently assured
him that she thought him very cunning, which she truly
did.

He reflected—gazing with comfortable benevolence
from beneath the pendant ends of his head-gear at the
two young people, who in putting away the tea things
had just hidden themselves, quite unnecessarily, behind
the closet door. " Neither," he observed at length,
brightening still more under the influence of a happy
thought; " it's a trifle different, and quite appropriate ;
your mother and I used to sing it when we were courtin'
Saturday nights."

So saying, he brought from the book-case, with fond pride, a certain venerable and battered singing-book, bearing " White and King" conspicuously printed on the cover, and still enveloped in the mists of those youthful memories, peered over his glasses a long time at the diabolical patent notes. Then he adjusted his children on either side his rocking-chair, and named the tune— Greenland—solemnly beating time with his thumb.

As you may not have the pleasure of familiarity with " White and King," I will subjoin this ancient ditty :

" When Adam was created, he dwelt in Eden's shade,
   As Moses has related, before a bride was made ;
   He had no consolation, but seemed as one alone,
   Till to his admiration he found he'd lost a bone.

" This woman was not taken from Adam's head, we know,
   And she must not rule o'er him, it's evidently so.
   Great was his exultation to have her by his side;
   Great was his elevation to have a loving bride.

" This woman was not taken from Adam's feet, we see ;
   And she must not be abused, the meaning seems to be.
   This woman she was taken from near to Adam's heart,
   By which we are directed that they should never part."

There had been some small by-play during the singing. First the good Deacon smiled a curiously compassionate smile at the young man, and poked him jocularly with his left forefinger, his right hand being occupied in marking the accents. Then Louis sniffed significantly at Mollie when submission was discussed in the second verse, and their leader also turned to her with some emphasis.

Then Mollie reached round behind her father's chair, and revenged herself on her lover by a little vicious pinch, as his duties came under observation, and all three burst into a delighted giggle when the happy consummation was reached.

"There!" said the Deacon, authoritatively tapping the cover with his spectacles. "That's the talk for me; an' all I've got to say is, that in this undertaking which you've entered upon, I hope you'll be successful."

The next day was warm and hazy, and Sunday besides. That is how the pair came to be spending it together in the orchard.

"Louis," said Mollie, knitting up a memorial of Pastor Harms, Wichern, and Kaiserworth. "I long for work—real work. I envy you your path among opposing circumstances. When your life is over, you will have borne mankind's burdens and accomplished something, and reared a better pillar than Absalom's—a structure tangible, created, done!"

"Done brown?" asked the other, looking lazily up at her earnest face from the support of his crossed hands, as he lay stretched out on the grass.

"Not exactly," said Mollie, too much interested in her thought to care for his quirks. "I think there is so much difference between real work, and such as tires us out, and never betters ourselves or any one else. It seems to me that women don't get the right notion of life as men do. I would be willing to suffer a great deal if I could only give the world a very small good. I can't seem to make a little study, a little music, a little German, a little sewing, and all the rest idling, come into my ideal of life."

"You ought to live for your friends," suggested Louis; much as to say, "me for instance."

"You can't," answered Mollie, with the air of one who has travelled wearily through an unsatisfactory train of thought. "They can't live for you, nor you for them—as an end. The minute you try it, you prey on your friend's life, and he on yours. Friendship is the richness of two busy lives flowing into each other; thereby both are strengthened for their own duties and battles. What I want is work; I must have it, or I can't be your helpmeet."

" O dear," said Louis, looking at her with a mixture of admiration and compassion. "Why aren't you satisfied to sit here passive, and sway with the shadows, and be quiet, listening to the beautiful voices the earth has for you, and not fret, out of harmony with it all. It makes me perfectly happy to lie so beside you. I never want the day to end."

This was very sweet. Mollie smiled at the dreamer; but she would not be put off. " Because," she said eagerly, " you are taking a man's earned rest after toil; and the charms of the day are half by contrast with the labor that makes you a firm-muscled man. But you would despise a life of lounging under the apple-trees, with no better end or purpose, and so do I."

" So I should," said the young man, with kindling eye, half rising as he spoke. " I too wish to be something, a man among men. I want to earn wealth and a home, and put you in it. And then we will go onward together. But I think you are wrong about the German and music and culture, they are worthy aims for a life's devotion. Think of Orlandus Lassus' epitaph: 'Here lies the weary who refreshed the weary.'"

" Well, perhaps," said Mollie doubtfully, and then brightening. " Yes, to excel, to help others on, to identify one's self with, as a master; but not to dabble in, Louis; not to dabble in. What I would choose would be to minister to my fellows as an end, and then bend every department of culture to its aid. I have been thinking a great deal about Enoch. You remember Enoch? He walked with God, and was not, for God took him. The idea haunted me, till I had to write it out."

"I don't like Enoch," said Louis, perversely. "I want to have a good time—and that dreadful suggestion of being hurried from danger to desert—and desert to danger—by a power outside of one's self, is too repugnant to be entertained for a moment. I'd rather lie amid some sylvan scene and be comfortable. Or, no," seeing a shadow play over his friend's face, "not that; I am glad to work; I am never idle. Now you know I'm not, Mollie "—she nodded—" but I want to choose congenial work. Please read the verses. I see them sticking out of your pocket; that's something I like. I'd suffer, as you say, if it would make me a poet."

Mollie produced her labor without any comment, and read the whole to Louis, who listened critically, and smiled occasional approval :

" And Enoch walked with God—known through the land
  As one all feared, few loved—Jehovah's friend.
  Mayhap thou'st slowly climbed the granite hills—
  Pushed through the dim fir woods that make their heads
  So wild and fearsome, and come out upon
  Some huge gray rock—the mountain's naked rib :
  Sheer below thee lay the matted tree-tops,
  Wove so close, it seemed a feather trembling
  Down the thin blue air could never pass their leafage.
  Towering in circle stand the hills,
  Joined, as if hand in hand, quiet as silence,
  And half veiled with cedar. Above, the summer sky ;
  Poised in its blue so high, a very mote
  Would hide its flight—an eagle. All the
  Faces of the hills full of a mastered sorrow ;
  A grand peace, a stilly power, vast as a thought of God.
  Akin in nature this to Enoch ; and the Presence with him,
  Even so lonely 'mid the crowd of life,

2

Kept him forever.   Yet the children loved him;
Those happy beings, still too young in life
To have a dread of God, walking with Enoch.
Sad it is that at one gate of earth
We should strike hands with God, our friend;
And, walking through earth's space,
Find at the other gate but a stern Judge,
Who says, 'I never knew you.' Can He change?
Or is it we who have forgot His face?
But Enoch walked with God, did not forget.
When from the grass, in the still summer morn,
Lifting himself, he turned to meet the sun,
Or when the romping children in the town,
Loving to hang upon his strong, firm hands,
Would frame their steps to match his bold, free stride,
And watch with questioning eyes his mouth so sweet;
Or when he bargained in the noisy arch,
Where surged the traffic from first morn till even,
There was a Presence with him all men felt
And feared, and, fearing, hated Enoch, who
Alone feared not.

    Not in wrenched nature, or rude risings up
Of power, this presence came.
He never trembled forth in purple mists
At the gray dawn, or, standing lone,
Forced to the desert by imperious power,
Enoch heard no inarticulate murmur of a loving voice
Call in his ear.

                Or in marches long
Resting an hour in balsamy cedar groves,
Stooping to drink from the clear running brook,
No loved grave face mirrored beside his own,
Thrown back in broken dimples from the spring.
It was a Presence deeper, grander yet,
Than these fantastic utterances would show—
A calm, full rest within his inmost heart—
A mighty stirring of his deepest self,
That moved the man to proclaim awful words—

Pity and wrath, vengeance and love and pain,
Felt by the Highest, touching Enoch's soul.
For 'twas with soul matched to the Almighty pulse
Of the Great Heart, that Enoch walked with God."

"Now, Mollie," said Louis, getting off his grassy couch and shaking himself, "that's theology, and you promised to stop flinging it at me. It's no fair."

He stretched out his hand for the paper as he spoke, and scanned the lines, with a provoking little smile that only made him more delicately handsome.

"I won't be pelted with religion," he continued, pettishly. "Baxter quarrelled so, the only rest the neighboring saints had was in his absence, and I don't believe in it, anyway. I love you, but oh! Mollie sweet, not your hobby. Let us have peace. Besides, how can I believe without a change of heart? and really I can't change it, because you've had it these dozen years. Now truly, honest Injin, is it fair?"

He was so playful, and so coaxing, and so really in love with her, that she gave a little sigh to the despised theology, and only looked at him with happy eyes. Brown-haired, brown-eyed, slender, with a cheek that paled and flushed with every varying emotion, she could find no fault in him, religionist or sceptic. It was all the same to her, in her craving, over-mastering love. "Come back! come back!" said she; "I'll be quiet while you read 'Phantasties.'"

"Ah! that's better;" and the stripling returned to accept the proffered book, and walk an afternoon's march further into Mollie's life. .

"I'll sing a hymn, if that will comfort you," said he, throwing down the volume, and studying her face, for fear a shadow might have come upon it from his resolved following of his own humor. I'm not a statue or bewitched, but I feel sore from the crown of my head to the sole of my foot, I've been so belabored with the Bible. From Aaron's rod to Elijah's staff, all the cudgels have come upon my back. He took up a guitar lying on the grass beside them, and set the strings vibrating among themselves as if they spoke by their own impulse, not his. Shall it be, " When marshalled on the nightly plain," or "Brightest and best," sweet heart?

"Louis," said Mollie obstinately, "I believe I was right in the matter of Enoch. I stick to it. If you liked you could see it too. I know the metre is wrong, but the spirit is correct, anyway."

"The spirit is willing but the flesh is weak. Eh ? " retorted he, airily. "Well, if I can't sing your Calvinistic theories asleep, I'll take to slumber myself. After all, Mollie, you are my best religion.

> 'Plus blanche que la blanche hermine,
> Plus pure qu'un jour de printemps,
> Un ange, une vierge divine.' "

His silver tenor half sung, half whispered the words, and before the Huguenotish strain was concluded, he had really slipped into dreamland—lying with his arm thrown under his head, in the careless, boyish grace of youth.

Mollie dropped her book to watch the shadows play to and fro on his upturned face, and indulge in the luxury of loving him—her own—never to be shared with another—all hers—and forever.

CHAPTER III.

"Humpty Dumpty sat on a wall ;
Humpty Dumpty had a great fall."

HE scene shifts from the McCross' pleasant orchard, in the heart of Millville, to the streets of its humble dependant Syllabub. Time—another warm autumn afternoon. Dramatis personæ—two ragged boys disputing over a pile of worm-eaten boards. In the foreground a small story-and-a-half unpainted cottage, with a hieroglyphical sign swinging over the door—

" Old Solomon Rodgers, with  ,

Affords entertainment to  ."

That sign had been put there in Revolutionary days, when the tavern was the resort of all the country-side, from the red-coated gentleman who called for his ale at the door without dismounting from his handsome steed, to the louting plough-boy leaning against the fence to stare at his betters. Old Solomon himself, a portly red-faced Englishman, who had watched the gentry build their quaint houses and plant their rambling gardens about his humble mansion, and had drunk to King George till the last of his patrons found a refuge from patriotic treason in the village church-yard, was fain to follow them loyally to the end. If any one cares to push aside the tangled grass that hides his weather-worn tombstone, he can read in mossy letters, deep cut in the glittering mica-schist (Latin to match the times):

HIC JACET SOLOMON RODGERS
OF THE
KING'S ARMS, WHO DIED A
LOYAL SUBJECT OF ENGLAND,
A.D. 1812."

And now that he and those he reverenced are alike gathered to their fathers, the brawling occupants of a factory suburb spank their children and anathematize each other amid the carved stairways and decayed grandeur of the gentle; and to-day, when our story begins, one Patrick Michael Mulligan dispenses goat's milk manufactured, and cherry brandy of suspicious parentage, at the stand of their simple neophyte.

The gardens where blue-eyed Faith and sparkling Prudence wandered and dreamed are crowded with uncouth brick tenements; and white-headed, dirty children play in gutters, which net the very thyme-bordered plots once sacred to the old-fashioned fellowship of the hollyhock and rose. Squalor and filth have reign; and decency, compelled by fear in daylight, leaves free course to folly and crime when once the shadows have fallen.

Nay the less, the old sign, as I have said, creaked through all these changes, and on the day when the events I chronicle befell, two weeks' rain had rusted its fastenings to a more mournful tune than ever. I have always thought these hoarse mutters had vast meaning, but time, alas! has made them as unintelligible as the blackened inscription which I can read only because my grandmother remembers it.

The conversation going on beneath its antiquated dignity had nothing of these reminiscences to mar its realism. Shade of gentle Lady Arabella, draw not near!

" If you don't tote them ere boards to the Cross-Roads, I'll lick you," exclaimed Amos Daley, who was tall, with black hair and gray blue eyes. He stood full half a head higher than Hugh, and looked able.

" I won't," said Hugh, setting his arms akimbo, much as to say, " Come on, if you dare."

The miserable, worm-eaten, snail-tracked, mud-crusted heap of contention didn't seem worth the challenge, but neither boy was insensible to the charming prospect of "punching his adversary's head," and, when he was subdued, crowing over him.

They were evenly matched. Hugh had the advantage of a better fitting dress and firmer flesh than Amos; he was, indeed, rather cat-like in motion and muscle; whereas Mr. Daley had just reached that stage of growth where his joints were loose, his motions sluggish and uncouth, and his bones gave the impression of being far too big for his body.

There can be no aggravation to a Syllabub boy equal to a clog-dance of defiance, performed by a little chap on the other side of an insignificant defence, such as the present heap of kindlings. Mr. Daley made a lunge forward over the same, caught his foot therein, and sprawled; while Hugh, who had darted clear round it and hit his foe a blow in the back, performed another dance, enlivened with whistling and snapping of fingers. A big dog also rushed from behind a pig-pen and took the nether integuments of our hero in his teeth, with vicious growls.

" Sheure for onctht yer gittin yer due, Amos Daley. An' is it to steal yer here? Hold 'im, Skip! " cried a ragged girl, appearing in the door-way. Little Doppy had not fulfilled the promise of her babyhood—lean,

skinny, freckled, with a pair of brown eyes large enough
for the Nova Scotia Giantess, she quite warranted Amos'
sulky retort:

"Yis, 'n more'n my due whin I have to look at yer
ugly mug—darn your pup, he's enough like you to be yer
own brother, he is." This was also true, if bony form
and ragged hair be likeness.

Doppy, however, felt the insolence of the rejoinder, the
more that Hugh added a rasping laugh at her expense.
She therefore sent the contents of a water dipper with
a vigorous aim full in the grinning face of the prostrate
foe, and shying the utensil itself at his accomplice,
banged the door; then instantly reappearing at a window
up-stairs, shrieked, "Larn manners next time," in flush
of victory.

"Oh, I'll be as iley as a barrl of kerrycine if you'll
call off the dog," said Amos, fain to retrieve by art the
losses of war. We may well say loss, for if Skip's attentions continued much longer, he felt that there would be
a separation from the garment of the particular blue
patch now tackled so vivaciously, and had a reasonable
dread of the next canine procedure.

"Do," said Doppy, with withering scorn; "but you
wouldn't be nothin' better 'n fish ile." After which she
complied with his request.

Enter Aleck Heffron, with boards.

"Where were yees after gittin' 'em?" cried Amos,
feeling inquisitively at the point of doggish attack, and
sighing with relief to find the aforesaid patch still there.

"You hain't missed 'em from the great River Hotel,
where you board?" inquired the new-comer with biting
irony.

"No, I'd turn up my landlord if he didn't keep better
at our house,"

"Town-house," corrected Hugh; "jest comin' from there, you'd orter know."

As Doppy was still within sight at the window, the trio shouted a stave in shrill chorus—just out of range from chance missiles, while they picked up their dusty burden, and they jumped and yelped long after the house was left behind :—

> " If I had an old wife to bother my life,
> I'll tell you what I'd do, woo-woo-wooow—
> I'd set her afloat in a leaky boat,
> To paddle her own canoe, woo-woo-wooow."

" Bow-wow-wow," chorused Skip, who, urged on by Doppy, had followed up the amiable serenaders. " You'd better git, or I'll go for you," shrieked she, shaking her dirty little fist. Hereupon the cavalcade took to their heels in good earnest, and arrived at the spot destined by their aspiring ambition for the store, much panting, and looking back fearfully; and we may as well follow Doppy's scornful example, and leave them to their work.

Just at this moment a riding party were moving away from Fir Covert. Mary McCross, in a sage-green habit, we know; and you may have met Mr. Cymbaline Adolphus Brown, nephew of Captain Slocum. He has accompanied friend Serena to the Catskills, and travelled in Euwope with a party, since the date of our present equestrian excursion.

The magnificent brunette, in maroon velvet, with a long white ostrich plume in her coquettish cap, is Peace Pelican, who has come down to Millville to visit Susy Jenkens. Francis Haythorne rides beside her, tall, spare, with clear, sharply cut features, and hair, eyes, and beard, all shades of the same splendid fiery hue. You know the old couplet:

2*

" With a red man, read thy read ;
    With a brown man, break thy bread.
    With a white man, draw thy knife ;
    From a black man, keep thy wife."

There *is* something profoundly repulsive in a white-
eyed, red-lidded, white-faced, white-lipped, white-haired
man, deny it if you can.   But all honor to the red people.   I never met one whose temper was not as true and
good as hasty, and the tale of whose virtues and freckles
was not exactly equal.   A red head may outlast its ruddy
color, the bright cheek it emulates may pale, but the hot
pulsations of the heart that lights them, can never cool
to generosity or faithfulness; or energetic kindness to its
loved, and quick forgiveness of its hated.   Yet, for all
this, do not pray for a red-haired millennium, unless you
are equal to a counter-irritative diet of Cayenne.   For
this people, the sun always rolls itself in thunder or in
smiles; the path of life leads either straight up hill, or
down.   Still, as only ruddy David could have assembled
about him a Jonathan, a Joab, a Bathsheba, and a Solomon, my opinion is firm.   There are two kinds of red-
haired : those, my favorites, who flame like lighted charcoal in open air; and those, better students, but less lovable, who smoulder like charcoal in the pit, ready to burn
bright on occasion.

Mr. Haythorne belonged to class number two.   His
hair had grown with years into a rich chestnut, and curled
slightly; his eyes were reddish hazel, like a fox's tail.
He rode indolently ; as if, being fairly on horseback, he
never meant to go to the trouble of dismounting, and
had grown there.   Here he made a sharp contrast to
Mr. Brown, who gave snobbish attention to toes and
elbows, and airily cleared his saddle at every step.   Peace
Pelican, too, displayed all the elegant graces of a Top

Town riding-school, while Mollie went on in her usually unobtrusive style, so that no one knew whether she performed her part well or ill.

It is delightful to whip Pegasus to a gallop when the day is cool and the roads are fine. So our troop thought, at least. The clear, white sunlight of New England lay over hill and wood. I have always believed New England's religion and Sabbaths were as much fed on her sunshine as the Bible. It's holy purity has something of heaven in it. On this autumn afternoon it penetrated the gray-green, granite-dotted pastures, the clumps of dark-leaved chestnuts, the pale willows by the water-courses, the lichen-decked fences, the gurgling, hurrying river, the black, fir-crowned mountains that framed the scene. Autumn butterflies floated over the haycocked fields, aged crickets wooed loudly in the meadows, dragon-flies shimmered above the ponds, bobolinks and blue birds and starlings aired gayly the mysteries of wings. All was as peaceful and strong and delicate as is the home of the Puritans in its very essence. It needs not Bret Harte's exquisite words to recall

> " Some boyish vision of an Eastern village,
>   Of uneventful toil,
>   Where golden harvests followed quiet tillage
>   Above a scanty soil."

The white-spired church with its row of drooping elms, the busy red mill nestled in a hollow half up the steep, the spotted lilies and dodder, and cardinal flowers of meadow and wood—how do they stand to us Godward, emblems of purity and peace, in all the weariness and wants of after life!

Still, as I have said, the secret is mostly in the sunshine, and under its spell our young folks raced and frisked and caracoled, till sheer lack of breath brought them, in a staid quartette amble, down the steep hillside.

Said Mr. Haythorne, pulling off his hat and letting the sun gild his auburn mane, "This afternoon is enough to make even poor Yorick replace his night-cap on his battered crown, and see beauty in life. On such a day as this, I am a saint."

Mollie surveyed him playfully. "I echo Sancho Panza," quoth she. "Thou art the first saint on horseback that ever I saw."

"Where else do you see them nowadays," said Peace, secretly tickling her indolent escort's steed, in the hope that it would give him a little shake-up, and venting some inwrought bitterness in her speech. The mettlesome animal shied out a couple of yards, and stood on his hind feet once or twice; but his rider was glued to his saddle, and only smiled a complacent "Thank you" at the attentive friend. "One hardly expects to find them among the Great Unwashed," resumed he, reining his horse into line again.

The relation these two held was peculiar. Something in his egotistic—he was egotistic—unruffleable, lazy tranquillity aggravated Peace to fever heat; and he, on his side, could never make up his mind to let her alone, in spite of her flouts and jeers, which she aimed so incessantly that some must needs rankle.

Now she eyed him with vivacious disfavor a moment, and then retorted, "For my part, I never see a broadclothed, self-satisfied biped, bestriding his sleek steed like a clothes-pin on a pumpkin, without remembering Oliver Wendell Holmes on the subject."

The color mounted to the roots of his auburn hair, but he gave a placid smile, and snatched from an overhanging tree a handsome cluster of wild cherries, which he tossed gallantly into her lap.

Mr. Brown, who had overheard the colloquy, pushed the other side of Miss Pelican, and cried artlessly, "Do repeat them ; I haven't seen anything spicy since I read Plurabustah in bed last week."

"I thought you meant to say, ' Boots at Holly Tree Inn,' " retorted she, facing round, and alluding to Mr. Brown's favorite topic of conversation. "No! if you want to hear them, ask Mr. Haythorne."

" Certainly, if smiling Peace wishes it," said he in a low distinct voice. "These are the lines to which I believe she alludes :

> " ' Come, gather your reins, and crack your thong,
>   And make your steed go faster ;
>   He doesn't know, as he ambles along,
>   That he has a fool for his master.' "

He looked square in her face as he repeated them, so that she reddened with consciousness of her unladylike implication, and giving her horse a sharp blow, sent him prancing and rearing up the road till he reached a little bridge over a certain pretty shady brook, where he turned round and round a full dozen times, and then shot forward like mad.

It was quite impossible to be long angry with Peace. She was so royally, piquantly handsome, and her malice was so childish, her storms so thoroughly the offspring of her own soul fret, which only broke upon their victim by accident—she was so generous and impulsive and true, one must needs forgive her from mere admiration of her beauty and amusement at her freaks. And Francis Haythorne forgot her biting tongue before he had spent five minutes watching her white plume dancing on before

him, and her tall, graceful figure swaying limberly to the
motion of her shying yellow horse. He was the most
thin-skinned of men, though he had never gauged his
strength with opposition enough to learn the first lesson
of self-distrust. But instead of wounding, she interested
his lazy complacency; so, without any apparent hurry or
intention, he was again beside her, calm and deliberate as
before.

She did not seem to have at all composed her ruffled
feathers, however; and rode along the stony margin of the
foot-path, leaping an occasional log, and holding her face
averted till they reached a second brook—this time shallow and sunny as brook could be. She might take her
road over the bridge beside her escort, who was politely
waiting her, or wade through the rivulet, which would
scarcely wet her horse's hoofs. She cast a quick glance
on his pleasantly smiling face, and resolved—shame inducing a certain angry meeting of her handsome black
brows—to give him the whole road though the stream
reached the saddle girth. Which it really did, for her
charming steed, after a vicious kicking at the clear bright
water which sent his rider in a hasty leap to the ground,
deliberately knelt down, and rolled, saddle, bridle, stirrup,
all—over and over and over in the refreshing liquid.

He was beginning a fourth revolution when she caught
the reins as they came uppermost, and, jerking his head out,
let the brute through the brook, which she crossed herself
with a prodigious jump, that nothing but the bitterest
wrath could have accomplished in safety. The smile was
so broad on Francis Haythorne's well-bred features, that
he beamed like the full moon turned sarcastic; and, ruling
his delight into solemnity perfectly maddening, he dis-
mounted and held the dripping stirrup up with the gent-
lest care.

"Do take my horse," said he; "this saddle is wet through. I can easily change my dress, and I know you can ride without the horns."

But Peace waved him off, mortified and stormy. "If you want me to mount, do so yourself," said she, flourishing her whip with suggestive vigor; and she led her own aquatic Pegasus to a stone wall and was on his back in a twinkling of the little viper's laughing eyes, which offered curious contrast to his muddy but innocent yellow nose. Her sympathizing friend had wisely galloped before; but the young lady followed him at a dead run, and reining Sandy almost upon his haunches, exclaimed in a voice quivering with passion, "You've made me lose my self-respect twice to-day! Now let me alone! I shall hate you just as long as I live—there!"

"I hope so," said he cheerfully; "I can bear anything but insignificance. Shall I lead your horse?"

"Don't you dare so much as to look at me," cried she, actually quivering with temper, and twice as handsome as ever; "and don't press too close, either, or you will get muddy, and that would break your heart, you know."

Francis Haythorne might perhaps be a wee trifle dandified in his dress—or would have been, if his taste was not so exquisite and quiet. He had therefore received a shot in his vulnerable point, and sulked in concert with the angry beauty.

"Here are the Cross-Roads," said Mollie, who seemed as little pleased with her ride as the pouting couple she joined. "Let's sweep past at full speed, and go home."

The proposal was received with favor, and the company prepared to ride rough-shod over the last resting-place of the unhappy suicide buried there, when a horrible noise smote their ears, and produced an unlooked-for catastrophe.

Hugh, Amos, and Aleck, having put up their modest booth, roofed the same with a probable remnant of one of Mrs. Noah's window-curtains, and sat in state over the stock-in-trade (two apples, six peanuts, and a mug of lemonade) till all was consumed. Tiring of this, they unconsciously forestalled Gilmore, and resolved to have a band. They therefore took to themselves other spirits, and, being fully equipped with whistles, bones, a conch-shell, and an old tin pan, inaugurated their minstrelsy for the benefit of our equestrians. Judging from the discomposure of the horses, they could not have been familiar with village instrumentation. In spite of Peace's endeavors (she was too proud to make a sound), Sandy betrayed his breeding by walking up to the booth, and, putting his fore-feet on the third fence-rail, endeavored to fire off an imaginary pistol; failing in which, he composedly knelt down, and dropped her over his head as he had learned to do little boys at the circus, and, entangled in her long dress, she was obliged to allow the complaisant Haythorne to lift her to her feet.

"There!" said she, "I hope you're happy now; that whole grocery store full of idlers and loafers is grinning at us like Cheshire cats. Go away! I'll never get on him again as long as I live—never!" But Sandy now stood with his nose at her pocket, searching for sugar, as meek and innocent as if he had never kicked a fly in his life, and she couldn't help forgiving him on the spot, and fed him all the sweets she had directly.

Old Mulligan's dog Skip, however, had a deeper rooted abhorrence of Amos. He came along just then, and rushed at his bare toes as he stood balancing himself on the sharp fence-rail, whither he had climbed to make the conch-shell more effective. The unfortunate boy hopped with surprising agility, brandishing his instrument in one

hand, and in the other the pole of the shanty, pulled up
in his fright. He made a fine figure, his tattered garments streaming in the wind ; but it could not save him.
A miscalculated leap, and boy and building mingled
in a confused kicking heap. At this Mollie's horse lost
his composure, and began bucking, which of course
brought her to the ground without ado. Mr. Haythorne, who, after his last Peace-ful repulse, had withdrawn a little distance, and stood watching the scene
with indolent amusement, heard a faint cry. Seeing
Miss McCross's saddle empty, he hurried to her aid.
But she was on her feet before he reached her, and shook
herself gayly. "I am not hurt; hurry, and help the poor
boy."

"He probably knows enough to get up," said Francis
Haythorne, casting a disdainful glance at the dusty ruin
from whence issued piteous howls. "Idle dog, he de-
serves a whipping for heading such a performance."

Mollie looked disappointed a moment; this didn't
realize her ideal man at all. After a short hesitation,
she gathered up her skirt, and dodging through the fence
helped the snivelling child to his feet. He might well
give way to tears; besides wounds and tatters personal,
the shanty of his pride was demolished, and worst of all,
there sat little Doppy astride the fence-rail, cold-piece
basket on arm, making faces at him.

The other lads gathered near, and glanced with unim-
pressible face, but active curiosity, from the elegantly
dressed young lady to their forlorn companion.

"Are you much hurt?" asked Mollie kindly, wiping
his bleeding face with her soft handkerchief.

"Not as I knows on," with a sullen shake of the
shoulder where her light hand rested.

But the sunny-hearted girl smiled down into his eyes

so openly and brightly, that every one was infected by
her pleasantness, and grinned in concert. "Don't you
think a big paper of peanuts would be some comfort?"

She never thought what a lovely tableau she made in
her graceful, girlish, dignified compassion. It was almost
a pity that the red-haired aristocrat should have had the
benefit of it. Peanuts? What music dwells in the
word! She slipped the money into Amos' hand, pointed
to the store opposite, and sprang quickly to her saddle.
Riding away, they found Mr. Brown judiciously halting
half a mile from the scene of tumult. And here Peace
had her revenge, for Francis Haythorne, who had insisted upon mounting her horse, was brushed neatly off
against a tree, by the incorrigible Sandy, who then turned
round and laughed, as the crestfallen horseman picked
his sprawling length from the dusty road. Two beautiful tortoise-shell kittens had been sleeping in the sun, on
the wide piazza of the grocery opposite the booth, and
in double fright of Skip and the racket, darted into
the great branches of the overshadowing chestnut-tree.
Now, entering the secret precincts, a scampering and
scratching ensued that all the cats in the Salem witch-
craft couldn't have beaten. Then came stillness, and,
with the pussies' reappearance, an odor that erected all
noses in anguish.

"Drat them animiles!" said the fat grocer, taking
his Irishman's meerschaum from his mouth; "they've
ben an' tipped over the whale-oil on to theirselves.
They beat all I ever see for worretin' an' cantankerin'.
I promised them to little Doppy, but I don't calkelate to
stand this. Yesterday I finds 'em asleep in the meal tub,
and to-day they gnawed up half a chicken. Here, Amos,
just you go an' kill 'em, and when you come back I'll give
you an orange."

The rosy merchant returned to his town politics with relieved mind, and Amos, nothing loth to do his errand, shuffled off with the doomed felines, holding them by the tips of their tails, as one would a dirty pocket-handkerchief.

" Amos—Amos Daley," called Doppy's voice, "give me them cats."

"Wouldn't you like 'em?" returned he, with the ugliest grin his bruised features could assume, and jiggled them up and down to "get the music out on 'em."

"Now you'll learn to throw water on me."

"O Amos! do give 'em here."

"Shan't; I'll cut their tails off and roast 'em for breakfast. Father's short of fresh meat." He went on with his occupation as he spoke, with the greatest enjoyment.

"You mean, dirty Irish boy!" cried Doppy, white with rage, and stamping hysterically. "Give me them cats; you hurt 'em."

"Good to make 'em grow long," returned Amos, varying his exercise by sometimes grasping a leg or an ear, careful to keep them always in full view.

Doppy made a rush at him, stopped half way, and, with a look of perfect despair, threw her apron over her head, dropped in a heap in the road, and began to sob in concert with the cattish howls.

Amos gazed at her, transfixed by amazement. He shifted the kittens to one hand, and scratched his head to wake himself, while mouth and eyes flew wide open. Was it possible that his ruthless foe was reduced to this? Was that curious complication of pink calico and brown pinafore, rocking back and forth in such bitter grief, really she? He advanced a little nearer; the kittens wailed; she sobbed afresh. He put his free hand in his pocket and felt of his jack-knife to bolster up his courage,

fast ebbing before this painful sight, and strove to preserve his stolid face. This being a dismal failure, he
shook the kittens with a virulence exceeding all previous malignity, but his heart still sank.

The little girl shuddered. "Amos," cried she, lifting
a face where the tears had washed two white channels,
"I hain't nothin' of my own but one bead ring, an'—sob-
sob—a-a china mug, but I'll give 'em to you if you won't
kill the cats."

Poor little Doppy! she was so nice crying. His
friends had no such fondness for their animals. Master
Daley's resolution vanished utterly. Perhaps he'd better,
—he took half aim, and threw one kitten at her, just to
try the effect.

She gathered it in her skirts and kissed its head passionately, and wiped and cuddled it, crying all the while.
And then, somehow, the other kitten was laid with its
fellow, and some one was saying soft words in a harsh,
boyish voice: "Don't cry now, sis. I hain't hurted 'em
of no account, and you've got 'em safe. Don't, there's a
dear. Say, I'll give you all my peanuts if you won't squall
no more." Amos adored peanuts.

It took some time to convince Doppy of his kind in-
tentions. But at last she dried her eyes on her oily apron,
and began to smile. It made a strange alteration in her
pinched, weary face. In its bright glory her best self
shone forth, womanly, sweet, and lovable. "I don't want
your nuts," said she, gratefully. "I didn't know you
were so good. I'm sorry I sprinkled you;" and a gleam
of roguish amusement tucked the corners of her mouth
into what should have been dimples, and still hinted at
beauty.

Amos laughed too, and answered with some remorse:
"I ain't good; it was mean to jigger your pussies; but I

won't plague you no more, never." His keen gray eyes were bent in very friendly sort upon the other party to this compact, for compact it was, and, when he asked to carry her rescued prizes, she gave them into his keeping with implicit confidence, and they were gently snuggled against his jacket all the way to the "Solomon Rodgers."

. . . .

"Mr. Hoskins, I killed them darn brutes as you telled me; will you give me the orange?"

CHAPTER IV.

" Can she make a cherry pie, Billy boy, Billy boy?
Can she make a cherry pie, charming Billy?
She can make a cherry pie
While a cat can wink her eye.
She's a young thing—she can't leave her mammy!"

WHEN Miss McCross descended the stairs next morning, she was stopped by Bridget, whose cheeks were streaky red with grief.

"Me cousin be dead, mum, and we want to give him a three nights' wake, and an illegant funeral. Would ye mind gittin' the breakfast, and lettin' me go now?" The young Celt's face was like a house with two tenements—the up-stairs half all smiling at the prospect of three evenings' fun, but the down-stairs part solemnly mourning the corpse.

Retiring visions of garden-work, sewing, letters, friendly visits, flitted forlornly through Mollie's mind. When did the prospect of a week in woman's normal sphere fail to strike the victim with disgust. Greasy dishes, crocky pots and spiders, aching bones, blistered fingers! Ugh!

Mollie resolved to put a pleasant face on the matter, since there was no help for it. Assuring the mourner that she would do the work in her absence, she made a few consoling inquiries about the bereaved family, especially a certain long-legged widower supposed to be sweet on Bridget. The bright-eyed serving-maid appeared extremely gratified at the friendly interest, although she tossed her head and said, "she hoped she was intirely too principled to think of a man as old as him—forty if a day!"

So she gave a little frisk up-stairs, and put on her best purple Sunday-go-to-meeting dress and a blue bonnet, and took a yellow sun-shade, and green plaid shawl with a red and black stripe in it, and hurried away to the funeral, leaving Mollie to wash up a great pile of tea-things which her grief the preceding night had induced her to set away dirty.

The doorstep to the back kitchen entrance is a great foot-worn rock. There we will sit comfortably, and play with the green and yellow parrot, while the new cook gets breakfast. We have known of her being high-priest at these altars before, and so are not worried at our prospects. Besides, the kitchen is a kind of architectural poem, good for lay contemplation, and we own to being not only lay, but lazy, and sniffing the fragrant coffee, and watching preparation of the tear-provoking onions with luxurious content of inaction. We feel a kind of awe of these hallowed precincts. We are gazing at a monument to the housekeeping genius of whole generations of Prices, called and chosen to their pursuit as fanatically as Lord George Gordon, or any other assassinating enthusiast. It is wainscoted with so many doors leading into pantry, store-room, sink-room, china cupboard, tin cupboard, and the like, that there is scarcely an inch of room for the yellow pine ceiling. It looks out on beds of herb garden, where Mollie's grandmother had collected every possible leafy medicine, from tansy and sage, to catnip and boneset, and sweet thyme, and African marigolds, these last—charming garnishes for soup.

Mollie was worthy of her ancestors. It is a pleasure to this day to eat at a table of her setting. We must dine; but let refinement, not pheasants' tongues, grace the board. Our heroine was a true artist. She didn't admire tongue cut into Chinese mandarins, and chicken pressed into lizards and elephants. But on a ground of spotless damask she liked to mingle pale-green cucumbers in cut glass, and red and yellow tomatoes glittering under ice, cress fresh and crisp from the garden, toast delicately streaked with brown, in its silver rack. When her work was complete, all was simple, inviting, wholesome. It would have been so without the handsome tableware that was the pride of Mrs. McCross' heart. She always insisted on using the solid silver tea-service, and accompaniments, on the ground that they saved crockery; her daughter washed them daily in a bright tin basin, with a little white dish-cloth, that had a long handle. Louis thought she never looked more sweet and lovable than when fulfilling this trifling duty; though he was firmly resolved that Mrs. Alwood should do nothing of the sort, except, perhaps, weed the garden of an evening, with himself to oversee and carry her watering pot, and after work trundle her home to the door in a spruce wheelbarrow painted blue. But Louis was boarding in the village, above the harness shop—had been for three months—and the cheerful song that Mollie sang over her cookery grew fainter as she neared the awful time of serving up, and finally gave place to a look of worried expectation, as she sounded the two-toned breakfast bell in the hall, and cast a glance of anxious scrutiny over her completed handiwork. A pair of daintily etched vases still wait their flowery burden, and Mollie hurries to the garden to remedy the omission. There is plenty of time; Mrs. McCross is always late.

It is a trite observation, that flowers and children, more than anything else, appeal to the good there is in us. This is partly because we soften when we remember the holinesses of childhood, which carries in its hand two symbols—a butterfly and a flower. In baby days a Marguerite, an acorn, a Jacob's Ladder, which we, happier than the Patriarch, could find on any summer hillside— toys of God's own making—satisfied our purer instinct. True, maturity and age prefer to give a high price for labored imitation, but our souls always see the cast-off treasures in a halo, rainbowed through the prism of a tear.

And poets who claim a kind of modern prophetic insight are faithful to the outgrown blossoms. Burns could dwell on the days when

> " We twa hae paidlit in the burn,
> An' pu'd the gowans fine ; "

and Hood lament, in more studied phrase,

> " The roses red and white,
> The violets and lily-cups,"

of innocent boyhood. What dabbler, even, does not fancy that mere mention of these divine flowerets that gem a familiar hillock is the password to the heights of God- like Olympus, and maunder about roses and tulips and violets in an a-b-c andrian style, that we forgive for love of his subject ?

The least-cultured instinct reaches out toward flowers. It is no association of cultivated thought and æsthetics that brings a pot of scarlet geranium to grace the humblest artisan dwelling—sets the felon's picciola against the barred windows that piteously contrast. It was no elegant refinement of taste that gave a matron in an English jail the saddest sight she ever beheld—a bold, bad woman gloating over a common field daisy stolen from the prison yard. There is some subtile relation between the good and true in the human soul, and the spirit of beauty whose vital force moulds the poorest blossom into harmonious shape and color, which gives these growing thoughts of God a language that needs no coarse intervention of sound, but conveys emotion independently to the soul.

Our truest friend can only imitate the fidelity of the flowers who follow us into every season of life. First, religion's Christmas holly, and the snowdrops and lilies of Easter confirmation; then love's rose-buds, and orange-blossoms for the wedding; later, separation brings the forget-me-not and pansy; and ere the sexton strikes his spade in the earth, our best-loved casts a bit of green into our grave.

Most things end with the tomb, and having reached this point, I don't see how Miss McCross' meditation could have gone any further, even if she had not seen little Doppy.

It was really a great mistake on this infant's part that her five-o'clock visit should have been so prolonged. She had pulled her onions, and stowed away her beets, and gathered her apples—they lay near in a dilapidated basket—but still she lingered.

Mollie came upon her crouching on the damp ground, ready to spring away at the very rustle of a twig, and

3

yet forgetting all in the scarlet gladiolus she held broken
in her hand.   The little sharp face bent over 'the fiery-
throated prize with an intensity of soul hunger as bitter
—*more* bitter—than death.   The young lady had her
hand on the thief's shoulder before she knew it, and, without any conscious thought labor, felt in her own soul a
sympathetic sentiment of pity.

But the culprit sprang to her feet with hardening face,
every trace of longing and reflected flower spirit giving
place to depraved anger, fear, and unchildlike survey and
mastery of her perilous situation.

"Le-me-lone; I hain't took nothin' o' yourn," she cried
with an oath, wriggling like an eel under Mollie's firm
grasp.

"I don't want to hurt you!" said her captor in her
clear pleasant accents; "let me see your face."

Little Doppy obeyed, with such a mixture of cunning
and class hate deforming her lineaments, as made the pure
woman who held her, recoil and relax her grasp.

The child felt it, and escaped with a cat-like spring.
"He! he! he! No, I guess you won't, bad cess to you,"
was her retort in her rude harsh voice, perching on the
fence post as she spoke with both blistered dirty drum-
sticks of legs hung outside ready to leap.

Mollie resolved to conquer.   "No," said she tran-
quilly, "but here's your basket, and if you'll stay and
talk to me a second or two, I'll give you some huckleberry pie to fill it."

"You won't put a hand on me?"

"No."   Mollie folded hers behind her.

These waifs are excellent physiognomists, and Doppy
felt in the inmost depths of her vicious little heart that
she had a "soft thing."   She came with circumspection
however, prepared to fly at the first alarm.   "What d'ye

want ? " said she ungraciously, but with keen-eyed observation of everything, from the hyssop, so to speak, of the
wall, to the cedar of Lebanon, or rather the Fir Covert
that shielded the house on three sides the flower-decked
domain, like a black fringe on a gay tunic.

"I want several things," said Mollie, smiling in her
friendliest guise. "Your name, for instance."

Suspicion at once rose rampant; visions of jail and
police-courts, to which her nine years of life were no
strangers, thronged Doppy's brain. She drew back,
dogged and defiant:

"Father 'll lick any one that meddles with us," cried
she.

"Oh, he will? Then I shan't think of attempting it,"
said Mollie, smiling again with an amused vision of
old Mulligan's defensive operations. "Do you know
Amos ? "

"I might." Doppy bit her finger-nails stolidly, but
never gave over her watch on the young lady.

"He's a friend of mine. I want to send a message to
him."

"Amos!" cried Miss Mulligan, with a little burst of
impulsive disdain—"he's a great 'un."

"Then you won't oblige me." Mollie looked disappointed.

"I might," answered Doppy again, looking apparently
straight at the fence, and surveying Mollie through the
corner of her eye, while she wiped her gnawed digits on
her scorched pinafore.

"Will you tell him that I have got some shirts and a
pair of shoes that will fit his feet, and want him to come
and get them ? "

"I might, if I should see him," said Doppy, carelessly,
and took a second secret survey of this curious person,

from her smooth brown hair to her morning slippers. And she smirked as she found that there was a button off her calico dress, and gazed at the vacancy so steadily, that Mollie felt the place, and looking down discovered the loss for the first time. Conscience-stricken, our heroine ventured to offer some flowers, by way of rounding the interview. Hereupon the child's old, restless face became greedy with longing; and snatching the bouquet from its'collector's hand, she seized her basket without a word of thanks, and scrambling over the fence, started up the street on a greyhound's run.

This wholesome mortification of philanthropy sobered its disciple; but she was only the firmer resolved to see more of the limber-legged infant, and so picked up Tabby, who had been permeowing around the little intruder the whole time, and ran back to the house.

I have always held it a breach of hospitality to talk about people who entertain me. In consideration, therefore, of the many good dinners I have eaten at Fir Covert, I will only say of Mrs. McCross, that she was limp and faded like a last year's print over-boiled and ill-starched.

She had laid herself upon the sofa, and sighed pertinaciously, while her daughter was absent, and Mollie, when she brought the breakfast in, and sat anxiously waiting her verdict, felt to the marrow of her bones that something was wrong. She ran over all her possible failures and sins, including her engagement, of which she had said nothing. Upright as she was by nature and principle, she had discovered long before that the easiest way for all parties at Fir Covert was to let things reveal themselves.

Mrs. McCross sat down languidly, and fanned herself with the table-cloth, as if the effort to breathe was too

great; but rallying after some minutes, began to pour
tea. She gave the creamer a vicious shake at the first
cup, and smelt at it.

"Mollie, don't you know any better than to put sour
milk on the table. Might as well call us pigs at once,
and feed us on swill."

"It's morning's milking, mother."

"No such thing! Don't tell me I don't know night's
milk from morning's."

"Mirandy, it *is* morning's," said the Deacon, deprecatingly; "I gave away every drop in the house last
evening."

"Then the pail's sour; you're just slut enough to never
look into it from one year's end to another, and the thriv-
ing Catholics, that'll burn us all in our beds some day, and
you're so devoted to, wouldn't wash it if it was green.
Why didn't you drain the fat out of this egg-plant? It's
swimming in hog's grease. That's always the way; weak
and sick as I am, I've got to be up the first thing in the
morning and the last at night, or there's nothing done.
Where's that milk pail?"

"It's on the closet shelf."

"You put it up dirty, of course. You never thought
to scald it, but just tucked it away. Always shiftless and
slack. It's a sin in the sight of God."

Mollie swallowed something lumpy, and looked steadfastly at the untouched meal, which was perfectly dainty
and nice, but made no answer. Her mother pushed
her tea-cup one way and her plate another, and tearing a
piece of bread began to eat it a crumb at a time, tucking
it in as if the effort to live were beyond bearing. "Go
and get me that pail."

Mollie rose and brought it. It proved as sweet as
a head of young clover.

Mrs. McCross glanced into its bright depths, and set it down as one would a hundred-pound weight. Hope and dignity were annihilated in its descent.

A long silence ensued, broken only by a faint permeow from Tabby, who was weakly petitioning bits from the Deacon.

"Mary, put that old cat out! I'll wring her neck! meowing and permeowing around me!"

Her husband gently shoved his pet toward the girl, and a green and yellow parrot in the kitchen greeted the dismissed favorite with hoots and shrieks of laughter. Poll having gnawed the fastenings of her cage door, ambled out, and made a rush at poor puss, chuckling and kissing, and fairly drove her to claw up the what-not, where she stood at bay on top, with tail enough for three, while polly climbed maliciously after her. Being cuffed on the head, she bit at Tab with her iron bill, till felina was fain to run down again, leaving the feathered victor singing and whistling, her tail spread and her wings shaking in commemoration of her glorious victory.

This hubbub was specially distasteful to Mrs. McCross. She angrily demanded why her daughter didn't answer her.

"I beg pardon; I didn't hear you."

"You did! What do you say that for? You heard me ask you if you'd washed that pail, and you never spoke. I'm not enough account in my own house to be listened to! You're a thankless, ungrateful, ill-tempered girl! Deacon McCross, I wouldn't pretend to have any affection for my wife when I treated her as you do!" The gentleman addressed looked mildly up from his dish of cress, and said, "Law! Mirandy, how ken you?"

"How can I?" Mrs. McCross burst into tears. "You

bring screeching poll parrots and everything into the house to annoy me, and then ask 'How can I?' There it goes now, with its 'dear Louis, dear Mary,' in a voice like a car whistle, and every nerve I have in the world on edge. Why don't it say dear tea-pot, dear mop handle? Might just as well. I know you'd as lief have me dead as not, and I will be some time; then, perhaps, you'll regret doing all you can to make me miserable." Her voice had a feeble wail in it that wrung Mollie's heart, though she had been brought up on such scenes.

She sprang hastily to her feet: "Mother, I didn't know Louis meant to give me the parrot. I'll keep her in the barn, anywhere, so she won't annoy you." Then she threw her arms around the sufferer's neck, and kissed away her tears.

"No; I won't have the poor bird abused," permitting the caress with disgust; "I couldn't be cruel, even to a dumb beast. I can bear it just as I do everything else. There isn't much of my life that isn't spent bearing something for somebody." She darted a look at her husband, who wriggled painfully. "Nobody ever had such a cold, heartless set of human beings around them as *I*. Every one seems to try how much he can pile on. Never mind; there's some one to bring up the rear. It's no matter how much she suffers; wear her out and get another; you'll find out the difference!"

The Deacon pushed back his chair and glanced wistfully at the "Millville Universe," but didn't dare touch its inviting page. Mollie left her mother and sat down, hopeless of stemming the tide, in a chair, the other side the room. "Don't talk so," said she gently; "we all love you dearly, and want you to be happy."

"There it is again! 'Don't talk so.' Shut up your head, old woman. You've served your turn; now you can stand aside. There's no more work to be got out of you! I've borne a great deal from you, Mary; I've loved you too much! You're paying me for it."

She sobbed, and covered her face.

Her husband snatched the newspaper in a convulsive dab. "You ungrateful girl," he began, "you orter know better'n hurt your mother's feelin's so. It's jest as she sez. You don't care for any one but your-self."

Mollie gave him a glance of silent reproach. His eyes sank. "It's no use," cried he testily. "You shan't have him, an' you might's well come to it first as last. I'll give you all the money—anything you want; but we must get done with this."

"I can't," said she, shrinking back with piteous, frightened appealing in her poor blanched face; "don't ask it, father; I love him." She turned from one to the other; but the Deacon drummed with one hand under the table, and looked at his paper; and Mrs. McCross' handkerchief came down quite energetically for a languid invalid.

"You can't!" cried she, in her thin, nasal voice. "This to me, that have brought you into the world! I suppose you'll be disgracing the family, and running away next. He's just mean enough to ask it. You needn't look at the door; you've got to hear what I say. How can you sit there, Elizur, and listen to her! *Running away*—do you understand? I tell you, Mary, I'd as soon see you dead as married to that fellow. Don't I know him? Haven't I had him here under my nose in this very house for years? You break my heart." And she began to cry again.

Mollie's lip held a curve that could be touching when it curled up, and trembled like a hurt child's; but there was a certain belying squareness about the contour of her chin and check, and her pleasant, steady eyes had no yielding in them. She rose sadly, as her mother's harangue was thus merged into another line of offence, and answered, "I'm sorry you feel so, but I cannot break my word to Louis."

"Well, run away then, and bring down your father's gray hairs to the grave! ungrateful daughter! If you hate me,—I'd care something for somebody, if it was only an old cat, just to see how it felt."

"I shall not run away, mother; you're forbidding to grease the horse's teeth to no purpose," said Mollie, with some heat, and then was silent to master herself, and repent her hasty speech. "I expect to wait a long time—years," looking imploringly at the small, blonde features, now crumpled into a peevish frown. But there was no impulsive motherhood lurking about Mrs. McCross' pinched nose and thin lips, the latter borrowing from some unknown source a bright carmine hue, not consonant with her thinned Batchelor's hair-dyed, gimlet-like ringlets. Alas! how could motherhood go hand-in-hand with such adornments? The wife-love that beautifies every stage of woman's journey among the silvery abeals and birch woods of shady afternoon, and makes her regret for the fresh young brightness of her morning descent from the hills, only a pleasant memory could not have union with that combination.

Without exactly saying this to herself, the daughter felt instinctively that her mother could not comprehend her soul cry—the χ in their mental equations stood for an unknown, not only, but a totally dissimilar element, which neither could hope to balance. Mollie's momentary beseeching gave place to a different emotion—it wasn't defiance—but a simple comprehension of their essential

3*

soul variance, that induced her to add calmly, " I *shall* marry him, because we have loved each other ever since I can remember, and we *are* married in God's sight now."

Mrs. McCross walked stiffly to the door without a backward glance at the culprit, and banged it in righteous anathema. Her husband lingered behind. There was something in him that vibrated in better harmony with his daughter's *soul-strings*, though their gamuts were no more identical after all. "You're strong, Mollie," said he, wistfully, "but she'll tire you out; I can't stand by you—I'm an old man, daughter. I must have some comfort. I'm willing—more, I'm glad—you like each other; I hope God means to right the poor boy's wrongs, but your mother won't have it so."

The girl was silent a moment, perhaps counting her strength; her frame—even-balanced physical to mental, had given her no experience of lack here. She felt *able* to her finger-tips, even while her vivid imagination portrayed an almost endless vista of struggles and weariness. She drew the fatherly gray head close to her fresh young face. "My own papa," she answered, her eyes deepening with love and earnestness, "don't mind me; I am strong —strong enough to bear anything for Louis."

Here the mother's querulous voice, "Elizur! Elizur McCross, haven't you any consideration for me, that I am left all alone from morning till night?"

His wrinkled face grew wearier. He dropped Mollie's fingers, which he had been caressing between his own, and with slouched shoulders and hands crossed behind him, went slowly into the parlor, where sat the wife of his bosom. Mollie, left behind, gave a tired sigh, that was repressed as soon as vented audibly to consciousness, and after a few moments' pensive sitting with folded hands, looking out into the battle of her life,—poor girl! she little realized *what* a battle,—rose, and quietly began her work. All the people near Mrs. McCross wore a heavy, repressed expression, that came over mouth and eye at her approach. Now, though Mollie went about humming a little song picked up among her Irish pensioners, a plaint of a poor exiled soldier boy who was homesick, and had no money to get back to fatherland, it was because she always checked a sigh by turning it into singing, on principle, and the stave of the queer jerky melody ran up and down, like a lattice raised to hide her busy thoughts.

Poppy meanwhile had descended from her post on the what-not, climbed to the second-best kitchen table by the corners of the cloth, and discussed a plate of putty with lively enjoyment. She was sharpening her bill on the edge of the dish, keeping her bright eye fixed with portentous brilliance on the cat, when Mollie entered, bringing a salver of dirty dishes, and poll invited her to view her work of destruction in every variety of pretty Poppyisms. The tray went on the table, and Mollie had the suicide in her hand in a twinkling; tears, that would not gather for hurt pride and feeling, filled her eyes. " I'm so afraid you're killed," cried she, cradling meddlesome poll, back down, in her hand, and kissing her soft green breast tenderly. "Poor! poor polly! How could you touch that horrid stuff?" But the bird, though she lay with her legs drawn up and her head ducked in, was embodying the passiveness of content, not pain. In short, she found the situation delightful, and said, " Dear Louis, dear Mollie," with unabated relish and vigor, the second she regained her feet. Her mistress could only caress her anew, and scratch the yellow cheek feathers raised so insinuatingly, and say, " Oh! what pretty wings!" when they were spread in all their red-and-yellow glory to her admiration. And though work must be done, her climbing by beak and claws up the calico wrapper, clear to Miss McCross' dainty head, couldn't well be helped, nor her services as hair-dresser, rendered with utmost care, refused. She pulled each filament gently at the point of disappearance in the heavy braids behind. Hairs rooted at both ends were puzzling. Feathers were not made so, nor Louis' fur, nor the cat's. Without doubt, the custom was vicious, and warranted lusty tugging, such as required a firmly planted claw, and Mollie, after twisting and turning in vain, was fain to take her down, still giggling, and chewing industriously at one long brown hair. If it had been the chief tail feather of her bitterest enemy, it could not have afforded more complete satisfaction. She played with it thoughtfully, when from her throne on the gas fixture she watched her mistress begin preparations for dinner, occasionally joining in conversation with any noisy kitchen utensil, or refreshing herself with a nibble of pine from the casement.

Mollie always cooked from a certain old, long, thin volume handed down from remote antiquity. It was once a library catalogue. You could still read, heading its pages, " Histories, Cyclopedias," etc., written in a stiff, tradesman's hand, and pale ink.

If the proof of the pudding be in the eating, this book must have been of the finest, for many generations of mice had nibbled its greasy corners. As Mollie took it from the pantry shelf, the air was filled with the aroma of nutmeg, cinnamon, cloves, and mace. It opened of itself to " Natural Histories ; " and passing by sundry recipes for brandy cocktail, pop robin, and Welsh rarebit, she was soon deep in marble cake, whence she passed to biography, in the person of Sally Lunn, and thence to tipsy cake and deviled kidneys, reposing peacefully under the heading of "Religious Works." Thus laboring, and clinging fast by her faith to Louis, albeit notwithout many secret tears, a fortnight passed. But one day, as she bends over her cookery, all of a sudden Mollie hears a faint squeak at the front gate, followed by a well-known boyish tread on the gravelled walk, and, dropping the iron cooking-spoon, throws herself into the new-comer's arms. Polly, looking on wisely, takes up the well-known strain, "Dear Louis! dear Mary!" and Tabby knows that there are no more tit-bits for her, and virtuously slaps the floor with her tail, and eyes robins on the mountain ash with fell purpose.

"O Louis, how I have wanted you!" cried Mollie, first breathing a long relieved sigh; then brightening into a dewy humble smile,—humble with the kind of humility that love makes it passing sweet to a woman to yield to her husband, and him only—humility born of our loftiest needs, and made possible by our rarest tenderness.

"I wish you had," said he airily. It was *very* charming to be a necessity to Mollie, who was the "one woman" in his mental amphitheatre. Something in Mollie's intensity was exquisitely fascinating to him. It stirred unplumbed depths of capacity in himself, and the first revelations of our power to ourselves are emotions of delight the gods might well envy. The poor gods, who can only know and do, it is not for them to imagine, strive, grow through striving, accomplish, and find in accomplishment the least element of the perfect joy of success. Mollie always seemed so rich a being to Louis. She wasn't round; she was all projections, and feelers, and filmy longings, reaching endlessly into the impossible. Louis didn't think round women nice on the whole; but the difficulty might have been, that most women are

round like circles, and very flat; whereas the right round-
ness (which who possesses?) is that of the sphere. But
Louis himself was very like a young barnacle, swimming
lightly about the blue oceans of feeling, and being, and
enjoying. It was a very uncertain matter what rock
would be the basis of his future solidification into a housekeeping and sedate shell-fish; or if he wasn't swallowed
up by some big-bellied monster beforehand, and so altogether robbed of the patriarchal barnacular possibility.

As yet, Mollie recognized this fact not one whit. Some
people *first* love *analytically*, some by *unconscious synthesis;* and though time may induce the opposite method
before we write "finale," or time writes it for us, its
choice belongs to our own proper *nature* at the start.
Mollie, like most women, was synthetic in such matters.
She loved Louis for his harmonious whole, not because
his face was delicate and refined, or his scholarship
finished and elegant, or his heart warm and lovely, but
because it was *Louis*. Here was her beginning; here she
was content to end. She had analyzed flowers, and their
structure could not be replaced; she had analyzed books,
to destroy their flavor; she had analyzed her friends, to
lose them; she was not *afraid* to subject her love to this
disastrous process, she never thought of doing it. If
you had asked Louis why he cared for Mollie, he could
have given you a complete catalogue of the things delightsome to his soul that had induced his fondness, and for
all their love, they seldom agreed, even in vital points,
just as on the present occasion.

"Make the most of me, sweetheart," said he, seating
himself on the table and drawing her to the same elevation; "the rose that blooms beneath the hill must shortly
fade away. I'm off to Top Town this afternoon."

"Well, I'm glad you're going," slowly; then, girl-like

(she was only a girl after all), confirmed her words with two large tears that fell warm and round on Louis' hand.

"O Mollie!" said he, hastily, with a warning huskiness in his own voice, that brought back her self-command at once. She couldn't have Louis cry; that would never do.

"Don't feel so bad, dear; I thought you liked Top Town."

She didn't like it—though it was her need of him that would be so bitter, so craving, that had induced her tears. Her tell-tale face would have betrayed her, even if her lover's delicate soul-feelers had not made him aware of her sentiments. Some people, like this pair, have a sixth mesmeric sense, as true and delicate a mood test as a magnet to the pole.

"You don't agree with me," said he, blankly. "I see it in your silence, and everything. Why, it's a splendid opportunity. Think of it! A partnership in only three short years, and then yourself in peace and plenty forever! Why, it is almost like a miracle. We can travel, collect pictures, indulge our poor starved art tastes to the full—live! But I see how it is: you would rather tie yourself to slave labor, and anxiety for daily bread. It is just your high-toned notion, but not business like, my dear."

Mollie thought that taunt very hard. When any one was going to take a departure from rectitude or nice feeling, were it little or great, it was always done on "business principles," which, being a woman, she could not be expected to understand. She grew very white about her lips, but persisted, "I hope it *is* all for the best, I'm sure." The glance she lifted to his was an odd mixture of deprecation, pain, and unconvinced opinion. "I work so hard to make people temperate

and good, and it seems as if this put you on the opposite side."

"Too bad," said Louis, playfully, yet with a certain
strong dissent underlying his airy way of treating the
subject. "I knew it was religion; your only fault is
piety. Sometime you'll learn to let people set fire to
one sin to light them on to the next in peace."

"I *never* shall," said Mollie, with obstinate decision,
"and your rhetoric is as heathen as your philosophy.
People can't be set fire to in a figure when sin is the
property under consideration. Sin is opaque in its
nature, and the result of darkness, and can neither burn
nor be a torch in any form, except *brûler en enfer*, which
we weren't speaking of." There was no windmill too insignificant for this Quixote, but here her lover oppor-
tunely sealed her mouth with his own.

"If it's all one to you, I'd rather sip honey from your
lips, *ab osculo rubescente puellæ*, to-day," quoth he; "the
process is sweeter."

It *was* provoking to have cold water thrown on one's
plans and prospects. Mollie felt it, and did not blame
him. "Louis, was that *osculum caritatis*, or not?" said
she, smiling. "I try to think well of Top Town, but I
suppose it's my duty to speak my mind."

"Very right; duty performed is a rainbow to the
soul. No, it wasn't *caritatis* at all; it was the very
passion of vehement adoration. Is that satisfactory?"
The words seem light, but the look that went with them
was tender.

"At any rate you are not in the sample room," remarked Mollie, with the air and feeling of one resolved
to look on the bright side of a thunder-cloud at his
zenith.

"That is just where I am," said he, coloring. "Peli-

can said to-day it was the only place open to me. I
wish it was another. But then, the prospective partner
of a concern holds a different relation to society in any
situation than a mere clerk. Your father discharged me
from my place in his office last week, so it's Top Town or
starve. *Don't* feel so about it, darling. What could tempt
me to leave you except the hope of speedy return?
Don't you trust me, that your face is the epitome of
wretchedness? Think it not unkind" (coaxingly) "that
from the nunnery of thy chaste glance I flee to war's
alarms."

"I *do* trust you!" said Mollie, all intensity. She
was trembling against his shoulder, in the violence of
her feeling. "Haven't I given you myself? But I can't
explain how I feel—so beset, and as if a hand were
stretched out to come between us—so untranquil—sun-
dered from my moorings."

The boyish figure, with his flitting color and dreamy
eyes, formed in graceful, unknit lines—so dear, so beautiful, so uncomprehending! Yet it was passing sweet to
have him draw her poor, perplexed head to his arm, and
kiss her eyelids smarting with bitter tears, and call her
his own dear Mollie. The gesture, the prompting emotion,
the tenderness—were all she craved. Yes, she was his
—nobody else's—forever. Top Town might bring untold
disaster, but they were one. Rising and standing before him, face to face, "Tell me," said she, "are you
quite resolved to accept that position?"

"Quite."

"I feel, I *know* trouble will come to try us both. I
want to say,"—she spoke with effort, for she saw by the
perplexed look in his gazelle brown eyes that her words
seemed to his view to be a criticism of him, and not
what she meant, "that whatever happens I am *always*

yours. You mustn't—*I* mustn't—ever put myself in one thought and yourself in another, nor in God's thought. We are *one*, not two, and mercy, blessing —whatever comes, is *ours.*"

He accepted the position, of course, Didn't he desire that very thing above all goods ? The proposition was sound. His face flushed and paled, and flushed again, all with pride and love, and delicate, sensitive appreciation of her worth to himself, and his exceeding riches in her. But for all that, it meant something different to him than to her. She was looking at it as a safety-boat in perils, and doubts, and storms; he regarded it as a pleasure skiff, wherein they two would sail always in dreamy, sunny seas.

"Say it again," she said, hungrily ; "say we are *one* from this time forth, forever."

He said it solemnly. It is a wonderful thing to say, —such as should demand bending knees and a beating heart before all its heavenly sweetness and obligation, and he knew and felt it. "It is true," affirmed Mollie, drawing a long breath and wearing a quietly satisfied peace in her face.

Enter Mrs. McCross.

This good lady having been taken with neuralgia directly after breakfast, had kept Molly waiting on her the whole morning.

First, she must leave her work to hunt the camphor bottle, which always stood under the mirror; then she must get assafœtida, and mould the pills, a mustard paste, and three different kinds of tea, for benefits unknown. While her daughter was within earshot the mother groaned aloud, and when at last everything a *malade imaginaire* can invent had been applied, and Molly gently inquired if she felt better, she answered that she presumed she should when she was dead, for then there would be no one to make her ill by selfishness and ill-temper.

Lastly, Mollie was summoned from her half-cooked dinner to read a comforting chapter, beginning, " Fret not thyself because of evil-doers," and to listen to a tearful prayer over her ingratitude.

The girl left the room, calm as always. Her mother sobbed loudly till she remembered another medicine. But Mollie for once was deaf to her call. Hence ensued a look through the kitchen key-hole and hasty entry.

The pair gave a dismayed start at her appearance, though they kept their position on the table, hand in hand. But Louis' heart beat fast and hard. He dreaded his prospective mother-in-law. She on her side regarded him with indignant disdain. "I should like to ask how *you* came here?" cried she, in cutting sarcasm. Now Mrs. McCross had been all the mother Louis had ever known —if such care as that lady would be likely to give can be called motherhood. He withered like the mown grass under the hot sun when she addressed him thus. With him loyalty and obedience went hand in hand, and he had been accustomed to submit to her from infancy. His childish tenderness was not broken with the rending of their familiar ties. " I came to see Mollie," said he, deeply hurt; " I am going away."

" I shan't believe it till you're gone; you're full of deceit as an egg is of meat. You needn't sneak in to try your fascinations on my daughter; she won't have you."

Louis might be sensitive and gentle, but he was very apt to be found, after repeated dislodgment, in his original position. "She has agreed to take me, however," remarked he quietly. But he was not quiet in his soul. She seemed to be jabbing him with a rusty knife.

" Promised fiddlestick!" said Mrs. McCross in her

most insulting tone. "Mollie, you can never want that puppy; I despise him! His very legs look mean."

Mollie had been standing silently, watching her lover's downcast face, but now she darted to his side and threw herself upon his breast. "This is my place," cried she; "no power on earth can part us."

Mrs. McCross saw that she had gone too far, and so uttered three shrieks, and fell fainting in a clean place behind the stove. She did not recover till the object of her abuse had pressed his good-by kiss upon the lips of the girl bewildered in the intensity of her sudden wrath, and left the house. Mollie followed him to the door and watched him go' up the road, and was surprised to find herself clinging to the handle for support. She could hardly stand. She began to be afraid of herself. She hadn't known that she *could* be so angry.

The remainder of the day was spent on her mother's part in audible tears. By long practice she had acquired a groan as resonant as a bell, and there was a particular place in Mollie's back where every one caught and quivered.

How it rained that dreary afternoon; as Francis Haythorne told Peace Pelican, "the angels must have been doing up a three-months' wash of dirty surplices in their leaky tub." Mary was in her room begging mercy for herself and Louis, praying comfortless prayers that seemed all wrong, and only settled heavily back upon the heart that had no power to wing them upward. Her tempest of longing, fighting, willing, had given way to a reaction. She couldn't feel sure of anything since that terrible soul-uprising against her mother—all the more terrible because it found vent in no kindred act, but spent itself silently while she rested upon Louis' heart. That very fact might have given her the wished-for clue to her

labyrinth of miserable, helpless reasoning. But religion
and love have to be rediscovered by every votary. They
are not sciences, but unknown worlds, where neither
atmosphere, nor light, nor one's friends' voices are like
those of the previous existence. Mollie didn't know that
she had a right to this perfectly radiant happiness of love.
She believed that in a case of two diverging paths the
thorny road was unquestionably the God-elected. But
any road with Louis was like heaven, and we must not
wish for selfish ease on earth; how could she say God's
will be done, when He might not be willing to give her
Louis? How could she have so little love for her be-
trothed, as of her own consent to leave a shadow of
possibility of his loss, by saying God's will be done?

Beside her religious indecision, was a second, equally
bitter. She would have followed her lover without a
doubt but for her parents. She would have given up
her plighted troth, if she had not felt from the depths of
her soul that it would be treachery to the man that
trusted in her. All her life she had taught herself to
feel that every act that brought a shadow to her
mother's face was sin; and now each sob that came up
from the room below made her feel like a murderer.
Could her happiness bought at this price be anything
but damning guilt? Would God bless such a union?
She couldn't be married without God's blessing. Mollie's
first lesson in life had been self-abnegation. She was
not the woman to weigh happiness against duty; it was
the rival claims that would not be measured. If for a moment the lover's scale seemed to descend, she spied *herself*
thrown in to turn the balance, and so had to begin afresh.
She could never get beyond her heart-rending premises.
Hour after hour passed. She had been over the ground
step by step a hundred times, and gained no result for

or against.   She *could* not be false to Louis.   She would
not be false to her mother.   Six o'clock struck, and she
rose from her knees, where she had thrown herself when
she entered her room.   Her head seemed on fire, or as
if a great wheel, with every argument a spoke, were
revolving there endlessly.   She was hardly conscious of
anything but this frightful, measured revolution, while
she got the supper, and sitting torpidly, with her own
untasted, waited for opportunity to clear the table.
Her father's remarks, put always in the mildest form of
humble suggestion, her mother's peevish fault-finding,—
were like the idle wind in her ears.   She scarcely heard
their voices.   Oh, if she could find a new argument!
If she could decide from the old !   She hurried back to
her room and cast herself again upon her knees.   " My
God, be merciful! what shall I do ? "

But God's answers are vocal in future circumstance.
We cannot always assure ourselves, in such moments of
mental upheaval, that we truly hear the still small voice.
She would have to fight this battle again and again, to-
morrow, and many to-morrows, before *the* answer came.
But in the midst of her agony she remembered the
phrase, "Bless the Lord, O my soul, and forget not all
His benefits."   Reason was worn out.   Mollie clutched
at the bare adjuration as a drowning man catches at
straws.   "Forget not all His benefits."   Would the
Giver of good withhold the *one* good she craved?   She
judged Him by herself, and nestled in to the conviction
of his pity, resting in the everlasting arms, and loving
Louis.   And between such moments of extreme mental
tension and corresponding nervous collapse, Mollie's
inner life vibrated for months and months.   Her balances
were too equally weighted to descend on either side.
Some new item must be cast into the scale.

CHAPTER V.

"'Good mistress mouse, are you within?
'Yes, kind sir, I'm settin' to spin.'"

ITTLE DOPPY was at home; no doubt of it. In the first place all her earthly possessions lay scattered about the room. Not the bar-room, but the one behind, where the family living was done. Up-stairs in the attic dwelt Johanna Haverty, with her father; and the back door opened on a little weedy garden that once fell in terraces to the river, and still boasted two or three knotty apple-trees, and a few fragments of stone wall supporting the ragged turf.

Our heroine's apartment held two beds, one in each corner; a rusty cooking-stove; a chest of drawers; one wooden chair; a greasy table; a picture of the Virgin with a spiky glory about the head; a market basket with a ragged edition of the "Police Gazette" in the bottom; a few musty cobwebs dangling from the ceiling; an old hat stuffed into a broken pane of glass; and —Little Doppy. Stay: I have omitted two kittens fast asleep on a dirty shawl. The little girl had been eating her forlorn breakfast—three or four cold potatoes, a bit of codfish, a piece of bread—all that ten cents would buy at the back door of the Millville House.

Presently she arose, gave the scraps to the kittens, and going to the hall stairs called, "Joe! Joe!"

In answer appeared a figure very unlike Doppy, for whereas the one was softly colored and weary in look, this new-comer's bold black eyes and scornful mouth, albeit a trifle stained with tobacco, were the personification of energy. "How's your father?" said Dorothea in a low tone.

"Sleepin', as you might say," she answered carelessly; "you needn't look down about it. I went through his pockets and he's got to come to himself. I bought a bit to eat last night, so I ain't hungry. Goin' pickin'?"

"I spose so. Must do somethin'," said the child in an old, spiritless way. "I be sick of livin'. I wish I was dead."

"Whisht!" said Joe, tossing her handsome head. "I ain't; I likes to live. It's jolly. So you've kept the cats?"

Doppy nursed one of them on her arm with a motherly motion. "Yes," said she doggedly, "when the old man comes, I puts 'em in the closet till he goes again;" and she glanced scowling at sundry blue-black lumps that decorated her neck and arms. "I'll have 'em now if I die for it. I *do* wish I was dead. [This in a business-like tone.] I see lots of children as has cats, and dogs, and oranges, an' I hain't got nothin'."

"You do look pretty rough," quoth Johanna, surveying her with a patronizing stare. She wore one brass ring, a string of beads, and hoops in her ears, and so had whereof to boast. "Be them all yer cloes?"

"Yis, an' that ain't the hull neither. I had a dacent bit of a dress, and when the old man come home he took it off wid him quicker'n that." Doppy snapped her dirty fingers in illustration.

"No wuss'n my old man," quoth Joe, her head in the air. "Divil a bit of work has he put his hand to for better'n a week, an' he drinkin' an' drinkin' the hull time. Pah!—I hates the sight of them liquor shops."

"You go yoursel' often enough," said Doppy. "Wasn't ye after lyin' dead drunk in the road last night, an' me callin' ye to return?"

"Have a chaw?" interrupted Johanna.

"No, I hain't none," giving up search in a pocket of complicated contents. "Here's a cigar end; will that do?"

"What's the picture?" asked Doppy, rejecting the proffered courtesy.

"Nothin' but some o' them things they gives away at Nickson's," said Miss Haverty with contempt. "They gives cloes an' a dinner onct in a while. Take it; only don't say where it come from, or I'll get licked."

Doppy nodded, and bending eagerly over the card formed herself a far more touching picture than the one surveyed.

"What does it mean?" said she after a pause.

"Dun know,"—Joe was ogling herself in a bit of looking glass; "all they say is lies, anyway. It might be a pilgring—a man as walks and walks," she exclaimed with superiority.

"Oh! a tramper; see his stick an' pack. Girl alive! it's a travellin' pedler he is," cried Doppy, a light breaking over her face.

"No," remarked Joe, sententiously; "them's his sins in the bag beyant. Them women ain't buyin'; they's angels, after givin' him clean cloes for his pack. I can't say what they does wid them rags. I've seen wuss at Goodheart's. Belike they sells 'em." Johanna carefully picked a pimple from her dirty face as she spoke. "Teacher said they was willin' to give 'em to us ef we was willin' to take 'em, but that's stuff."

"Gosh! I'll try," said Doppy with resolution.

"They'll no more'n put their noses inter the door ef

4

they come," remarked Joe, rising from her knees with a laugh, and setting her arms akimbo. "When they see the dirt of ye, and how nasty the floor be, 'I knows they ain't good,' they'll say; 'folks as poor as this is always bad.' That's true fur ye; I heard that Miss Pelican criticisin' on us so, myself."

"Then I'll fix up; I took a broom the other day that'll just do." So saying, she dragged it from its hiding-place— a new one, with E. McCross cut in the handle.

"You'll have to quit that ef you expects folks to give ye so much as a pair of stockings," quoth Joe, swinging her basket on her arm preparatory to starting forth. As she drew her shawl over her head she paused. "Ef the old man wakes, tell him I'll bring him his pint soon. It's better to give it him at home than let him go out, the job to get him in bein' so hard."

Little Doppy presently completed her task with satisfaction, and had just put the broom up in the corner when Hugh and Amos entered.

"How's the kittens?" said the latter, hanging himself awkwardly against the side of the house and blushing his freckles out of sight entirely. "I wants to know of 'em sometimes."

"There they be," returned Doppy with dignity, "layin' on that shawl. Hain't I fixed the room nice?"

Poor Doppy, her labors were unappreciated.

"Nice!" exclaimed Amos; "well! that's a good un! Why the dirt's under the stove, and the quilts is crooked on the beds, and it's as nasty as pizen."

Dr. Johnson says the truth is the meanest thing people can speak.

The child's face fell like lead. The pink glow which her happy thoughts had raised faded from her wan cheeks. Her brown eyes sought the floor and filled with tears.

But when Amos concluded with a mocking laugh, echoed boisterously by Hugh, she suddenly regained her self-possession, and grabbed the broomstick, on inhospitable thoughts intent. " Git out, you mean, dirty Paddies," cried she, banging the door after them, and jumping up and down on the floor with rage. Her blazing glances fell on the offending couches ; so she tore off quilts, sheets, and feather beds, and stamped on each separately, unheeding the howls of her beloved kittens, thus suddenly hurled from their resting-place. Then, finding no further food for her fury, she threw herself atop the heap, and screamed in concert.

"My eye," quoth Amos from without. " Ain't she a snapper ! " and he did a double clog-dance with Hugh on the door-stone, where all the flings hit the frail boards scarcely held together by their rusty hinges.

After a while silence reigned without ; but Doppy's sense of her wrongs grew with memory and vent. Suddenly she met with a stoppage to the auricular index of her woes, in the shape of a great lump of molasses candy, which Amos, who had entered unperceived, stuffed into her mouth as she opened it for a bigger howl than usual. Unclosing her eyes, hitherto tight shut in the extremity of her grief, she beheld a good-natured grin on our hero's freckled face, and the remnants of his soothing application in his hand.

" When be you goin' to stop them yowls ? " asked he in an agonized tone. " Hurry up, do ; there's a dear."

Little Doppy, taken by surprise, melted at the kind act, and proceeded to unburden her heart.

" So you want to be respectable, do you ? " quoth he, when she came to an end. " That's my mind. I've wanted to iver since day before yesterday, when Miss McCross told me an' Hugh—we bein' up to her house at the time—that she hoped we'd have as nice gardings as her'n, when we come to be growed. Punch my head! jingo Pelters! if I don't mean to!"

"Poh!" said Hugh, "All you'll ever see flowerin' is a whiskey blossom ou the end of yer nose."

Amos shook his fist. "Git out, darned son of a gun! I'm in arnest;" whereat the intruder vanished, to return with a sick, featherless chicken, picked out of the gutter. "There!" said he, hurling it at his friend; "there's the first beginning of the poultry-yard. The best you'll see, be jabbers!"

This cruel taunt led Doppy to resort to the broomstick, which was an effectual weapon in her hands.

"Now let's be respectable," said Amos, as she came back triumphant, unmindful of the familiar strain loudly chanted at the corner—

"If I had an old wife to bother my life,"

whereby Hugh revenged himself in exile.

"I'm in wid ye," returned Doppy. "How shall we begin?"

"Spose I've got to go to work," answered Amos, reluctantly, after an ominous pause. "Father's been blowin' this six months cause I don't do nothin'."

"I can't," said Doppy. "I'm too little for the mills."

"You can keep the room clean," suggested Amos, grinning in spite of himself at the demolished beds.

"I don't see how I can iver be gitten them things back," with an oddly humble face for Miss Mulligan.

"I wouldn't mind helping of yer," said Amos bashfully. "'Tain't nothin' to lift."

"You're a broth of a lad," smiled the little damsel; and so awkward Amos tried his hand at making beds, and other household lore, with wonderful gentleness, and great comfort to both parties.

"Oh, how dirty the flure bees; sure it's a log flure, an' niver smoothed at all," said the maiden, surveying it with a disgusted face.

"Why not wash it? I see mother doin' her'n last month."

"Who's to lift the heavy pail from the well?" said Doppy despairingly.

"*I* will," answered Amos, with heroic resolution—thinking inly how he would sprinkle her.

But Doppy was no bird to be caught with chaff. Meeting him at the step, she took the great wooden bucket in both hands, and shut and locked the door in his face. "Ye'll be tracking the place all over if I lave ye in. So go 'long wid ye."

In vain Amos called and grumbled. She was deaf to his entreaties. He had to content himself with making faces at her through the window. But, as it was necessary to stand on tip-toe to do it, the amusement soon lost its zest, even though Doppy returned each contortion with a worse.

Joe came back in due time, and, compassionately offering her services, the two dined together on the contents of her basket, in the only corner not deluged through Doppy's energy.

Under her treatment, though streaky, the floor became tolerably clean. The stove, too, on being brushed, showed faint signs of blacking. The kittens frisked gleefully in the yellow sunshine, and by this time old Mulligan came in, and was pleased to say that he didn't mind about them. Doppy cooked his supper and he went out directly. Afterward the two girls sat long in the renovated apartment, talking, till Joe said she must see to her old man; whereupon Doppy fed her kittens, and laid them and her tired self into bed, and presently began dreaming that an angel made her wing-feathers into brooms for her especial benefit, and then cleaned the room, and festooned the walls with white dresses and aprons.

CHAPTER VI.

" Jack and Jill went up the hill."

" The filmy gossamer now flits no more,
  Nor halcyons bask upon the sunny shore,—"

 STATE of things—frequent to busy people when they indulge in circumspection,—the sad outlook of every heroic life, as a matter of course. But hopeless indeed must be the existence to which all places for pleasant soul loitering are forever closed. The limitations of humanity forbid the bare possibility of such a case; least of all was Mollie, whose feet barely touched the entrance of earth's sorrow-filled labyrinth, to grieve utterly. One may sing,

" And like the mountain's golden ore,
  Changeth my sorrow nevermore;"

and even in the complaint unwittingly own to a possibility of brightness, a capacity for glitter and shine in the sunlight; so now.

It is true that the evening after her lover's summary expulsion she cried herself asleep; but the very next morning she came back from slumber on the swell of a Baltimore oriole's matin hymn, sung under her window. Moreover, it was no common bird that parted her dreams. The mellow notes had a certain dear familiarity, the result of frequent and admired repetition. In short, Louis had not been able to leave her thus in sorrow; he had climbed the maple that veiled her window from the road, and was administering comfort peculiar to himself.

"He's neglecting his business to console me; I mustn't let him," was the instant self-reproof that came to his promised, as she opened her eyes and smiled with pleasure. She therefore rose hastily, and donning a daintily embroidered dressing-sacque at hand, threw open the shutters, and greeted him with a blush, and glance from her bright eyes meant for reproach, but in fact only happiness at their reprieve.

"What! not gone?" cried she, forgetting dignity to carry the kiss he tossed to her lips.

"I was left," responded Louis, penitently. "I saw the time-table in the morning, but at noon I forgot when the train started. Then I said to myself, 'I ought to go; it's my duty; but if it turns out that the hour is three, not four, I shall have made a dreadful mistake.' I shall have to take the owl. Meanwhile, I know you are panting after the water-brooks, Heart. The one on Turk's Head I mean. With your parents' permission, we will start at three o'clock."

"Come in," said Mollie, beaming approval.

"You forget I am forbidden. I had to climb here in the tree because I wouldn't enter the gates of—call it Eden."

Mollie looked at him a moment as he leaned forward, half hanging, half resting upon the great maple, his lithe youthful frame bending to the position with easy grace; his soft, gazelle eyes meeting hers with mixed sorrow and laughter.

"That's a pity; I was just comparing you to un oiseau de Paradis. But you confess yourself nothing but a hangbird after all," she said, playfully. "I don't see how I can talk to you out of the window, either, if you consider yourself tabooed. It would spoil our love if we did anything by stealth. I shall tell mother, and you can ring the door-bell when you arrive."

This prim little speech, delivered with naïve resolution, seemed quite satisfactory to the stigmatized oriole, for he swung himself lightly to the ground, and made obeisance.

"With equal souls and sentiments the same," laughed he. "Farewell, sweet-heart." Then he hastened gayly up the street, humming Schubert's song, "To thy chamber window roving, love hath led my feet." He always appeared and disappeared thus on Mollie's horizon; ever delicately gleeful, or, in the inevitable dark days, suffering in the healthy ingenuous way that belongs to unsullied natures,—a kind of pain that too many of us look back upon as a lost luxury. Perhaps she ethercalized her conception of him overmuch. But, even if she did, she had all her life been doing the same office to his ideal of nobility and rightmindedness. He only lived the grace of her love.

That afternoon, accepting her mother's sullen silence for consent, and sealing her father's irate lips till they yielded a furtive blessing, she sallied out. Louis made haste to hold up a great brass key, when he saw her open the door.

"Right off St. Peter's bunch, the Congregational string," cried he. "I borrowed it as I came along for a parting melody."

Half a mile away, across the river, on the road to the Turk's Head, stood the queer old wooden church, with its huge, carved mahogany pulpit, its open belfry, whose floor was thatched with sailcloth, since the conical tower yielded scant protection from the elements, and its singer's gallery fenced with faded red moreen curtains, behind which Roaring River youth chanted "There is a fiery, dreadful hell," long meter, and coquetted in all forms of measure from time immemorial. In these sacred precincts stood the common darling of saint and sinner, the minister's pet, and Louis' idol—a new Odel organ, with three banks of keys, and innumerable stops.

Dulcet Petibone, the schoolma'am, presided on Sundays, but young Allwood, who borrowed Fred Growing's key and played there many an hour every week—clerk's hours before seven o'clock summer mornings, felt no envy.

Mollie's office was to blow; she often shared these musical matins. This was a good leave-taking. Louis would tell her all his soul on the keys, in a tongue she had learned to understand from childhood. She was almost his only confidant in these tone revelations, but she used to think that no words could explain her lover's moods half as well. Commonly, when he was troubled, and obstinate about confessing the cause, she led him to the nearest instrument, and unravelled his secret with facility. "He feels thus," she would think; "only this or that cause could have induced *precisely* such emotion."

To-day, the prelude was a fuge of Sebastian Bach's, for practice. Next came a morsel or so from Handel. Then Louis drew a roll of manuscript from his pocket, and called his faithful ally from her post.

"See," cried he with boyish exultation, "here is a pot-pourri from Der Freischütz:

> " ' Would you question, would you ask me,
>   Whence these tones so wild and wayward,
>   I should answer, I should tell you—Me.'   .

4*

Me, who sat up till two o'clock last night to copy;" and he laid his hand on his heart and bowed theatrically. "When I gave back the piano arrangement to the Gonecusset scythe-maker (he brought it all the way from Fatherland), he little thought that I had the best of it safe on paper. This is for Sweetheart—a remembrance of her poor music-scribbling lover. First the waltz,—now the soldier's solo,—here your favorite prayer. This is the place where they cast the bullets. I have put in every air—soldier's, tenor adagio, orchestral flourishes and demoniac machinery to boot. Finally, the Hunter's Chorus, Rosy Wreath, and so on. It was *tout bien ou rien.* Now listen."

He had indeed done his work well. The whole emotional and descriptive intention of the author had been preserved, and he put it on the organ with an artist's instinctive coloring.

Mollie mentally followed the story, and shutting her eyes, fairly saw every picture. The entire scene in the Wolf's Glen, so faithful a copy of midnight in the forest, seemed to have had a fascination for Louis. His listener shuddered as he called up the black sky, the wind sighing among the trees, the water dashing down the steep, the devilish counting and laughter of the soldier, the frightful apparitions, and in the midst, the lover's tender little mother vision.

"Do you know," said the musician, suddenly breaking off, and speaking with an eager flush on his cheek, as if he wanted to be reassured, "putting myself into that huntsman's place—smooth bore—hunting match—loss of skill—Agatha, Casper, and all—I think I should not have refused the bullets? I couldn't rest last night, the music echoed my thoughts so. I felt as if Top Town, and money, and the liquor trade meant just the same to me

that the Wolf's Glen and compact with Zamael did to
Max. And you, dear trembling conscience, are a real
Agatha."

Then it came to Mollie that she ought to make a final
protest. Not that Louis would stay at home, but for
principle's sake. But she had spoken her mind, and acquiesced in the decision, and she dreaded to renew the
conflict. Moreover, she by no means classed her lover
with that weak-minded hunter. Though she had resolved
to be strong for the future, she had already yielded the
present, and even now had begun to look at the Cereus
with eyes of hope, and to defend it to her own sense of
right. She therefore kept a miserable silence.

Louis' delicate intuition caught the phase of affairs at
once. "O dear!" cried he in a pretty, harmless petu-
lance that was quite his own, "never mind! We are
going to the Turk's Head; you will hear the woods tell
another story, and I'll just improvise a wee bit, to take
the incantation out of our minds. America is not the
land of superstition, and mission-struck Mr. Pelican cannot possibly be metamorphosed into an ill-natured fox-
hunting spirit. You are to be *Mrs. Allwood*—Top Town
must furnish the wherewithal."

Thereupon he gave his lovely head a wilful toss, and
began to play. I have never heard such another master
of the art as Louis. His long, nervous fingers wandered
among the keys, waking from them a coherent language—
a tale all fresh and simple. Not a "random business pat-
tering and groping up and down from one stop or key to
another," like Ritter's lament over the prelude, but a con-
sistent following out of the subject of thought uppermost
in his mind, enriched by brilliant cadences and ornaments
indeed, but never yielding to them the central idea.
This afternoon, the adagio, and the soldier's ferocious

"Wie, Was, ensetzen," were persisting themes. Ninths, sevenths, elevenths—nothing would lead away from the dismal glen with its mantle of black firs choking and shutting out the sky, and the incessant plunge and gurgle of water. Runs, trills, cadenzas, began and ended just here. He pulled the Vox Humana and struck into the prayer, but no less followed the vision—to represent itself in the accompaniment of the recitative with weird persistence.

"Tell me, Forget-me-not," said he, abruptly, "do you believe your thoughts would follow me into danger in this fashion, as Agatha's did Max? Would you hear the forest murmur in your ears every hour, if I was in a Wolf's Glen? O, I know you too well to doubt." And, as if the answer had exorcised the demon, he took up the duet in Spohr's Psalm: "Children, pray this love to cherish," and in returned faith in his untested strength, hurried into exulting harmonies.

His confidence and his foreboding alike brought a pang to Mollie, this sad afternoon of leave-taking, as she sat filling the organ lungs with the breath that he made exhale in melody. This had always been her part. Their world seemed to her like a Pygmalion's statue, which she fashioned and he made live. Now he was going away; elsewhere he must find nutriment and stimulant. Hitherto, their emotions, their labors, had been one. His very attainments in his art were only *her* longing for him, which *he* realized. He was her boy lover. In the tears she wiped, gathered as much motherhood as selfish pain. Soon Louis throws by his revery: he has guessed that she is heavy-hearted; he will comfort her. Then he plays a volkslied, strong, earnest, free. Isn't that noble, darling? That's Mendelssohn's last Lieder ohne Worte. It means that earnestness, however withstood by fate, will make way and conquer at last. You shall learn it; it is not difficult. It will be a prayer, we will say on the piano. Now sing "He shall give thee thy soul's desire," while I blow.

These were Louis' devotions. Mollie obeyed, and the pair silently closed the instrument as the last note faded away, and together they went back into the sunshine. Louis' gayety returned the instant he regained the open air. "Mollie sweet," coaxed he, "let us be merry to-day. We were miserable all night; but this is time I saved to cheer you. You must smile!" He caressed her hand, half imperious, half imploring, and then ran a bit up the road, and frolicked back again airily, to present a captured Camberwell beauty, the fruit of the chase.

"Let us make a scapegoat of him," suggested the young girl, watching his struggles with a pity partly born of her own soul pain. "See, some one has already brushed the blue and gold from his pretty maroon wings, and we have several specimens already."

"Agreed; wait a minute and I'll offer the invocation," said Louis, stopping, and moving the fingers of one hand up and down on the back of the other, as if working up a difficult piano passage—a trick he had learned by doing German lessons while he practised exercises. "Ah! I have it:

> "'Go, harbinger of Autumn, thou mimic of his robe,
> Fly hence, and bear upon thy wings
> The care my Mollie on thee flings—
> A burden very light to carry,
> Since care's no care that doth not tarry.'

That's not so bad for an impromptu epigram—you smile! Then it was worth inventing. You are lovely, so. Now I can be truly gay. We are going toward the brook;

there is dear old Atlas—I can see the name we carved
on him, plain as ever."

He pointed to a huge square rock, full fifteen feet high,
which towered from the centre of a bit of granite-strewn
pasture, like a gigantic monument among a host of little
tombstones, perchance as a memorial of a wrecked life
among its poor dead joys. But neither of the lovers felt
any longer in the mood for such sombre fancies. The
stern patriarch seemed indeed transfigured by the afternoon sunlight reflected from his gray sides; a flock of
birds assembled for southward flight were twittering on
his summit, and bits of green fern nodded from all his
crevices, and scarlet creepers trailed from his wider
fissures like favors worn at a ball.

So said Mollie; and then laughingly followed up the
simile: "An *Irish* ball, I declare! You wouldn't be a
quarter so sweet, Louis, if it wasn't for the emerald in
you. See! the two peach-trees we sowed beside the old
darling are all grown and handsome. He takes good
care of them, because his playmates planted them. Do
you remember how we tried to worship the sun on top.
It's black and streaky yet, where we had the altar."

"Yes, but we roasted corn and potatoes there a good
many times afterward. I stole, and you cooked."

"Magnum est Vectigal par simonia," laughed Mollie;
" but see! to-day is all omens; here is this lovely brake
with two perfect heads—one for you, and one for me—
on the same stem."

Shrill, childish voices followed the stillness that ensued,
while Louis eagerly examined the rarity, and a boy and
girl, tattered and dirty, emerged from the wood. Marks
of a tussle with the blackberry bushes did not improve
their sunburnt faces and arms, and, though the inevitable
basket carried by the damsel was filled with masses of

fern, golden rod, and purple-fringed daisies, these coarser
spoils were evidently taken for lack of better, and failed
to satisfy.

"They bees all gone," was the boy's melancholy reply
to some forlorn complaint. "Bad luck to them cows
that browses on 'em. They bloomed white all over when
I came this way froggin' in the spring. Seein' yer so set
back about it, I wish I was a field of roots so you could
dig me up and be satisfied."

"I don't want to grub thistles," was the tart rejoinder,
in suggestive thickness of tone; then repentantly, "but if
you was, sure I'd still be the bumble-bee to buzz about you."

"Why, that's Amos and Doppy!" cried Mollie, from
her perch aloft. "They stopped after Sunday-school last
week, to ask Peace if she thought roots lived this time of
year. She told me of it. Of course there are no flowers.
She's ready to cry with disappointment. They think of
nothing but the garden of the 'Solomon Rodgers.'"

"And if I've a grain of fellow-feeling, I'll go to show
that shambling donkey where they grow," added Louis,
ruefully. "Mollie, I believe you'd coax me to hunt
truffles for the Dennis pig, if you thought the McCross
refuse didn't fatten him well enough! Well, I shan't
get another opportunity to do your pleasure—to be useful is my wish."

"You certainly are one that loveth all things best,"
answered Mollie, fondly meeting the smile into which his
assumed expression of injury melted, with a bright one
out of her heart. "I had only got as far as compassion,
but you spring to relief! Here, Doppy, climb upon the
rock with me; Mr. Allwood knows where the roots are.
He is going to show Amos. Amos won't mind your
leaving him; gentlemen always like to wait on their
lady friends."

"Thar! look at that now!" cried Doppy, in full approval. "Yer to go and dig, Amos, while I play leddy long wid Miss McCross. Be keerful of me basket," bestowing the horrid wickerware with a lofty imitation of Mollie's method of granting like favors. An agile shinning up the huge boulder followed, but, flushed and triumphant at last, she took her place beside her new friend with a grand spread of her tattered skirts.

"You like Amos better than you did yesterday?" suggested Mollie, when *her* eyes came back from watching the pride of her soul disappear on his friendly errand.

"I've seen worse bys," admitted Miss Mulligan, as she played a kind of solitaire peep-a-boo with her bare toe and the hem of her dress. "I'm not in a peck o' nettles 'bout him same as some 'ud be. And if I said I tought him bully, you'd go and tell, and he'd make light o' me. It ain't best to own carein' for the best o' min." Her ten years' skin and bones made absurd contrast to this astute remark; but Doppy was far too earnest to notice the twinkle in Mollie's eyes. "Who put this rock here?" inquired she, diplomatically changing the conversation. "It's a whoppin' big un! Amos and me made out, comein' up, that them little lookin'-glasses all over the stone walls must be for the Good People, though we don't believe in 'em noway, if Mrs. Dennis *do* have a silver pin they left in her clane milk pans in Ireland."

"God put it here," said Mollie, "when He made the mountains."

Doppy sniffed.

"It's one part of them," reasserted Miss McCross, gently, "but not so pretty as some of the other kinds. They are full of little red stones that shine—garnets. Often these are bedded in white sand, and are very bright. I shouldn't wonder if there are a few hidden here," and with the thought she jumped up and uncovered a shelf-like fissure ingeniously thatched with sticks, moss, and pebbles. "Ah, yes; so they are!" fishing up a nondescript mass of chrysalids, beetles, geological specimens, odd mosses, birds' feathers and wings, and squirrel skins. "Mr. Allwood and I used to hunt for such things a great deal when we were children. We made our hiding-place here. This green stone is tourmaline; this thin, glassy bit is leaf mica, the same as the fairies' mirrors. See these large garnets! This red stuff is iron ore. We found some greenish, once, that we thought was hornblende."

"In the rocks?" cried Doppy, her eyes as large as saucers.

"Yes. I'll tell you all about them, if you like."

And the botanists, returning with their baskets full of muddy spoils half an hour after, found the little figure still sprawled contentedly on the summit of Atlas, kicking its heels, and watching Mollie with unabated interest as she knelt expounding her treasures.

"May I present you with some sassafras?" said Louis, from the base of their citadel. "Avourneen delish, come down, if we are to go to the brook. I have helped Master Dalcy to hepaticas, lupines, cardinal-flowers, gentians, triliums, mocassin-flowers, clematis, white violets, adders' tongues, enough to restore the 'Solomon Rodgers' to its old splendor."

"If you please, ma'am," said Doppy, rising and making a quick knee-bend, like that she did before the altar at church, "I am very much obliged to you." Mollie was astonished at the soothed, courteous manner of the child and the modest blush with which she made her thanks.

"Would you like the stones?" asked she, instantly putting herself in her eager listener's place, and anxious to rivet her wedge till another opportunity offered for driving in.

"If you would be so kind," answered Doppy, coining the polite little phrase anew in literal reply,—" the ones you've explained, till I tell Amos the story."

"Come down," cried Amos, all bound up in pride of his well-stocked basket. "Sure iverything 'ull wilt, if yer so schnaly."

"Why don't you stand at the foot to help me, same as Mr. Allwood has Miss McCross?" asked his young lady, her soul expanded with desire to live experimentally her new ideal, and woman's longing to teach the recreant swain his duty.

"Cause he's a gentleman an' I ain't;" and Master Daley set down his burden, and leaned against the wall, hands in his pockets, with invincible obstinacy.

"Thin ye can go 'long alone. I'm going to be respectable, and respectable people don't shin down."

"But *I* have been waiting for the honor," interfered Louis, much amused. "Would it be too great a loss of dignity for you to be lifted?"

"You should take better care of your little friend, if she's kind enough to ask your help," admonished he, as Miss Mulligan was deposited beside her basket.

Doppy's large brown eyes sparkled with pleasure. "Do ye mind that, Amos," she enforced proudly. "Jest give me holt of that handle; it's too heavy fur the likes of you."

"I cackellate, I'd best take care of my little friend, and do my own liftin'," parodied Amos, accepting the reproof good-naturedly. Then he slyly turned the tables. "I'm waiting to hear you say, 'I bees obligated to the likes of ye, Masther Daley, fur yer perliteness,' same as Miss McCross 'ud do in yer place."

How could poor Doppy but answer, meek in woman's humility, " That's thrue fur ye—ye have me gra-ti-tude," and feel in the depth of her soul that even the long word, well drawn out, could not compare with the profound wit of her shambling admirer.

Meantime, Louis and Mollie had already pushed toward their destination. Black Turk's Head rose loftily on one side the road, to be confronted by the Christian's Lookout, over across. And beside the path, in the little valley between, flowed the brook, bending downward, sylph-like, as if to lay her bright hands on the laughing face of Roaring River, busy about his work far below.

" She trips on rarely," cried Louis. He loved the dainty stream—so wild, and yet coy and gentle, beneath its arch of maples and alders, ever straying blithely among its huge, green-mossed boulders, with the unfretted strength of persistence that nature had given to seem fairest of all to him. " Why should we walk stupidly where humans plod along, when we can just as well frisk on the granite floor of that Nixie's palace, yonder?"

" Why, indeed," cried Mollie, yielding easily to his fancy. How many, many times had they already traversed together the stepping-stones, worn round by the incessant pressure of the nymph's feet!

No lovelier palace ever had elf. There was the brown water itself, with here and there a sunbeam resting like a topaz upon the Lurline's vesture. The autumn golden rods and daisies bloomed in the open, beyond the faintly turning arch of willows, maples, and alders. But over their heads tangled clematis hung in sprays, and great bushes of poke berries vied in richness with the graceful masses of bitter-sweet, and even more brilliant clusters of red and yellow nightshade—for it was a patrician Lurline, that must not be without its wicked ways. Here,

too, trailed scarlet woodbine, in its fervid flame, another
Dido, mourning after her lost birds of passage. Daws
were cawing in the woods; nuts untouched by frost, but
shaken by overmuch wind o' nights, dropped through
the hazy autumn air. Now and then a partridge roused
from its cover whirred past, or the sharp crack of a rifle
on the other side the hill warned of farmers' boys on
holiday.

Louis looked about him with an air of perfect relief.
"It hasn't any resemblance to the Wolf Schlct," cried
he, drawing a long breath. "It is our own dear little
stream, in our familiar New England solitude—no
vinous Neckar, or cascade in grim fir-mantled, bear-
haunted Hartz. Do you know, I was worked up to that
extent when I finished Der Freischütz last night, that the
sight of an honest American rattlesnake would have been
delightful, as reassuring my miserable bewitched self?
But see how the Nixie is offering you a seat upon this
great rock in the midst of her possessions, and this little
one covered with moss is for a footstool ! Hear the water
dive under its arch with a gurgle of welcome, to slide
shyly forth in that clear pool below—

> " ' O solitude, if I must with thee dwell,
>   Climb with me the steep—
>   Nature's observatory, whence the dell,
>   Its flowery slopes, its river's crystal swell,
>   May seem a span. Let me thy vigils keep
>   'Mongst boughs pavilioned where the deer's swift leap
>   Startles the wild bee from the foxglove bell.'

Ah! thanks, Mr. Bullfrog; I was just wanting your
place."

Mollie sat silent and happy. She loved to watch her
lover in this mood. She revelled in his delicate sim-

plicity, his bright-hued fancies, his culture, faultless in a
school whose standard and strictness were equivalent to
worship of beauty as the revelation of law; or law as
that sole arrangement of things which could produce
beauty, and hence had the undying joy of knowing them
to be the same thing. *She* was formed for activity, for
resisting adverse tides of thought, habit, mayhap fate.
She was his repose, because she did not waver or falter;
but she sought in him an every hour outlook into regions
of upper air, where he seemed in these days to dwell.
Words from her would only mar his delightsome humor,
since diverting it from its own path. She had no need
to speak.

"I am going to relate a little ditty, if you'll forgive
the expression," said he playfully, prisoning her with a
long wreath of brilliant woodbine he had been braiding
deftly during their walk; "all about a Lurline here in
this very brook. She had brown hair like the withered fall
leaves, and the bits of blue sky mirrored in the water were
exactly the color of her eyes. She had lovely red lips,
too, like the cardinal-flowers; and the trailing arbutus
that grew near her banks was the very perfume of her
breath; and her tunic was emerald green, spangled with a
border of golden rod and yellow buttercups. A poor
bullfrog lived in a hole of the bank. After he'd spent a
long time admiring this beautiful sprite, he presumed to
offer himself; and she looked with favor on his bright
eyes set in a ring of brilliant topaz, the only beauty he
had, and let him spring to her arms in a transport of
bliss.

"But it began to be winter time before long, and he
had to bid good-by to the lovely Nixie, and seek protection elsewhere; and she promised to be true—"

"Well, she was," interrupted Mollie.

"I'm afraid not. I shouldn't wonder if when the poor fellow returned he found another fatter frog than he squatted here on this very stone," persisted Louis, half teasing, half foreboding.

"Never!" cried Mollie, ardently. "Lurline's true name is Forget-me-not; and she always binds their turquoise in her hair and on her breast; there are some now just where we planted them."

"That was what I wanted to hear you say, laughed he roguishly.

"Oh," said Mollie, piqued, "how *I'll* allegorize!"

"If it's a water nymph, wouldn't alligator be a better word?" suggested Louis. "It would be a hint of warmer weather."

"Just as you like; the only part of the story I look at is the moral. Nixie was a man with teeth as white as blackberry-blossoms and sharp as thorns, and he got tired of his poor froggie-wife—like Johnnie Sauds, and one day he caught her nose under a stone and held it there till she choked."

"Do you know," said Louis reflectively, suspending his occupation of knitting a blade of grass around two straws, while he deliberated, "I am not settled about Mr. Sands. Don't you think that in spite of the joy he undoubtedly felt at his release, the horror of that desperate act must have pursued him through life?"

"I should suppose it might," acquiesced Mollie, much amused.

"Yes; think of his remorse, and the shudders of his friends, and the disgrace accruing to the Sands family. What a weight to bear!"

"Perhaps they were Quicksands, and didn't try," suggested Mollie.

"That's a fact," said Louis, receiving back his coin composedly; "that will hold water."

"That kind of soil usually does," agreed Mollie again.

"At all events, I should say J. Sands ruined his prospects of happiness by that fell deed," concluded Louis, rising as he spoke, and tossing the knitting into the stream, to watch it whirl hither and thither, till it finally caught in a knot of orchis, and rested quietly, thus moored. "That's a good omen, dear Lurline," resuming his gayety, and springing lightly ashore. "See! true love knits our separate lives as the grass ties the straw, and our fate has come to good harbor."

Mollie gave him her hand, and submitted to be helped over the rivulet, though she could have crossed it alone with perfect ease. It was her choice luxury to be tended by Louis, equally as she abominated such casual gallantry from others.

"If I was a bird," said he, smiling to her thanks, "I'd rise and survey that chipmuck I've heard rattling behind us this last half—Oh!"

The exclamation came down to his listener from the designated height, and she was naturally too much startled to divine the meaning of it, till a strange voice cried out,

"Well done, my Fejeee Bruiser! I never landed so big a fish more successfully. Chipmuck, indeed! what do you take me for? Hope I didn't damage your coat collar."

"A bear, or a condor! Charley Pelican!" answered Louis with a gasp, "I'll never think out loud again."

"Or court, either," suggested the intruder. "But I intend returning to terra firma. Are you similar?"

Louis therefore swung himself to the ground, followed by the handsomest Hercules Mollie had ever the hap to meet. That he was Peace's brother, she did not need his prey's exclamation to discover. There was the same imposing stature—Charley was at least six feet four—the blue-black Spanish hair curling a little in ringlets, not kinks; the bright dark eyes of a perfect almond shape; the brilliant complexion, even the Castilian mouth, with its haughty curves, equally handsome as Peace's, since it gained in mobility what it lost in delicate strength. Peace repeated line by line, in short, with this difference: Mr. Pelican exchanged sister's stately refinement for infinite dash, levity, audacity, that seemed not quite so reprehensible in the brightness of his magnificent beauty, as they do in uglier men. He bore himself so grandly, and tossed his head so wilfully, like a war-horse impatient of rein, and expanded his broad chest with such an air of power, that a mere look at him quickened one to the same enthusiasm one feels in survey of Niagara, Bierstadt's Rocky Mountains, the Strasbourg Cathedral, or any other masterpiece.

Now the two characters of life Mollie hated most in those days were Absalom and Lothario. Louis therefore watched in some trepidation to see how the heir of the Pelicans would find place in her good graces. She was full of pleasure at the friendly relations augured by her lover's sudden elevation, and, with her face bright with laughter, turned to meet the young giant of whom she had heard so much. Poor Mollie! He favored her blushes with a stare as full of curiosity about his sister's pet friend, scrutiny as to her points as a specimen of her sex, and merriment broad to insult over the gathering of his eavesdropping, as utter carelessness of his own behavior allowed to concentrate. Mollie's cheeks exchanged the flame of enthusiasm for the more painful brilliance of anger. She drew herself up with dignity, and said as reply to the condescending cap-lift vouchsafed, that she would walk toward home; Louis might follow at his convenience.

Mr. Pelican seemed not ill-pleased at her wrath—indeed he chuckled audibly—and told Louis he envied him his sweetheart, and would like to present to her the results of his shooting, the more as she could undoubtedly freeze the birds without other ice than herself, and still stared.

"No, thank you," cried Mollie indignantly. "I am quite as well aware as yourself that you consider us as much objects of sport as the woodcock and partridges. It is a mistake. I accept nothing from strangers whose manners are equally lacking in delicacy and self-respect."

"Mollie!" gasped Louis, perfectly aghast at a phase of character new even to his experience of her. The rebuff didn't embarrass Charley at all. But having raised the tempest, it occurred to him that the task of allaying it would be exciting. "I beg your pardon," said he, revolutionizing his tactics. "I stand corrected, and now implore your acceptance. I dare not make game of you and Allwood, or the birds either, any more. A worse hunting ground I never saw. One no sooner spies a fowl than—Jerusalem—he's mired in a quag, or choked with alders, or tripped on a nigger-head, or has the gristle of his nose torn out in a blackberry patch; and by the time he gets straight, he's been despoiled of every bit of boots, shirt, skin, temper, bird gone, all lost, and then he can't even comfort himself with the sight of a pretty girl. Now will you have 'em?" He gave his magnificent shoulders a contumacious shake as he spoke, and defiantly drew his three plump partridges from his game-bag.

"I am not pretty," said Mollie, in a matter-of-fact tone, "and I am offended because you had the impoliteness to eye me over, just as if I was not entitled to re-

spect. I do not wish any of your killing; there isn't salt
in Millville to make the dish palatable." The words
were spoken in a low, even tone, not expressive of anger,
only conveying an ordinary piece of information. When
ended, she turned to Louis as if intending to depart
immediately.

"Snooks and sneezers!" said Charley, watching her
with enjoyment by no means malicious, with very much
the pleasure a big dog has in chasing a ball, and rubber
failing, takes up with chicken as substitute. He snatched
up Louis thereupon, and holding him fast as one would
a kitten, jumped upon the stone wall, thence to an overhanging chestnut, and with his free hand steadied himself in a squirrel's climb toward the top.

"Now say you'll eat my birds, if you don't want him
dropped," he called, triumphantly.

"Not if you carried him into the clouds," retorted
Mollie, beginning to descend the hill.

"Jam diu, jam dudum!" said Charley, laughing easily. "She's as perverse as a thermometer! Which is
the most humiliating to her delicacy—to bandy words
with her slave, or forgive him?" and he returned to
earth, and keeping fast hold of his burden, pursued her.

Either Mollie must run, or allow herself to be overtaken. She preserved dignity,—held her first pace.
Charley only made a dozen steps before he reached her,
set Louis gently on his feet in her path, and said entreatingly, "See! I've brought him back. Now, please take
my game," and smiled as he looked down at her. No
one ever defied the fascination of that coaxing mouth;
not even Mollie, who held out her hand for the spoil in
silence, half sharing for the moment in Louis' manifest
admiration for the trickish giant.

"I'm going on the owl with you to-night," resumed

Mr. Pelican, addressing the young man, as he drew a long breath of exultation over his success with the lady. "We'll hunt the buffalo together. By your leave, ma'am, I'll pair the odd partridge before I give him up. Just tell Peace you don't like me, if you dare!" and he threw her a kiss, with unmatched impudence, and ran away into the fields.

The path toward Millville was directly opposite, and Mollie went along wrapped in thought. She had paid humanity's tribute of submission to embodied perfection of beauty and power. But the reflection that this potent spell-master was to take her place beside Louis was at least disagreeable. And Louis himself followed her reverie far too closely to care to ask its subject.

"The sun is set. See the mist settle over river and valley. It is so still and bright here! if we need never plunge into those shadows below!" said Mollie, breaking the rest-full stillness, and pausing on the brow of the steep.

The spire of the church below pointed directly to their feet. It seemed as if one of the yellow walnut leaves, fluttering down from its tree overhead, would cover half the town—fold the mills, the shops, the white village homes, the century-old elms, in its tiny mantle.

" Then let us loiter a little on the wall the other side the road, so we won't disturb that red squirrel. Millville looks exactly like the enchanted city going under its lake for seven years' sleep. To-morrow morning not a tree beneath crest will be visible; silver fog will make a suggestive water study of it. One might remember Baucis and Philemon, and shake in his shoes."

" I dread to go back. How calm and happy we have been this afternoon ! The very noise that ascends from the streets is refined to music. That bird sings twice as clear. But the mist will hide our way, perhaps make each other's faces dim. O Louis, how can I let you go ! "

He took her hands in his, and bent over them, his eyes full of tears, sorrowful, earnest, albeit he was boyish and simple beyond his years. Theirs was the simplicity of unity, and alas! the half-comprehended misery of their parting was, that it made twain of what God's Providence through a whole childhood had joined in one life.

"This is like the Mount of Transfiguration," said Mollie, accepting the clear western sky with its one fair star shining serenely in lucent æther,—way beyond the river, the solemn hush about them,—the peaceful memory of their hours together, as a Heaven-given whole."

"That is true, but one cannot build tabernacles there," answered Louis reverently.

Nothing more was said till they reached Gonecusset Street, when Louis threw off the burden with a jest. "Aren't you sorry your capitalist has been so generous?" inquired he. " I was thinking that since I own the whole avenue, pity we can't occupy any of it. Here is Deacon William's; he begged it of me till he should be so blessed as to become a widower; and look at his wife now! Then there's Mr. Bizby's next, my especial friend. I had a singing-school attachment for his grandmother."

"But see 'Squire Hitchcock's! that would suit me," cried Mollie, demurely.

" I really couldn't ; " and Louis stopped to lay his hand tenderly on his ribs, as it happened. " He was my messmate in the war of 1812. I couldn't be severe toward a comrade. You needn't look across the way either; that is the saddest case of all. I deeded it to the village for a common, but the Spiritualists were the only people willing to enjoy it, on account of the name. So I offered it to the Presbyterians, on condition of their calling their edifice the 'Short Cut.'. But they said such an idea would undermine the great doctrines that lie at the foundations of their system. So it had to go to Snip the tailor to get anything cut out of it but myself."

"In short," said Mollie, smiling bravely as she opened the Fir Covert gate, "it is like your pet psalm, 'Ye gentle spirits, the world is all your own.'"

And so it was—as much as any part of it. God be with 'em.

CHAPTER VII.

"'Old woman, old woman, old woman,' quoth I,
'Whither, oh whither! oh whither so high?'
'To sweep the cobwebs from the sky.'"

IN a wild-beast show, my dear readers, it is needful to have an arena—Patience of Hope is our arena. In a wild-beast show they bring the animals from far and wide. Similarly the participants in this chapter come from the four quarters. To a geographical mind, how commonplace would seem attendance at a cock-fight, were the preparatory circumstance of smuggling the fowls to the pit in carpet-bags unnecessary. But how delightful, on the other hand, to watch a polar bear chew up a tiger.. Here is variety! The poetry of antagonism! Precisely like is the habitual enmity of the sleek tiger of warm prosperity, to the shaggy bear bred in the frigid experience of want. Why do the tiger and the bear fight? "For 'tis their nature to," Mr. Chadband; and the opposite factors of a mission school take no new departure from the old rule of class hate.

Christ love affords a tournament ground for more passions than amity comprehends, all the world over; and the bears growl and show hug to the tigers; and the tigers lick their gilded coats and wash their complacent faces after banquet on the ruder foe, six days in the week; and the seventh do like unto it. The real Christ in a mission school is a lamb, equally the antipodes of the sleek or shaggy—a lamb cradling in his master's bosom, and bent on errands of simplicity and peace.

I am indebted to Peace Pelican for the above disagreeable statement of the situation, and while I proceed to marshal my forces into line this Sunday morning, I will remark, *en passant*, that the originator thereof prided herself on being a tiger, but admired Mary McCross as a lamb, and considered it a root of offence in Francis Haythorne that he manifested no agnus of nature or habit. She had, moreover, been heard to mention wolves and sheep-skins, and similar objects, unconnected (?) with Mr. Nixon, the superintendent; and his habit of knocking down his scholars with a heavy fist invariably induced her to add bête to the list of his descriptive nouns.

The Sabbath of our chapter dawned clear and breathless, laden with the heavy spice odors of great beds of tuberoses and chrysanthemums at Fir Covert, stifling amid the squalor and pigs of Syllabub.

But it was Lord's Day down there after all. The white sunshine streamed over the uncouth comfortless buildings, into greasy windows, and reeking cellars, as brightly as ever it did upon the broad bend of Roaring River, fringed with willows and nestling among softly sloping pastures. . Here and there a yellow butterfly fluttered across the road. The very gutters sparkled; and the great heap of dock that flourished by Doppy's front door was brilliant with dew-drops. Devout old women in

a double head-gear of cap frill and sun-bonnet; spruce
young girls in their stiffly ironed muslins, and gay young
fellows in Sunday broadcloth, wended their way toward
the church, whose far-off bells you could hear. As
Bridget told Mary McCross, "that same whose spire
reached nearer to heaven than ary another in the place."

There is something about the Sabbath atmosphere
that marks it from common times. We may philoso-
phize it away, but our souls acknowledge it. Sunday is
the Rachel's Child in the week, and now, as of yore, goes
clad in the festal garment; its sweetly discordant bells
sound in our hearts, calling to rejoicing. Under our
windows comes the joyful tramp of the multitude that
keep holiday. Through the open gates of heaven streams
the sun, whose beams are equally strength and peace.
Looking thereon we feel the Son of Righteousness arise
in our hearts, with healing in his wings. Our voices are
soft, for it is the Sabbath ; and our faces calm, for this
day God dwells recognizably among us. The heat and
cold, the breeze and calm, are in no wise changed. The
grasshoppers shriek in the fields, and the swallows stir
under our eaves, as alway; but once more peace and
good-will toward men enact their miracle ; and Ambrosia
foams Bancis' earthen pitcher, and Philemon's poor
cottage stretches away into marble halls.

The above was the *ipse dixit* of Mary McCross, as she
looked out picture-books in the library, whereon to hang a
thread of moral story at Patience of Hope.

I am sorry to add that no similar train of thought
occurred to Amos Daley, as he swaggered toward the
meadows so much affected by his penny-pitching associates.

It had been too hot for Amos to sleep that sultry Sunday. When, therefore, he had drawn on his trousers

and scratched his head with his mourning finger-nails, he was ready for action. He lived in the third story, left hand, back tenement, of the Chain Locker on River Street. He had six younger relations, including an orphan cousin—and but one shirt.

Nor was our rhapsody fellowed by any single idea in the indolent brain of Francis Haythorne : outstretched on his chintz-covered sofa, and combating a dreamy intention to practise Lohengrin ; making the rose-water in his nargileh bubble and boil the while, and occasionally glancing at a copy of "Origin of Species" in his hand. Just then the door-bell rang, and a serving man entered the room.

"If you please, sah," said he, wiping his dripping face, and smiling, perhaps in delight at breaking in on so much cool comfort, "Missus say Mary Ann be's sick, and she wants you to come and proscribe."

"What is the matter with Mary Ann?" said the disturbed physician, keeping his finger on a pigeon experiment page, and surveying the intruder languidly.

"Missus 'clare she have a high fever, and she be in great flurry. She thinks her eyes is rolled up in her head. She said for me to wait and bring you." The darkey grinned again.

Francis Haythorne looked at the thermometer, and wished it was cool enough to kick his black insolence out of doors. It proved only a passing feeling, however, forgotten while he caressed his curling beard with his soft white hand, and reviewed the conflicting claims of Wagner, temptingly open on the flower-decked piano, and Esculapius hot, dusty, and beset with worry. "Rolled up in her head!" What if the detested infant had congestion of the brain, and should die on his hands, to make him turn cold on hot days, and hot on cold days, forever.

"I'll tell you, John," said he, calmly, turning just enough to look the man in the face, and not a hair's-breadth more; "you've made a mistake. The person you were sent to lives just across the street. Don't you remember it was Jenkens? Here's a quarter for your trouble;" whereupon he returned to consideration of rock pigeons and pouters, and the bubbling nargileh seemed to murmur approbation of this settlement of the case.

Peace Pelican, screened behind the Jenkens' half-closed parlor blinds, looked straight into the shady window opposite, saw the colloquy, watched the man approach and ring the home door-bell, and listened attentively to a redescription of the wretched infant's situation, which by the way was obviated by a dose of eau sucré. The young beauty's lip curled with contempt. She felt glad to find a chance to despise the self-sufficient red-haired. True, she held it unladylike to walk down town in a hot day. She liked to array herself elegantly, and practise the fan exercise to admiration, and smile at the moths caught in the current; she revelled in perfumes, and exulted in her ivory nail files and powders. But somehow the two sorts of goose did not seem exactly benefited by the same sauce. Peace could not help thinking toughness a virtue in ganders, whatever might be the case with the pretty white feminine fowl she compared to herself. She resolved to set this delicately before the eyes of the lazy medicine man; and arranged herself with extraordinary care for "Patience of Hope," as she thus decided. When Peace wished to strengthen a good purpose, or unravel a knotty problem, she always began by adorning herself to a perfection of toilette. It facilitated her reasoning.

. . . .

Everything about the McCross mansion seemed to

have fallen asleep long ago, and to be still drowsy with its long nap—taken while the outside world had gone on changing its face and fashions in its own scrambling, pushing, bustling way.

It was a quaint wood cottage, set some distance from the street behind its hedge of fir-trees; a cottage full of angles and additions that rambled back, growing less and less, till it ended, like most human handiwork, in smoke. And the hams and shoulders, done in this humble termination of greater things, were not without fame in the country thereabout.

A wide piazza ran across the face of the house—disorderly beyond parallel in the presence of a forgotten broom corn. Its front was overhung by wisteria and woodbine, clematis, and a rare Miller's Burgundy grape, now spreading its small compact clusters athwart the entrance half shyly, and yet withal in the modest boldness of merit. About the piazza lay a narrow, box-edged bed, full of tender crimson-tipped daisies, violets, and heart's-ease. A patch of camomile green and aromatic reposed near by. Away one side stretched an old-fashioned garden full of roses, and portulaca, fritillarias, escholtzia, painted ladies, and Turk's caps. There grew flaunting crimson cock's-combs, and great African marigolds in autumn, and early crocuses, and hoop petticoats, and snow-flakes, at the first vanishing of winter.

At this moment Mary McCross was descending the steps on her way to mission school. Her arms were full of books and her hands of flowers. Patience of Hope was to shine right brilliant with its Lord's Day Blossoms. All Millville and Roaring River taught there, and a dear, delightfully wicked school it was. Deep in a brown study, touching the story of Goliath as an illustration of faith, Mollie approached the scene of her labors.

"Darned if she don't study all them books," cried a voice in her ear, and waking up, she found half a dozen boys staring at her. The trumpet unquestionably gave no uncertain sound. Prepared thereby for battle, Mollie instantly smiled, and invited them all in.

"Might as well go to hell, and I'd as lief," shrieked a ten-year-old theologian. But Amos, who had loafed up to the school, overheard, and knocked him down on the spot.

"I'm goin' in, boys; who's afeard?" said he, scoffingly; and in a minute they were all seated about the young lady, as ragged and dirty a group as ever happy teacher possessed.

The chivalry that led Master Daley to insure the class, prompted him to keep it in order. He had a charge on his mind also. Little Doppy, whose imagination was still fired with visions of "clean cloes," had resolved to attend and win. Indeed, a scuffle, and blows, and shrill childish curses, at the foot of the stairs, already betrayed her vicinity.

Amos, in fact, might have been seen at the "Solomon Rodgers" that morning, detailing the delights of Patience of Hope, with a tortoise-shell kitten nestling in his neck, and its mate curled up in the crown of his hat. The picture of the caressing furry pet rubbing her sides against the apple-cheeks of the awkward lad, was sweet to Doppy, though Joe Haverty, who was present, *did* turn up her nose. It was the pleasantness of the memory, more than anything else, that brought Dorothea to the *salle defendu* of the mission-school.

"She shall come up! let her 'lone, or I'll punch your head," cried Amos, leaping the balustrade and darting to the door. Then, suiting the action to the word, he drew Doppy, sobbing defiance, from the smutty clutches of

Aleck and Christie Malone, and half dragged her in his hurry to the class of Mary Ann Williams. "You be a good lady, and she'll rest content wid ye," said he decidedly, and vanished without further preamble.

The people teaching in the room that day were our old friends. The Irish beauty with a whole seat of boys bigger than she, was Sonsie Eagan, and Sabrina Bradshaw sat next, with another just like it. Opposite her was Miss Williams, and beyond *her* Zoe Walsingham. Jan Vedder kept the door, for quiet was not the order of the day at Patience of Hope, Chris Goldsmith's name, and decidedly appropriate.

School opened with a song—White Robes. Amos intoned all on one note, and looked complacently at his agonized teacher. Then Mr. Nickson offered a prayer— a long one. Directly a stream of whispers came over to Miss McCross. "Go away, musketer. We has enough of ye at home. Say, Miss, I had a musketer in my hand once and I squashed him." Alas for Mollie! insect jewelry was all the rage in Millville. Just then Zoe gave a convulsive giggle. Chancing to steal a look at the unbowed heads before her, instantly each black little hand sought its owner's face, and one bright, mischievous eye blinked through in merry mimicry. Mr. Nickson closed with Our Father. We give the version Hugh repeated :—

> " Our Father who art in New Haven,
>   I paid all my debts square and even.
>   Thy kingdom come with a big jug of rum,
>   If I didn't pay all, at least I paid some."

"Say !" said a tall boy in Miss Eagan's class, when the devotions were over, "Nickson, an' Vedder, an' Bradshaw, beats all the fellers I ever hear pray."

"Pooh !" returned his comrade. " Never mind him,

Miss Eagan; he's jest greased his head with his mother's lamp ile, an' don't know what he's sayin'."

Meantime, Mary McCross was surveying her wriggling, uneasy, mischief-loving, sham-hating urchins. Most people would have been intimidated by their ring-leader alone. You must have seen Amos to appreciate him. Preparatory for school he had assumed full dress, and his long, wide-skirted coat, of ministerial cut, was built for a Falstaff. It was ornamented profusely with horn and white porcelain buttons, he had turned its sleeves back half up his arms, and its collar was ripped off, and hung down his back. His trousers were fastened to his waist by an old rope, and their tatters but half concealed his sturdy limbs. His keen, blue-gray eyes sparkled under their heavy black brows, and his lips closed over a row of tobacco-stained teeth as regular as beads. In any but his present attitude of protector, he would indeed have been formidable, for he possessed the resolute will and quick impulsive daring that makes a lad a leader anywhere. But Miss McCross was impressed with the idea that he would give her a quiet class, and had her own theory of insuring this result.

"Boys," began she, "I'll tell you about David to-day."

"We've heard that once," said Hugh, with strong disapprobation.

"Well, of heaven then. What do you suppose they live on?" A dread pause, till Aleck suggested "peanuts," with a giggle, whereat Hugh brought out some in a paper and passed them round. But Amos nabbed and suppressed the dainty in calm resolution. "You shan't plague the lady," cried he, a warning flash in his eye. "They don't have nothin' to eat there."

Mollie smiled encouragement, but Hugh rejoined, with great composure, "Then they must be thin as shadders."

"Tell us the boat story," said Barney O'Hara, who had been there often. But Noah's adventures were brought to a sudden stand-still.

"You say the whole world was one big pond, as deep as Roaring River pond?"

"Yes, indeed, deeper," said unsuspecting Mollie.

"O! what a bully place to swim," cried Aleck, drawing a long breath.

"They chew tobacco in heaven, don't they?" said Hugh, offering Miss McCross some.

"Why, I'm surprised; I thought they did."

"I chew to keep the hunger off," put in white-faced Barney. Seeing the drift of the matter, Mollie began a long story about Anderson's "Match Girl," and Kingsley's "Three Fishers," and soon pointed her morals to a thoroughly interested audience.

"This picture is about Ananias and Sapphira," said Cymbalinus Adolphus to his boys. "Ananias is the man, and Sapphira is the woman. They told a lie and fell down dead! Suppose you should tell a lie and fall down dead! Now!" said Mr. Brown, solemnly, "what do you believe became of them?"

"Went to hell, and be d—d to 'em," said a rough-looking fellow. "Bet they're hot enough now."

"If you please, sir, I burned myself all over once with kerrycene," put in a lad with merry eyes. "I was awful sick."

"Oh, I'm *so* sorry," said Mr. Brown, doing the sympathetic. "What did you put on it?"

"It's the biggest lie I ever told in my life, and I ain't dead either."

Old Miss Petingil came grimly in one day and took a class. "Do you lie?" quoth she.

"Yes'm."

"I stole your tom-cat's kittens," confessed one rascal.

"Peculiar! how folks ken," said the maiden, drawing back from the faces that were eying her with malicious grins.

"Mebbe you swear too?"

"Look-a-here, old woman," said one, "I'll lay ten cents agin your best bonnet, that I can beat you any day."

"Dreffful strange, I allow!" quoth the spinster. "You wicked boy, don't you know liars and swearers are an abomination to the Lord?"

"No, I don't, but I'll tell you one thing; ef you don't speak civil, you'd better git, fur we ain't goin' to stand it."

Thereat the poor lady rose in a fright and ambled away.

Rosy-cheeked Peter Bradshaw was energetically explaining machines to a large class, who listened, chin in hand, in motionless attention. His prosperity was short: one boy had conceived a spite against another, and to-day the train was laid. Suddenly a large piece of pumpkin pie struck the offending party full in the face, and hung a ludicrous attachment to his upturned nose. In the derisive shout that greeted the missile the blow was returned, and the fray became instantly general. So sudden was the rise of the scrimmage, that it must have been planned beforehand. "Don't be afeared, Miss Bradshaw," said her boys, gathering about the Silver Lake Goddess, who was very pale. "We'll take care of you."

Hymn-books and picture-cards were flying about, and some one threw a stool with no bad aim at the gallant Superintendent, who had taken refuge behind a black board, and trembled visibly.

"Sit down!" cried Peter Bradshaw to the pumpkin-pie victim. "*Sit down*, I say!"

"That red-haired cuss shan't stay here; he's the devil himself."

"It's because your sister's head is so red that you'd excuge him."

The laugh that rose at this sally was by no means ill-humored, but the participants hurried to obey the cry, "Out! out!" that proved the signal for a general stampede toward the door. Then Jan Vedder, coolly holding his post, exclaimed loudly: "The first fellow that comes near, I'll pitch down-stairs!" and suiting the action to the word, he seized a six-foot Irishman who led the malcontents, and deliberately flung him to the bottom.

"Well done!" "Couldn't have beaten that myself!" were commendatory exclamations from the crowd thus boldly faced, and a little undecided pause ensued. Hoots below warned the teachers of a party of roughs assembled at the gate; but still the scholars within, bent more on fun than mischief, hesitated to force their way out. The result seemed an even chance, and there was a moment's silence before the decision came.

"The devil! they're cowed! the fools!" cried a stranger in Mary McCross' class, who had been urging on the tumult with missile, voice and stamp. "Let's go, Christie Malone."

Mollie recognized the danger. A word would rally the party and break up the school. "No, you'll stay here," said she, quietly.

"Who's to stop us?" retorted he, all braggadocio. "I don't see the man."

But Mollie was not quiet within, for Francis Haythorne, who had been sitting on the visitor's bench, the picture of indolent, high-bred amusement, now approached her, and offered his assistance.

The angry blood surged to her cheeks, as she exclaimed, in a haughty tone, *very* natural, and yet uncommon, to Mollie, "*No*, sir. If I can't take care of myself, I've no business here."

"Bully for you," shrieked Amos, approvingly. And when she turned toward the angry agitator, with an entirely different air from that used to her sybarite protector, and said, in an even, sunny tone, " Will you please take your seat ; " bending on him a glance that implied, " Don't you see what impertinence you expose me to ? " he dropped meekly to his place without a word.

It was nature, not generalship, that won her the day, and her victory was the settlement of the whole disturbance. Even the victim of Jan Vedder's prowess picked himself up, and, holding out a hand fit for a blacksmith, exclaiming, " I admire to know you ! that was a hunki shove ! I'll be quiet if you leave me in," showed no trace of malice.

Francis Haythorne, in fact, was the only one wounded. He had not only proved of no use, but he'd been told so. Nothing less than Mollie's perfect unconsciousness of having given ground for offence could have saved a rupture of their friendship. As it was, he had to pocket the affront, and, thoroughly piqued, resolved to put his hand to the plough, and looked to her for approval. None, however, came. Mollie was too deeply immersed in her own work to bestow any interest on the matter.

Peace, on the contrary, wanted the amusement of walking home with him, and was liberal in her praise, and let him carry her sun-shade as a reward. But even Peace had her root of bitterness. " Mollie," said she, stopping suddenly, and speaking with an intensity of emotion nearly amounting to fierceness, " I hate that school ! I've five little girls in my class, and every one of their fathers gets drunk ! "

" Well ? " said Mollie, who was very fond of Peace Pelican, and interested in all her thoughts.

" *My* father sells whiskey."

CHAPTER VIII.

" ' How many strawberries grow in the sea ? '
I answered him as I thought good—
' As many red herrings as grow in the wood.' "

 WEEK or two after this, Peace Pelican, who was visiting in Millville for the autumn, found her way up to Mollie's room.   I don't say " found her way," because she was a stranger there.   On the contrary, her calls were so frequent, that Mrs. McCross was accustomed to tell Mollie they might as well board her at once.   Mrs. McCross had all the dislike of a careful parent to those of her daughter's friends that she did not select—Euphemia Hitchcock being a fair sample of her choice.   She said she wanted every bit of Mollie's heart herself. · Accordingly, Peace was scarcely seated when she called from the foot of the stairs :

" Mary ! Mary ! it's time for our morning season of prayer.   Perhaps your friend will come down, too ; anyway, she can't expect you to give up *your* religious duties."

Mollie cast an ashamed and anxious glance at Peace, whose black brows bore an ominous contraction.

" Go down, don't wait," quoth that lady, maliciously. " Tell your mother I've done my stint this morning."

Mollie went patiently to the door, and then stood still with her hand on the knob.

" What are you stopping there for ?   Don't you know

" ' Satan trembles when he sees
The weakest saint upon his knees ? ' "

He'll have an ague fit this morning.   I won't join you out of sheer pity.   I dislike making my friends uncomfortable, and two is enough to set at him !   Go ! I want to read Gil Blas." She settled herself deep into the easy-chair, and elevated her magnificently arched foot to the dignity of a worked ottoman. It was a lovely stool, a slender, womanly hand, holding by their stems three golden apples and a leaf or two adhering. But, though Miss Pelican's eyes were bent on the booted member that tapped an angry accompaniment to her thoughts, she saw neither it nor its dainty rest. Presently her face cleared and she smiled. Peace had a wonderful smile : not sweet, nor gentle, nor tender ; but affluent, and brilliant as ver-milion. I suppose it was an index of repentance, for when Mollie came softly in a few minutes later, she exclaimed :

" If you don't forgive me I'll pay you the half peanut I owe you, and we'll dissolve partnership."

" Then I'm afraid I must," said Mollie dryly, and she too smiled, a womanly, gentle gleam, that gave an honest radiance to her face. Mollie's laugh was the most re-liable thing about her. It only answered to pleasant or ten-der emotion. She could not summon it at her will at all.

" Goody girl ! Grin' for a huckleberry ? " dancing something white before her.

" A letter ? " Mollie was not matter of fact now. She fairly trembled with delight. Peace eyed her cynically, and thought up cutting remarks. Peace was altogether fancy-free, and prided herself on a brain fever and two marriages of desperation, which her heartless charms had brought about. " I should think you were reading num-ber one, instead of number twenty," said she, when the eager, happy face above the paper had worn her patience threadbare. " I believe Louis sonneted to you every other night while I was in Top Town. I made a point of looking over his shoulder on purpose to see him blush."

" You are mistaken," said Mollie, uneasily ; " this is the first time he has written ; in fact, my only love letter." She folded the note as she spoke, and carefully laid it away among her ribbons.

"Well, if 'my precious Mollie' applies to any one else, perhaps they were destined otherwise. I didn't read far enough to see

Love-sick
Pickwick,'

at the bottom. They were probably penned for effect, as mamma's morning's scribble declares that he is punctuality, helpfulness, good temper, and all the virtues done up in a bundle."

Mrs. McCross, habited in a large straw flat, cut in on this pleasant theme with the announcement that Cymbalinus Brown and Francis Haythorne were both coming to tea, and she wished to persuade Miss Pelican to remain also. She was not sorry for her late rudeness; but convenience was more important than consistency. She therefore cooed the invitation to her "dear child," and then, embracing Mollie in a gush of motherly tenderness, exclaimed: "I feel that the Lord has given me the leading of His Spirit in pointing out Adolphy Brown to be the husband for you. He is a man that will be no hindrance to your Christian course, and I desire you to sparkle up to him and get the most out of your opportunity."

Peace, who really wished to make amends to Mollie, and, moreover, had not forgotten her resolve to expound the gander theory to the delinquent physician, assented blandly to Mrs. McCross's plan, and instituted a mental comparison of her hostess, in her present accoutrement, to a pale toadstool, which was quite apt enough to console her for the enforced amiability.

"Come and kiss me, sweet creature," said Mollie, turning round from the mirror and a dish of magnesia and water. (She had been applying it to her face to remove freckles, in obedience to her mother's parting command.)

"No, thank you; I don't touch whited sepulchres," retorted her friend.

"Oh!" said Mollie, laughing and plunging her dainty head in the wash-bowl, emerging thence fresh as a flower. She had abundant strength and will in those days, and *small* maternal shafts couldn't find a flaw in her armor. Besides, there was her talisman,—her first and only love-letter. Ah! none but God, the divine love, can tell the passing sweetness of that shyly worded, half-hinted, half-implied, testimony of honest affection, to the woman that cherishes its source as her best good.

"Let's go to sewing society, as a preparatory work of grace," said Peace, finishing aloud an internal reverie about the impending tea-party. "I feel dreadfully snippy. If I expend the impulse on pants and shirts, the nearest circle of my friends may be the gainers." Whereupon she shook her skirts vivaciously, and glanced in the mirror. Peace couldn't help testing the propriety of an emotion by its effect on her face, any more than she could help breathing. But she never remembered to assume the right expression away from her Urim and Thummim, so it was little consequence.

It had grown well into November, and the day was chilly and sombre. Under foot lay damp heaps of leafage, brown and shrivelled, and the overhanging clouds closed near and gray upon the look-out. The shivering passers-by showed cold pinched, and were mottled blue and yellow. But Peace loved the faces of her kind as yielding a delightful excitement, and viewed humanity generally as affording arena for practice preparatory to dazzling a more limited selection of bipeds. She, there-

fore grew gradually into geniality and brilliance as the
walk proceeded, and entered the sewing society gathered
for victory. She beamed with majesty on her friends,
struck envy to the hearts of her enemies, and, demand-
ing shears and cloth, began blocking out work in graceful
dignity of attitude, and accurate performance of her
task; for she was "capable," as well as elegant, and
prided herself thereon.

Mary McCross was provided instantly with work—
something ill-made and thrown aside by the unskilful
seamstress,—and settled unnoticed into a corner. Her
mother's training had not permitted her many friends;
the little handful of mission people, who had, like Peace,
unearthed her at Patience of Hope, being the extent.
Outwardly calm, she was much given to inward trembling in "society," and nobody remembered to look
her up.

Miss Petingil generalized conversation on their entrance, by asking if they knew of the tableau Mrs.
Deacon Williams proposed adding to the Christmas
entertainment;—Mrs. Williams—Mary Ann's mother;
you remember her?—Mrs. Ramble's half-sister. Shortly
subsequent to this her husband died, and left property
to Sonsie Eagan.

"Yes, indeed," spoke up Susie Jenkens, "Mary Ann
is to stand for Flora, crowning Payson as little Samuel.
Her mother called on Mrs. Bradshaw, the other day,
when I was there, to ask for the flowers. Mr. Nickson
proposes to appear as Mercury or Delilah, I forget
which, in the background."

"Pooh!" said Miss Petingil; "I've got a wreath of
orange-blossoms I might ha' let her had—real French;
I wore 'em at Semanthy's wedding. They'd ha' done
just as well."

The girls giggled, for Semanthy had married the missionary so long before, that her sister uniformly refused to tell the date.

Then Zoe Walsingham asked if they had given up having the Proddy twins stand for Raphael's cherubs.

"I don't like cherubs," said Peace; "I wouldn't be ' a little cherub here below,' for anything."

Miss Petingil craned up and sniffed, disgusted at the speaker's youth and beauty. Peace had an eminently antagonistic atmosphere about her, for all her charms and bewitching little ways. "Wings on babies must be dreadful!" put in Mary McCross, coming to Peace's rescue. "You couldn't hug them, or squeeze them, or spank them, because their feathers would always be in the way. Why, one wouldn't be able to enjoy them a bit ! "

" But they're not children; they're cherubs," objected Susie, who was inclined to keep to the letter.

"They must be somebody's children," insisted Peace, perverse as usual. "Don't tell me God is hard-hearted enough to make them, and stunt their growth too, if He didn't provide some compensation ; nothing short of having a mother could induce me to be a baby ! I believe all the infants that die and go to heaven are cherubs."

" I hope so," said a pale woman, softly. "I don't exactly want God to let my children know so much they'll despise me."

The girls looked down in silence. She had that winter buried her last babe—a bright-haired, bright-eyed boy. That was why she worked so patiently in the mission school.

"Niver fash yoursel' about that," spoke up Sonsie Eagan. "I've heard my mother say that sometimes her dead little ones came back and slept in her arms, warm and loving. And often o' summer nights she felt their sweet breath on her cheek, as she sat lookin' toward the stars and thinkin' of 'em. Perhaps they're seein' ye now."

It was pitiful to watch the lady instinctively smooth her collar, and dress her wan lips with the "mother smile."

" Peace," said Mollie, withdrawing from the mourner her eyes violet, and with a hungry craving in their depths, " I'm not sure but heaven is a sorry exchange for that woman's arms." Then, after a stab from conscience, she added, " But after all, God is the great type of motherhood; we can always find it in Him, in the flesh or not."

Meanwhile old Mr. Pelican, who was in town for the night, having first perused the modest columns of the " Millville Universe," became so much interested in the election, that he resolved to purchase the New York " World" for further information. He put on his coat, buttoned it tight to his chin, fastened his gloves, elevated his stove-pipe to its proper position, and then went downstairs in his stockings, forgetful of the glaring deficiency of his toilet. A decided numbness of toe made him aware of the lack, and, still in oblivion *temporibus mundi*, he hastened to draw on his boots over his pants, and sally forth again. As Charley had spent some time that morning in ornamenting the fronts with two large white paper death's heads, he presented a startling appearance. Peace and Mollie met him strutting along in all imaginable dignity, his portly person held carefully erect, and his bedizened legs advancing with majestic stride. His daughter struggled between vexation and mirth, but felt the former predominate, as she caught

sight of Charley skulking the other side the street to
enjoy the scene. Miss Pelican held herself specially in
charge of her brother's ideal of propriety, and flew at
him, and set him down with judicious severity. "How
perfectly disgusting!" exclaimed she, with superb scorn,
as she met him on the crosswalk; "the trick is boorish."

Thereupon Mr. Pelican forgot his six feet of dignity,
to the extent of thrusting his tongue into his cheek, and
winking at her with his left eye, a proceeding far from
soothing to his sister's feelings, to judge from the extreme
hauteur with which she elevated her handsome nose,
and sailed away.

But Mrs. McCross' tea drew on apace.

Francis Haythorne, first arrived, was immediately ab
sorbed by Peace's inevitable love of coquetry, and
carried off to the garden to pick bouquets, and be twitted
with laziness, and spitted on eyebeams, till he was too
dizzy with her spells to know black from white. This
was all the greater fun, because Miss Pelican was perfectly well aware that Mollie was his feminine ideal, and
believed his worship at her shrine too constant to be
broken up by radiant smiles and dazzling looks. Her
line of tactics left the field free to Cabby, who arrived in
lavender tie, and tea-rose button-hole bouquet, the pink of
sartorial art. Mollie, chafing at the necessity of enduring
his presence, received him coldly. But he was intent on
business. A gentle squeeze of her passive hand, accompanied by a killing glance from his small, shallow eyes,
acquainted her with the fact instantly. But this young
lady had a way of congealing—or to all appearance addling
—her brains till she looked like a mantis playing 'possum.
She immediately took refuge in this state of mental syn-
cope, stared vaguely, and murmured something unintelligible about the weather.

6

Mr. Brown was not surprised at her evident flurry, hung his hat on the rack with a neat and appropriate flourish, and on entering the parlor took up the guitar, and struck chords with a sentimental air.

" Do sing," said Mollie, stolidly, from an uncomfortable chair in the corner.

" Oh! I can't," responded he, using his lovely infantile drawl. " My name it is Josephus Orange Blossom—I can't sing."

" So sorry," remarked Mollie, without changing a feature.

Mr. Brown was not embarrassed, but, as she began making edging with no further attempt at conversation, he lay down at full length on the sofa, and piped in affected falsetto, with marked emphasis:

> " 'Oh, no, dear George ! not just yet awhile—
> Mother says I mustn't—mother says I mustn't—mother says I
>   mustn't—,
>   ' But father says you can.' "

Here he smiled enchantingly, and played chords to give Mollie time to take in the beauty of the idea.

" Oh ! " said Mollie, assuming an expression vacant enough to be imbecile in any one else. " What a relief to find *that one woman* possessed of a little common sense ! "

Her suitor vouchsafed her a gentle and patronizingly inquiring stare, and continued to extract a buzzing effect from his instrument.

Now as Mollie was inwardly enraged at his sacrilegious handling of Louis' dear music pet, she revenged herself by despising his slender little legs, so sweetly laid out, crossed, to contemplation, and became more stiffly erect, and emotionless in face, every moment. The entrance of Peace, beautifully decorated with vines and china asters by the attendant doctor, suggested a diversion, and the four sat down to euchre. The glowing faces of the new-comers, fresh from the keen autumn wind, enlivened our discomfited wooer, and he secreted a full set of face cards in his vest pocket, with view to aiding good-fortune. Mollie, who cared nothing for games of chance, but abhorred cheating, and always played her best as matter of conscience, detected her partner's little plan, and writhed inwardly.

The game was stupid, in consequence of much coquetting on Peace's side, and bad play on Mr. Brown's. Mr. Haythorne—who was a scientific and devoted euchre man—frowned; and Mary, who could get no leads answered, and was assisted repeatedly on left bowers unguarded, felt insupportably ennuied.

"What a spirited game you venture!" said Peace, with a mendaciously approving smile, and a view to ameliorating the situation. Then, as no one remembered whose turn it was, she put down a heart on Mr. Haythorne's left bower of next suit, and was not detected in the mistake.

"I ought to," responded he, much flattered. "I was taught my system by a blackleg."

Mr. Haythorne felt too much disgusted not to be obtuse to the malicious twinkle in Miss Pelican's beautiful eyes; and Mary, who had a habit of punching a hair-pin in and out her coiled shining braids, when in a brown study, forgot what she was doing, yielded to the custom, and finally dropped the implement on the carpet. Cabby immediately picked it up, and sticking it in his mustache, observed the effect in the opposite glass, holding his head on one side, and assuming several varieties of smile.

"Ah!" said he, ogling himself all the while, "Diamonds

trump? Allow me, joker. This picture looks exactly like the pulpit last Sunday, with the two ministers on each side supporting the colored brother."

"I don't see how you can do that," cried his partner, suddenly vitalized. "You've played once before, and I hold the card you've put down, in my own hand. The trick is Mr. Haythorne's. That euchres us, and gives them the rub." Mollie was indignant for two reasons. In the first place, she was beaten by his slovenly playing; and in the second, considered the company insulted by the attempted fraud. She rose directly, but Mr. Brown lifted his artificially prolonged eyebrows, and remained wrapped in affectionate study of the effect of the black hair-pin on his lily-white complexion. "Oh, you play a strict game?" said he. "Quite correct." He increased his angle of neck-crook as he spoke, and slightly varied the position of the ornament, with another smile of self-approval.

Mrs. McCross now entered, followed by her husband.

"Why don't he get a kernel of corn, and call the hairs together?" said Peace, aside, after a survey of the suitor's scraggy blond ornament.

"That one on his little toe he 'acquired from wearing expensive patent-leathers,' perhaps," suggested Mollie.

The "entre-nous" style of conversation obtained through the room. Mr. Haythorne was monopolized by Deacon McCross, who was bent on obtaining useful information.

"You say you've been in Africy?" said the old gentleman, eagerly.

His guest assented.

"When Dr. King, the missionary, travelled in those parts, he said he discovered some people without much of any clothes on, an' they came at him, an' 'were going to eat him up.' 'Spose you didn't see nothin' of that sort?"

Mollie, who loved her father too dearly to mind his peculiarities, listened in some amusement for Mr. Haythorne's answer; but Mrs. McCross exclaimed immediately, "Elizur, *will* you have the goodness to hold your tongue?" which broke up the colloquy. The old man said he guessed he'd go out in the garden, and scald a few ants and uncles, and wandered mildly off, leaving his wife to conduct the conversation.

"Did you attend the 'Read and Sew' at Mr. Growing's?" said the young man, snatching the first topic likely to interest.

"No," replied the Deacon's wife, in a disparaging tone; "in my opinion, Mr. Growing and his idol of a playwriter are alike. I consider it out of character to read such things at a church society. When the youth of the congregation are dead in trespasses and sins, Baxter's 'Call,' or Doddridge's 'Wives and Progress,' would be so much more profitable."

(Her auditor smiled with complaisance, mistakenly supposing it to be a joke.)

"The author and reader are nothing but a couple of whining sentimentalists, to my mind." This was winged for her daughter's ear. Mollie loved her earnest young pastor for the help he gave his people, and was often at his house.

"I always supposed Shakespeare a great writer," said Peace abruptly, forsaking her friend to egg on the critic.

"Nonsense!" answered the lady, in a decided tone. "Why haven't people discovered it, then? He might have found material well worth study in Chesterfield, who was a truly great thinker."

"Come over here, Mr. Haythorne," said Peace, from

the tête-à-tête sofa, where she sat with Mollie. "Mr. Brown is dying to have Mrs. McCross show him tho Père Hyacinth geranium in the library; he wants a slip."

"'There's many a slip 'twixt cup and lip,'" said Mollie; "she won't cut it. But Peace has a conundrum for you."

"I give it up, à priori," said the doctor, sitting down with the air of a man who expects to be amused without any trouble or energy on his own part.

"Pooh!" retorted Peace. "Guess who Mr. Brown has been warning us against as dangerous?"

"Himself, perhaps," Mr. Haythorne suggested, with the contempt a tall man feels for a little one.

"No! in spite of the blackleg companion, he assures us he is wild no longer, by which he proposes to increase our respect on considering the possibility. It's *you*, dear cherub! He says you are a tough knot; you belonged to a Kneipe in Germany, and sent your friends to kniptions in consequence."

It is impossible to convey the intensity of Miss Pelican's delight at this bit of gossip, and Mr. Haythorne was as tickled as a correct young bachelor conscious of power and irreproachable bringing-up would ordinarily be. Mollie, who thought it unfair to join in the laugh against her own guest, interrupted: "I have a conundrum too; it's my turn. We've been talking about L'Africaine. Was she weak or strong?"

"Do you think I am going to take sides?" replied he, smiling, and caressing his curling beard. "By no means. You can argue the case and I'll decide."

"'I'll be judge and I'll be jury, said cunning old Fury,'" quoted Peace. "Never mind! *I* say she was weak, and a fool to love him." The dash of defiance with which she delivered her opinion was equally pretty and piquante.

"Strong," asseverated Mollie. "But she was wrong to die."

"Weak," persisted Peace; "weak as water. 'Malgré moi, je regrette á peine auprès de toi mon doux pays; et mon palais au souveraigne; et mes dieux dans mon cœur trahis.' Isn't that fairly contemptible folly? And all for the most callous-hearted, egotistical wretch ever put into an opera."

The self-constituted umpire writhed under her somewhat personal glance. "I pity him," he remarked sweetly. "Between two women he must have been beside his wits."

"No doubt of that," cried Peace, twisting the meaning.

"She was strong," said Mollie. "She knew how to suffer. Love is capacity for bearing sorrow for our friend. Her pain was nearly infinite; therefore she could not have been weak."

"I think so," agreed Francis Haythorne. "It is true I can't understand such love, but I believe every true wife feels it."

"And husband too," put in Peace.

He was silent.

"You disagree?" Mollie lifted her eyes thoughtfully to his face.

He laughed behind his beard, with the quiet self-reservation men cultivate in conversing with women and their other inferiors. "You remember Hood's dictum," was his suggestion, after tantalizing them with silence.

"Go on," quoth Peace. "Let him say his little verse, Mollie."

He bestowed a glance of oddly mixed annoyance and admiration on the unquenchable, and repeated:

" Our love it ne'er was reckoned,
  Yet good it is, and true;
  It's half the world to me, sweet,
  It's all the world to you."

Peace grew angry under the cool gaze he fixed on her. "Is that your idea of a wife?" said she, hotly.

"Yes! I want a woman whose heart will be mine all day long at home, while I'm away, and certainly mine when I come back to rest in her constant tenderness, tired of the outside world."

"In fact," retorted she, "Mr. Haythorne's model Griselda is a 'she ministered unto him.' I'll never be that for any man."

Whereat he smiled again, exasperatingly.

"Peace," said Mollie, her gravity unmoved from the earnest hold she had of the question, "you've never been in love."

"Yes, I have, scores of times,—with ideals. Do you know," remarked she, with engaging candor, " I always hate a man I've been half in love with? I took quite a fancy to you the first time I ever saw you."

Poor Mr. Brown's wooing sped very ill that afternoon. Mrs. McCross brought him back, a sprig of the gallant reformer's namesake in his be-ringed fingers, and gave him a seat beside Mollie, with too ominous an expression of face to be ignored by her daughter. His twaddle, always annoying to a girl whose intensity was carried into every detail of life, became absolutely painful under the circumstances. Cabby, however, interpreted her silence as bashful modesty, and was fired with ardor in pursuit of the gilded prize. But what Mollie's refusal to be complaisant could not do for her, accident effectually accomplished.

Deacon McCross had stolen in, and now sat beside

Mollie's corner of the tête-à-tête, with his hand content-edly clasping his daughter's. He was fond of resting thus, and sunning himself in the pleasure she was able to give her friends. He was at his proudest then.

Mr. Brown, who was not equal to the discussion of L'Africaine, felt it necessary to lend a hand. His forte was something he denominated a "widdle," and invention came to his aid.

He winked at Mollie, and next winked at her father to point the joke, then propounded it: "Why is an old man's head like the sky? Because there is a little bear there."

Deacon McCross, who was sensitive about his age, grew red. He satisfied himself that Miranda was absent, and remarked severely: "Young sir, remember Elijah, and say no more about bears. I am no longer youthful, but I respected years when I was."

"I think it is a blessing to grow old," cried Mollie; "that is, I think wrinkles are a blessing."

Peace elevated her eyebrows, and Mr. Haythorne exclaimed, "How so?" from the opposite side of the room.

"Because," said she, slowly, as if spelling out the thought, "they are remembrances of the covenant, '*I* will be with thee even to gray hairs.' They seem to me a sort of hieroglyphics that contain the story of a man's life."

"That's no blessing," said Mr. McCross, uneasily.

"I think it is," answered Mollie. "Isn't such a record Heaven's memorandum of what the new man shall be? Every touch by which the sculptor corrugates the marble is a preparation for the statue, every peg driven in the cast, the measure of chiselled perfection. Old age is the witness God gives of our future. Bless God for wrinkles, say I, and let us rise up, every one, before the hoary head."

6*

Her auditors gazed at her in astonishment, and drew a sigh of relief when she paused; as one sighs after the fourth scene of the fifth act of a tragedy—something in joy at what is passed—something in fear of what is yet to come.

Molly hadn't meant to crush Cabby with this burst of eloquence. She was still awake with the pleasure of the late discussion, and brought her graceful thought to defend her father's position from mere impulse. But she had proved herself original and earnest; and the little dandy was afraid of both qualities. He shuddered to see her bright eager eye, and lips parted with her quickened breathing. "No, she should never be Mrs. Brown; never!" He snatched the hair-pin from the blond fringe, and tossed it and Mollie's opportunity in the fire. And she never was.

It is as odd as true, that for wife or love, men are more afraid of a woman of talent and culture than of a shrew, a fool, or a flirt.

.   .   .   .

Both my heroines were childish enough to keep extract books. I subjoin the selections they made that night.

Peace wrote :—

> " No drede hem not, do hem no reverence ;
>   For though thin husband armed be in mail,
>   The arowes of thy crabbed eloquence
>   Shall perce his brest and eke his aventaille.

.   .   .   .

>   Be ay of chere as light as lefe on linde,
>   And let him care and wepe and wringe and waille. "

Mollie wrote :—

Though weary, love is not tired ; though pressed, it is not straitened.

Love is active, sincere, affectionate, pleasant and amiable, courageous, patient, faithful, prudent, long-suffering, manly, and never seeketh itself.

For in whatever instance a person seeketh himself, there he falleth from love.

Without sorrow, none liveth in love.

CHAPTER IX.

"High diddle diddle, the cat got the fiddle,
   The cow jumped over the moon;
   The little dog laughed to see the sport,
   And the plate ran away with the spoon."

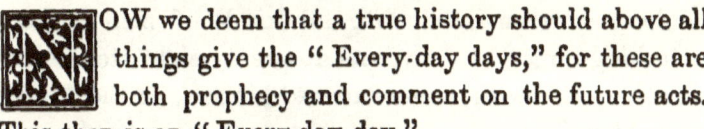OW we deem that a true history should above all things give the "Every-day days," for these are both prophecy and comment on the future acts. This then is an "Every-day day."

It was several months after the events last recorded, that Mr. Haythorno walked into Fir Covert just in time for dinner. Since Cabby's rebuff, Mrs. McCross had fixed upon him as the desirable suitor, and spared no pains to domesticate him. Mollie was not charged with great burden of his entertainment when Peace was at hand, and neither helped nor hindered her mother's manœuvres, finding her great excitement in Patience of Hope, to which she regarded him as a useful adjunct. She knew now that her unmarried life was to be the scene of such mines and countermines, and said to herself, that, as his impenetrable egotism would doubtless keep him heart-whole, he was a nice lay figure, in room of a more vitalized element of the studio; in short, harmless. No man, ascetic or ease-loving, is averse to having a well-appointed house open to him at all times, and, when a fresh, sweet maiden shelters there, the charm is complete. In this case there were two maidens, for Peace continued her stay at the Jenkens', and, to Mrs. McCross' manifest disgust, spent half-her time with Mollie.

Francis Haythorne was a citoyen du monde. He had travelled much and at leisure, been at Heidelburg University, studied music in Leipsic and composition at Vienna, drank beer in Bavaria, and tried opium at Constantinople—this last unsuccessfully.

He had done a little sledging in Russia, but, finding it uncomfortable, spent the allotted time at Rome. He never cared to climb the Alps, but vastly enjoyed the American-like society at Interlachen. With little exertion, and in the most gentlemanly way possible, he had contrived to become acquainted with all kinds of men without attaching himself to any, and at twenty-eight stood alone in the world, with, as he flattered himself, neither duties nor obligations.

To such a man it was a rare pleasure to discover in the friends two people at once cultured and earnest. He had drifted into Millville, and met them both at a sewing society, where his art was called in aid at a fainting-fit Belle Brandon got up to show the perfection of her features in repose. The acquaintance had ripened fast. Molly, absorbed as to love in Louis, saw all mankind in a halo in those days; and, debarred by her parents' peculiarities from association with friends of her own age, except under protest, found his refinement, delicate breeding, and high scholarship a source of constant enjoyment; while his mind, no better than hers, but trained in argument and stored with German thought, proved a form of high mental stimulus. She learned how to arrange the factors of a conclusion, and analyze a formula of reasoning, with precision new and delightful. He drew her out for the pleasure of watching her rapidly evolved and unhackneyed thought; and she relished his visits because he helped her to understand herself.

Thus agreeably situated, with Peace to point the arguments and be snippy in the pauses, he carelessly permitted Mrs. McCross' transparent management; taught in the Sunday-school (pure morality, nothing more, as he carefully explained); read history with perseverance; cut his bell-rope so patients shouldn't call him up at night; in short, wasted his time to the entire satisfaction of all parties.

This morning the dilettante found Fir Covert parlor empty. Voices up-stairs, in the thirds and semi-tones of animated but pleasant discussion, informed him of the whereabouts of the mates, and a talkative parrot, hung above the plants in the window, called out "Good-morning." "Pretty cold," said she, conversationally. Then, holding up a claw, "Poppy want to come." Concluding Mr. Haythorne resolved to negative the proposition, she asked why the men didn't propose, with extreme interest; said something about dear, dear somebody several times, and kissed vociferously. The visitor still continuing self-absorbed, she emptied her seed cup on his head out of revenge, and remarked that her father was a drunkard and her mother dead, in hilarious accents.

Mr. Haythorne was not the man to forgive in a parrot things objectionable in humanity; he annihilated her with a glare, which led her to make a dab at him so energetic that she got her head out of the cage, and had hard work to pull it in again, and so lost her temper as to make pie of her furniture the minute she succeeded.

But the object of her ire had taken refuge by the piano. There lay "Songs without Words," a few bits of Schumanu, a fair sprinkling of Beethoven, and on top a copy of Overture to the Midsummer Night's Dream, and the Der Freyschütz. He whistled the latter smilingly to himself, till the young ladies entered.

"Who plays this?" asked he, keeping fast hold of his treasure while he made his greetings, and losing no time in spreading it carefully on the rack, his face expanded in anticipation of a treat.

"Unless you can render it, no one," said Mollie. "That is Mr. Allwood's music. A very simple air, without runs or trills, is the utmost extent of my ability."

"And yours also, Miss Pelican?" looking disappointed.

"I have a reasonably good ear for melody; let us have the tongs and the bones. I can bring in Bully Bottom's bray," retorted that damsel. "But as Sybarites like you detest such minstrolsy, you'd better put the piece away, unless you choose to read the verses you've hidden in the leaves." She picked up a folded bit of paper as she spoke.

Vexed at the imputation of scribbling, he caught it from the little hand mischievously dancing it before him, and crimsoned with annoyance to find its contents really in rhyme.

"Go on, Mr. Sybby dear," said his tormentor. "You ought to have written it on a doubled rose-leaf. Remember next time."

"The verses are not mine, as you can see by the Greek initials in monogram at the bottom. I could neither draw the one nor write the other. You must ask Miss Mollie's permission to have them read."

"You are welcome to the perusal," said Mollie quietly. "Mr. Allwood scribbled them one Sunday, to console me because my boys all went off to play, and I had no class."

Now if a man hates anything, it is to render another man's poetry; but Peace would insist, her maliciously beautiful smile daring the poor victim to his task. Being both a fine elocutionist and a gentleman, he accordingly gave the simple lines with grace and taste, which momentarily disarmed the gad-fly, and made Mollie's heart swell with memories of her absent lover.

"On the shelf in an oaken cupboard high,
 Lie six little balls of brown,
And every day a maid trips by,
And watches very anxiously
 Those dainty nests of silken down.

"Six pairs of wings flit to and fro
 In the depths of that cupboard old—
Six pairs of wings that quickly grow;
And their giddy owners long to go
 Out into the wide, wide world.

"The door is open. Why should they stay?
 No eyes their doings view.
Off they dart in merry play—
Off to the fields and the flowerets gay.
 And wouldn't you do so too?

"As for the maid they left alone,
 She mourned them long, and she wept them sore.
But the faithless butterflies didn't return;
They flew too gay o'er the grass and fern;
 And she ought to have shut the door."

"There!" said Peace teasingly. "Don't you wish you could write poetry like that?"

"No," said Francis Haythorne, "I don't think, and I know Miss Mollie agrees with me, that this *is* poetry."

Mrs. McCross had once heard him say he loved to see

woman about her feminine occupations, and henceforth made Mollie darn the whole family hosiery in his presence. The seamstress looked up now from an immense web she was stretching across a heel to answer: "You are right; but I think also that the language scarcely counts ten true poets. The rest are only poetasters."

"What becomes of the long row of worthies on your shelf?" asked Peace; "Holland, Owen Meredith, Longfellow, Campbell, and the rest?"

"I don't mean that there are not *many* charming writers, and that the world isn't better for possessing them. Their work is sweet, tender, and often inspiring. But I only call that poetry, which would have found expression from its own imperious nature, if nothing poetical had ever been written; which moulds its own form, and is instinct with thought, power, passion, and even revelation; which carries its hearer out of himself, and for a moment makes him live unconscious—I had almost said independent—of his own existence."

"Such as this," cut in Peace, in aggravating sing-song:

> 'I'll slip an' slide dem golden streets,
> Silver slippers on my feets.'

Or this:

> "'Lord called Daniel; Daniel forgot to hear him.
> Lord called Daniel; Daniel said, 'Here I be, Lord.'

They're not spurious imitations. I heard them at negro camp-meeting myself."

"Miss Mollie," said Francis Haythorne, frowning at the impertinent interference, "you should read one of my German authors. He claims that all poetry first seeks to find expression in muscular action, and metre is the softened form into which it resolves itself."

"Mrs. McCross, isn't dinner ready? Out of the depths have I cried unto thee."

"That's wicked," said the madame, shortly. "I came to call you."

"If you'd waited any longer, then you might have quoted Punch's epitaph on a candle : ' A wicked one lies buried here.' Such avalanches of learning!"

Francis Haythorne caressed his curling auburn beard with lazy grace. The act, which showed well his soft, beautiful hand, always exasperated Peace.

She walked across the room. Peace was especially handsome in motion, and began a conversation with Deacon McCross, who was aimlessly turning over sonatas at the piano, in his usual attitude of spectator at his own house.

"Are you musical?" said she.

"Not enough to lie under the fence to hear the slivers rattle," he returned, pleased with her notice ; "but you, my dear, look as if you might make music."

"So she does; like Euphemia Hitchcock, by the pound," interrupted his wife, overhearing. Mrs. McCross stood in awe of her tall and energetic guest, but hate sometimes got the upper hand.

"Nineteen, twenty, my stomach's empty. Please, mammy, give me some dinner?" quoted Miss Pelican, saucily.

"Where did you buy your dress," asked her hostess in confidence, on the way to the dining-room.

"Mamma and I picked it out at Starbird & Pedlow's. Isn't it pretty?"

"Yes—rather," hesitated Mrs. McCross. "I thought, on account of the size of the figures, I'd get some for a bed-quilt."

Deacon McCross sat down at table, and handed Peace

to her chair as he did so, which gave his wife opportunity to exclaim : " It would, perhaps, be as well to stand while Mr. Haythorne says grace."

" You didn't pray long," remarked Peace, with a wicked sparkle in her eye, after he had yielded a doubtful and hesitating compliance.

" No ; brevity is the soul of wit."

Now Mrs. McCross fancied her guest unregenerate, and desired his conversion. " I noticed you read from Chronicles, the other day at prayers," began she, seeking opportunity to scatter good seed in his sceptical mind; " do you like them especially ? "

" I chose what promised to be least offensive," he returned, following his constant habit of playing upon the peculiarities of all, and silently enjoying the developments that chanced to ensue.

" Then you don't believe in the Bible," seizing her chance, with alacrity.

" The Old Testament is as reliable as any collection of fables.   Reason teaches the absurdity of most of its miraculous machinery."   He sipped his coffee with the provoking ease of the incredulous amid a circle of believers.

" He that is in the way of life, keepeth instruction," replied his would-be opponent, as she poured herself a cup of tea, and smiled, conscious of hitting him hard. " When men throw away the Bible, it's because they want liberty to do wrong. Shall a man know more than God ? "

" Instruction is the application to the mind of metnal stimulus, thereby inciting it to labors whose end is wisdom.   I have not always found this in the Bible, though some do.   Goethe, you know, says, ' Every man must think after his own fashion; for in that fashion he always finds a truth, or sort of a truth, to help him in living.' "

" No matter if his boasted reasoning makes him an infidel atheist," said Mrs. McCross sarcastically.

" Atheists have the same right to their own methods of thought as Christians. But I am as much a deist as yourself."

" Deist! I'm nothing of the kind ; I have no taste for heathendom," cried the defender of the faith in genuine horror.

" Better think wrong honestly, than not think at all," put in Mollie.

" Nonsense," repudiated Mrs. McCross, and annihilated her with a glance. " *You* don't know what you're talking about."

"Do you eat olives, Mr. Haythorne ? " said the Deacon, feebly attempting to arrest the tide. " Does he, Miss Peace ? "

" Yes, he was weaned on them," responded she, promptly.

" I think Miss Mollie quite right," the young man continued, unconscious of the addition to his fare. " To quote Goethe again : ' Piety is but a means of reaching the highest culture through the purest repose of mind. The inactive, ignorant superstition, which often passes for piety, is worse than striving, earnest scepticism."

" Solomon," quoth the madam, waiving the *ipse dixit* with just contempt, " says the wise man dies like the fool."

" That was when he had dyspepsia," remarked Peace.

" He says a fool is wise in his own eyes," their hostess retorted, wheeling round. " He advises us, instead of leaning to our own understanding, to take fast hold of instruction, and what is the beginning and end of wisdom but the Bible ? "

"What Solomon got his from," said Peace. "The cedar of Lebanon, and the hyssop that springeth out of the wall."

"He who is satisfied with pure experience," went on Mr. Haythorne, seeing Mollie interested, and disregarding this side issue, has truth enough. And Goethe adds to the thought: " ' In this sense the growing child is wise;' misunderstood dogmas are the scourges of honest piety."

"If children are wiser than grown people, I'll give up," said Mrs. McCross, disgusted. "Let's put away the rod, and kick out our schools."

"Schools are useful to furnish the mind with correct data, and also to train the constructive faculty; but their learning is not always wisdom: a one-ideaed child is often more clear in thought than a fact-burdened savant. It was Solomon's reasoning power, not his collection of information, that made him great."

"If you don't believe in schools nor religion, you might as well be—a—a Manichee," said Mrs. McCross, snatching at the first big word. "You'd better set up a fetich house at once."

Peace suddenly beheld a mongrel vision of elegant Mr. Haythorne equipped in a Congo garment of gnus' tails, doing a bit of fetich worship, and gave a convulsive giggle, which was scarcely quenched by Mrs. McCross, who exclaimed:

"As the crackling of thorns under a pot, so is the laughter of fools."

Mr. Haythorne's fastidious face wore, hereupon, an expression of polite astonishment, and Mollie was ashamed of the turn the argument had taken. He noticed it, and endeavored to right matters by saying quietly:

"You mistake me, madam; I uphold both schools and religion; but they should be animated by thought—not cramming and superstition."

"Popular thought," said Mrs. McCross in triumph, "is unnecessary. It requires no reason to do one's work, —to wash dishes for instance. The less time people idle away in dreams, the better for them. The whole duty of man is to fear God, and keep His commandments."

A long pause ensued, broken by Mollie, who observed modestly: "I have been thinking of late, that education was best gained from experiences. I have met a few men whose stock of facts is limited, but who can reason on abstract questions with much clearness. For this reason, having acquired learning enough to observe intelligently, the English gentlemen go from home to put themselves in new conditions of life; to discover, by the working of their own minds in unaccustomed situations, the feelings and wisdom of those who habitually dwell therein, and by wise reduction of these thoughts, to learn the meaning of existence. It is inability to put themselves in other people's places, that makes men narrow-minded, though by simple following of God they may have become very good. Hence books, even novels, are a great blessing. They enable us, who are chained to one spot, to know the experiences of all classes, and learn, though less vividly, what others get from travel, and varied habits of life."

Mollie stopped, her eyes bright with excitement, and her whole soul shining out of them upon Mr. Haythorne, who looked at her admiringly, and was about to answer in kind, when Mrs. McCross exclaimed with energetic displeasure: "Novels! I was piously brought up, and taught to read my Bible, instead of wasting the precious moments upon paltry romances, and hyfalluten trash. It is my belief that novels breed atheists. What saith Solomon: 'Of making many books there is no end.'"

"I do not wish to throw down the authority of the Bible," remarked Mr. Haythorne to the Deacon, who was listening rather blankly. "What I look at, is the enormous mass of folly people feel obliged to take in with its gold."

"Ye-es," the old gentleman made answer; "young man, ain't you rather blowin' yourself up with the wind of them big idees?"

"Not a bit," interposed Peace. "The cold goose has gone to his head!"

"Your own Goethe says, wisdom consists only in truth," said Mollie. "The Bible appears to me a faithful account of the wants and errors of mankind, with the means of cure. In this light it is always infallible, whether the traditions be correct or not. 'For this reason,' writes he, 'the Bible is an eternally effective book, and for all time no one can come up and say, "I comprehend it as a whole. I understand it in details;"' but we say modestly, 'We reverence it as a whole; we apply it in particular.'"

"Do you understand German, Miss Mollie?"

"No, sir," she replied, blushing. "I speak no language except my own; but Louis, I mean Mr. Allwood, used to be fond of Goethe, and would often translate him to me."

"May I ask who this Mr. Allwood is?" said Francis Haythorne; "after reading his poetry, and seeing his music, my interest is excited."

"A young chap that used to clerk it for me," answered the Deacon, stiffly.

"And do chores on the place," chimed in his wife.

Peace flamed up. "He is my friend, and one of the

nicest people I know. You should hear him play. His tones are all pearls."

"No such thing. He's shiftless, and an atheist" ("deist," corrected Mollie, with flickering color, but voice steadied by intensity of anger), "and poor as Job's turkey besides," went on her mother; "I have no respect for him, nor confidence in him. I would speak good of him if I could, since he grew up in Christian influences; yes, under my very eye."

"That last is what the donkey said of the cabbages he could just see over the wall of the next garden," said Peace, in a loud aside.

"I call it ill-bred to gabble before my elders," retorted Mrs. McCross, aware of the sting.

"You'll have to sharpen your chopping knife, if you're coming at me," returned Peace, nothing daunted. "I'll always speak up for Louis as long as I live, for he is as good as gold."

The Deacon, after sitting absently awhile, with his fork in the air, now put on his hat, and ambled from the house.

Peace, glancing at Mollie to adjust her tactics to propriety, was startled to see the tired, worn, gray look that had possession of her young face—a look that the old, brave, friendly smile did not banish, only ennobled. And Peace had no reserve of strength to meet her friend's need. "Poor Mollie!" was the best, the sole word she could give.

Mr. Haythorne proved a man of penetration. That he had drifted upon a family snag, was too clear; and that both his friends had lodged there, seemed equally certain. He therefore paddled his own canoe into calmer waters with all speed, and, though Poppy said, "Dear Louis, dear Mollie, ptchoo," every time he appeared, never, even in thought, permitted himself to make a voyage of discovery in that dangerous neighborhood. Notwithstanding this *laisser aller* behavior, however, he failed to get the Midsummer Overture as he had intended, and henceforth regarded minor poets with even more disparagement than before, and what is still odder, never analyzed the feeling.

CHAPTER X.

" This is the malt that lay in the house
    That Jack built."

FRANCIS HAYTHORNE continued to find Fir Covert to his mind. The girls soon discovered, or thought they did, that his egotism was the outgrowth of a sense of propriety too fine for American rudeness, and so compelling him into isolation, and that he was, therefore, the rarest of all rare men; one that a woman can safely meet, without that vigilant outlook upon the movements of Sir Felinus with which our maiden Mousalina is compelled to arm herself in his company.

True, Mollie missed the graceful, naïve characteristics that she so loved in Louis. He had the air of a man who had seen the world, which means nowadays that simplicity is an abandoned charm. He was, however, haughtily delicate, and not only scholarly and industrious, but cultured. He worshipped the words "good taste," and never for a moment lost his self-poise in rampant enthusiasm.

His inspectresses were always longing to see him come out of his reserve, trying to find some key to unlock his innermost; and they tacitly agreed that, if the shell of their fascinating oyster sampled the pearls therein concealed, theirs was a Ben Trovato, indeed.

Peace's mode of conducting her observations was strictly aggressive, and such as laid herself open to study quite as thoroughly as her subject. She was in a constant state of irritation at his dogmatic criticisms and assertions, and persistent refusal to endorse any favorable opinion she happened to offer, be the subject what it might.

Their meeting was always the signal of a wordy battle; their tête-à-têtes being usually conducted in this style:

" Have you read Charles Anchester ? " begins Peace, laying down the volume in question, with all the delight it excites in young people vivifying her face.

" When I was a boy," very condescendingly. It *is* chilling, at least, to be made to feel that we have only arrived at a point left far behind in the dim past by our companion; but Peace is not discouraged.

" I am fascinated with it. I wish I was Seraphael. I wish I was at St.Cecilia's. I'd like to use up my old gloves on stupid Sebastian Bach, and know Florimond, and see Jennie Lind, and hear the unprincipled violinist, and—"

" Have Jewish finger nails, and a face like a fiddle, and write a horrid hand. Most young musicians go through a Mendelssohn period, just as one has lettuce and asparagus in spring."

Though begun teasingly, the dictum came to an end with extreme loftiness.

" At least own you liked the book," persevering, but beginning to show annoyance.

" Ah! ye-es, up to the average of that style of literature, I believe."

7

By this time the *livre condamné* is clasped protectively against Peace's magnificent bosom, and she exclaims indignantly, "I'm thankful enough that *I* haven't grown so mature that I prefer baled hay and carrots to honest pasture. I'd rather munch my proper nutriment of thistles." With sniffs of disdain Miss Pelican retires, to establish a system of coquetry between her dainty feet and the andirons supporting their blazing burden, and thereby to offer an extremely artistic coil of blue-black hair to Francis Haythorne's observation. A considerable pause ensues, broken by the critic:

"Miss Peace;" in a conciliatory tone.

Silence.

"Won't you please answer? what made you go off so?"

"Because you spoilt my pleasure in the book. No matter what I like, you always snip it down, and ask if it's deep. I don't care anything about it's size. I want to enjoy pretty things, and receive sympathy. You don't know what sympathy is! all your culture is cavilling!" The shining coiffure gives emphasis in tosses, but, except one crimson ear, she shows him nothing of her face.

"I didn't mean to take the zest of your enjoyment away," cries Francis Haythorne, really remorseful; "the truth is, I have forgotten about the book. I remember liking it as a boy. Let me have it to look over to-night; perhaps I found fault for nothing. I don't read English enough to keep up, truly."

Peace is thereupon mollified, and lends him the volume, which he lays down somewhere about three o'clock next morning, and owns, as becomes a man of honor, that no better musical novel has ever been written.

After a few months of this sort of warfare, it began to dawn on the critic's brain, that, though carping and appreciation are poles, just estimation does not lie in the middle. Moreover, Peace, whose aggrieved soul was not prone to inactivity, made him an offer of a sugar-plum for every sincere praise he might allow himself to utter. As the result of six weeks' faithful observation, she one day brought him a mint-stick, and a caraway seed picked from the candy ornaments of Mrs. McCross' Scotch cakes. "This whole piece is because you said you thought Mollie's pot-pie perfect, and this teenty taunty one is what you remarked about Thomas' Orchestra."

The implication of the rewards was even more disgusting to the refined gentleman than their paucity. His conscience, however, forbade vanity's rankling wound to deter a wholesome introspection, as result of which he said in his heart that the young lady's malicious strictures were merited. But his self-elected censor busied herself with fresh plans for his discomfiture.

One day she entered Mollie's room bearing a letter directed, in her large, artistically looping hand, to F. Haythorne, Esq., M.D.

"There," she exclaimed, raising the gilded, monogrammed lid, and drawing forth the enclosed note with a face expressing perfect satisfaction, "if this don't prove a soothing application, I'm disappointed. He'll have to call and have it explained, and there'll be a scene. I know I've fixed a delightful recreation. I'm nearly seventeen, and have never had a spark of a flame, not a snip on a proposal. One can't be expected to live thus: read! read!"

She glanced in the mirror, and readjusted the fall of her cashmere skirts. Peace was partial to woollens (when she didn't wear silk). The graceful curves delighted her sense of beauty.

"What! you want to pin it to the wall 'tother side the room to decipher? Then I'll give you the contents myself!

" DEAR SIR :—I found a black-and-brown striped caterpillar out to-day. He is very anxious to be put on the
list of your patients. I offered to telegraph him, but he
is afraid it will injure his constitution. He says he has
only two objects in life: to see Gen. Grant hung, and me
settled in the world. He wishes me to state that, if you
will tender me your heart and hand, he will die happy.
I don't in the least wish to marry you, but I *am* really
pining to refuse somebody; and, considering how often
you have evinced solicitude for my welfare, I know you
will hasten to give me the opportunity.

" Furry-striped Caterpillar, Esq., wishes me to add that
he only waits the pleasure of giving us his dying blessings, after which he hopes to take his place beside Mrs.
Furry-striped Caterpillar, long since deceased.

" Yours, obedient to his commmands,

" PEACE.

" P. S.—He's afraid this evening will be his last."

" Realize it!" concluded she, walking up and down
in extremity of her elation. " Picture what a fret he'll
be in! He'll have to come out of his shell, now! He's
in a case without German precedent. What a stab in his
precious dignity! I think I see him writhe, impaled on
that missive like a fly on a pin."

" But if he should stay away, offended," suggested
Mollie, who longed to have the note sent, but felt bound
to lay open the difficulties.

" He won't," answered Peace, positively. " He thinks
it's a sin to pause long enough in the street to examine
the contents of a shop window; and he wouldn't pry into
the affairs of his dearest friend, or bitterest enemy. But
he is full of curiosity, for all that; and he couldn't forego
the pleasure of studying us scientifically for the world.

He'll be here at the earliest possible moment, never fear."
Whereupon she turned a pirouette, and hurried down-
stairs to play "Three Jolly Brothers" in triumphant
measure. How light-hearted was Peace in those days of
early girlhood! Life's sombre shadows showed themselves but shadows; her one reality was her own gay
humor.

It is needless to add, that the tormented swain appeared
punctually, to be welcomed at the door in effusive rap-
ture by Miss Pelican.

Entering with an air of speculation, laughably mixed
with dignified offence, he exchanged his position for intense disgust, when she gave him a languishing glance
from her great black eyes, and exclaimed: "So affectionate of you to come! My kind protector has even now
breathed his last; but let me assure you, my sentiments
are unchanged."

He leisurely doffed his dove-colored overcoat, and a
certain cashmere scarf of palest, heavenly blue, which he
had bought because he couldn't resist its temptations,
and wore tucked in, in an amusingly shame-faced manner; also his cap of richest sealskin; also his gloves, of
Quaker dye. In short, he was a quiet-tempered man
with a grievance, if he understood himself; the gypsy
of extreme fascination, and boundless audacity, awaiting
him at the door, should feel the cost of assaulting a German scholar, musician, M.D., and man of taste.

"You've come at last!" pursued the would-be object
of his regards. "I was just practising—

' How slow the hours are gliding, while here I wait in vain ;
  Love seems my sad heart chiding, and gives my bosom pain !'

But that is ended now " (tender sigh, and then rallying).

You must see the sad remains of our mutual patron. He makes a sweet corpse."

The aggrieved would fain have hung back, but she was inexorable, and led him to a bell-glass, beneath which she had laid out a not only deceased, but suspiciously dry, caterpillar, impaled on the stem of an ivy leaf. Being the heaviest of the two, the funeral decoration tilted the stiffened form in mid-air, displaying its double row of black legs and its ebony face to great advantage.

"His features are quite composed—such a beautifully paternal expression!" said his mourner, sadly.

"Are you a candidate for a lunatic asylum?" gasped the Sybarite, retreating, shocked to her full wish.

"Don't be agitated, I beg," entreated she, with tender solicitude. "Believe me, I share your suffering. I, too, comprehend the excessive delicacy of the situation. You tremble! Rouse your strength of mind in this trying moment: he! he! he!"

"Excessive indelicacy of the situation," retorted Francis Haythorne, his drab garb actually seeming to darken in his gravity. "I can't imagine how a young lady could—"

"Oh, you do not rise to the largeness of the necessity!" interrupted Peace, gently. "You need time to rally your thoughts," sympathetically. "I understand the magnitude of the generous act." Here she broke down in a weak giggle, more irritating than any preceding part of the performance. "He! he!"

"I came to demand an explanation of that absurd missive!" cried he, getting angry. "I must have it."

"There! there!" said Peace, in a maternally soothing tone. "I see I must be strong for both—true enough:

'When the little heart is full,
A little sets it off.'"

" I'll not submit to this! " cried he, striding wrathfully to the hall. " I will not be victimized in this way; I'll go at once."

" If you're a victim, what am I ? Break, heart of stone, my Thisbe's gone. Alack! alack! alack!" Executing a magnificent shriek, Peace fainted *à la* Miggs, against the parlor door, so he couldn't get out.

As there were two such means of egress, he fled through the farther one, but she was too quick for this.

" Stop him, Mollie! stop him. He's going to propose when he brings his mind to it; reassure him; pat him on the back; anything. I must have the comfort of refusing him. I will! I will! "

Thus cut off (for Miss McCross darted from her place in the sitting-room, where she had been enjoying the scene, by Peace's advice), the young man strode back to his tormentor, glowing with vindictive ire through his self-drilled quietude, like a coal red to its heart, through its feathery film of ash. "Miss," quoth he sternly, " since you will take no denial, I can't. My principles forbid me to entangle any simple and unsophisticated girl in my fate, till I've worked up a medical practice, and [here he reached a superb tone of triumph] *that'll* be a long time hence, let me tell you."

Instead of sinking beneath the blow, the object of this crushing rejoinder leaned against the door frame to laugh; and Francis Haythorne unconsciously accepted the support of the opposite casing, speechless from bewilderment.

Here was he, the student, the man who believed that a well-bred person always lived in isolation, conscious to himself, though unfelt by his associates,—who even reverenced the atom that moves freely among its mass, and is touched of no other atom,—here stood this faithful adherent to the truest traditions of fastidious self-reservation invited to furnish sport to a school-girl, and totally without the proper method of showing his resentment.

By good luck, Mollie came in to find them thus, *hors de combat*, and help them upon neutral ground.

" If Peace will promise not to pursue her attentions, will you make full confession about the kneipen ? " asked she, bringing up a side issue. " Since you evaded the question so shamefully the other night, Cabby has gone to the length of looking up an account of them in an encyclopædia, to convince us of your degenerate morals. He made out that American students, with hazes, rushes, secret societies, blowing up of pumps, and all incidental follies, could not equal the practice of frequenting those frightful kneipen. Come, of how many were you a member, honor bright ? Cabby was mysterious, and gave us to understand that he is up in ways that are dark and tricks that are vain, himself."

" One ! " said Francis Haythorne, glaring at Peace, whose mirth was by no means allayed. " We did nothing ungentlemanly; we never drank too much, for that reason; we despise such things. No ! their attraction to me was the absence of the abominable sex. I wish I was there now ! " and he glared again.

" Do remember one of the songs," begged Mollie, whose curiosity was stimulated by Louis' adoration of everything German, as much as her pacific duties.

" Yes," cried Peace, wiping her eyes. " I'll try to forgive you if it's good, not verdant and loud, mind."

Now it was one of the amateur's peculiarities, that he never used his musical talents, when he imagined his circle of listeners not enough up in culture to appreciate his skill. He openly said that few people cared for anything better than omnibus pictures, and if a good painter wouldn't degrade his pencil to execute such daubs, why should he, Francis Haythorne, lower his fingers in the same fashion? Indeed, he had once given this very reason to the friends for refusing to play to them. Whereupon they had made common cause of the plain reflection upon their taste, and fought the battle to victory.

Since that date, he went to the piano with perfect docility, when asked; but this evening he flew thither on the wings of wrath, and sang Heidelburg's song with gusto:

" Old Heidelburg, thou fine one,
All wealth of honor's thine,
On the Neckar or on the Rhine
None other comes thine equal.

City of merry comrades,
With wisdom heavy, and wine,
From the clear flowing stream, blue eyne
Sparkle to woo thee.

And comes from the mild south
The spring, over mountain and lea,
Out of his blossoms he weaves for thee
A glittering bridal garment.

And with me, close in my heart,
Like a bride, dost thou ever stay.
Like the spell of young love is the sway
Of thy name so fondly dear.

When pierced sore by life's thorns,
Or the world all to bleakness fail,
I'll spur my horse back to thy vale,
To thy gentle valley, O Neckar."

He hurled every couplet at mischievous Peace. She

7*

had indeed played her joke, but he was not without weapons.

She was listening with due gravity to the pretty air (so much better in harmony and melody than our rattling college songs), to which Mollie was hastily supplying the alto. Even the invidious vision of the wife-like valley couldn't move her.

"Mollie," said she, thoughtfully, "you know when he said he was tender-hearted? and that while he was a little boy he stole away and wrote 'Francis Haythorne's Lamentations,' because his Pa had hurt his little felinks scolding him, and he'd seen those poor Jerry put in the Bible? Don't you believe these are the very ones?

"Oh, you were tender-hearted to pen those, as you say;
But now you're mean, and won't propose, to while my griefs
        away."

The doctor's hasty exit from the house precluded the resumption of hostilities. He *was* vanquished.

But it was more than one half hour later when the girls finished talking over their experiment. That is, Mollie ceased listening to Miss Pelican's comments.

And the burden of all was, that she repented teasing him, and had liked him better every moment, because his courtesy had fully stood the strain upon it, proving its rare metal; and because she had laid herself open to rudeness, and he had not for a moment thought of such self-degradation, and because—because—because, *he was too good to be trifled with.*"

Whereby the doctor will be seen to have won the day.

CHAPTER XI.

" The cat's in the cream pot.
Run, boys, run ! "

 WEEK after Peace's pleasant divertisement, Mollie met her on Gonecusset Street.

" My day is done," said she, solemnly. " Upon the stroke of twelve I must depart."

" What do you mean ? " asked her friend, who never knew quite how to *expect* Miss Pelican.

" Why, you are aware I am attending school at Rosenbloom; have been all the autumn, only I dreaded to launch away *in propria persona.* But yesterday came a letter from madame, stating that as it is already December she will not suffer me to eat the bread of idleness any longer, and I must either give up my room or my Millville visit. So you see—

' Time the churl had beckoned,
And I must away—must away.'

In future I shall spend my time digging German roots to pelt you with—not to speak of French—*per aspera ad astra.*

" Oh dear, do be more merciful to me than you were to the cat. I know you were swearing at her in feline tongues, the day you meowed and frightened her so."

" Pooh ! " said Peace, " pet names always have a contrary effect on animals. I told Charley that, when he called me a donkey the last time I saw him. I shall weep in all languages," she added, soberly, " if I don't find you well and bright when I come up for monthly holi-

days. I have taken a scunner at Top Town," avoiding
Mollie's honest eyes, "and shall not go back this winter."
By the way, Peace was evidently hurrying to change the
subject. "Father writes that he was put out by the
condition of business when he got home, to that extent
that he went to bed in his bosom shirt by mistake, and
mother woke him up in the middle of the night to tell
him of it. He eschews board at the Millville House
henceforth, and tarries by the stuff."

So Peace went to school, not as light-hearted as she
wished to appear, and leaving a vague uneasiness in
Mollie's mind. With her went Susie Jenkens. Sonsie
Eagan joined her friends at Rosenbloom soon after, and,
bereft of these efficient laborers, Patience of Hope would
have suffered sadly if Mollie had not thrown herself into
the gap. Most people teach Sunday-school as a pious
interlude in the real business of life; but to Mollie the
place was holy ground. She went softly, and with un-
shod feet. It was awesome, and yet passing sweet. She
spoke to her people by day, and stood facing God by
night, and carried His calm tenderness as Moses brought
away His glory.

The school gradually worked out of the Nicksonian spirit
into her own. Gentleness and tenderness replaced shaking and cuffs. The craving poverty that Louis' absence
made in Mollie's heart comfort became the riches of the
poor. Their lacks and longings were like an open book
to her clairvoyance, and she loved them out of the over-
mastering, all-pervading love she bore one slender boyish
absentee. There were other loves and hungers at work
in the school, moreover. Jan Vedder, a robust type of
muscular Christianity, remained faithful to Sonsie Eagan's
parting trust—six rollicking boys; and Peter Bradshaw
did his devoir to Zoe, and so far converted his scholars,

that they waged deadly war over the superior use of cams in machinery to any other modes of modifying action ; and he worked till one o'clock Saturday nights upon knotty problems in hydrostatics, to which science he and the class devoted themselves every Sabbath. Mary Ann Nickson had kept the hold on Doppy's heart gained from Amos' introduction, and every Sunday tried her best to tell the young band how to find the one thing valuable in the dusty and stony walk of life she must tread as well as they. And it was Christ, Sonsie Eagan's Christ, who was her comfort, and made her know how to overcome her poor plain face, and numbed intellect and harsh training, and, in spite of all, win the confidence of these waifs, whose life was like a shadow of her own.

But, though the individual classes grew quiet and orderly, the noisy element was continually refreshed by new-comers, and the singing still croaked like a frog-pond, and the lessons hummed as a swarm of bees.

After Christmas, Francis Haythorne went on a three-months' trip to Alaska, inspired thereto, perhaps, by Peace's contemptuous statement, that a man who never took a chance to freeze his fingers wasn't worth looking at, accompanied by a gift of jaunty white mittens with red tassels, the lovely work of her own hands.

The winter and summer, and the next winter, wore away without notable event. Only two letters reached Mollie from Louis. Captain Slocum saw them at the office accidentally, and brought them to her. He had written regularly, and wondered that she didn't answer his questions. It was no use to tell him that her nearest and dearest were these that played her false. At least she could not. So she was brave in keeping it to herself, though it gnawed at her heart; and she beat it down, and went quietly about her soup-kitchens, and temperance society.

The second Easter vacation brought Peace, and, since swallows never come singly, Miss Petingil one day made them a call, which has its importance in this history.

Peace, who was bending over a fragment of the graceful, womanly work she loved—I forget whether it was embroidery, canvas, crochet, or tatting; she did them all, and to perfection—Peace saw her coming, and exclaimed, "Don't tell that horrid old thing I'm here. She has a natural hatred of guileless innocence like mine. I'll hide."

The wilful lassie, work-basket and all, was ensconced behind the heavy dun curtains in a trice, leaving Mollie to her fate. Miss McCross, in fact, watched, with equal vexation, the approach of the prim black alpaca, stalking solemnly up the walk. Every fold in that thrice-turned dress was primed with gossip. Gossip and snuff fought hard in its spinster pocket to come out first with the starched kerchief, and the blue yarn stocking everlastingly in the knitting. Gossip perched on every thin curl that decorated the maiden's hard-favored noddle, and peeped with equal zest and malice from her shrewd, greenish-gray eyes.

I have had a somewhat extended acquaintance with the criminal classes. I have dealt with reformatories, and reflected much upon the phases of regeneration. There is but one crime incapable of cure—for only one brings no remorse. The scandalmonger is a hopeless subject.

Miss Petingil felt no compunction as she rang the door-bell. She was intent on the occupation of a lifetime. Funeral, wedding, christening, she attended them all; and if any thereat lacked information, it was her misfortune, and not her fault. Was she her own fashioning, or society's? On whom lay the blame? Who bore the greatest curse?

To-day her dignity was tremendous, and her mission therefore, proportionably important.

"Mebbe your ma's at home," said she, when Mollie opened the door. "Never mind, I'll jest come in and set a while." And she dropped into the new mosaic chair, to which Mrs. McCross' sickly fingers had given the finishing touch a week before.

"I don't b'lieve the gel cared a mite," she told Mrs. Williams next day. "She didn't look put out, though I sot on't the fust thing." But the patchwork cushion was a small consideration compared to that into which the tailoress plunged without preface.

"I want to know if you've heerd the way that All-wood, that used to work fur your Pa's, been agoin' it? No? Dew tell! You needn't perk up your head so pert about it. I s'pose you ain't in love with him, nor anything. You won't have any snuff? I guess I'll take a pinch; it's real comfortin'." Miss Petingil always snuffed when she gossiped. It gave her opportunity to note any little symptom in the subject.

Mollie warily drew her arm-chair in front of Peace's hiding-place, and played nervously with the tassels of her loose dress. She had no shade of distrust of Louis, but the woman sickened her. What right had *she* to mention him?

"I s'pose you know," continued Miss Petingil, spreading the gathers of her dress straight with her left hand, while she still plied her nose with the "yarb," in all the pauses,—"the feller went into them Pelicans' licker saloon up in Top Town. I das to say that ere Peace gel was settin' her cap for him. But she's seen the folly of it. Peculiar! I must say."

The young lady had been sitting with a mixture of
amusement and disgust on her clear features, over which
every feeling glided as the light wind plays on the surface
of a lake, but troubles not its calm depths.   Now a new
emotion, strange to Mary McCross, ruffled her face, and
taught her for the first time to drop the lids over her eyes,
made violet with fear.   But she held her ground.

"Miss Pelican is my dear friend," said she, with gentle
gravity.   "I don't like to hear her lightly spoken of."

"I cackellate I know them Pelicans as well as the
next one," pursued the old lady, in no wise abashed;
"and I ain't at all averse to speak my mind about 'em.
Codfish aristocracy, I call 'em.   Made all their money
out o' delirum tremens, an' sich."

Peace muttered something wrathfully behind her curtain, and Mollie trembled in anticipation of a sudden descent upon the tale-bearer; but for some good reason the
angry girl kept her place.   This very self-restraint alarmed
her friend.   Her visitor's next words told the story.

"It's no more'n charity to let you know how your folks
hev ben imposed upon by that Allwood."   Miss Petingil
put on a pair of round spectacles as she spoke, that she
might watch her victim's face more closely.   "Young
Brown, Cap'n Slocum's nephew, came from town yesterday, and I heerd him tellin' Squire Hitchcock about it.
You see the chap's habits ain't nun too good, an' Brown
met him an' Pelican holdin' on each other, up about midnight.   Adolphy said he had to laff to see Allwood
hoppin' over the shadders the lamp posts made on the
pavin' stuns.   Ef you'll b'lieve me, he cleared every
one, thinkin' 'em logs, or suthin'.   Wan't it peculiar?"
She wiped her snuffy fingers on her stiff handkerchief,
but never once moved her gaze from Mollie.

The latter had learned self-command in too hard a school to wince. She answered calmly, " I should think so ; but, as I hinted before, I do not wish to hear about it ; " and rose to end the interview.

The spinster didn't stir. " Oh, you needn't go off, Moll. I ain't agoin' till I finish my visit. I thought you'd be shocked " (she gave a relieved sigh). " As I told Adelizy Euphemy. 'Adelizy,' sez I, 'ef Mollie McCross is settin' store by that feller, she'd orter be warned, an' I'll put on my bunnit an' go over this very afternoon, an' she'd do wrong not to thank me for't.' "

The old thing brimmed with malice as she proceeded ; but her listener didn't yield a jot. She sat, her graceful hands motionless in her lap, her position easy and unconstrained. Her muscles had not contracted a hair's-breadth in that whole fifteen minutes' agony. Only fifteen minutes—it seemed a lifetime. Her face was gray and weary, but simple will set her firm, womanly mouth close, lifted her clear, unflinching eye to her tormentor's, and made her say in her cool, liquid voice, " Do you think so, Miss Petingil? I'm sure Louis and I feel the obligation equally. We will always bear it in mind."

" Well, I dew hope," advised the tailoress, patronizingly, moving as she spoke toward the door, " you hain't no hankering after that feller. He's a gone coon. Brown said it was wuth five dollars to ha' seen him reelin' an' skippin' along the street. Take a friend's counsel, an' drop him like a hot potato." Miss Petingil let fall the big jointed forefinger, with which she had been gesticulating, in illustration.

" I *never* drop a hot potato. I should hold it till I was ready to lay it down, if it burned me to the bone," said Mollie, *hors de combat* on the weighty matter, and glad of opportunity to let out her antagonism in a side issue; and she shut her lips, so firm and handsome, and stood, her muscles tense now, her nostril dilating like a stag's—a very type of power.

Miss Petingil felt the pleasure dear to the hunter when his game turns at bay. She admired bravery, with a scientific taste. "Now I think on't, your ma' promised me some Egyptian poppy seeds, an' ef you'll fetch 'em I'd as lief wait as not,"—she parleyed at the door.

Scarcely was Mollie out of the room when the gossip re-entered it, and hurried toward the curtain where sat Peace.

Her design was anticipated, for that young lady stepped out with blazing eyes. " You miserable mischief-maker, I look at you in astonishment. Have you any woman in you ? "

" Massy sakes ! " screamed the old lady, " ef you don't want to know what you are, don't set listening. As for that McCross gel, I come up here to see ef it was true she was goin' to marry him. Folks say she is, an' I bet it's so. She's wuth two of you any day, for all your paneers behind, and your disgraceful, low-necked, dress waists in front. I thought likely you was listening, or I'd ha' said more; an' now you've come out, I *will* free my mind. Ef I'd ha' been Mary McCross, I'd ha' sent my lover anywhere, ruther than to Charley Pelican, that all the world knows never could do nothin' but sing political songs, an' git drunk. There! Ef you don't like it, you may lump it! "

Peace shook from head to foot. " I despise you," said she. " God do so to you, and more also."

Mollie, coming in, heard, and ran to her. "Dear Peace, *dear*, dear Peace, don't ! " cried she. " We mustn't curse her. Go away, Miss Petirgil ! " and she

pressed the seeds into her hand, and pointed to the door.
"Don't you see the harm you've done? Don't stay to
tempt us any further."

"Harm!" screamed the old woman, pocketing her
prize, and then shaking the liberal hand at the maddened
sister; "she's the harm! blackguardin' me, an' listenin'
in such ways as no lady 'd demean herself to come to!
You'd better read your Bible, miss! 'The child that de-
spiseth its mother, the ravens of the valley shall pick out
its eyes, an' the young eagles shall eat them."

"Are you the vulture to finish the bones?" said the
poor girl, bitterly.

But the tailoress was now intrenched in dignity, and
went her way, condescending no reply. I trow Nero
himself might well have envied her afternoon's work.

When she was gone, the two young sufferers stood
looking in each other's face, speechless. But at last
Mollie's rigid self-command gave way. "O Peace!"
she exclaimed, passionately, "can't you say it isn't
true?"

But Peace leaned her haughty head against the win-
dow-frame, and sobbed aloud. "It *is* true," said she,
fiercely, "every word, and more! I hate them, I hate
my very being, everybody; I wish I was dead, I wish
everybody was!" She gasped once or twice, and then
rushed from the room.

As her footsteps died away, Mollie, my dear Mollie,
sank on her knees, to begin a new, bitter battle with
pain.

First came the fierce, intolerable sense of misplaced
love, and shame, amounting to physical agony. They
swept away the very framework of her existence—her
faith, her world, her God. She clutched at each for support, and grasped emptiness. There are moments in

some lives when every experience of the past, every hope of the future, every nerve, every vital power-generating organ, seems to concentrate its force in one intense pang; at that point the mind must either snap or relax. Mollie's relaxed; numbness, vacancy, ensued. Then she rallied a little, and fell to thinking how she and Louis used to make poppy shows, and shake her grandmother's forbidden tulips for their brilliant spoil—Bangutter's leaves they called them, in memory of Mrs. Price's indignation at the mistaken title bestowed in Mollie's earliest speech.

The foolish memory brought tears. Her dear, gentle Louis, whom she had thought so noble! Alas! alas! Mollie never struggled with herself after those bitter drops baptized her love. He was hers now; hers through all, her very own!—to love, suffer with—and, highest, holiest privilege, to save. Louis and ideal bliss she dared not claim, but Louis in need of her, sinning and wounding himself, could not call vainly. He had a right to look to her to bind up his hurts, and, with a free, exulting sense of strength, she realized how she could joyfully shed her heart's blood, drop by drop, for him—all for him. She knelt, full of this new joy, and pledged her life for his before God; and the old, almost forgotten "peace" filled her soul, supplanting alike the long war of duty, and the delirium of first regained liberty.

Then she remembered their common reproach: it was she that should bear his sins and carry his sorrows henceforth; and, sighing and blushing with shame, and crying hot tears of misery, she went up-stairs to pray for him, and write him a letter, without a word of reproof, full of love, and hope, and blessing.

At length Charlie's sister came back. She had tried

to walk her passion out, and returned faint and weary, but with stormy face.

"I cannot bear it," said she. "They have no right to do so. I hate them! I could curse them for their folly —and myself for caring about them. O Mollie! what shall we do?"

Just then Mrs. McCross' scolding voice came sharply from below, and the Deacon's "now, Mirandy, do be easy," in feeble expostulation. Mollie shut the door; the old suffering grated on the new. Peace was frightened by the gray, pain-drawn face she turned toward her. But Mollie's firm, pleasant voice reassured, as she drew her friend to a seat, and, with a few caresses, brought the so much needed tears. "Dear, dear Peace," said she, "God can teach us how to suffer." Then, after a silence, as the poor girl's sobs grew fainter (her head rested against Mollie's shoulder, and Mollie's magnetic touch was on her hand), the lover added, "Without sorrow none liveth in love."

CHAPTER XII.

"Here we go, up-up-up,
    Here we go, round-round-roundy,
Here we go this way and that,
    And here we go down-down-downy."

"MISERY," said Mary McCross, "is the result of too great self-concentration. I am going to spend the morning in Syllabub." Peace made a horrible face. She expected to return to Rosenbloom next day; and, besides, was filling in a canvas copy of Powers' Greek Slave, and disliked interruption. Privately, I think such caricatures of art monstrous and disgusting; but they were all the rage, and, in spite of her strong, good sense, Miss Pelican as often did the things *à la mode*, as the things *à son cœur.* She didn't object to personal charity, *in a small way,* and she was lavish in money-giving; she had even experienced a degree of pleasure in the Patience of Hope class, especially the part where Francis Haythorne walked home with her. But the smells that particularly belong to poverty, the drunken women, and the pigs, were her abomination.

However, Mollie was set on the walk. She had a pie for little Doppy, a shirt for Mr. Heffron the piper, and a shawl for Mrs. Dennis, all of which were needed at that precise time, so there was no way of escape.

On the road they called to see the Rev. Mr. Growing, whom they found at the Bizbys' solacing himself with his third pipe and Shakespeare. He was revisiting his former pastorate, and welcomed Mollie warmly. His sunny, open face was a great uplift to her. She felt better before he said a word.

Few appreciate the comfort and rest a real pastor gives his flock. Out of office he may meet them but seldom, but as he lays holy things before them Sabbath after Sabbath, he gets to occupy a vast importance in their souls' economy. The weak quote him. The strong renew their strength in him. Through him, God supports the mourner, and confirms godliness. He embodies, moulds, and wields the moral sentiment of the community. He bears in him the power of God, which is the more often forgotten because of its silent strength. Though perhaps a timid thinker, he harnesses the runners in the race; though no genius, his warm Christ home is often the nursery of genius. In a word, he says of his people, with a depth of truth only he himself can know, "My little children, for whom I travail in birth."

But, to Molly, Mr. Growing had been more than even the minister. He was her tried friend, fellow-worker, and confidant. With a suggestion he had often helped her out of her unspoken troubles. It was to him that she, with great difficulty, told her heart, touching her new-born Christ; and though she never asked sympathy or aid again, she unconsciously held him as a physician, only to be applied to in extremity, but certain to cure.

He, on his side, rejoiced in her energetic love of truth and helpfulness, and, though it was sweet to carry his lambs over the rough places, felt a comradeship with this sturdy pilgrim, who feared to breast no storm. He quietly watched her in what Goethe would call her apprenticeship; incited her aspirations for culture and experience without her knowing it, helping to direct them wisely and happily; and, if he sometimes shook his head over the battles she was certain to fight, he forebore to dishearten by criticism or prophecy.

Mollie had missed him since he went to Cannadasset. She would feel his loss more in this crisis of her life. It was her need time. She told him so, only half realizing it as she spoke. "No! no!" answered he earnestly; "remember Don Quixote. Pray devoutly, hammer on stoutly."

"I shall," she said with her customary quiet intensity, and he didn't doubt her.

On her side she asked about Cannadasset, in a grave, ministerial fashion, as if knowing the weak spots in parish work by instinct.

He told her all the pinches: the hitch in the prayer-meeting, the difficulty in collections, the impracticable plans for reaching the proud poor, the crying want of *culture* among Phil Penhurst's operatives, which last he and the young manufacturer were trying to meet by night schools and woman's societies. "If I can only get the widows to pray for me, I'm all right," said Fred, winding up a *Harlequin* of ministerial puzzles, which Mollie evidently understood, and had hung up for private tilts in future leisure. In fact she was not waiting for time coming, but, absorbed in consideration, rose, shook hands abstractedly, and wandered away still deep in thought, leaving Peace, whose share in these weighty discussions had been amused listening, to carry off the shirt and pie and shawl, all, including herself, being totally forgotten.

The slush of a parting snow-storm was under foot. The spring, as Miss Petingil said, "was drefful late an' tejus;" adding, "for her part she found if she lived through March, she noticed she was pretty apt to last the hull year."

On wading down to Syllabub, Peace judiciously woke her friend just before they reached the "Solomon Rodgers," and they entered, to find Doppy in a state of tear-streaked despair. Since Mrs. Nickson's death, the waif had transferred her allegiance to Mollie, though Francis Haythorne nominally taught the class; and Amos highly approved the feminine selection, for the elegant and fastidious physician was rather despised by the muscular young Hibernians. Mollie with a woman's instinct, which teaches her to still her heart pang by some helpless care, drew the hot-tempered little emerald into her soul, and gave her liberally both affection and aid. She would have done the same by Joe, had not Miss Heffron disdained such effeminate guardianship. Johanna, poor thing, regulated her ideas by the standard of her boy associates.

This day appeared to have been a sad one for Doppy.

Her visitors discovered her plodding hopelessly through jagged seams of a half-made chemise, "whose conthrariness was," she affirmed, "beyond belavin';" and its bulgy gores, raw-edged hems, fulled fells, and stitches all dotted from needle-stabs, were enough to provoke pity even in Mrs. Williams, who was notably the hardest woman in Millville.

Mollie was on the alert now. She seated herself on a promiscuous chair without ado, and gently twitched the garment away to look at its workmanship. It smelled as if it had been used as dish-cloth and duster, and its damp condition rendered it probable that it had dried its seamstress' eyes.

"How much better you sew!" said the examiner, assuming the battered brass thimble, and beginning to rip, baste, and hem, with every appearance of content. Doppy, who was kneeling beside her to observe the process, gave a comforted smile, and watched the amendment of a zig-zag place in intense interest.

But Peace considered the ravelled, silken seams of her life too badly frayed to admit of reformation, and attempts at bettering the poor, time-garment of a street-child, appeared weary adding to misery.

Having therefore pelted the cats, secretly turned up her nose at a horrible, all-pervading odor of burnt potatoes, and studied the fly-specked Madonna till she began to feel as if the end of her nose was equally sharp and crocky, she vented her ennui in patting her little foot on the bare floor with vehement protest, and indulged in indignant coughs as Mollie entered upon a third long fell with unruffled placidity.

But though Miss McCross paid no attention to Miss Pelican's fidgets, Doppy was much exercised thereby; and, after brief consideration of the ameliorating means at hand, resolved to sweep. She had kicked up a mighty

8

dust, when she remembered the " E. McCross " on the broom-handle, and dashed the tell-tale implement into the cupboard, with an impulse of burning shame and regret.

Mollie sewed on quietly; and, looking at the little girl, who stood rooted in the middle of the floor twisting a lock of hair, ready to cry, asked in her pleasant sunny voice,

" When did it happen ? "

There was neither anger nor reproof in the tones. Accordingly Doppy did not feel called upon to turn dogged or defend herself. She crept humbly toward her friend, and hid her face in her dress without a word.

The teacher whose heart was very sore with her own pain, experienced a strange throbbing sympathy for the repentant reprobate trembling against her knee. She laid her hand gently upon the bent head; when Doppy ventured to look up in her face, she saw her eyes full of tears. Something in that frightened, appealing glance stole all Mary's power of repression, and, helpless in the grasp of emotion, she rested her head against the battered chair-back, and wept in spite of herself. It was all one bitterness, and all gates opened the prisoned fountain.

Doppy had never seen a lady cry before. It was different from any confession of pain she had witnessed; *so* noiseless, *so* imperious, *so* resolutely combated, *so* plainly only *hurt;* *so* patient and uncomplaining. She was frightened, and, forgetful of her remorse, laid her friend's hand against her hot little cheek, and begged her to be happy once more, and kissed the passive fingers again and again with all the fervor of her impetuous Irish nature. And, when Mollie regained her self-control, and sat up pale and weak, she could not rest till her caresses were returned, and her peace made ; and, still in the bitterness cf inner suffering, Mollie took the little comforter on her knee, and laying her head against her shoulder, gave her the taste of mother-love and mother-fondling the poor child so craved and needed, and found again her own strength thereby.

Miss Pelican, quite forgotten by the actors in this drama of penitence, had felt her own composure much shaken, and retired to a corner to give them a free " outing." Finding calmness now to reign, she gathered up her scattered bundles, and remarked sarcastically, " Let thy moderation be known unto all men—in going home," when the door opened to admit Joe's old man, drunk.

With never-tiring charity, Mollie had provided him coal and food and work. The more she gave, the less he did. He labored two days out of six, and raved in drunken delirium the odd four. At length he threw down his brush, declaring that, as he had labored for the benefit of humanity, humanity was bound to support him. A trifling habit of painting all around the spiders he met (on the crazy supposition that touching them would make trouble with Joe) had somewhat decreased the value of the little toil he brought himself to endure ; and his daughter, who begged, stole, or starved, as it happened, felt no loss as the result of his lapse from duty. He now went straight to Peace, and tried to stand upright and look at her.

" Don't mind him," observed Doppy, as the lady shrank away. " There's a window broke where he works, an' he's a cold in his eyes, so he can't see straight."

" Hev you observed my girl anywheres ? " demanded he, fiercely.

" There, lay down a bit," interfered their hostess again, in a soothing voice, pointing to an old lounge as she spoke; " she's comin' directly."

"I'll smash her," remarked he, as he pitched toward it. "She hain't taken care of me. Here I've ben drunk all day, an' she hain't come near. You see she's drunk all the time, and I'm (hic) never sober (hic). She'd orter have more oversight on me 'n she does. I'll wallop her. I'll—" he had reached his couch by this time, and whiskey got too much the upper hand for speech.

"Mary McCross," said Peace, in angry dignity, "I think it's positively unladylike to stay here a second longer."

"Just wait a little," pleaded her friend, who was accustomed to such doings, and had again become busy at the sewing. "If I baste in this sleeve, she can finish it for Sunday; he isn't going to wake up."

While Peace was gasping in astonishment at her coolness, Joe, Christie Malone, and Amos returned from a "pickin'" expedition to divide the spoil.

"By Jingo Pelters," said Master Daley, holding up a broken champagne bottle, "that Miss Williams is the gol darnedest mean woman I iver see; jest think of askin' pay for a spilt bottle like that, an' three chicken-bones! Doppy, how's your buird?"

She smilingly produced a miserable canary in a cracked tea-pot. "He don't sing 'ary a note. I believe it's the sades you giv' him."

"Nonsense," said Peace, examining the poor thing, which had almost lost every feather, and peeped feebly. "How could he in the dark? I should think he'd have sore eyes."

Doppy looked miserable. "It's a bootiful buird," said she, "an I vally it as the gift o' frens, but I hain't nowheres else to put it."

"Thrue fur ye!" said Amos proudly. "I sawed

wood the hull day at Square Hitchcock's fur him. The crookedest sticks them wos! But I didn't make no account of it, fur the pleasure ov givin' him to Doppy. 'An' here's the singer that'll take the top off Syllabub,' sez Miss Euphemy, an' me carryin' him off."

The girls exchanged glances. They had heard Adeliza regretting only the day before, that she hadn't raised a song-bird in the whole nest. Something about defrauding the laborer of his hire crossed Peace's mind, as she caught a happy thought.

"You bring him, tea-pot and all, up to Miss McCross this afternoon, and I'll put him in a cage. I'll engage he'll whistle when he comes home."

Mollie smiled gratefully, fathoming the generous intent; but the expression of dissatisfaction with which she had been watching Joe and Christie increased tenfold, as their relations to each other grew more obvious. They seemed on terms of greatest intimacy. She snatched a coil of rope from his pile : he took her about the waist, and twisted it from her hand. She kicked him. He stood back, and struck her a violent blow.

"For shame!" cried Mollie, indignantly, "to touch a woman!"

"She's my wife, or goin' to be, an' I've a right to lick her if I like," said he, in his sullen accent; then under Mollie's compelling power, "You *are* my girl, Joe?" in half apology.

"Yes," she answered, apparently impassible.

Doppy, however, did not share in her apathy. "Ef so be's yees can't be dacent, in a respectable" (Doppy dwelt on the long word with deliberation)—"respectable house, ye may lave straight, Christie Malone. I keep a *quite* place—thank the saints." She snatched the poker, and, big boy as he was, Master Malone departed without ceremony. Mollie followed him out. She had been waiting, partly in hope of seeing him. He was a tall, white-faced fellow, with watery red eyes, a shock of fiery hair, and a mouth like a potato-hole. The only thing that marked him among the degenerate types of humanity bred by destitution, was his foot—so handsomely arched, small, and slender; sole heritage of gentle blood for generations back. He was not strong apparently, and turned sixteen.

" Have you any work, Christie ? "

He stood with his head down, kicking the door-step, and shook his shoulders.

" What made you leave the Gonecussets ? "

" I ain't agoin' to kill myself workin' for any man."

The teacher sighed. It was up-hill toil. She had looked after him patiently, begged him places, clothed, not him alone, but his family; not for a few months, but two long years. She had tried to teach him to read, prayed about him in private, exhorted him in public, and this was the result ! He had been constantly in her class since the memorable disturbance, when she enforced order; but his tricks, lies, rudeness, sly whispers to a blushing neighbor, tried her very soul.

" Why do you come here ? " she cried once, desperately.

" To set where its warm," retorted he.

To day the incubus weighed more heavily than usual. She let him slip sullenly away, and Peace lost no time in joining her, really thankful to have got out in safety. Miss Pelican was not properly constituted for a Bible reader.

" That boy is a load of lead to my soul," said Mollie, as if announcing a recent conclusion.

" His head is curiously shaped," rejoined Peace ; " it slopes right to a point on top, and has no back at all."

The home missionary looked worried. She remembered hearing a former instructor assert that a man all face, and nothing behind it, *couldn't* make a decent member of society. Thenceforth her eyes rested on the lad with an uneasy, fascinated glance. Was it possible to save a boy with no back to his head? She didn't despair. Said Peace in the most serious voice possible, " I often call to mind the baby's epitaph:

> " ' When Gabriel's trump shall wake the dead,
>   And souls to bodies jine,
> · Too many there will wish their lives
>   Had been as short as thine.' "

" My dear," said Mollie, having as usual shelved both remark and quotation for future thought, " I find great comfort · in that verse touching Christ's triumphant entry."

Peace looked up now in honest sobriety, to hear the Scripture: " And thy King came into Jerusalem, riding on a wild ass's colt ! "

CHAPTER XIII.

" To one she gave porridge,
  To another gave bread."

THE sitting-room at Fir Covert was large and circled with oak, and the carpet was brown—all the way from yellowish to chestnut. When I looked in, the heavy, dun curtains were unlooped, for the sun had long since gone to bed, and with him retired

the top-knotted fowls, scolding wrens, and melancholy
robins, who roamed daily about the place. The late frost,
which had surprised them, brought out the old andirons,
and set them holding a stick or two of hard maple. The
wood hissed and snapped in the red-throated chimney,
and the bright flame danced fitfully, making gay the
dark frames of the water-colors Mollie had done when a
little maid, and falling with weird brilliance upon a great
copy of the Court of Death that hung opposite the fire-
place.

Beside the hearth lay a pair of slippers, whose seven
ugly monkeys stood out distinct against a scarlet ground-
work. On the dun-rep arm-chair, wheeled close to the
fire, hung the cashmere dressing-gown, with its long tassels. Poppy swung from her silver perch, and Mollie
sat on the floor, watching alternately the red shadows
playing over the wall, and listening for the well-known
step on the flagged walk, thinking the while such maidenly thoughts as properly lodge in comely brown heads
that stand erect, like brave annunciation lilies on the
stem.

At last he came for whom all waited. The gate swung
with its customary squeak. "Papa!" cried Mollie, lifting her cheek from the chair-cushion as the door un-
closed, and running to meet him. Now the old gentleman was hurried forward to the blaze, bereft of his
coat and hat and boots, and invested in the gorgeous
dressing-gown and slippers. Next, Mollie spirited away
the cast-off garments, then came back and took his gray
head in her hands, looking into his eyes, and kissed his
withered cheek. After this she sat down contentedly on
the cushion by his knee. The old man smiled a comforted smile, and seemed to grow a little plumper, a little
younger, a little less careworn, just as he always did

when the familiar dialogue was performed, for it was a very old scene, though it never seemed old to these two.

"Where's your mother?" said the Deacon, patting Mollie's soft hair, and stretching his black-stockinged feet to the fire.

"Gone to mother's meeting, and we'll have tea alone," answered she, gayly. "She is to sup with Mrs. Hitchcock. Won't we have a nice time ordering our meal! What shall we cook for you?"

"I'll take a pair of parrot's tongues," said this easily suited individual, after considering awhile.

"No tongue to spare," retorted Mollie, with due gravity.

"Then let it be bear's feet, fried," he went on, in the same tone.

"No," said she, pinching the loose skin at the back of his small, wrinkled hand (the Deacon was still proud of it, though it began to earn its living fifty—sixty—years ago). "I haven't killed the animal I've got; he's too lean. Hadn't we better have Welsh rarebit?"

"I guess so, little girl," smiling into her loving eyes. He always called her this when they were very happy together. She was his pride, his sole delight. He watched her as she rose to give the order in her dignified, maidenly way, and his heart grew lighter when a positive foot-tap heralded her return.

So they had the Welsh rarebit, and Mollie poured tea from a quaint Japanese teapot, and fed her father with muffins served on the choicest illuminated plates.

The cakes despatched, they told each other's fortunes in the bottom of the teacups.

Mollie twisted hers four times on the saucer to give the tears chance to run out; and her father found therein

beaux and diamonds, not to mention a horse and buggy.
As a reward, she discovered him addressing a vast concourse of people, which she knew must be the eleven
o'clock prayer-meeting, but he felt sure was an audience
to his Fourth of July speech.

After this was decided, they went back to the parlor,
and she dropped into her old place at his feet. They
talked a long time about business and gossip. If Mr.
Nickson had been heard from; if Dr. Perfect's last sermon was really to be printed for circulation; if Mrs.
Perfect had prayed the crippled darkey to full use of her
limbs, as had been hinted.

These questions being settled, she became absently
thoughtful, and fell to playing with his fingers. "Little
Pete, Peter Rue, Rue Whistle, Whistle Dossel, Gobble-
gobble-gobble." She told them all one by one, shaking
each absently, and then began again. "Father," said
she, with an effort, after he had snatched her wandering
hand and prisoned it in his own, "do you know anything of Louis?"

A change came over Deacon McCross. He ceased to
be the loving parent, sunning himself in his daughter's
affection. The dun arm-chair held a spare, old man,
with a mixture of fear and remorse in his weazened features. It was only a moment; the expression passed
away as he answered, "Nothing, daughter." Mollie
heaved a stifled sigh, and stared hard into the burning
coals.

He was miserable, seeing her suffer, and cast about for
some means to comfort her. He only knew one way—
to give her something. "Mollie," said he, hesitatingly,
"suppose I deed you the 'Solomon Rodgers' Tavern?
Would it please you? You've often asked for it." She
knew the motive that prompted the gift. Her poor,

weak, loving father! She was very sorry for him, and so made much of the matter, and set herself to chase away his trouble.

She perched on his knee—very lightly, because the time was near when the grasshopper would be a burden to those once stalwart limbs—and hugged and kissed him, and tickled his cheeks to make dimples. As he still looked sober, she snatched a newspaper, and proposed to burn it to see who would marry first. He smiled and agreed; so she got down before the fire, and lighting its severed leaves (the "Millville Universe" was not a large sheet), laughingly blew her own fragment to make it blaze. "See, cruel papa," quoth she as the last spark died from off his blackened fortune, "you will be out of the market first. But settle your mind to one thing— I shall claw my step-mother."

Doubtless the Deacon knew too much about claws and clauses, to be charmed at the prospect; so she felt it plain duty to play "Pease Porridge Hot" with him. Before the game was done her brown hair rippled away over her shoulders, a mass of wondrous beauty, her cheeks reddened into a soft blush, and her firm, supple fingers burned with their fairly earned punishment.

In the midst of this, the door opened, and Mr. Haythorne walked in. Then Mollie arose from her ottoman, brought him another arm-chair, poked the embers, and, having added a stick or two of maple, took her seat opposite, just where the flicker would play upon her serene face.

"I have been reading the 'Spectator,'" said he, settling himself for a chat, and warming his white hands at the blaze. "The weather is unseasonable—a frost last night, and now heavy rain."

"We are always glad to give the hearth-cricket chance

to chirp," answered she, punching a stick to make the sparks go up chimney. "What did you find in the 'wicked novel-book,' as mother would call it: 'man is born to trouble as the sparks fly upward'?"

"Not precisely. 'The division of troubles was the theme of my meditation. I read from three to five, history or classic literature; one can never know enough of either."

The young girl was looking toward him, but she saw not his handsome, curly auburn head and flowing beard, nor yet his hazel eyes, that glanced so full of fire to hers. She was watching in thought a dearer face, with eyes of purer, softer light, and a lip whose remembered curve was scarce darkened by the down of manhood. If the recollection could not now come free of anxious pain, it was a dear pang, loved for whose sake she bore it.

"Things in this life are equal," said she, as if she wished to believe it. "There's a balm for every wound, and," after a pause, "every honey-bee carries a sting."

"Heine says, there are sweet peas for all. That is a better song than one more orthodox the little German maid sang with false voice but true feeling, as he relates."

"In that case, 'full many a flower is born to blush unseen,'" said Mollie sadly. The troubles of this world compassed the poor child to-night. "He would have said more truly, thus: 'thistles and night-shade grow n every man's garden. If he pull the night-shade first, he is happy.'"

Her tone, very hard for Mollie, so startled the gentleman that he dropped the tongs wherewith he was building up a castle of red coals behind the forestick.

The clang awoke the Deacon, who always dozed comfortably off when Mollie talked literature, and Poppy

withdrew her head from her downy wing, blinked sleepily
at the trio, and failed not to murmur ere she closed her
brilliant eyes, "Dear Louis, dear Mollie, pchoo;" a sentence which continued to make a disagreeable impression
on the guest's mind.

' He fell to talking of Europe; how the German maidens waltz and drink Rhine wine, and Mollie seemed to
him fairer than any German maid. Then he told of his
beloved Goethe, of his long bachelorhood, how he
thought to wed a lovely young girl, but was so frightened
by the cradles his mother rummaged from the garret, that
he broke the engagement.

Mollie lifted her clear, fathomless blue eyes to his face.
"It would be my dearest wish to have a merry, noble boy
to love, caress, and bring up into honorable manhood."
She thought the while, with a sigh, how far off seemed the
blossoming of her fullest wife-love.

But Mr. Haythorne rambled on, talking of Coriolanus
and Virgilia, Faust and Marguerite, and patient, lovely
Undine, and every noble type of woman seemed to find its
breathing-life in the young girl sitting so womanly modest beyond the blazing maple-sticks. But Mollie's heart
flew with every picture of devotion to her absent lover,
and panted to be all this and more to him.

CHAPTER XIV.

" Ride a Jack horse
To Banbury Cross."

MIDSUMMER eve fell warm and breathless. The lazy stars blinked through the thick ether, and the moon put on her parti-colored garment, and sailed quietly through the cloud-banded heavens. The trees swayed sleepily to and fro, as middle-aged chaperons nod at the eleventh hour of a grand ball. At sunset the very cat-birds sang heartlessly. In fact, the only creatures which managed to brave the leaden heat were a chorus of frogs and cicadæ that kept up their Handel and Haydn Society till long after humanity was making spurious imitations in bed.

If fairies were abroad, they had chosen a bad time for their revels. I wish I could have found them and begged a sleep-philter. Every evening Mollie's light stole through the dusky evergreens, till the last straggling footstep died into stillness; then she breathed a weary sigh; she hoped her lover's truant feet had brought him home.

When the labors of life were appointed, man stepped up first, and on him was laid to plan, to work, to take the headship of the family; and he went away, supposing he bore the whole burden. After him came woman, willing to share the misfortunes of her race; to whom the angel said pityingly, " The man, thy husband, fancies he carries *all* the curse: he has only left for thee, powerless to cope with the rough toils of life, to weep his failures unavailingly and in silence."

Careless of the sanctities of the night, you might have

noticed a quartette stealing through the Millville streets about eleven o'clock, Mrs. Williams's well-filled garden being the goal. Amos, like a famous scion of his profession, carried the bag,—a large one, that went with a string,—and they all walked softly as if afraid of waking such echoes as still lingered amid the flat respectability of this Gonecusset's Eden.

Silently the boys dropped over the sharp-nailed fence wherewith the woman sought to shut out Syllabub.

Cucumbers mildly growing by the pale moonlight, warty squashes, and odoriferous onions, returned to earth to ripen, all passed their examination, to be pronounced too young.

But there were lettuces and seed-onions and early raspberries in plenty, that found community of experience in the wide-mouthed sack.

"Ain't they whoppers!" said Hugh from the pea-vines, when the pressure of business was somewhat abated.

"Hush!" returned Amos, revelling in a bed of late strawberries. "I tought I seed a light some'rs."

"Boy alive!" returned Aleck with a contemptuous sniff, "she never 'luminated when Grant was 'lected, an' she ain't likely to use up kerrycene for such 'umble perfessionals as we, mean old granny!"

"We've got enough for here," said Hugh, anxious to be on the safe side. "Let's go some'rs else."

"Oh!" cried Aleck in anguish. "I be caught, sure's grief!" Even so. Payson's steel trap, baited for Gracie Jenkins' rabbits, had snared bigger game. With much subdued groaning, the member was released, and Amos threw the bag over his shoulders preparatory to departure, when Hugh cried "Hist!" in a frightened tone, and immediately a dull thud was heard in the distance.

"Run, fellers, she's comin'!" said Christie hurriedly.

"Pooh!" returned Aleck, "she's jest ben lickin' the young ones. Golly! how she did lay it on! They squalled too loud fur her to be hearin' ov us."

"But I noticed a noise like the poundin' I see Miss Petingil givin' her cloes in a barr'l," whispered Hugh.

"Most likely it's the ghost of all them lickin's you've missed," returned Christie, whose notion of Payson's late sufferings was for some reason quite vivid.

"Give us a rest now," put in Aleck. "Didn't I hear Miss McCross explainin' how nothin' was iver lost: so all them are laid up for ye yet. By the same token, ye'll get 'em soon, for you're growin' so tall they can't wait much longer."

"I'll pass that," whispered Hugh ruefully; but he had scarcely said it when the same ominous sound smote their ears.

"What shall we do?" said Amos, promptly circumventing an attempt, of Hugh's to run away.

"Let's go! Where does it come from? This way— no, that! Dear, by goll, it's all over!" quoth the latter, sitting down in a miserable heap on the ground.

Thud! thud! came the remorseless monitor. They looked into each other's faces in horror.

"It's a Banshee to warn us of death!" cried Aleck in a choked voice. "We've one in my family. See, there he stands! He allus appears afore any on us is took."

They all looked where he pointed. There, amid the long shadows cast by the fruit-trees and the chequered moonlight sifting through the trellised grape-vines, geamed a white figure—erect, motionless, with averted face.

"Deuce take your Banshee!" said Hugh, half dead with fright, "it's a Bugaboo goin' to carry us off for

stealin'. He stamps three times, an' thin switches his
tail an' moves his horns an'—"

"An' if so be's you ain't good, you git a darned
lickin'," interrupted Amos. "I heerd mother doin' that
this mornin' to my little sister. I don't believe a word
on't. It's a Banshee, an' you're goin' to die, Aleck.
Golly, I'm glad it ain't me!"

"That's so! Do run, or I'll have to lose a mornin's
work by your funeral," said Christie, trying to laugh.

"You must be smart. I'll bet it's the old woman,"
cried the doomed individual uneasily. "Any way, I'll
have my share in the truck to-night." But, in spite of
the brave ending, his teeth chattered, and the awful
figure with upraised hand pointed to the miserable lads,
inexorable as fate.

"Amos, do go an' see if it's anybody," gasped Aleck.
"'Tain't nowise likely he wants anything o' you."

"Go yourself," retorted the person addressed, indignant
at the suggestion. "I'd be ashamed to be afeard of my
own relations."

But Aleck shook his head. The moon went behind a
cloud; the wind stirred the trees; the terrible premoni-
tor of the ghost sounded at uncertain intervals, and still
the pale figure moved not.

"I'll be darned if I stand this any longer!" cried
Christie. "Move up to your Banshee, or I'll thrash
you well."

"An' I'll help," said Hugh, advancing with the jig-
step of habit, curiously at war with the feelings of cowardly fright.

"An' so'll I," chimed in Amos, doubling up his fists,
preparatory.

Thus urged, the unhappy lad stole slowly toward the
gleaming horror, till he suddenly uttered a shriek, and

dropped to the earth. "O boys! I'm kilt. I'll never steal agin, long as I live!"

Christie picked him up. "What are ye hollerin' about, ye fool? Were ye gassin' us the hull time, that the fallin' ov a few apples an' a couple ov towels on the bushes should set ye to takin' on so? Git up, or I'll lick ye."

"Ain't I killed?" asked Aleck, opening his eyes. "Something hit me on the snout worse'n I was ever hit afore."

"Don't ye know an apple when ye feel it, ye jackass?" said Hugh, sending a half-grown early over the fence with a vicious kick. "Now you've raised the old woman."

Sure enough, the stout figure of Mrs. Williams appeared from the kitchen doorway, still habited in her night-cap, and in her late husband's old boots, which she was wearing out to save shoe-leather. Long before her tallow dip had explored the intervening space, the boys had safely climbed the fence. "I swan dumb," quoth she, stumbling over the sprung trap, "here's the track of the nasty Irish. Got hurt! I'm glad on't;" and she forthwith retired to her matronly repose.

The boys had run full half a mile, when their fears abated enough to permit a halt.

"It'll niver do to go into Millville at once," said Christie, with his customary sly caution. This was the kind of a boy who will talk to you about religion, with his eyes earnestly directed to yours, hungry longing filling them, and be holding a second conversation in deaf and dumb language about a gambling row that very moment. "You give me an' Aleck the bag," continued he, "and we'll hurry home, while you go round t'other way."

"Not for Joe," retorted Hugh instantly. "I'm

intendin' to see the dividin' of them fruits. Aleck can walk along wid Amos."

"Suit yerself," rejoined Christie, "only make haste. It's goin' on twelve now."

Five minutes afterward Amos and Aleck reached the stone wall that surrounds Bradshaw's meadows.

"Hurry, an' git over," whispered Mr. Heffron, who had his own reasons for distrusting young Malone. "We'll cut through the lots while they're partin' the stuff, or we shan't git nun."

Amos mounted the stones slowly, for the wall was of good height, and protected, moreover, by a superstructure of rails.

"Jump! jump!" cried Aleck, with a poke; whereupon our hero gave a spring.

"Ugh! what's this! O Aleck! what am I on? The divil's got me this time, sure."

"I'll bet he has," replied that still ruffled ghost-seer, glad the incredulous Amos was likewise in grief. "You'd better say your prayers. He's jest spreadin' his wings to take you to the bad place. Such horns as he's got!"

Amos, looking before him, sure enough saw two immense things erecting themselves as his dreadful bearer rose from the ground.

"Hail Mary, full of grace! Do let me come down, Mr. Devil, please!" he cried imploringly, not daring to move a muscle. "Speak! speak! only speak."

The satanic emissary, true to his instinct, laid back his pseudo *horns*, raised his tail, and, planting his forefeet forward, gave vent to a series of he-haws that echoed strangely through the still night.

"Oh! do speak English, Mr. Devil!" shrieked the unhappy rider, too thoroughly frightened to recognize his unsought steed; while Aleck, remembering Pauline

Bradshaw's donkeys, burst into a peal of discordant laughter.

The noise awoke Daisy, who responded to her mate's call from the other side of the field, and Dandy took to his heels, Amos still clinging to his seat, in bolt upright, rigid terror, and muttering alternate petitions to the saints and Diabolus. Behind him streamed his immense coat-tails; before him lay unnumbered horrors, and the night air bore the sound of Aleck's retreating footsteps, fainter and fainter in the distance.

.   .   .   .   .   .

"If ever I'm caught in that ere line agin, I hope, yis, I *hope* I'll jump onter them nasty beasts, same as last night," said Amos, with awful solemnity, when he had finished confiding his woes to little Doppy.

"Airnest?" inquired she, with the brevity of doubt.

"Airnest," responded he, laying his stubby fingers together in heartfelt devotion, and rolling up his sparkling eyes till only the whites were perceptible.

"Now, that's rale good," said the confessoress heartily. "I hope I may get licked ef I don't do the same. Miss McCross has found me work in the mill, an' I'm to go every week to her house to learn to sew n' read, n' be a lady same's her."

"How hunki!" commended the devoted Mr. Daily, without a shadow of misgiving as to the result. Then imagination retraced its steps through the interval. "Ain't you goin' to be at home, or pickin' no more?" queried he, doleful at the prospect.

"Jess so," returned she, in a dignified tone, "an' you'd best do the same, n' quit wastin' yer time, n' makin' a lazy lummox of yersel' same as ye be."

"You're awful hard on a feller. I don't like to work no how," said Amos meekly.

"Wimmin takes to it, I s'pose!" retorted Doppy, in sarcasm. "Learn a lesson from me as has kept her house clean, an' washed her cloes all summer."

"If you say so, I will," he assented, in rueful awe of her energy. "What a tiger you are! Vedder'll find me a job, 'cause he said he would."

"Then don't be settin' lookin' at yer fingers," exclaimed the active damsel, beginning to put chairs and tables in forbidding groups, and glancing at a scrub-brush with portentous meaning.

Amos accordingly saw no alternative, and sallied forth to clinch resolution.

"That's the woman it takes to bring me to terms," was his admiring soliloquy as he strode manfully toward Millville.

"There," said Doppy, closing the door on him, and feeling the bristles of the scouring implement in a bustle of pleasure. "I knew I could make him! He's the best-meaning chap in Syllabub, and the darlin'est!"

CHAPTER XV.

"Three wise men of Gotham
Went to sea in a bowl;
If the bowl had been stronger—"

PUT this down because of its extreme pertinence. Only the wisest take as substantial a ship as that named. Even Diogenes had nothing better than a wash-tub. In the sea of life one meets but leaky craft: broken beer-barrels, dismantled

paint-boxes, cornstalk fiddles, muck-rakes, pea-shooters, represent the rafts that float most of mankind. Our own canoe is only paper. On the whole, the Pelicans thought it a much more refined method of sailing toward the better land to take a bowl, which they accordingly did—a first-class affair, called the "Night-blooming Cereus."

I regard it as a paltry trick in an author, to tell the perusing stranger the whole family history of the book-people, and so prejudice his mind with scandal—a thing altogether unlike the healthful and inductive method of acquaintance in real life. Fortunately I am here spared the temptation, for I know nothing about the Pelicans, except that they one day settled in Top Town, opened a distillery and sample-room, which flourished abundantly, and in due time Peace and Charley grew into years of discretion. I always suspected that the old gentleman had a touch of Spanish blood; for the children were Castilian brunettes of the most pronounced type. As for their mother, she was small and fair-haired, very gentle, very conscientious, very winning, very much afraid of Mrs. Grundy. She was either a Perkins or a Pitkin or a Norton, or a Hooker, of Connecticut, I don't know exactly which, and any one learned in New England genealogies can tell why.

Of late years Mr. Pelican had interested himself in benevolence and religion; had donated to orphan asylums, and given cottages at the sea-shore to struggling ministers, and sent poor students through college; had become instant in prayer, attendant on the preached Word, and widely known through the columns of the local newspaper, the "Cereus," meantime, piling up the wherewithal to indulge himself in these pious bonbons. If he had begun with a saloon and ended with a still,

he would only have been the successful rum seller; but,
starting with the manufactory, and gracefully adding the
sample-room, Peace and Charley held their heads among
the nobles of the land. Indeed, there was a legend about
a Spanish buccaneering ancestor, with bars of gold and
silver tankards (represented by a certain golden-lined
silver sugar-bowl that stood on three solid bear's claws,
still in the family), and an oratory and a big crucifix, inlaid with diamonds, and a black mustache on the
father's side, and divers more reliable tales of Indian
encounters and revolutionary episodes, such as found
vent from Mrs. Pelican's patrician lips. So, after all,
they had whereof to boast as much as any, and there the
young folks intrenched themselves, and sniffed at come-
up-over-night Top Towners, particularly those who
" pushed by Miss Craydock," which sort of thing pride
helped them to despise.

Mr. Pelican had long held dealings in real estate with
Deacon McCross. He happened to see Louis in his
office one day, and was struck by his modest bearing and
truthful, refined face. He was on the look-out for a clerk
at the " Cereus," who would make up for Charley's irregularities, and, hearing young Allwood's history with emen-
dations from Squire Hitchcock, at once set matters in
train to engage him.

Our hero accordingly went to Top Town, to be received by Peace's mother with delight. She must needs
show him kindness, for her heart was very tender; but
from the moment the gentle, impulsive, spiritual enthusiast entered her household, they found a sympathy between
them that her own haughtily imperious children were not
attuned to share. Louis was the sort of man delightful
in a house. He was modest, pure, unselfish, scholarly;

full of delicate ways and artistic tastes; always busy, always cheerful, and instinctive in generosity and tact.

Mrs. Pelican was the sort of plant easily compressed into a corner by the vigorous growth about her; it really proved a godsend when this kindred shoot enticed her over the wall into a more congenial garden. Louis' deference to her, as the representative of that dear, mysterious motherhood his lonely boy-life had never known, was complete. She answered it by taking him into her heart as her own son. The inside witness of this was strong solicitude in the matter of his church-going, and opinions on episcopacy as the one inspired form of Christianity, and soundness on the creed commonly called Athanasian. The outside evidence was her mending his clothes, and, there being little but books and rags in the tiny brass-nailed trunk, the *omnium gatherum* of his treasures, the shy replenishing of the same. But this was only ventured upon after a piteous tussle with the rents, which were faithfully and curiously patched by Louis' own manly fingers. "My boy may sometimes be motherless and a stranger," said she, in a note written in her old-lady's round-hand, and pinned to the additions as a timid precaution against hurt and rebellious pride.

Thereto Louis straightway yielded, and brought his beloved volumes into the sitting-room, and spread his music over the piano, and played her the "Battle of Prague," because she said it reminded her of her youth, and expanded and basked in the genial atmosphere. If he ever felt doubts as to the benefit of the "Cereus" to society at large, ever at soul loathed the ruin he saw at work in heart or body of its frequenters, or the spirit that pervaded its precincts and caused that ruin, he kept it all to himself. Indeed, after the first day or two he didn't think much about it. He was released from the wearisome pickings and fault-findings of Millville, set in a life of luxury and friendliness, with the dazzling hope of easy success in business, and the enervating sense of having every man's *good* word in a situation where he was secretly conscious he deserved it less than when he supposed he had their bad one. For it was a peculiarity of Mrs. McCross' discipline, that its subjects not only detested themselves, but believed everybody else held them in dislike. Even Mollie was not without a trace of this feeling, and it had gnawed Louis' heart for years. The men who frequented the sample-room were both well-dressed and respected; Charley, though wild, was a hearty sort of fellow; his father, the soul of benevolence; and he himself did all and more than was required of him.

Old Mr. Pelican, passing through the sitting-room one day, saw "Elective Affinities" in the original on the table, and examined its mysterious characters critically. His nose elevated—"Slotch!" he said in accents of deep disgust, and then ran away. But he held up the student as a pattern to Charley not the less, and regarded him as a rare and delicate curiosity which he had been lucky in finding.

And Charley, handsome as Absalom, petted, spoiled, took a most pernicious fancy to Louis, and they came and went together as David and Jonathan. A general favorite is seldom the best of the flock. Charley had been the family idol. He had run away from school and driven a canal-boat six months in boyhood; won silver cups in memorable boat-races; was up in trapeze exercises; could perform the giant's swing, and hold a chair with a man in it, at arm's length, by the bottom round. He was a connoisseur in ballet-dancing, and held

9

pronounced opinions on the proper size of the feminine ankle. He was, I reiterate, absolutely beautiful; and had two fetiches in the persons of a billiard-cue and a pair of huge iron dumb-bells.

Possibly it would have been better if the business hours had not gradually stretched, and the quiet evenings, when, the father being away at charitable meetings and the son in society, Louis translated the "Wandsbecker Bote," played his beloved Mendelssohn, and discoursed of Wagner to the well-pleased old lady knitting fancy socks by the table, been exchanged for long stays at the sample-room, and longer visits to a gaming-saloon opposite; not that Louis was learning to love gambling; he had no bump where such temptation was temptation; he went because, as Charley said, it was necessary to know the patrons. But his notion of the "relation of values" was in a way to get dreadfully mixed.

As time passed, Mollie's letters came less and less frequently; she, poor child, often saw them thrust into the fire, and, though she writhed under her mother's espionage, yet strove to endure without a murmur. "Love," she said very often at this time, "is the Spirit of God. We should therefore be careful not to wound any human love, lest we grieve the Holy Spirit." Wherefore she suffered in silence.

While, then, Louis' affection for his *fiancée* was as fervent as ever, he grew gradually unable to locate her memory in his new, full life; and her influence was daily buried deeper beneath its confused impressions, hurried acts, half-formed estimates of the all-important *worth while*. And Charley, energetic, variable, full of exuberant vitality in the every-day contact, usurped her *outside* place.

Matters had been sliding and slipping down-hill in this

way about a year and a half, when something occurred,
as is usual in such cases, which gave them accelerated
speed.

Mr. Pelican had the greatest propensity for asking
people home from his religious and charitable conven-
tions to spend the night.   On this occasion he had picked
up the Rev. Dr. Perfect, late of Nansook Junction, now
of Millville, who was nothing loth to save a hotel-bill,
and become acquainted with the rich and eccentric
Abimelech Pelican, Esq.   He even talked late that evening with him over a pitcher of sweet cider.   The doctor
refused all more intoxicating beverages, but ate up a very
full saucer of brandy excused by a wonderfully minute
peach, mischievously dished out by Charley as a tester.
It is only justice to say that he sanctified the viands by a
grace long and all-embracing enough to equal a spiritual
bear-hug, closing with the hope that the Lord would
strengthen them by and help them to grow through the
same ; which Charley misconstrued into " Strengthen us
to bite, and help us to go through it."

The doctor was a large, pompous man, with a bass
voice and shaggy gray eyebrows.   He might be a fervent Christian and a burning light, but Charley told Louis
in a loud aside, " It was whale-oil, smoky."   "Is it,
Brother Allwood ? " cried the worthy man, dashing at
his victim in a glow of religious feeling.

" I don't know that you'd think me worthy that appel-
lation," said Louis, shrinking away like a sensitive plant,
in double disgust at Charley's snickers and Dr. Perfect's
" word in season."

During the meal, the reverend gentleman talked much
of the higher Christian life, which he and his wife
illustrated so well that they had neither of them sinned
for a twelvemonth, and further argued the possibility of

performing miracles, hinting at a more than speculative
knowledge of these gifts of the Spirit. He also made a
touching personal appeal on the subject of religion to
every one present, beginning with poor Mrs. Pelican,—
whose timid faith was fruitful of more goodness than
comfort, and who felt a rude home-thrust to the bottom
of her soul,—and ending with Charley, whom he besought
to be warned in time.

"Yes, sir," retorted the young man gravely, "in the
touching words of the poet, I feel

> "'Youth forward slips,
> Death soonest nips.'

I've often thought what a pity it was we couldn't shorten
up the lives of our Christian friends to lengthen out our
own. It would be clear gain to both parties, you know."

The clock cuckoo cried twelve warning notes before
Dr. Perfect offered to retire, so interested was he in
expounding the spiritual view of the unilluminated
Christian's shortcomings to his sleepy host and hostess,
the boys having pleaded business and run off. He had
been sitting some time before his bedroom fire, toasting
his feet, in very airy costume, previous to a departure for
the land of Nod, when the bell below began to ring
furiously. In nowise averse to learn the family secrets,
he hastened to the hall to listen, and, hearing men's voices
on the steps, resolved to save the household trouble, and
open the door himself.

In company with a stream of cold air, the gentlemen
dashed in, shaking the snow from their feet and coats;
and Charley, who had stood treat quite too often that
evening, made a dive at the visitor, and caught him in
his Arctic embrace. Indeed, the poor man's white dra-
pery rendered him a conspicuous object in the faint light.

"O Romeo! Romeo!

> "'When marshalled on the mighty plain,
> When shall we three meet again?'"

cried he, hugging him fondly. "What's in a name, old cub? We'll sleep together at the foot. Bully boy with a glass eye!"

"Anathema maranatha!" exclaimed the doctor, trying in vain to release himself. "Let me go—*put me down*, you young reprobate. Touch not the Lord's anointed!"

> "'Maid of Athens, ere we part,
> Give, oh! give me back my heart!'"

murmured Charley, clasping him still more fondly. "Alas! how vainly I sigh; as soon make a whistle out of a pig's tail, as get anything back from a priest's clutches. At least we'll have a farewell break-down before I say adieu, pretty waltzer, adieu."

"Dance!" gasped the divine, who looked like a well-thumped pillow in the clutches of a housemaid. "Dance! Avaunt, Satan!"

> '"Once there lived a man in Balninacrazy
> Who wanted a minister to make him onazy.
> And thus the gentle youth he bespoke him,
> "Will you dance with him, dear Ally Croaker?" 'Hem!'"

Charley was suiting the action to the word, and they were flying about among chairs and tables with fury.

"Do you know what you've got, young man?" thundered Dr. Perfect. "Verbi divini minister! Servus servorum Dei. Omnia ad Dei gloriam. Monstrum horrendum informe ingens cui lumen ademptum."

> "'I've got an old Tom-cat, although one eye is staring,
> I've got a Sunday hat a little worse for wearing!'

Come, Louis, beat time with the shovel and tongs;
this deuced darling is so heavy I'm out of breath. You
know the tune 'Barney Brallaghan,' te dit de, de de,
diddle de." They had whirled into the library by this.
"Never mind," as the poor man gave a series of agile
skips, remarkable for one of his ponderous proportions,
"you'll soon catch the steps. One, two, three, hop!"

"Let me be! It's wicked!" gasped the doctor.

"Oh! do not be discouraged, never too old to learn,"
urged Charley between his rapid gyrations. " I can take
the tuck out of any dancer living. Oh! your toes?"

Round and round they spun, dashing among tables,
knocking over chairs; Louis performing the music with
tongs and fender; Charley, carolling snatches of songs
at the top of his voice, till the family, roused by the ter-
rific din, rushed down *en masse* to part the dancers.

Dr. Perfect left directly after breakfast next morning,
shaking the dust from his feet, and predicting "wrath"
laid up for Charley, whom he denominated a worthy type
of "Jeroboam the son of Nebat that made Israel to
sin."

Though Louis' share in the above proceedings had been
small, he wandered about the "Cereus" next day in an
agony of repentance and disgust. His friend attempted
comfort.

"Have some whiskey? This on hand is most as good
as water. That's what the old fellow said about his root-
beer, after he'd drunk half the keg."

His repentant partner shook his head. "I detest
myself—the business—everything. How could I ever
be such a fool! I am ashamed to look any one in the
face."

Charley lifted him up by the strap of his pants and
shook him, but, when he set him down after this trifling

admonition, his face was as solemn as before. Thereupon
Mr. Pelican treated him to a glance half-remorseful, half
bitter.

" ' Champagne Charley is his name.' Why don't you
say it and tell the truth ? " said he.

" I'm not going to blame any one but myself," was
Louis' friendly answer; " one's enough to be disgusted with
at a time."

He had hardly got the words out of his mouth, when
Hercules picked him from his chair, and, regardless of his
kicks and struggles, consigned him to a long drawer that
happened to be open near by, whence he only emerged on
solemn promise to pull no more sad faces. But stopping
the foolish boy's mouth didn't rest his conscience. After
this, feeling disgraced in his own eyes, he plunged eagerly
into Charley's pleasures. Mollie was too closely watched
at home to find opportunity to write many letters, and
the *closer application to business,* which is the usual result of a good woman's epistles to her engaged, was their
very worst outgrowth possible, in this case.

Mrs. Pelican sighed, but couldn't make up her mind to
undertake remonstrances with a stranger that she had
already proved ineffectual with her son. Mr. Pelican
was laying plans for a soldiers' home, and poohed at her
fears.

"Nonsense, woman," cried he, pushing up his glasses.
" I don't believe it. Boys will be boys. Must sow wild
oats some time. Don't fret yourself. I was a great deal
worse than they."

His wife knew this perfectly ; she had had the task of
rooting up his early planted weed-crop all her life, but
she was too true a woman to own even to her secret
soul that Bimmy could be altered for the better. Her
only doubt was whether a second edition of herself would

be found to undertake the like work for this youthful chip of the old block.

Peace came home but seldom. She had here the skeletons of her life, which she knew neither how to command out of sight, nor destroy, and so stayed from Top Town more and more, and tried to find comfort at Millville—at school—travelling—anywhere among strangers. This was just as well. She acted like yeast on Charley's latent possibilities of evil; everything wrong in him began to ferment the instant she sailed into the house. "She sniffs so at a feller," the aggrieved youth complained to Louis. "I say to myself, 'Jam din, jam dudum! I'll bust for two and a half, if I don't cut up something,' and then I vamose and free my mind."

In her flying visits, she scrutinized Louis closely, her dark, brilliant eyes seizing every alteration, and her handsome lip carelessly indexing the scorn and angry contempt she felt.

"He's a dissipated fool," she exclaimed to her mother, as she watched the pair sauntering down the street, cigar in hand. "His gentle brown orbs, that poor Mollie dotes on, wander to the ends of the earth rather than meet mine; the very clothes he wears have replaced their former modest poverty and boyish grace with the fashionable, exquisite airs of 'our set.' I could spit a chicken on the waxed ends of that dyed mustache, and he parts his hair in the middle. If a hung Punch in effigy would look like a warning to him, I'd rob the poor-box to buy the puppet."

"Oh! how dreadful, my daughter!" exclaimed Mrs. Pelican, thoroughly shocked. She never could give her feelings the relief of a mutual outpouring with Peace. The vehemence with which the excitable girl vented her emotions, made her literal, conscientious mother shrink timidly within herself, afraid. "It's all Charley's fault," said she, with a sigh. "Don't hurt his feelings, daughter; he seems like my own boy."

"But some one ought to do something!" fumed Peace. "Don't you see how that everlasting bottle is just soaking all the man out of him? Think of Mollie! I wish Charlie was dead! I wish I was dead! Everybody!"

She was accenting this declaration in her usual way, when she saw two tears course down her mother's face below the gold-bowed glasses, and fall, round and glistening, among her forgotten, tangling worsted balls. The raw recruit in the camp of pain stopped, remorseful and terrified; she knew her mother cared as much, but she had not seen her in her veteran's uniform before. A young girl may well tremble before an old woman's tears. "Women can do nothing better than suffer in silence," said the little lady, hastily composing herself. "It is their only defence, my child."

So Peace thought better of her half-formed resolve to remonstrate with Mr. Allwood, and worse of the liquor trade, and kept away from Top Town altogether, leaving Louis to go on unwarned. Toward summer Euphemia Hitchcock came up to spend a week or two with some friends, and Louis sought her out at a sociable, and asked after Mollie. But Miss Adeliza had not seen her, though she opined such constancy to mission-work was "likely to make one peaked."

Even this doubtful news was the source of misfortune; for, being obliged to return to the "Cereus," he confided her to Charley, who undertook to see her home. Notwithstanding her confidences with Miss Petingil, the fair Hitchcock started forth triumphant in the exchange. But her escort, tiring of her inanities, halted in mid-road. "If you aren't afraid to go alone the rest of the way, I'm

9*

not," said he, and left her: a circumstance which she neither forgave nor forgot.

A lowered view of life; a distrust of one's fellows; a thirst for excitement; a settling back from the race, are not surer signs of folly than precursors of fall. Into this state Louis was now come, and the result was inevitable. Neither Mollie's letters nor her love could now stem the current. Indeed, Mollie seemed a long way behind in his life-journey; it was hardly more real than a dream to him that he had ever known her. But his one possibility lay in the fact that the memory was a *blissful* dream.

One Sunday night, about this time, the family were all collected in the library around a green bass-wood fire. This same fuel was a speculation of Mr. Pelican's. He had bought a large quantity because of its white and beautiful appearance, in expectation of a fine blaze.

"I declare!" cried Charley, after poking and punching the sizzling stuff in vain, "if father'd give up benevolence and buy two or more cords of this, he could put hell out."

"O my son!" exclaimed his mother, disquieted by the profane allusion.

"I solemnly believe it," reiterated he. "That reminds me. Father, have you told the Sunday-school lately about the pious old lady, who was so poor she was obliged to read her Bible all night by the moonshine coming down chimney? He did, mother; I heard him myself."

Mrs. Pelican's delicate soul-machinery was very sensitive to the endless jars of her robust household. She felt that her husband's corns were trod on, and looked at him with helpless concern. The wicked twinkle in Charley's eyes was ominous of a worse onslaught, and, anxious to change the subject, she insinuated mildly, "Bimmy, dear, let's sing a hymn."

Now as her good man had superintended a Sunday-school, led in a prayer-meeting, presided over a missionary society, and heard three sermons that day, he had no further appetite for honeycomb. "Peace, woman, peace!" he exclaimed, pushing back the suggestion with both hands; "I loathe everything good."

"Mother'll have to hang her harp on a willow-tree," said Charley in a bantering tone. "Father's had too much whang-doodle."

If Mrs. Pelican's vocabulary of proper names had included that legendary bird's, she might not have felt hurt. As it was, she supposed the allusion was a term of opprobrium especially referring to her proposal, and sat, meek and forlorn, in the corner.

Louis, who was seldom included in the family misunderstandings, presently opened the piano and began to play quietly, and, after a few minutes' hopeless survey of the prospects for pious union, the old lady drew her rocker toward the instrument and composed herself to listen.

This would have been good policy in Louis, under ordinary circumstances. Mr. Pelican immediately leaned back in his lounging-chair, and stretched out his feet for a nap, and Charley, who had a tremendous bass voice, proceeded to improvise a vocal accompaniment. But malignant fate has swift revenges for people who undertake to baulk her plans for being disagreeable. She suggested artfully to Absalom, watching his mother as she swayed back and forth to the rhythm of the music, that Louis was supplanting him in her affections. The more he glowered at the picture and compared his brusquerie to his chum's thoughtful tact, the more obvious became the sequence. Delighted at the thought of giving his old friend a nice evening, the musician was laying himself out

to please.   Variations of the " Swiss Boy," " Buena Vista
Polka," " Postillon of Lonjumeau," " L'Enfer Quadrilles,"
Gluck's " Gavotte," all the old-fashioned favorites he could
remember, followed each other in animated succession, and
Charley's new-born jealousy augmented every moment.

" Small herbs have grace ; but great weeds grow apace."

It was actually eleven o'clock when the minstrelsy
ended, and long before that, C. Pelican, Esq., after throwing the whole contents of his pocket at the performer, bit
by bit, gave up the hope of stilling his energy, and retired to put snuff on his pillows, in small attempt at revenge ; and he actually arose at three next morning, and
stole to Louis' bedside to hide a hair-brush in his boot
and add alum to his tooth-powder, before his mischief-
teeming brain would rest.

The day following, as these little ebullitions had not
eased his mind, Charley planned a double visit to the
opera and the youth's prayer-meeting, in company with a
young lady better known to his male acquaintances than
their sisters.   Unfortunately old Mr. Pelican happened
to preside at the latter, and, spying his ill-doing heir, he
took early occasion to administer a tremendous raking
over, which, under ordinary circumstances, would have
been received as a matter of course.   But the main burden
of it was to hold up Louis as a pattern, and this gave a
second turn to the snow-ball.   Henceforth it grew
mightily.   Louis could not issue a direction in the store,
whose management was largely in his hands, nor open the
door for Mrs. Pelican, nor pick up her handkerchief, nor
talk confidentially five minutes with his father, without
spurring it with fresh impetus down that steep hill on
whose tops sits distrust frowning upon confidence asleep
below.

CHAPTER XVI.

"Pease porridge hot, pease porridge cold ;
Pease porridge in the pot, nine days old."

 FEW weeks after Amos' donkey-ride, Mollie and Mr. Haythorne planned an unprecedented entertainment, the same being nothing less than a tea-party at little Doppy's. Since Mr. Haythorne's assumption of Doppy's class it had multiplied in numbers, and shone in erratic verses above all others. There is a tradition of one of the latter still handed down, supposed to have been produced by a very juvenile member of the sisterhood :

"Plenty of fishes in the brook,
Daddy ketch 'em wid a hook ;
Mammy fry 'em in de pan,
Daddy eat 'em like a man."

But whether, as Peace insisted, this novel Bible recitation was the result of Mr. Haythorne's industry, this deponent saith not. Peace, who was again in Millville for the summer, seemed delighted with the tea-party idea, and invited herself. It would have been wise in you to have done the same.

The fact is curious that we owe to the agents of our worst ills their occasional alleviation. *Par exemple,* if old Mulligan, whose drunkenness was the source of his daughter's troubles, had not got very drunk that morning, and so absented himself for a week's spree, her tea-party might have lacked the successful termination insured by his absence. As it was, a town election the day previous being the indirect cause, and corruption of the ballot, and the consequent folly of certain wretched husbands, fathers, brothers, and sons, the direct, his pocket was full, and he started for Top Town instanter, to spend the contents.

Then began scrubbings and sweepings on the part of Doppy, and comments and good advice from Master Daley, who had begged holiday and immediately transferred himself to his friend's hospitable door-posts.

"Now, Amos," said the maiden, as she tucked up her beds resplendent with two green-and-yellow patchwork quilts, " ain't them splendid ! The colors is so cheerin'. Do ye mind me tellin' ye yesterday that father give me the money to git' em from the pawnshop? Mother she made 'em jest afore she died."

Yes, Amos minded; and how came the glass out of the window?

" Them's the fruits of timperance," said Doppy in angry irony, bestowing a kick on the coals that old Mulligan had scattered over the floor in a drunken tumble. " Yis, timperance ! An' why don't ye ask where the fine new curtings has gone that me and Miss McCross made no longer ago'n Saturday week ! Whin I meditates consarnin' the meanness of min, I could hate 'em all, even you, Amos ! "

" Thin I wouldn't think on't," said he, not much alarmed, to all appearance. Doppy, however, did think on't, and a still more emphatic kick preluded a flood of tears rather stormy than beautifying. Her freckled swain eyed her awhile with an extremely puzzled air, then took one hand from his trousers' pockets and scratched his head thoughtfully.

" An' was it Goodheart's ? "

" Yis, it *were* Good Hearts," with a stamp. " If you don't quit gawpin' there at me that's so miserable, I'll shy coals at you." Whereat he found it best to disappear, first, however, enticing the pet hen into the room to act as comforter.

It will be hereby perceived that Doppy's struggles after respectability had produced their invariable meed of heart-ache, which, by the way, her friend Mollie shared to the full.

Peace remonstrated with the indefatigable missionary, once, on discovering a certain straw work-basket, lined with rose-colored silk and daintily furnished, in process of manufacture for Miss Mulligan—"In the first place, it's wicked to waste such lovely things."

"Waste?" Mollie was going to lift her eyebrows in superior wisdom, and let it go, but womanly love of self-defence got the better. "This only cost four dollars; I made the emory and pin-cushion and needle-case and cotton wagon. I saw you pay *five* for the turkey you presented Barney O'Hara last Christmas. That only lasted a day, and this will be useful a long time."

"Who cares for a commonplace turkey!" said Peace, "fat, long-legged thing! But this is so delicate and ladylike. It is out of taste for such people to have such things."

How provoking in Mollie to laugh.

"I know what you will say," continued Peace, coloring with vexed sense of defeat. "'You wish to excite aspirations,' but, as Francis Haythorne says, 'contentment is better than wealth.' If you don't fret them with sense of lack, they'll never know the difference. What if they live like pigs? That's all that's asked of them. I think you do them a positive injury when you put such ideas in their heads. They're a great deal more unhappy than they were before you meddled with them."

"Perhaps they are," said Mollie gravely, "though I don't believe it. But that does not prove me wrong.

In this life, or the next, we have ultimately just what we earn. Success fairly pays for our efforts, and I think any amount of misery worth enduring, if we may thereby struggle up into a higher state of existence. The fact is " (she spoke with the conviction that comes from experience), "every step we gain is through pain, either ours or another's—sharper in direct proportion to our advance. It has come to me lately, that Christ's best gift was the power to find in pain, formerly the curse of life, a ministry of blessing."

Peace, like most people who prefer this world's joys to the other's, and instead of taking trouble for its worth, refuse to take it at all, and so have it forced on them,— Peace looked uncomfortable, and edged off.

We return to Doppy at the same moment with Amos, and find her still gathered into a disconsolate heap on the floor, absently smoothing the pet hen with one hand, and arranging the scattered cinders in gray squares and triangles with the other. She jumped up ashamed of her emotion, and hurried to the sink for the water-pail, intent to escape to the well. But he, no whit abashed, displayed the missing hangings, and called her to come and look, in proud triumph.

"No, I won't!" resolutely. "I'll not be in no one's debt; I hain't no money. Father takes every cint I airn at the mill. Them as borrers, sorrers—mind that." Doppy bowed her head on the handle of the bucket and wept aloud.

Amos dropped his bundle, and eyed her in blank misery. "I say, Doppy, I hain't asked ye to borrer," said he, after revolving the case doubtfully awhile. "I thought ye wanted to be respectable, so I got the curtings. If ye hadn't had the pawn-ticket on the floor stamping on't, I couldn't ha' done it; so it's all your

fault, an' I shan't take 'em back." The good-natured
fellow looked ready to follow his friend's example and indulge in damp emotions.

"Amos, how *can* I ever be respectable?" said the poor
girl, appealing to him as a refuge of strength. "What
with father, an' livin' here in this nasty hole, an' havin'
Joe upstairs, an' bein' so ignorant myself, it's too much
to ask. I'm wretched!"

"Now, Doppy, you'll come out ahead," said Amos,
drawing closer, and evidently believing his own words.
"I'll tell you what I'd do," speaking with great effort;
"I'd—I'd—" He hesitated.

"Go on," said Doppy expectantly.

"I'd do the best I could."

This advice may seem trite, but not to Doppy. The
want in *her* heart was as well filled thus as ever were
Barbara Farquhar or the "Wide, Wide World" heroine
or Aurora Leigh or Guenevere or Ursula Halifax or any
other written-up ladies sustained and comforted by their
devoted adorers. It is the manifested desire to lift the
burden, not the way in which it is handled, that helps
women to bear. As for the weight itself, that can seldom
be more than readjusted at best.

"I guess I will," said Doppy, with a light-hearted resumption of her armor, and a certain tender, sweet curve
of her red lips, not yet quite steady.

"Doppy," pursued Mentor earnestly, "you'd best take
them curtings; seems like we wos relations, 'n't don't
count."

She crossed her arms over the water-pail, and reflected,
—Amos watching in some anxiety. "Them's true
words," said she at last. "We is relations, fur we're
tryin' to be somebody, 'n I'll do it for you, Amos Daley,
which I wouldn't fur no one else."

So they had a grand cleaning frolic, that even a few sighs over the sadly deteriorated appearance of the window-hangings couldn't sadden, their owner consoling herself, after the manner of house-keepers, by remembering that every one had seen them clean once, which proved that they might be again.

It is worthy of remark that, in squabble or making up, Master Daley never laid so much as a finger on his little friend. Mollie had given vent to too many strictures regarding such trifling indecorums, to have them seem pleasant or honorable to Doppy. Once only, months before, Amos had put his arm around her in a fit of enthusiasm; but the result was disagreeable.

"An' is it to take advantage of a poor girl's tears you're here, Amos Daley?" cried she, springing to her feet, and dashing aside his hand vehemently. "An' haven't I enough sorrer on my heart, not to be makin' it run over wid sufferin' along o' losin' me likin' for meself? n' that's what yer caresses is leadin' to. Go long wid ye for a sneakin' Paddy, n' not the brave b'y I thought at all, at all." And he never got so much as a glance for a week.

Mollie and Peace had prepared for their festivity in methods peculiar to themselves; the former by an hour's Bible reading and prayer, the latter by a new set of extremely becoming ribbons.

These friends, so completely antagonistic, yet united, made a curious couple. Peace, with her dark, imperious beauty, snapped her fingers at circumstances, and fascinated everyone as a matter of enjoyed opposition thereto; while Mollie quietly compelled her surroundings into harmony with herself and each other.

Their arrival, however, put a quietus to the housekeeping of their young hosts; and a hasty exit, via the window, on the part of Amos, awoke momentary misgivings in the souls of the detecting guests. But his speedy entrance, in a clean collar, through the door, calmed their fears; and they concentrated their energies upon unpacking the baskets, setting the table, and reviewing the household crockery, viz.: one gravy-boat, landscape pattern; an egg-glass with half a standard; three teacups inscribed to "my wife"; four tin plates, with the alphabet on them; and a tin soup-dish, that Mollie recognized as having once been Mrs. Bradshaw's, —the relic of a happy anniversary. And she smiled, even in the arduous duty of setting forth the salad, when she remembered the ride on the ox-cart with Peace and Louis tête-à-tête, and the fun that brimmed its now battered concave.

Diligent counting of noses, however, revealed a deficiency in even these bountiful stores. Doppy came to the rescue. With her hands on her hips, she told of Joe, "a broth of a girl intirely," that would like to come and bring her crockery; and that young lady, bashfully belligerent, made her entrée.

Peace and Mollie both shrank back thoroughly uncomfortable under the bold black eyes unwaveringly fixed on them. But the critic manifested no embarrassment. She seated herself at once, stared contemptuously, extracted some soothing compound from her pocket, which she chewed, and kicked her bare, dirty heels, and squared her elbows, in haughty silence. Perhaps this love-forgotten waif had depths of heroism and constancy in her nature; but, if so, these clean, high-bred girls held no key thereto. She hated them, as matter of course, while she calculated shrewdly whether anything could be got from their strange dinner-party freak.

Meanwhile the feast was made ready, and if not set out

> " Wi' sauce ragouts and sic like trashtrie,
>   That's little short o' downright wastrie,"

yet, what with the parsley-garnished ham, a trifle hacked from a jackknife in Amos' pocket, the great heap of parti-colored candies, the crisp salad, the snowy biscuit, and, last but not least, the fragrant tea, it made no poor display.   When once the party were fairly seated,

> " Dire was the clang of plates, of knife and fork,
>   That merc'less fell like tomahawks at work."

A few minutes before dinner Doppy's protégée loquitur : "Please, ma'am, won't you' gi' me some shoes? my feets is all bare."   Amos interposing, "You sha'n't plague 'em askin' fur things."   But Mollie beckoned the child toward her : "Are you too old to be cuddled?" said she pleasantly.

"Dun know," quoth Joe, action and tone alike new to her, and suffered herself to be drawn close to Mollie, as she sat on the old settle.

Full of her craving instinct of mother-yearning, my darling was smiling, in her own guileless, winning charm, straight into Joe's poverty-scratched soul, and the stubborn girl had no defence to keep her out.   She didn't say much; these old want-twisted children never do. They are always observing, calculating, learning, suffering; but to their gently reared friends they have few words.   Yet after that day, Mollie never met this poor little one when a smile did not overspread her face and soften her great black eyes.

But Peace, who wasn't much given to petting, least of all such repulsive specimens, observed a cloud on Doppy's face.   A kick levelled at Chaw-em-up suggested jealousy.   Of the clutches of the green-eyed fiend, friends, dogs, and kittens are alike made sensible !

"Won't you sit by me?" said Miss Pelican, on pacific thoughts intent.

"I ain't a baby; I got done such child's-play a long while ago." Doppy drew herself up, and accented the Yankee compound word with dignity.

Joe was on her feet in a moment. "So did I! she held onter me."

Amos whistled, whereat Doppy poked him viciously in the ribs, eliciting a grunt, while an expression of stupid astonishment crossed his good-natured face.

Luckily Mr. Haythorne's entrance concentrated all attention on the feast, and for the time green eyes was forgotten.

The new arrival was mainly attentive to Mollie; but Peace touched his hand airily. "Be not familiar with any woman, but commend all good women in general to God," quoth she.

After this hint, he bestowed his cares on Doppy, who was not deceived thereby, and told Amos, who had several times during the meal bestowed unmistakably disparaging glances at the red-haired Sybarite, that Miss Peace wanted Haythorne herself, but she reckoned he liked Miss Mollie best. Meanwhile the supper as a totality was joyous and brave, and Doppy's loquacity grew greater every moment. Having once learned to trust her friends, she had perfect repose in them, and not a shadow of thought seemed to her worth reservation. Encouraged by her fearless freedom, Joe ventured a little, and the talk ran on the wonderful garden at Fir Covert, and the treasures thereof, not excepting Poppy in her green and gold coat. Doppy was accustomed to read fairy tales aloud to her friend in her Saturday visits, and the limits of the McCross domain contained the whole stock of stage machinery with which she was able to drama-

tize in her thought the wonders and beauties she found
described. For stories, tell them aptly as you may, go
on the theatre of every hearer's imagination, to be furnished with such scenery as memory may have picked
up, and fitted with such passions for actors as Heaven
and the experience of your critic may have provided.
What wonder, then, if our tragedy is stale, or our farce
drags! Figure the Pacha putting John Halifax in rehear-
sal! Alas! poor Yorick!

But it was Poppy who filled Doppy's conception full.
What had she not stood for—" The Singing Bird," "The
Enchanted Princess," "The Malignant Fairy," "Pooh-
Pooh's Brother Phœnix," "The Ugly Duckling." To
her dying day Dorothea loved her. What wonder she
waxed eloquent! " Only to see her ways, perliter than
anybody's, and her rid eyes."

" Yis, she allus kisses when you gives her anything,
and eats it right away," said Amos, applying his remark
by a kick at Joe's toes.

" I can do that myself," said the disconcerted damsel,
putting an enormous piece of sponge-cake into her mouth,
in effort to appear at home. " He says, ' Dear Louis, dear
Mary, ptchoo ! ' that's a kiss, you know. I've often heerd
him in your garden afore any one was up." Then becoming conscious of what her confession involved, Joe turned
very red and took refuge behind a biscuit. " Mr. Allwood's name is Louis," added she, reappearing. " Mr.
Allwood is the nicest man ever I see. He has the littlest
foot entirely, and the voice of him so sweet like a melo-
deon. He allus give me a penny. He ain't here no
more, is he, Miss McCross ? "

Peace, who enjoyed such complications, stole a look at
Mr. Haythorne, and smiled benevolently at the unconscious Malaprop; and Mollie answered, " He's in Top

Town with Miss Pelican's brother. I haven't seen him for a long time. I wish he was home." The remark, more to herself than her questioner, need not have been so disagreeable to the gentleman opposite. Mollie had forgotten that he existed.

" Likely he's sick," said Doppy, with a view to consolation, while Joe, being admonished to hush by a poke from Amos under the table, flushed with wrath, and exclaimed :

" I won't keep still! I'll talk if I please, darn you! He's her feller. Haven't I seen 'em walking together lots o' times, when I went by begging rags of old woman McCross, as never gave me a thing at all for me pains, bad cess to her!" Having done her worst, she escaped from the room.

Then succeeded an awful pause, broken by Doppy, who exclaimed apologetically, " Don't mind her; she hain't no manners nohow, an' I'm most sure she was drunk."

" I wouldn't feel bad about losing my little secret," suggested Peace with profound malice ; " such trumpery is like the ointment of a man's right hand which betrayeth itself."

" It has never been a secret," said Mollie, a trifle haughtily, the rude exposure of her inmost springs of act and feeling seeming almost like a public shame put on her. " I supposed all the world knew that I intend to be Mr. Allwood's wife."

Peace could not resist a second glance at Francis Haythorne, whose cheek showed a slight flush, as well as the tips of his small, shell-like ears ; but his eyes met hers with their usual serenity.

" Did you say you were going to wash the dishes, Miss Pelican ?" in an insinuating query.

" Your noblest natures are most credulous," she retorted, curving her handsome lip, disgusted. Then her eyes began to dance: "Prithee, peace!" in a taunting tone. "I dare do all that may become a man; who dare do more is none;" and handed him the dish-towel, which he held as if he expected it to explode.

This is the way some small sprinkle of fate reduces to smoke our delicate catherine-wheels, rockets, and fiery crowns and daggers: all rough imitations of the star of true love revolving close and constant about the great beneficent source of flame. Or if, as the liberal reader may insist, they be imitations rather of Mars than Venus, still, inasmuch as any real ambition, be it warlike or peace-ful, is still a matter of true love, I beg leave to retain the figure. But the discolored flame of fancy, evanescent— of no more substantial source than a quarter teaspoonful of strontium burned in a few grains of gunpowder—bears little resemblance to the torch of affection. Mr. Hay-thorne found so excellent consolation in this *reductio ad veram*, that in a week he wondered how he could ever have wasted so much good time about such unprofitable pyrotechnics, and, before a fortnight passed, observed many things in his former admiration that could be altered for the better.

Dishes being at last put away under Miss Pelican's directions, they played, "Button, button; who's got the button?" and Doppy never went empty-handed when it was Amos' turn to say "Hold fast."

Peace moved about the homely room stately as a fir-tree, and Mr. Haythorne noticed her fascinating ways and be-wildering eyes with new interest—the interest of appro-priation. She was in the mood for "sharpening her toma-hawk," she told Mollie, and his Sybarite inertia was very provoking. So they played a beautiful scene of exquisitely refined flirtation in high life all the evening, which Doppy and Amos admired very much, and Miss Mulligan more and more regretted Joe's flight from the whole premises, and consequent loss of the improving spectacle. For Joe's ideal already diverged almost to polarity from her mate's, and this was a grief to Doppy.

Mollie didn't care at all about her admirer's desertion, but sat smiling and happy, reading motto-papers to the delighted Amos, who looked and felt all arms and legs, saying pleasant things to Doppy nestling fondly to her side, and bestowing an occasional approving glance upon Peace and her recreant knight, absolutely unconscious that she ought to feel hurt. She felt able, and liked to please, in her simple, earnest fashion; but coquetry in its lightest form was a riddle to her. The extenuation is at hand—Louis was hers; Louis was all she asked.

Toward the end of the evening, Peace whispered confidentially to Mollie, who thereupon proposed to play a new game, and blindfolded Doppy. Miss Pelican handed out a trifle of a kerchief, and pointed to Amos. But Mr. Haythorne protested that he could easily look it into shreds, and producing a cambric monstrosity, the size of a small table-cloth, tied it about the boy's head with impressive solemnity.

"All's dark and comfortless. Where's my son Edmond?" he cried, in a menacing tone.

If you want to give people a sense of perfect helplessness, take away their eyes. Doesn't Aldritch say so? Accordingly our ruffling Amos was meek as a lamb. " I don't know, sir," he made humble answer.

This tickled Peace into continuing the farce. "Dost thou squiny at me?" she exclaimed in a hollow voice. "I remember thine eyes well enough. No! do thy worst, blind Cupid, I'll not love."

"I'm not doin' nothin'," said Amos, turning pale.

10

"What be yees about there? If ye say much more, I'll snip this darned blinder off, n' leave."

After a brief season of twitching and turning, pinning and laughing mysteriously, and pulling off and putting on, the knotted muslin was unfastened from the subjects' heads, and their metamorphosis became apparent to themselves. To be sure, Mr. Haythorne, hampered by the difficulties of the case, had only pinned Amos' new shirts on behind, and suspended the trousers in front, but that was no consequence. As for Doppy, one would not wish to see a fairer sight than she presented in her dainty dress and jaunty straw, from beneath which her curls strayed in so charming confusion.

"My!" said Amos. "By hooky, ain't you sweet-lookin'!"

"Give us a rest!" retorted Doppy. "Your own mother'd mistake you fur an up-town chap, just you wance git inside them things."

Then she threw her arms about Mollie's neck, minded equally to kiss or cry; seeing which, Mr. Haythorne hid himself behind a door lest Amos should do likewise. He needn't have taken the pains, however, for those handsome garments seemed to have transformed rough, blunt Master Daley. He eyed them wistfully, hands in pockets, as they lay in a pile on a chair, where they had been put in the general excitement of pleasant bustle; then, with a final furtive grab, slid from the room, to reappear in full bloom of elegance.

"How is your health, Miss Dorothea?" said he, in the diffidence of modest propriety, advancing with unwonted grace; "n' may I have the honor of seein' ye to the minstrels' Monday night? We'll have a parquette seat."

"Yis, certainly," replied she, with equal dignity. "It would give me great pleasure;—ain't them the words,

Miss Mollie? O Amos! it pays to be respectable, don't it? And you mind I was right about the white clocs." Then she laid her little red hand in her friend's lap. "You mustn't ever mind Amos, Miss McCross; he's rough, but he means well, and we've made it up together always to do just as you say;" which is the Celtic idea of gratitude.

Much to his astonishment, Francis Haythorne had enjoyed the affair hugely. He was a trifle ashamed of it, too; and told Peace by way of apology, as they went home that night, that ennui as well as wit sometimes tempts a man to play the fool with great courage.

"That remark makes me add vanity to the list," she retorted pointedly.

"You are unkind," said he, blushing to the roots of his auburn hair. "I really think with Goethe, one is only properly alive when he seeks the good wishes of others."

"And I, with myself, that no man is to be so much despised as he who is ashamed of his own virtues."

"My idea was, that out of so many I could afford to cut off a few," he averred, with outward effrontery, and inward wrath.

"On the contrary, I'd smoke those I had left in hope of their preservation," pursued Peace malignantly, resolved that the contemplated cigar should be no calm to his ruffled soul.

"Goethe says nothing to the point," he replied, striking a lucifer on his knee, and preparing to light the odorous Habana between his handsome lips.

"Yes, he does!" blowing out the match, as he sheltered it in his hollowed hand. "He says every one has something in his nature which, if openly expressed, would insure dislike, and that's you when you fumé. Now, how are your little feelings?"

"I can only fling away my comforter, and protest with John Knox against the awful regiment of women."

CHAPTER XVII.

"Pussy said to the owl,
'You elegant fowl.'"

THE season in Top Town promised to open very brilliantly. Charley, indeed, had made up his mind to have nothing less than a masquerade.

"Snooks and Sneezers!" said he, in confidence to Louis, who was for the time being restored to favor, "why should one wait till one's all fagged out with gayety and ready to bust for two and a half, before one ventures on the best thing of all? We won't, my gentle swain."

Accordingly Peace was written to, and she, in her turn, summoned Francis Haythorne, and Mollie, and Susie Jenkens and her father. Mrs. McCross wouldn't hear of her daughter's complying, but the others were glad to accept the invitation.

Peace, whose mission it was to improve Charley, lost no time in taking him aside and bestowing a little sisterly criticism. "Please to be as quiet as possible, and, above all, don't neglect your table manners," said she. "I don't want the idea carried back to Millville that we live in a wigwam. The other day, I know, I saw you put something into your mouth with your knife, and I've often spoken to you about your right elbow, which you frequently lean on the table. For mercy's sake, don't!"

As a matter of course, Mr. Pelican shut his left eye flat, and executed an ominous wink with the other. "Teach your grandmother!" cried he. "That snip of a Herr is the root of all this anxiety. I'll lay myself out to show the family breeding, dear, don't be afraid;" and thereupon ran off without more ado.

The Top Town Dancing Academy Hall was hired on account of its tiny gallery, so nice for viewing the dresses; and all the élite were borrowing costume-books at the Institute, and Hazeltine's picture-gallery was besieged for foreign prints. Wigs, trussing points, padding legs, and choosing knee-breeches were objects of paramount importance to the male youth, while gauze wings, trains, wire masks, and rosettes upon infinitesimal slippers were of similar weight upon the hearts of the fairer sex.

The Millville people arrived in season for tea, and Francis Haythorne met Louis for the first time. It took only two minutes to bring them together at the piano. Once there, Louis' perfectly delicate and tender legato touch wrung praise for his adagios from the critic, in spite of himself, and Francis Haythorne, who had the pearl-like execution of Hummel's students, and yet despised Hummel, played Liszt's fantasias till Louis was radiant with enthusiasm. They had begun improvising together in true brotherly fashion, although the doctor's style herein was labored, when Charley beckoned Louis away.

"It's tea-time now!" was Absalom's vexed exclamation. "My cake is all dough! There's my costume—that magnificent devil," pointing to a sable heap of horns, bats' pinions, and hoofs lying in a chair. "If you don't help me, I'm ruined. Gizzard has found out about it, and told every one it's my rig. Just change with me.

I know your robes and mantle will go. There's a friend."

"No, they will not," said Louis, pulling over Satan's skin; "they wouldn't cover your shoulders. The idea of your prinking yourself as Jeremiah! This is a very complete devil. I'll tell you what: if you choose to loan him to me, I'll fix you up a nobby thing. You must go down-town and get a complete set of flesh-colored tights, five or six woolly sheepskins, a quantity of doll-babies to hang by the hair at your belt, sandals, a huge club, and that one-eyed mask we were looking at this morning, with a long beard attached coming down below your waist. The cloak and breeches will be of the rough hides. Won't that be a divine Polyphemus? 'Monstrum horrendum informe ingens cui lumen ademptum?' Remember?"

"Exactly," said Charley, with brightening face. "I'll make a meal of any one that denies it. Just what that old Gospel-grinder dubbed me that night. What a lark it was! This is the tucker."

So it was settled; and Louis had the oddest sensation of casting off his identity when he donned his satanic garb, with its great, round red and yellow eyes, a forked tail that trailed on the ground and could be made to switch by pulling two tapes, immense branching horns, a goat's beard, cloven hoof, claw gloves, and a pair of bats' wings big enough for Icarus' aërial flight, not to mention the equally unfortunate excursion of Darius Green.

He was even sorry to defer the pleasure of assuming the new personality till after supper, and, descending to the table, he found Peace equally excited. She was carelessly arrayed in a loose crimson *négligé*, which enhanced the brilliancy of her face; her jetty hair, twisted into a

knot, had half slipped from its fastenings and uncoiled in
all its richness upon her shoulders as she conversed
eagerly with the immaculately clad physician, who was
toying with his dish of Louisiana figs.

Dr. Jenkens was talking about specie payment with
Mr. Pelican, senior, at the lower end of the table, and
Susie sat watching the handsome Absalom opposite her,
whom she met for the first time since childhood, as he
was always Jan Vedder's guest in Millville, and never
called at her home.

"So you do not think me like a rose or a hyacinth or a
violet or a tulip," Peace was saying a little anxiously;
the fire in her intoxicating eyes and the flush on her
damask cheek brighter than usual, as always when she
was coquetting.

"No," he answered, watching her, fascinated; "I cannot say so with truth. That gorgeous spike of flowers
in the vase yonder, so upright—majestically haughty—is
more akin to you."

"Oh! gladiolus," cried Peace, smiling at some inner
agreement of wish. "I am quite satisfied with the simile.

"Not gladiolus, but gladius," laughed he. "You are
no *little* sword. I was sure the scarlet beauty was one
with you in that keen, trenchant quality of which I have
so often been the victim. Pray, tie such a knot over
your domino that I may be on my guard to-night."

"As derivations are in order, I do not arrogate to myself the pretensions of a domino," said Peace. "But I
detect the aspiration in you—do you wear the favor? for
I own no *lord*, nor ever will."

"You are keeping Mr. Haythorne from his supper,"
said Mrs. Pelican. "He eats nothing at all. Louis, is
there anything German doctors fancy?"

"They are fond of snails and cockchafers," answered

the one appealed to, laughing. "Is it not almonds that they taste like?"

"We paid the children for picking the beetles from the fruit-trees so many groschen a dozen—I forget the price —and they ate them themselves. I never touched one."

"Peace might produce her caterpillar," said Charley, on purpose to be tormenting. Then having gained the attention of the company, he began to air the forbidden table manners. "Did you ever try catches?" addressing the dainty Haythorne affably. "This, for example," drumming with his knife-handle. "He can do little who can't do this." As he had been showing Susie how to drop a napkin-ring from his closed fingers, and divers similar tricks, every one was interested to attempt the puzzle, and a prodigious clutter ensued. "The silver moon goes round and round" was next brought forward, in spite of Peace's frowns; and then Absalom produced his best card, and asked Susie Jenkens if she had ever heard the "Chorus of Fiends."

"Oh, no! How is it? Do give it," was the inevitable answer.

"It's nothing without Peace: she invented it. I've taught Louis, but it needs three. It won't go off without her help. She leads, you know."

"No indeed!" cried his sister tartly, vexed as much as he wished. "I hoped you'd outgrown such nonsense."

"Hopes are deceitful," responded Charley, with a wink of aggravation.

"Do, I want to hear it," begged Susie, curious; and Francis Haythorne endeavored to be polite by emphasizing the request. Even Dr. Jenkens looked interested. There was no escape without rudeness to her guests. Peace covered her wrath with a smile, and the performers counted "one, two, three," on their fingers. When the time had been well marked thus silently, they burst into a triad of sepulchral ha! ha! ha's!

Mr. Pelican, who, absorbed in the money question, hadn't noticed anything that had been going on, now started up at the horrid racket, exclaiming, "What's that?"

"Your daughter's serenade," said Francis Haythorne, and unawares avenged Charley, which he wouldn't for the world have done willingly.

Mr. and Mrs. Pelican were going to keep Dr. Jenkens company as the Boffins. The good physician had made up his mind to indulge the wish of his lifetime, and personate William Tell, his boyhood's hero. The various members of the family being quite as anxious to remain unknown to each other, as the world at large, made quite a procession of carriages. First came the married people, then Peace and Susie, last Charley and Louis. Francis Haythorne had started previously in search of a friend, a certain German, Dr. Max, who he heard was in town. The lights at the ceiling of the pretty hall were reflected upon as brilliant and grotesque a scene as culture, taste, money, and love of pleasure could devise. Louis, attired in his fiendish costume, found himself confronted by at least a dozen of his race. There was a devil in shining golden scales with amethystine horns; there were two fine bronze devils, and one veritable poet's Satan, with red coat and blue breeches. Moreover, a bluebottle fly was at hand, with a velocipede—certainly young Gizzard.

A white, muslin-robed immortality with gauze wings, and a butterfly, fluttered about with St. Agnes in blanche merino, bearing a lamb. Jan Vedder, as Sycorax, bore a small Roman matron on his arm, who proved to be his mother. A colony of frogs and mice strutted here

10*

and there as perfect as real denizens of pond and field; while old Mr. Gizzard, gotten up as a Bologna sausage, and Hazeltine the picture-dealer, as the ace of spades, lent character to the company.

Charley himself made a magnificent Polyphemus. He expanded his chest, swung his dolls, flourished his club, and stalked about, glaring through his huge eye as to the manner born.

Every one was flitting about guessing the identity of the disguised, and examining the costumes. Laughter and jokes were everywhere heard, and the oft-remarked peculiarity of masquerades—that no one ever wears the character that might have been expected—was evident here in Top Town as elsewhere. The band played Verdi's bal-masqué music. The atmosphere was perfumed, the hum of merry human voices thrilled through the air, and Louis took in the ensemble with an eager delight. It satisfied his imagination; he felt as if he must be dreaming. There was no difficulty in recognizing his own household. William Tell's blue blouse did not ill assort with the professional manner of good Dr. Jenkens, to be sure, nor did benevolent Mr. Pelican make a poor golden dustman. But his wife, a very, very timid Mrs. Boffin, had already sunk into a corner beside Jan Vedder's Roman mother, where the two found pleasure enough in watching their children. Never was there a plumper, sweeter Fleur de Thé than Susie Jenkens, who was walking about on the arm of a magnificent Teuton with yellow eyes like smoky topazes. Keeping out of the range of these worthies, and totally occupied with each other, were a pair of revellers, whose superb costumes made them the cynosure of all eyes.

The lady,—a gladiolus,—over a green petticoat of quilted satin, embroidered down the front with tiny golden tassels, wore a crimson silk train, cut in five pointed gores, each finished as perfectly as a gladiolus petal. Her belt of pale yellow satin supported a golden network hanging in five tasselled points over the scarlet,—as the yellow heart of the gladiolus melts into its ruddier tints. The waist was likewise made of gladiolus petals, so disposed that the shortest came in front, showing her smooth neck in a sort of heart-shaped cutting. The sleeves, barely to the elbow, were gladiolus flowers, and their flaunting curtain displayed her well-turned arms, albeit the vicious little scolding-bone was there, though rather as a suggestion than a fault. On her head perched a satin hat—the same flower inverted over the blue-black tresses, that, braided with green ribbons and gladiolus blooms, strayed below her girdle. There were more of these flowers fastened by massive gold bracelets upon her wrists, and she wore them at her bosom, in her belt against her slender waist. At her side hung a sword-scabbard, formed of the martial leaf; a superb curving spray of the knightly blossom even finished her hat as a plume. She was indeed a flower personified.

Her attendant was Goethe, exactly as he stood in the famous suit of pike gray with gold lace in which he bade farewell to Frederika. He wore stockings, shoes, and a brown powdered bag-wig, to which was affixed a queue; carried his three-cornered hat under his arm, and, hanging by his side, he, too, bore a short sword. Art had aided nature in producing the noble swelling chest, and pencilled delicately the lines necessary to add Goethe's immense brown eyes—for he wore no mask. His own complexion was quite as brilliant as the bard's, and constant dwelling on his master's thoughts had unconsciously added to the student's every-day manner somewhat of his dignity. In short, it did not need the exquisite bracelet of cameo heads of Lili, Lotta, Frederika, Ottalie, Mignon, Frau von Stein, and Christiane Vulpius, which he wore, where the Herr Geheimrath once bore his order of nobility, to reveal his character.

Louis hastened toward them at once, but his poet shrank away. "Avaunt!" said he, "thou commonplace devil! Mephistopheles is the only imp I acknowledge as correct."

> "Du versuchst, O Sonne, vergebens
> Durch die duestern Wolken zuscheinen," *

retorted Louis, in the soft but pure accent of Middle Germany, which he had contrived to pick up Heaven knows where. "I must remain the fiend I was born. I thought Goethe too wise to attempt reforming the devil."

"I certainly stand corrected," rejoined the poet. "I do indeed believe in the metamorphosis of plants—but not devils."

"Kennst du das Land?" interrupted the gladiolus uneasily. "That is the only German I have at hand. If you must talk in foreign gibberish, do address me."

> "Ich denke dein, wenn mir der Sonne schimmer im Meere
>   strahlt;
> Ich denke dein, wenn sich des Mondes Schimmer in Quellen
>   mahlt.
> Ich bin bei dir; du sei'st auch noch so fern, du bist mir nah.
> De Sonne sinkt, es leuchten mir die Sterne,— O! wärst du
>   da!"

obeyed Goethe with characteristic gallantry, and smiling.

The flower shrugged her shoulders, dissatisfied. "Is he talking the poet, or himself, and what's he saying?"

"You shouldn't appeal to the foul fiend," retorted the

---

* In vain, O sun! thou strugglest through dark clouds.

versifier. "Ask *me*. I spoke the sentiments of my heart in the language of Wolfgang Von Goethe. But I decline to translate, and should this devil meddle, let him beware. I'll vibrate toward Christianity, and adopt St. Anthony and the good St. Dunstan for exemplars."

"Just tell me," persisted Louis, "now you've come back to earth, whose theory of optics is correct."

"Avaunt!" retorted his opponent indignantly. "The only discovery I take pride in is the identity of this enchanting gladiolus. Get thee hence! You have sufficiently proved that you are clad according to the proper blazonry of nature."

"True enough," acknowledged Louis, falling into speculation. "I no sooner donned it, than I felt myself suddenly free of the restrictions binding upon plain Louis Allwood. I knew myself able to do, be, experience anything and all I liked. Within this satanic mask a thousand impulses, all my life sedulously repressed, have reasserted themselves. More than this, this whole evening suggestions of action completely out of my habit—as I have heretofore supposed, my nature—have been pursuing me. I am half afraid of myself."

"All that frees our spirit and does not yield us self-control, is injurious," said Goethe, interested.

"If I was unknown, responsible to none but myself in this odd mental chaos,—which would then be a conviction that I had no reputation to sustain," went on Louis,—"I wonder what I would do! That must be the exact state of mind held by blacklegs."

"I have often reflected that any system which lessens the sense of responsibility bearing upon any class of individuals, no matter in what direction, or which class, is absolutely injurious," answered Francis Haythorne. "Why, what worse word does language contain than irresponsible? No; only the pressure of individual need matures conscience, and since conscience is simple recognition of law, and, to return to my character, 'only within the circle of law is the fullest development of liberty possible,' hence it follows that the more labor and anxiety is put upon an acting people, the higher types of excellence they will manifest."

"This is certainly the diet of snails and cockchafers you longed for," cried the disgusted gladiolus, a second time forgotten. "Methinks I'd like a bottle of hay for company." She was abetted by the velocipede, which dashed toward the group, scattering it to right and left. Flying before its dangerous parabolas, Louis stumbled against an umbrella.

"It never rains but it pours," said the mask, with a lisp certainly Cabby's. "But for pity's sake keep your pinions out of my stretchers. I always heard that the devil longed for a drop of water. Will you be kind enough to turn a little, or you'll hook Abraham Lincoln. You have samples of all the costumes on your prongs."

"Ship ahoy! shiver my toplights! lend me thine implement!" said the Cyclop, coming up, and hoisting poor Umbrella on his shoulder as easily as one would a kitten. "Suooks and sneezers! how did you leave the Son of Heaven? It is time to rescue Fleur de Thé from that leonine German. He has what I call physique! Come, umbrellas are certainly as near relations as Chinamen have; go and do the paternal. Fee, fi, fo, fum! I smell roast meat! I say, Satan," abruptly dropping Cabby, who hurried to make good his escape, "I vote this mighty slow. I've waltzed with two fellows by mistake, and Martha Washington asked me plainly if the Latin liquors hadn't gone to my head. Gizzard's so; when we asked him to say 'There was a piper,' he got as far as 'consider cow,' and then went on 'tehider tow, tehider tow, tehider tow, tehider tow,' and for the life of him couldn't hit the way to stop. Let's have a quadrille together. I'm a little too happy to ask a lady, myself."

"What do Germans do when they are merry?" asked Susie of her yellow-eyed companion, filing into the quadrille places opposite Polyphemus and the devil.

"They sing sad songs," he answered, "like this: The morning is red; yesterday I was on a brave horse, to-day I am shot, to-morrow I am in the grave."

"How hilarious!" said gladiolus, taking the head side-couple with Goethe. "How did you come to know Mr. Haythorne?"

"We belonged to the same Kneipe at Heidelburg— we went over the river every Saturday night, and smoked late as we liked." The new-comer had a very pleasant, simple manner, and spoke with polish and ease.

"Tell me truly, did you ever drink too much? Honor bright, I am not curious. I have a reason." Poor gladiolus was very eager; her voice showed it. Goethe leaned back upon the piano carelessly, and seemed lazy and amused.

"Honor bright, then, *I* sometimes might," owned Dr. Max in his pretty foreign accent; "but your partner, so insouciant yonder, never did. His head is as hard as a stone, and, besides, he was a good mother's boy. Weren't you, Franz?"

Peace didn't quite know whether to be pleased or not at this revelation; especially as the poet gave a little sniff in answer that might mean assent or anger or triumph or contempt. She therefore kept silence, and observed Susie's idea of sustaining a conversation, which seemed to·be the asking of questions.

"Oh, yes! we had gay times at Heidelburg. We went

to our museum ball every year, and danced in fancy dress. The year Franz was there there was a very fine mask. We had the court dancing-master from Hesse Cassel to teach us this old potpourri that we gave. It was a cotillon performed once a year at this court, and combined minuets, sarabands, and what not. There were five sets. In the centre of the room was Shakespeare: your friend was Slender, with Annie Page; at each corner of the set was another, making a star. The first was shepherds and swains; the second, Scotch; the third, cavaliers and their ladies. I was in the fourth, which was in the costume of Henri Quatre. I went to Vienna myself after the print containing the dresses."

"What did you wear?" cried both ladies at once.

"Let me recollect. Ah! I have it; the couples wore red, yellow, green, and blue, respectively. I am a Suabian, and asked my partner to wear my national color—orange. She was a very obliging young American, and consented. We exchanged our things when the ball was over, I remember. The ladies wore black velvet basques, with fulness at the back in a little frill, and the front all reversed and trimmed from throat to feet with slashes of gold-colored or other satin. Their petticoats were colored, too, with a band of embroidery. Their sleeves were slashed, and at the wrists were two huge muslin-like puffs; and they wore muslin at the neck, and tiny hats and feathers, and gauntlets, and we gentlemen had loose-topped boots, white stockings, breeches slashed and trimmed with lace, doublets slashed, and steeple hats with broad brims, and plumes, and lace collars. We all came in dancing from the ante-room, formed in sets like magic at a signal we knew in the music. But Franz kept us very late; he was waiting for his hair to be curled. Then afterward we were asked to a party to dance it all again, at the house where our set practised, and there the servants, dressed as clowns, came in and gave us bonbons, billet-doux, and the like from we knew not whom."

This was so nice that Peace cast a discontented glance over the gathering there present; but she had ample cause for wrath in her own neighborhood. William Tell danced with Sycorax, and made the fourth couple finishing the family group, and all went wrong in the quadrille. Louis had found his garb extremely inconvenient throughout the evening. But now his discomfort amounted to positive misery. He bowed to Fleur de Thé, and impaled her on his antlers; he squared about to avoid this, and prodded Francis Haythorne with his whalebone wings. Sycorax lost no opportunity of tripping over his tail, and every one was saying, " Avaunt thee, wizard ! " " Satan, avaunt ! " " Fly, fiend ! " " Get thee hence, devil ! " till he wished himself safely underground. Annoyed quite out of his presence of mind, so awkward were his endeavours to be harmless that Jan Vedder, unconscious of his identity, inquired if they found malt liquors keep well in his hot cellar; and William Tell wanted to know if he could say " truly rural." The evils of his position were heightened by the antics of Polyphemus. Though, as he owned, not over-steady on his legs, he had the audacity to indulge in cuts two at a time, and in pigeon's wings, and varieties of heel-and-toe step unheard of. And, worse than all, young Gizzard, quite too drunk to know what he was about, persisted in mounting his velocipede, which he had carried at first only as an ornament, and heading into every one. Peace's face was a study of hauteur, pain, and contempt during this ridiculous scene. Francis Haythorne watched her with less of pity than curiosity, expecting an outbreak, but none came. Not a glance at the buffoon acknowledged mortification or interest in him ;

and in the pauses of the dancing she looked away into the centre of the ball, ignoring her surroundings altogether, a vivid crimson spot on each cheek and a slight dilation of her delicate nostrils alone confessing emotion. But Parisian varieties is not performed in a moment, and when the velocipede dashed among them, and, but for a grasp at the friendly piano, would have fallen at their feet, Goethe felt her light touch on his arm tighten to an unconscious clutch like a vice.

"Take me away," said she, her voice sharp with nervous tension; "I am ill. Where is there a chair? Help me there."

Louis was thankful to give up the set, but it seemed like his blame to watch the poor bruised gladiolus sink on the bench, and strive in vain to stifle her hot rebellious tears. Her escort quietly placed himself in conversational attitude, and, spreading the huge scarlet fan she wore in her scabbard, shielded their faces from observation while he waited for her to recover her composure in silence. He was a man who, once opening the gate to an emotion, can never again recall it to command. Sincere pity was fast making way for affection, when Peace looked up gratefully, that soft brilliance tears give a woman's eyes illuminating hers. The strength that lies in silence and reticence seemed invaluable to her now. It helped her to her own self-poise. But when, obeying a man's first impulse, to snatch suffering woman from pain, not help her subdue it—he offered to call her carriage, Peace shook her head. "No," she said, all her defiant hauteur returning as she roused herself to speak. "I'll die first! No one shall ever tell that I couldn't stay out a pleasuring prepared by my own brother. I won't have it go that I'm ashamed of my blood and bone. Find him, and say I am recovered, and the next waltz is blank on my card. I've muscle enough to hold him up, luckily," and she laughed in bitterness and scorn. Three minutes after, she was on the arm of foolish, tipsy Charley, and the tour of every set was made with unerring skill before she suffered herself to return to Goethe, who had meanwhile been watching them with admiration of her spirit, and a kind of shiver of its metal, such as one has in examining a sharp dagger and feeling its keen edge.

Louis, heart-sick and ashamed, crept away from his friends, but only into fresh cause of misery. It appeared that all had taken the velocipede for himself, and comments were in the making on every side.

" Did you ever see anything so disgraceful as the capers of that Polyphemus, let alone young Allwood? " said the Ace of Spades to the Bologna Sausage. " People say they are regular sots."

Now old Gizzard was just that himself, and he had been heard to remark, that his hopeful son was nothing but a demijohn; nevertheless he agreed cheerfully to the proposition.

" True," said he, " the piety in that family has all gone in Pelican's missionary cause to China. Sad case, but it shows the necessity of implanting religious principles in early youth. I am very strong on this point, very. Let's have something."

Fighting his way through the crowd, the unwilling listener passed gentle Fleur de Thé, only to overhear her telling Mrs. Vedder that rumors of the disgraceful state of things at Top Town had long since reached Millville, and were killing Mr. Allwood's fiancée, whereupon Judge Sistaire, who completed the trio, nodded gravely, as people do over sorrows that they regret on general principles.

But even this was not the end, for Mrs. Gizzard came hurrying up in her usual happy-go-lucky style, exclaiming: "Every one knows you, Charley Pelican; where's your friend? If he's sober enough we want him to play. The whole room is agape at the ungentlemanly doings in your set. I can't find out my son's costume, but I conclude he headed it." Mrs. Gizzard's troubles had become too patent to seek concealment, poor woman!

"He is perfectly sober, and at your service," answered Louis. He followed her, trembling with confusion, to find Dr. Max and Susie, Goethe and Peace, conspicuous among the expectant listeners. "What flower shall I celebrate," he asked, drawing off his mask and claws, and trying to recover from his agitation.

"The one you have forgotten," said Peace coldly, but aiming her stab with deadly accuracy.

"I can recall the song, at all events, and will perform it;" he felt as if betraying his Mollie as he made the retort. She seemed to him to have no place in this scene —as well hang her picture in the "Cereus." But he had been dared to it. The music was a little minor barcarolle, whose plaintive melody and simple rhythm varied with the feeling in the verses, and were mixed and companioned by a gurgle of piano, like the noise of a river fretted at its banks by stones. The singer's perfectly flexible and musical tenor voice took a sadder tone of reality from his own unrest.

"I seek my love in sheltered grot,
  She is so modest and so fair.
Down in yon little meadow-plot,
  The brook it winds and babbles there;
  This is the song that fills the air:
Forget-me-not; forget-me-not.

"My barque it floats over river and sea;
  But, oh! our little moss-thatched cot

And my blue-eyed love are more to me.
   This is her parting, ne'er forgot,
Made sweet with velvet lips and warm,
As fond she hangs upon my arm:
   Forget-me not; forget-me-not.

"Together o'er the verdant lea
   We stray at sunset, plucking flowers;
There where the river floweth brown,
And blossom pranked his banks adown,
In this lone mountain-sheltered spot,
We seek the blue forget-me-not.
O traitor blooms! that sued our gaze!
Ye on the border grew so fine
All in her rainbow wreath to twine,
My love's bright glance upon ye stays.
O greedy stream! to snatch my flower
That had such riches in his own;
As some fair leaflet downward blown,
So fell my darling on the wave,—
My darling that I couldn't save.
Tear-blinded at her piteous lot,
Her wreath on the false rill was strewn,
And, sinking, thus she made her moan:
Forget-me-not; forget-me-not."

"Now it's your turn to make music," said gladiolus, turning on Goethe with acerbity.

He had been too much browbeaten in such matters to venture upon refusal: "If Satan will play Mendelssohn's Rondo Capriccioso—I have heard so many praises of his rendering."

This was another stab from memory, for it could only have been Mollie who admired. But accustomed delight in the lovely music soothed Louis; he played it enchantingly.

The andante—a dreamy lover's complaint, mirroring the motifs to come—was full of caprices. Then the Rondo began.

The presto opens with the most delicate possible staccato movement, the two parts imitate each other with fairy-like rhythm, and give in their tiny emphasis a frolicsome, fantastic utterance to the theme, climaxing in the double trill. Then comes that plain, entreating air, sustained by its monotonous pianissimo accompaniment, until, abandoning its style, it rises in something nearly anger, and perseveres in its argument in the left hand, while the right belongs to the wilful elf, frolicking up and down in arpeggios that are equally feminine and defiant. Then, as if wearied by the outburst, the theme creeps back, settling down exhausted between every half-spoken phrase, and scarcely gathering persistence to assert itself entirely, when it falls into a lower key, and, murmuring unintelligible words, fairly sinks into slumber, waking at intervals, as if to say, "I am so tired, I am so tired!" as a child might nestle in its mother's arms.

But elfin children never sleep. Suddenly it springs forth in the wildest merriment. It is neither naïvely playful among the flowers, nor coyly seeking rest. It is a mad chase round and round upon the sward, into which the elf drags her graver friend. Wilder and wilder grows the pursuit. Then a half pause, a little regretful memory of sweeter quietude, a faint leaning toward his human strength, a yearning even in midst of her play for something more earnest. But she tosses it all off, and sways him into the most heartless, breathless of fairy dances.

That was what Louis got out of the Rondo, and his sympathy reproduced the thought, for Francis Haythorne turned to the gladiolus and said something about the maiden Undine sporting on her flowery peninsula with the Knight of Ringstetten, and looked volumes. But she drew herself up with gladiolus dignity, and professed a failure in detecting Undine's fondness. She had been thinking of Tennyson's poetry beginning,

"Airy, fairy Lillian, flitting, fairy Lillian."

"I quite identified the emotion in that little half adagio phrase, where he seeks pleasance in love-sighs, and 'where, through crimson-threaded lips, silver treble laughter trilleth,' is certainly next." This was quite true, but the vision of the heartless flirt was not intended to soothe Francis Haythorne's feelings. Peace had no mind to be mastered through her momentary weakness.

Francis Haythorne took the place Louis offered him, and, gathering his ruffled feathers into order, began to play Liszt's Spinnerlied on Wagner's theme. The highly colored work of the authors suited him well, giving of necessity the warmth his style needed, and loud were the admiring praises of his hearers. Peace, in especial, was angry because Louis' playing forced her soul to respond in kindred emotion, and consoled herself by warm encomiums on his rival.

Charley had provided a dozen black dominos in each dressing-room, and, after the excitement of discovering the costumes subsided, general recourse was had to them, and, secure in their sable folds, every one launched his shaft at Achilles' heel.

"I heard that your Millville practice had got well. You shouldn't have let him, it was a mistake," said a lisping bat, attacking the Sybarite.

"Oh! you mean my friend Haythorne's patient," said Goethe lazily. "The wound was in his pocket, too close to his vital organs; I didn't dare keep it open."

"You should have given that snip the retort courteous," cried Dr. Jenkens, "and related that the whole family felt so badly to lose your visits that they got up a chronic whooping-cough, and have been obliged to receive regular attention ever since."

"That suggestion from you pays me for withholding it," replied Francis. "I think it ill-taste to defend *one's self* from rude slurs."

Peace, however, had taken him under her wing, and was much incensed. She therefore sallied forth as domino noir, intent on retribution.

"I wanted to ask about that young lawyer, Mr. Brown," cried she, stopping the jester. "Is it true his business success is so great that he's hired the Millville House billiard table to keep the run of his points?"

As soon as he had complimented Francis Haythorne, and himself been told by the smoke-topaz-eyed doctor, with German musical enthusiasm, that he was a " true musician with genius," Louis had shrunk away from the party, longing to hide himself from human view. He had come upon the inevitable result of his last year's doings, but it was with such a frightful suddenness as the traveller experiences while descending a dangerous mountain pass, and all at once slipping down the precipice whose terrors he had been braving. An air the band were playing seemed to follow Louis with reproaches. We have seen that he was so sensitive to music that it was to him *the* language of emotion, but often his own mood gave it shape. This was only a strain from the Eroica, but he remembered it too well. He stole unconsciously into Peace's corner of refuge, and fell into a reverie, led by the poor, belittled theme. How plainly came back the time when, with shut eyes and soul concentrated upon the revelation, he had first understood this wonderful vision of a heroic life and death, and been uplifted into mighty longing for the same nobility! He saw again the white-robed, ethereal concourse grouped in bright clouds about the choir, like space before a vacant throne. There on all sides stood rows of shining winged cherubim, waving slowly to and fro their mighty pinions as do butterflies new-born to aërial life, and seraphim whose intensity of adoration for their King made their hearts to pulsate, even to sound; and, since all in celestial space is harmonious, their love thus became music, and in the reverent hush of heaven rose the ineffable sweetness of melodies tending toward their own true centre—God. And in the midst of their place before the throne, were conquerors gathering about the hero, whose faces bore upon their gravity, gentleness, as flowers were girded by warriors over their struggle-tested armor, and they carried laurel crowns on their thoughtful brows, and they had woven one such for the new-come brother. Then the beholder trembled in awe, as the Perfect Heroism, higher than thrones or crowns, entered to acknowledge kinship with the soldier who had braved death, but bent all timid before the source of his bravery, the principle so far greatest in his being that it had absorbed his life into itself. Then swept the seraphic music through the courts of the hereafter, and all the solemn assembly cried Amen, and the illustrious brotherhood lifted in their arms the weary, toil-spent Hero till he should come to refreshing. And from their touch and the touch of the Highest sprang Heroism into the full health and might of eternity.

Louis recalled how he had turned to Mollie in enthusiasm of delight and cried, " If this was the Christian heaven, how gladly I'd die ! " His eyes fell on his hideous dress, his cloven hoof, his fiend's wings; to his excited imagination it seemed a fit symbolizing of his fall. He groaned aloud.

Then came Francis Haythorne to beg help in getting

11

Charley home, and poor Mrs. Gizzard on similar errand for her graceless son.

And this was the end of Absalom's merry-making.

CHAPTER XVIII.

"Old King Cole was a jolly old soul,
    A jolly old soul was he :
He called for his pipe and he called for his bowl,
And he called for his fiddlers three.
And every fiddler had a very fine fiddle,
And a very fine fiddle had he."

HE next morning Peace took the early car for Millville, accepting the Jenkens' invitation to their house, and she was careful to slip out before Charley was half awake. Francis Haythorne was glad to escape the unpleasantness of meeting the family scapegrace, and accompanied them. But he bade Louis a friendly farewell, and offered him the loan of Ritter's seventeen volumes on the Philosophy of Geography, which was accepted by the young man in a transport of gratitude ere he bestowed the party safely in their seats on the train, and withdrew to the " Cereus."

" Misery " (which Shakespeare was probably in the habit of looking upon as a synonym of fate) " brings us acquainted with strange bed-fellows." That is why old Mulligan bought his fall stock of rotgut at Pelican & Co.'s. Facts have a terrible inclination to mix themselves with our personal history. If you go over a block of buildings in '69, you do it at your peril, for in '73 your wife's brother-in-law, buys it, fails, and leaves you with his debts to pay and nine small children to support. If you cross a river in a ferry-boat with a pretty girl, and carry her bag, she turns vindictive twenty years afterward, and shoots at you,—verdict, sudden insanity. If the printer's daughter stands at her father's door watching the dusty journeyman with his two loaves of bread under his arm, that fact has had its noose around their poor necks in a twinkling. What thrones have not yearned for the tears and blood of Josephines, Carlottas, Antoinettes, or Lady Jane Greys! Who is there who has fought ill-fortune and perished at its hand, but has likened his fate to that of the unhappy wretch slowly drawn into the vortex of the whirlpool by the current once not discernible beneath the water's glassy surface?

How does a man's grave through his whole life silently compel him toward its maw by pressure of its intangible, all-pervading, ever-groping filaments! Facts are furnaces that must be fed with histories. They are soulless Un-dines in the ocean of existence, striving to perpetuate themselves by union with humanity. Woe to a man if a political office, or a big speculation, or a pious chap that runs a Sunday-school or a modest country place, gets an eye on him!

In the light of all this, it is plain that malignant fate had deliberately been narrowing the orbits of the Mulligan family and the McCross family and the Pelican family, until the failures and shiftless points of each came to react in misery on the others, and here the worst off had the best of it, for misery and comfort stand generally in the relations of heat and cold. The latter, being a negative thing, sucks up its positive, as negatives will.

After Mollie's gift of peanuts to Amos Daley in years past, it had been determined for all time that old Mulligan should buy liquor of the Pelicans, refuse to pay, and thereby necessitate Louis' presence in Millville. Charley's reason for accompanying him, though simple in appearance, was only part of the same infernal machinations of facts.

The past summer had brought its inevitable experiences. Experiences are like sheep: if you start one, you may know beforehand that the whole flock will follow. Hence day by day the brow of Pelican père grew dark, and the face of Pelican mère sorrowful, and the behavior of Absalom worse, till now the storm broke—where storms have a propensity for breaking—at the breakfast-table.

"You are a weariness to me," cried his mother. "You kill me;" and her gray curls trembled with her earnestness as she affirmed it.

"You disgrace the family," said his father.

Now for the "governor" to blow was quite correct, in Charley's opinion, but no such liberty was permissible to the maternal head. He resolved to punish her.

Mrs. Pelican was a nervous woman. She lived in the most aristocratic house in the most aristocratic street in Top Town. The very market-wagons went through alleys behind the residences, to spare their plebeian rattle to the ears of the inhabitants. "Gramercy Place"! The name alone was a tradition of refinement and elegance.

Early that morning appeared a hand-organ, playing "Kathleen Mavourneen," under Mrs. Pelican's window. Being of a charitable turn, she gave the man a quarter, and bade him move on. His place was instantly supplied by a "furriner," who sang about Cara Italia to a tuneless fiddle, and had a monkey. Mrs. P. thereupon bestowed a handful of nuts and ten cents, for which he invoked that amount of blessing and withdrew. She had not closed the door, when a man and two dancing bears claimed her sympathy; and, upon refusal of same, intimated with

tears that the others had been remunerated. Now Mrs.
Pelican was a person of spirit, at least in reference to
beggars; and she remarked pointedly that she had no
idea of satisfying all the tramps in Top Town. She felt
at once that she had done a foolish thing. The fellow
had a bad eye! What if he should burn the house!

He smiled a smile full of malevolence. "Too late,"
said he. "We have all hear, and we come dis mornin'
to play, every one of us."

> "Alas for maiden, alas for judge,
> For rich repiner and household drudge!"

The threat was well kept. The first two hours the
children in the square held high carnival; the next the
older inhabitants advanced to doors and windows, and
watched with anguish the constant stream of musicians
before the ill-fated house. One family proposed to put
out a small-pox flag; but after a short search, it was discovered that not an inch of so vulgar a color as yellow
was to be found among the patrician Nile greens and
lavenders in the piece-trunk. In vain Mrs. Pelican entreated, threatened, scolded; the swarthy Italians couldn't
—wouldn't understand. The gentlemen, all on the street,
were down town at their stores. She dared not leave the
place. At the thirty-first hand-organ, the cook, whose
temper was violent, gave warning and quitted the house.
This was entirely owing to the pleasantries of the dancing-bear man, who had amused himself all the morning
by setting his Bruins to climb the alley-fence and carry
off the eatables. The hapless mistress stuffed her ears
with cotton, and retired to bed and tears of vexation.
But rest was not in her day's programme.

At half-past eleven, a polite note from her right-hand
neighbor, requesting to know if she would as lief have

her orchestra play all at once and get through. At half-past twelve, the family opposite—total strangers—offered her two bull-dogs, and a pistol if she could load it. At two o'clock, five gentlemen called, one after another, to rehearse the various kinds of nervous illness imminent to their households, and to hint that their love of music had been satisfied. And when she assured them of her help-lessness, they went so far as to say that it was d—d provoking; which, in a lady's house, indexed a frightful state of mind.

It was no use to drive away the players; one no sooner disappeared round the corner than another took his place. By noon a crowd had begun to gather, and before long the street was jammed with loafers, musicians, half-clad women, drunken men, and a starving, hallooing, stone-throwing legion of children. It was impossible to force a horse through the tightly wedged multitude, and every one trembled in fear of a riot.

Mrs. Pelican's condition can be imagined, however, when her left-hand neighbor arrived to insist that she should address the crowd and send them away. The lady was clearly demented, but the thrall of scandalized Mrs. Grundy! think of her! "Indeed! indeed! I cannot," gasped she; "anything but that!"

"Madam," said a choleric inhabitant, who had just entered, "you acknowledge paying them; you refused the bull-dogs and the pistol. It has a bad look."

Thus adjured, she took the cotton from her other ear, having been too much agitated to remember it previous to this, and, pushed to the fore, extended her head from the window, and coughed several times to attract atten-tion. Failing, she would fain have withdrawn, but this the choleric gentleman, whose presence of mind was lost, and who strode fiercely up and down the parlor with his hands supporting his coat-tails like black fins, would by no means permit.

"Go on, madam!" said he, not ceasing to tear up and down his beat. "Go on! it's your duty."

"Man," gasped Mrs. Pelican, looking round for countenance, and happening to catch the eye of a platter-faced German,—"man, won't you please go home?"

He lifted his great blue eyes stupidly to her face.

"Please go home," urged the lady. "I think, indeed I'm sure, your wife wants you," she added, becoming suddenly conscious that she must give a reason.

Here something that looked like a drowned kitten was thrown at the window, and the object of her eloquence put his fingers to his nose satirically.

"Come in, dear Mrs. Pelican; come in and tell me the meaning of this," said a voice behind the shutters, and Louis pulled her gently back into the room.

"Meaning!" said the choleric gentleman. "Why, this good lady has been paying all the tramps in town for their abominable discords, and our lives are in danger in consequence. Hear them howl!"

It was true. Tired of music, the crowd were looking for more exciting amusement, and stones and menaces were beginning to fly about.

"Why not sound the fire-alarm, and distract their attention;" suggested Charley, who had arrived, in great astonishment at the whole thing. "A crowd always runs to a fire."

The choleric gentleman actually started off to act on the advice.

"Let me out. Let me pass!" he cried, finding the front door blocked up by the press. "You miserable scoundrels, what do you mean by stopping a gentleman's progress?"

" Lor' ! " said the man—it proved to be the dancing-bear man—" we love yer too much to let yer go. Come, Jock, show the gen'l'man how yer loves him."

The biggest bear rose to his hind feet at the word of command, and advanced to give the fatal hug, when the front door opened, and Charley hauled the burgess inside by the seat of his pants.

" From what a fate have you escaped, dear sir," cried he, wildly shaking his hands.

Louis, who observed that Absalom was a little elevated, and who had, moreover, grave suspicions as to the origin of the affair, called the rescued man aside, and begged him to take care of Mrs. Pelican while he went for the police. Top Town, let me state here, was too large to make it possible to patrol the whole city without greater expense than the denizens cared to incur. Moreover, a habit of reappointing delinquent and dismissed officers to each other's places increased the usual proclivity for peace, manifested by these white-gloved dignitaries; and it is universally allowed that a man absent from a quarrel can't possibly be killed therein.

Louis walked calmly out of the door, up through the street, almost unnoticed in his exit. The crowd had been dancing the bears nearly to death in the interim, and were now busy with the monkey. In a few minutes fifty blue-coats marched quietly the length of the square, and aristocratic silence descended, dove-like, and sat with folded wings in this, its favorite and natural habitat.

In consequence of the trifling pleasantry, Charley, though his guilt was merely conjectural, deemed it wise to pass the next succeeding days in Millville, a decision which was hardly welcome to Louis. Jealousy does not linger amid practical jokes, and young Pelican had long before, almost unconsciously, passed the boundary of good-fellowship, and with slights, pettish insults, or hard words, made the clerk sensible of his inferior position, whenever drink or remorse set the pair at odds. Mollie, watching, fearing, praying at home, was less to be pitied than Louis, delivered up to the alternate torments of Charley Pelican and his own conscience.

Charley had reached that point where his friends began to look askance at him. The experience was a sour one to a man who was in the habit of considering his admirers thick as blackberries. Hitherto his handsome person and lavish expenditure had invariably attracted, and his effervescing love of pranks been the every-day basis for approving mirth. But now he could not help seeing that his cronies at the Cereus were getting sifted down to such men as the Guises and Gizzards, who gave themselves to bitters before breakfast, and their families to bitterness all the year round ; and who looked at the company of young Pelican as the personified good-fellowship of their faithful bottle. It irked him, stung him into recklessness, this quiet unconsciousness of him beginning to obtain among the discreet, this appropriation on their own platform, already recognized among the notoriously indiscreet. Absalom was getting ready to go down to his own house and abide there alone, under a ban, and this our Absalom as well, with his loud, hearty laugh, brilliant skill in games, elegant dress, and fondness for jocular, easy-going companionship, so well fitted to shine at the ultimatum of his ambition—a prime good fellow. Now, on the road to Millville, the young men had not been on the cars half an hour before Charley had gone the length of the train, made friends with all the gentlemen, and informed himself of the business and estimated the standing of every individual on board. It is worthy of remark that no woman ever spent half an

11*

hour in his company without experiencing an intense desire to reform him, and an inward conviction that she herself was especially fitted for the task.

Deserted by his companion, Louis approached Millville with oddly mingled feelings. Here was his love, here the scene of his vows and resolves—broken vows and resolves, which, he could not help acknowledging, were lamentable failures. According to Goethe, no one has conscience but the reflecting man. The ride to Millville was absolutely the first two hours' continuous reflection Louis had allowed himself since his departure to Top Town, four years before. In all those months he had scarcely seen Mollie half a dozen times, and then in stolen visits of a few minutes each, at Dr. Jenkens', or, as happened once, on the cars; brief unsatisfactory interviews, that kept alive his longing, though they failed to quicken his principle. But this time he meant to claim her for a long tête-à-tête. It was a twelvemonth since their last. He had looked forward to this little greeting space with pleasure, but the nearer he approached Fir Covert, the greater became his dismay. He was ashamed to face the woman that had gradually grown into his incarnate ideal of virtue and true womanhood. He seemed to see her pleasant, steady eyes diving down into the memories his own would fain conceal. He erased the fashionable part in the middle of his graceful head, and tugged recklessly at the ends of the cravat, whose bow was a model of Top Town art. But it wouldn't do. He had gone away a simple-hearted country boy, without either vices or a conception of them; he was returning with the polish and experience of fine Top Town world—in spite of himself one with it. And Mollie, to whom he was hastening, could not be altered; his faith in her was firm as the foundations; she had only been developing consistently with the theories by which he so well knew her to live. What would she think? What would she say? She had a way of speaking her mind freely, and worst of all, acting on what she thought. What would she do? Between love, and remorse, and foreboding, he was rather glad than otherwise when Charley joined him. Mr. Pelican, in fact, had been taking a review of the situation, and was inclined to regard this projected visit of Louis' to his girl as a going of a lamb to the slaughter. Perhaps his being himself a trifle remorseful at the bottom of his heart, led him to propose adding his company in the necessary business tour. "And don't you think," said the poor fellow (I always pity a repentant scapegrace), "that two tumblers of something cool in our rooms, and a good smoke, would be a comfort to the inner man?"

So they had something cool, and then something cool again. On the whole, it was a measure of precaution as well as pleasure for them to start out together.

CHAPTER XIX.

"Granther, granther long-legs,
Wouldn't say his prayers."

F all weary days, it seemed to Mollie that this had been the weariest. For unknown reasons, her mother had taken it into her head that the poor lassie was not sound on the doctrines, and the erring girl had been catechised on all the dogmas of Calvinism: Predestination, Justification, Regeneration, Total Depravity, and the Perseverance of Saints. Now Peace defined

the difference between her ego and Mollie's thus:
" Mollie," she said, " is timid, conservative, in regard to
methods of darning stockings; and agitator, radical—
leveller, in every question of time-honored orthodoxy;
whereas I am a reformer, touching darns—and darn
reformers generally." This, like most sparkling generalities, admitted question, but had a kernel of truth. Accordingly, intense fondness for religious speculation and
unlimited indulgence thereof, with a sceptical friend at
one's elbow to make the points, were not conducive to
Miss McCross' tenure of Calvinistic ideas. Mollie was
a devout Christian, but a liberal one, as her mother hereupon discovered.

In consequence, Mrs. McCross had argued in her peculiar manner, menacing her offspring with wrath, fire and
brimstone, and appealing to her alike by maternal
anguish, tears and Bible texts. Also Mollie had come
upon her in an attitude of prayer behind various doors.

When the Deacon, whom an argumentative state in his
wife invariably rendered meeker than usual, stole with
noiseless and guilty step to his dinner, he was posted up
in the subject, and set on his daughter, who, wretched as
she was, wouldn't give up.

" Just think," said his wife, " she says a man need not
be clear about the Trinity to go to heaven ! "

Thus urged, the poor gentleman began rather blindly :
" You'd orter be ashamed of yourself to do so ! " while
his wife chimed in, " I'm ashamed for her ! denying the
faith to which she was born ! a serpent's egg ! a cocka-
trice's nest ! she actually had the impudence to tell me
she must think for herself. I'd like to know what
mothers were given for, nowadays. She'd better be
circumspect. She might be excommunicated for less.
Mary McCross, how dare you look at me so ? I won't

have it " (this with tears). " I don't know what I've done to deserve such a burden, but it seems to be the Lord's will, so I'll try to be reconciled to it. *You* needn't talk to her." (Her husband had relapsed into absolute taciturnity, and was meekly eating his mashed potato.) " She don't care the least thing for what you say."

" Now, look a here, Mollie," quoth he, a sparkle of anger lighting his faded eyes,—he was tenacious of his personal authority—" you'd better right about face, pretty quick, do you understand ? "

" Don't, papa, dear," she had said, hastily putting her arms around his wrinkled neck, and sealing his irate lips with a kiss; " you know obedience is my strong point."

" So it is, so it is," gasped the old gentleman, conscience-stricken ; " but you'd orter be careful.

> " ' For 'tis but care saves timid hare,
>   When dogs are bent upon the scent.' "

Looking over to his wife, he saw a darker storm menacing after the delivery of this soothing distich. She was still lachrymose. On similar principle to little Alice's, this good lady wept while she was thinking it saved time. So great, however, was her husband's agility, that he had dodged into his white stove-pipe, and out of the door, followed by Mollie, whom he secretly beckoned on, before the first flash appeared.

Mrs. McCross, thus left to herself, put on her sun-bonnet, and hastened to the mansion of Mrs. Dr. Perfect, intent on entreating her Christian sympathy.

She interrupted the worthy couple in the fabrication of a " Higher Life " tract, where they detailed the marvellous effect of believing one's self to be sinless, when one isn't at all; but either the subject had run dry, or Mrs.

McCross was a favorite, for they welcomed her cordially, and read her the article.

"Yes, indeed," said the Deacon's wife, piously, when Mrs. Perfect laid down the manuscript, "it is all in believing. Since I believed, I have the inward witness that I have not sinned. As you say, it is a blessed thing to live without sin."

Thereupon her hostess rolled up her eyes religiously, and coughed interrogatively, which indicated that she considered one topic finished, and was ready for the next.

Thus encouraged, Mrs. McCross told her story. "You see what a dreadful condition she is in," she said, in conclusion; adding naïvely, "I can't think what to do next."

"Suppose we reason with her," suggested Dr. Perfect, who, in gesture and theory, scooped up indignation and burning enough every Sunday to effect the cremation of a universe. His favorite sermon was from the text, "And the wrath of God abideth on him." "There are, my brethren, three kinds of wrath," he would say, digging it up from the pulpit cushions. In his presence one felt how true was the old adage about Millville, that there hell was only six inches under ground.

"It is useless," replied Mrs. McCross. "She refuses to have any argument upon the subject."

"What contumacious! obdurate!" said the doctor, sternly. "I fear it should be brought before the session."

"That would never do," cried the lady, who was willing to torment, but had a family pride in the matter of church discipline. "Think of the scandal! Mr. McCross would not forgive it."

"Ah! well," said the worthy man for reasons of his own, not wishing to disoblige his Deacon. "Patience sometimes avails in the room of harsher weapons, but the camp of Israel must be kept free from spot at any cost; yes, madam, I repeat it, at any cost."

"Suppose we go together and labor with her?" proposed Mrs. Perfect, briskly. "You can give me the jar of strawberry marmalade and the recipe at the same time."

Accordingly Mollie, who had been trying to forget the disagreeables of her lot in some work for her loving old father, beheld the yellow, anxious faces of the two saints intruding upon her privacy, without even a knock of warning. Mrs. McCross didn't believe in civility when religious interests were at stake. In former years, she used to drive Mollie to the verge of distraction, by opening her letters, or compelling her to leave them unanswered for weeks, alleging that if she wrote too often her friends would get tired of her: by mutilating her favorite books, slandering her schoolmates, and proscribing visits with them, on such Biblical grounds as "withdraw thy foot from thy neighbor's house, lest by thy continual coming he weary of thee, and at last hate thee;" a text particularly applicable to callers at Fir Covert.

Mrs. McCross' theories of parental rectitude had not altered with her daughter's growth. She still searched her drawers, pumped her friends, and listened at the keyhole.

Mary rose politely to receive her unexpected guests; but Mrs. Perfect did not wait her request to be seated. Planting her stiff figure in the most comfortable armchair in the room, she loosened her black cambric bonnet-strings with one bony hand, and then demanded a Bible.

"It would be proper to begin with a reading from the Word," quoth she. "Is that your mind, Sister McCross?"

Her young hostess brought her the required volume. It chanced to be a Douay Version; but Mrs. Perfect read notes and all in blessed unconsciousness, and smacked her lips over the wholesale denunciation of unbelievers, the latter contained.

"Shall we have a season of prayer?" she inquired in a tone nicely impregnated with business and piety.

"Do, Sister Perfect," quoth Mrs. McCross plaintively, from her place near the door. "What doth Saint John say: 'If any man sin a sin which is not unto death, he shall ask, and he shall give him life for them that sin not unto death.'"

"Will you join us, daughter Mary?" said Mrs. Perfect, this time in her oily, entreating voice, dropping on her knees as she spoke. Mollie, who had suspended her work while the reading was going on, now arose outraged: "You must excuse me: I have all these bulbs to sort;" pointing to her basket full of monstrous hyacinths. "I cannot spare the time."

"I told you she was in a very unchristian frame of mind. I am fairly sick with grief at her obstinacy. Oh! resist not the Spirit, my child," cried Mrs. McCross, still kneeling, and applying her handkerchief with one hand and her smelling bottle with the other.

"Come, lift your troubled heart to the throne of grace," said the minister's wife, seizing Mary by the arm, as she bent to collect her scattered labels, and attempting to pull her to her knees.

"Indeed, you must excuse me," said Mollie, freeing herself from the Christian clutches with some difficulty. "It will be only a minute's work to pick up these papers, and then I will leave you to your devotions."

"If your poor bruised heart is fixed in its waywardness, I suppose we shall have to be the more earnest in

intercession for your imperilled soul. Here is a tract."
Plunging her hand into the pocket of her black-and-white
calico, she brought out, "The Giddy Heart Reproved," by
the Rev. Jonas Perfect, D.D., LL.D. "I hope you will
read it carefully, and then send it to that bold-eyed young
girl I see with you so much. She comes of a godless
house, and pays little heed to the preached word. My
husband considers her in a dangerous state."

"I have no desire to read your tract," replied Mollie,
annoyance rapidly getting the better of her self-control.
"I will not deceive you by taking what would only go
into the fire; and, Mrs. Perfect, allow me to say that I
do not wish a recurrence of the scene. I cannot feel it
my duty to bear a series of similar insults from an almost total stranger."

"Dislike of saving grace is a common feeling of the
erring heart," said the home missionary with a snuffle,
growing exasperatingly meek. "I will go, since you seem
to wish it. No, my poor friend, I will not stay," as Mrs.
McCross made an effort to detain her; "I had best not
intrude. But rest assured, dear child, my husband and I
will make you a special subject of prayer in the closet."
Still meeker, she stole down-stairs, having tied her bonnet, destitute of ruche or flower, with a mildly sorrowful,
drooping bow, and imprinted a clammy Christian kiss on
the cheek of her unwilling hostess; and she left a strong
savor of Christian meekness and sour hair all the way out.

Mrs. McCross followed her, weeping audibly. Once
such tears would have brought Mollie to her feet in an
agony of self-accusation. To-day the daughter sat down
and reasoned the case out faithfully. However wretched
she might be at these passages of arms, and she was very
wretched, she was conscious of her own rectitude. She
felt her position to-day to be one of propriety. Whatever

her mother might consider due to her relation it was no
part of her duty to bear the insults of that odious woman;
and she did not propose to.

"It is a hard case, as you say, sister," said Mrs. Perfect in leave-taking; "we must have faith.   Did you
forget the marmalade?"

Mrs. McCross presented it, and then withdrew to her
apartment, showing symptoms of convulsions. She had
strength enough, however, to call Mollie down-stairs to
make her hot toddy, and hunt the camphor. She divided
her attention latterly between sling and valerian.   Rein-
forced by their spiritual consolations, the poor lady declined supper, groaning loudly throughout the meal; but
habiting herself in a green-and-red double-gown, she appeared soon after to Mollie and her father, as they sat
taking a little comfort in the twilight.

They were singing Puritan fugue tunes, and had just
reached the line, "Did he rise? He rose, he rose,"
which they were reiterating in triumphant excitement,
when Miranda took it upon herself to illustrate in person,
and her husband stopped dead short on "He burst," a
second and forlorn parody.

"I always knew you cared nothing about your wife,
Elizur McCross," she cried hysterically. "You encourage
that reckless girl in all her unkindness, her cruelty to me."

The Deacon dropped the hand he had been fondling as
if detected in a crime, and scratched his gray head to
cover his guilt. "Although you defy my authority,
miss, and have ceased to regard me in the light of a
mother, it is my opinion, if I am to be permitted to have
any opinions hereafter, that you ought to retire and see
if you can't wake up in a better frame of mind."

Mollie bent over and kissed her father good-night
without a word, and after a little struggle with herself,

offered her suffering parent the customary salute—a courtesy refused in grim anger. Then she ascended the stairs obediently, her heart heavy, her eyes full of tears.

A moment after she reached her room, her father called her softly to open the door, and entering, discovered himself laden with a battered stove-pipe hat, and a bunch of keys. He set the former on the table, and jingled the latter with emphasis. "I have come for the one that locks the hen-house," said he, with perfect sobriety. "I want your mother to understand it," and shook them again. "Here is a lemon and six lumps of sugar; six is right for lemonade, isn't it?"

Mollie's smile, though difficult to call, was very sweet, as she said he was correct.

The Deacon laid his offering with the keys, and sat down on the bed beside his daughter. "Don't spoil your dear eyes crying, darling. Your mother" (Deacon Mc-Cross always spoke of his wife as a negro mentions his fetich,—with mingled uneasiness and reverence) "is peculiar." He drew the girl's throbbing head to his bosom, and wiped her eyes with gentle, albeit trembling hand, on a small corner of his pocket-handkerchief. "That's right," with childish satisfaction, as she sat up and began to laugh. "I like to see you so—I'll tell you something nice, too," smoothing back her soft hair. "Louis Allwood is coming here to-night to serenade you. I asked him to, because you hanker after him, you know, and your mother stops his letters."

"O papa! how kind!" said the girl, fairly beaming with delight. "I can't thank you enough. I know you want to be squeezed." This was the most sacred and delightful caress in which the pair could indulge. Mollie gave it on the spot, and Mrs. McCross, hearing the noise, pounded a vicious signal to be expeditious.

The Deacon put away his merry air instantly, and caught up his garden hat and keys with nervous haste. Half way out he stopped, set down his burden, came back, and took his daughter's soft throat in his hand. "You love him better'n ever," said he, half in interrogation, half regret.

"Better than ever, father."

"Wall" (slowly), "I hain't no objections, fur my part."

He paused again at the door, and fumbled nervously for the knob. "'Twouldn't be no use to let your mother know I asked the feller up," said he, and relapsed from the loving champion into the gaunt, bald, meek, everyday Job.

Mollie gave him the parting kiss he wanted, and stood watching his stooping form out of sight. Her poor, weak, tender-hearted father! How her heart went forth to him! True love, all agree, has in it an element of pity and an element of protection. Conceive love divested largely of complacence, infinitely pitying, infinitely active in relief, and it becomes the divine attitude toward us. Which, it seems to me, makes the Atonement very simple, for the syllogism stands thus: to love is to pity; pity is suffering; God loves; *i.e.* God suffers, and Christ lived his thirty years to let us know it.

"I want you to be happy, daughter," the Deacon said, as he slowly descended the stairs—and so he did. When he returned to his faithful Xantippe, he felt his old heart warm with that heroism that makes men God-like. Oh! if it had only held out! That is the point with us humans. We all of us have a few divine impulses, but the self-sacrifice that seals the flasks in which they are kept is such inferior stuff, that the precious elixir all breaks out, and at the important moment there is nothing there. Between this time and ten o'clock Mrs. McCross' tongue had *decanted* every drop of her lord's prowess.

Meanwhile, the vexations of the day forgotten, Mollie abandoned herself to delightful thoughts. She was to see her lover. No matter how fear would teach her to think of him, his image always stood fair and noble in her mind. How she had longed to see him, to listen to his voice, and look into his frank, gentle eyes, to nestle passive beside him, in the fathomless rest of his presence! Now in a few hours he would be near. She would feel again the subtile, witching fascination of his dear self. All the weary vigils of the past slipped into oblivion; all the distress and anxiety that preyed upon her fled at his approach. Her mind, suddenly relieved of its strain, relaxed. She fell into a calm, happy sleep, so deep that she failed to hear the soft cadence of harmony flowing in through her vine-latticed window. Even Louis' well-known tones only mingled with the phantasies of slumber.

> " 'Forget-me-not dreams in the moonlight,
> Her eyes are fair to see.
> Ah! gentle eyes, open to me,
> That I may know if love there be nestling.' "

Her lover had written the lines when the blue blossoms were unfolding from their crumpled pink buds, and Mollie had worn them in her chestnut braids. That was long years before. The two had set them to music, and sung them together a thousand times since, and now she was become his forget-me-not. Awake, Mollie dear. Go down into the shadowy garden, among the asters and balsams, dark in the pale moonlight. Go, and forget, if only for one brief instant, that time exists, save to bring happiness.

"You moonstruck whipper-snapper, if you don't quit these grounds, I'll make you wish you had," screamed

Mrs. McCross from the parlor window, in a voice some-what husky through anger, but more from the absence of false teeth.

At the sound her daughter started to her feet, broad awake, and held her breath in terrified anticipation.

"Mirandy, Mirandy, where are my stockings?" cried the Deacon feebly, from the bed-room. "Do come and help me find 'em."

"You keep away from here, meddlesome ninny," quoth his wife to her lawful head; then to Louis, "Do you mean to budge or not? Elizur McCross," bringing herself into the house with a snap, "do you hear me? Go and get into bed this minute."

"When all the clouds about the sun lie up in golden creases, I'll think of departing," answered Louis from the walk close by the window. His voice sounded strangely to Mollie's sensitive ears. It wasn't a boy's direct utterance. She couldn't instantly analyze the jarring peculiarity, but he ended the sentence with something like a hiccough.

"You have no business on my premises," shrieked Mrs. McCross. "Why do you skulk about the house at this time of night?—to steal?"

"Don't alarm yourself unnecessarily, old lady," said the young man; "I haven't come for the property my father left in your care."

"Drunken puppy! I'll teach you to talk so;" and her daughter heard the splash of water, and the sound of a blow, followed instantly by a sharp crash of glass.

By this time Mollie had reached the garden, and run to her lover, whom she found dripping with the contents of the well-water-dipper, which lay shining in the moon-light at his feet. He was gazing remorsefully at the shattered window, and evidently took no heed to the torrent

of wrath the lady in the parlor was pouring upon him,
or to her menacing gestures. He didn't even notice
Mollie's quick step, or see the frantic Deacon aimlessly
flourish a long knit stocking, as he hurried to his better-
half, and drew her from the casement by main force.
But soon he turned, and beheld the woman he loved standing near. When quiet, or deep, or earnest natures, are
once irritated, it takes a long time for the disturbed substrata to return to repose. Accordingly, though his
wrath had passed, he was still in the gall of bitterness.
As for Mollie, her whole soul was possessed with a blind
instinct to be near him in the trouble.

"I've broken your window glass, insulted your mother,
and made a fool of myself; now I guess I'll go home,"
said he, sulkily.

The girl's nerves were unstrung from long-continued
anxiety and vigil. She was trembling like an aspen, with
excitement. In such a state the merest touch destroys
our mental balance. The whole scene, from the struggling couple in the parlor, sympathized with by Poppy,
who thought it a free fight, and danced on her perch, and
shouted "go in, lemons," at the top of her voice, to
Louis' angry face, contrasting oddly with his boyish announcement, was very funny. She must cry or faint, or
somehow vent her emotion. She laughed.

He turned on her almost savagely. "If you enjoy it,
go on," said he.

It came to Mollie in a flash that this meeting would
determine their two lives. If she let him go thus, he
was gone forever, and she loved him.

"Louis, dear Louis." Only a woman can put her
whole heart into two words, as Mollie did into these.

The man felt it, but he wouldn't yield. The woman
close at his side lived his thought twin with her own.

"Louis," said she gently, "I love you at your best. Is to-night your best?"

He stood perfectly silent, looking away into the shadows so long—so long, it seemed to Mollie as if he would never come back to her again.

She concentrated her whole being into an intense, passionate throb of love; he must be hers, he *must.*

By and by the man faced his opponent. She trembled —now with fear. Had she won? She raised her eyes timidly to his, to meet them full of affection and honest purpose.

Then she held out her hand with a happy smile. He took it in both his own. The old dear touch, so missed, so well remembered. His pulse throbbed fiercely against hers—the only trace of the struggle. "You have won," said she, softly.

"Won," he replied, his eyes answering, with true manhood shining in them.

That was all they said; but they stood together a long time comforting each other, without need of words. By and by he drew her fondly into his arms, held her close a minute, and then hurried away.

CHAPTER XX.

"The pig was eat, and Tom was beat."

HAT night's sowing made bitter reaping for my poor children, just as the handful of tares good people scatter always does, though their wicked neighbors may harrow them in over a whole-wheat field, and yet never seem to get a ripe head for their pains.

Mrs. McCross rose early next morning, her aches and
ailments gone ; the white curtains poets wot of, albeit in
this case something red at the edges, rolled up from her
pale eyes to their farthest extent. She chalked her face,
donned a silk morning-gown, brought out her gossipy
patchwork, and enthroned herself and aromatic salts in
the cosey green sitting-room, in state, for she had a thing
in hand.

Before twelve o'clock she had blown a tale of midnight
attack and intended villany all over Millville ; for Susy
Jenkens came to get butter—the McCross dairy being
celebrated ; and Mrs. Captain Slocum called on Mary ;
and Zoe Bradshaw dropped in on mission business ; and,
best of all, Miss Petingil arrived in pursuit of bread and
butter, and Mrs. McCross failed not to send her up to
the village fully primed and early in the day. Miss Petingil, like a wise diplomatist, had two strings to her bow.
Her immediate object was getting a pair of pants to make
for the Deacon ; her secondary, interesting Mrs. McCross
in a moral periodical of which she was agent, called "The
Flag of Humanity."

"Hev you ever seen it ? " she asked, fishing it out of
the bag she wore tied about her waist with a piece of thin
black ribbon. "If I dew say it, there ain't a better magazine took in Millville. There's poetry *an'* there's prose,
an' lectures on health, *an'* everything that's good to read."

"We subscribe for several religious papers, to send to
the home missionaries," remarked her hostess ; "I don't
believe I could afford any more."

"But this is such a nice one," said Miss Petingil, with
a sigh. "When I go home all wore out tailorin', I rest
myself perusing it. There's one piece of poetry that
can't be beat no way, on tobacker. It's reely beautiful !
It tells how dirty it is, how much a man spends in his

lifetime, an' how high his heap of quids would be if he lived fifty years. It's splendid poetry," she reiterated, resting her forefinger on the page, and carefully wiping her glasses on her knitting. "I used to make poetry myself, but I couldn't come up to that, no way."

Peace, who was visiting Mollie in the next room, overheard, and resolved to become possessor of this effusion of genius. But Mrs. McCross staved off the contemplated reading by a characteristic remark:

"We had quite an adventure here last night. My husband's former ward came round and smashed our windows!"

The news-carrier's face, which had fallen a little, as she slipped "The Flag of Humanity" back into the faded bag, now grew bright with anticipation, and she rejoined briskly, "You hadn't no plate, nor nothink around, had you?"

"A mere trifle of the Lord's blessings, some of which he has seen fit to reclaim," said Mrs. McCross, humbly. "He feedeth the ravens, and the young lions do lack and suffer hunger."

"Jess so!" responded the spinster, whose eyes anticipation had greened like leeks. She chewed a black thread gradually into her thin straight mouth, and waited developments, meanwhile folding the broadcloth pieces with care, for she was particular about her work.

Mrs. McCross' gentle brow clouded with sorrow. "I have nothing to tell about our losses. Don't ask me. It *may* be a mistake. How can we worms know the secret acts of our brother-worms? Mollie, poor child, thinks he came to serenade her. It is as well to let it go so. It won't bring back the money to ruin him."

The look in her pale eyes was almost too fiendish to come within the united capacity of her Christian and motherly benevolence.

"But the example! your duty to society!" gasped Miss Petingil, not too much horrified to forget her snuff-box. "I know just how bad your feelin's must be "—sniff sniff. "But it's a devolution upon you "—sniff—" to sacrifice even your right eyes for the safe "—sneeze—" ty of your neighbors."

As Miranda's only answer was a plaintive smile, the advocate of justice pocketed the tobacco, to exclaim with sympathetic emphasis :

"He's ben takin' on awfully in Top Town, an' that ere Peace gel sticks up for him. Wa-ll, you needn't tell me men break into folks' winders fur nothin', an' yourn too, that have ben a mother to him. It's reely peculiar. Don't you think so ? "

Mrs. McCross agreed that it was peculiar ; and added, with a sad shake of her head: "Divine grace, as I've always maintained, is the only thing that will ever make a man of Louis Allwood."

So she started the story, and Cymbalinus Adolphus Brown heard it. He had gone the rounds of his acquaintance matrimonially intent, but none of them, even Euphemia Hitchcock, had buckled to ; and, being himself impecunious, he had lately gone into the law for a living. He therefore hurried to Fir Covert in search of a job. Since the tea-party, he had been very shy of Mollie, though Mrs. McCross, who was a great admirer of "the young gentlemen," in secret, lay in wait for him, and brought him in whenever she could. The household were therefore neither astonished nor otherwise to see him pay the mistress of the house a long call at an un-fashionable hour, though the two bolted their doors, and Mrs. McCross let him out of the gate, with her own hands, at close of session.

Louis meanwhile had accomplished nothing less than a

bitter quarrel with Charley Pelican, who was too little at ease with himself to be able to hold any one course of behavior toward those depending upon him. Louis, alternately snubbed, and made boon companion, or father confessor to pranks he was ashamed to hear of, was already at odds with his condition; and a few hours' sober reflection, well lighted by the candle of self-reproach, sufficed to disgust him with the very thought of the Night-blooming Cereus, and its genteelly drunken frequenters. Those nice ideas of honor, which he had felt too thoroughly natural to need cherishing, and unconsciously laid aside, reasserted their supremacy over a remorseful and humbled man. Such vigorous mental action produced a state of nervous exasperation, little fit to ensure a cordial meeting with the companion of his last night's spree, the less after a little recreation in which that young gentleman was indulging himself.

Peace breakfasted with Charley, and then donned her new charity uniform; the same being the remarkably elegant garb upon which the fair sisters of the Order of Sackcloth and Ashes prided their gentle hearts. Thus clad, the budding saint set forth, intent on teasing Mollie, who disapproved of charitable flummery; and her brother, left to himself, strolled through the village in search of mischief.

He had not gone far, when he met Francis Haythorne, so perfectly arrayed in soft brown, that he seemed to have just stepped from a bandbox. Charley, who had a style of his own, embracing a bright blue cap, scarlet necktie, "coatie all too short," and huge cigar, eyed him over and sniffed with scorn. He despised his sister's male friends on principle.

"Lend us your flipper, Haythorne," quoth he.

The person addressed sniffed in his turn, and gingerly extended his well-gloved fingers.

"Darn snippy weather for quadrupeds!" remarked Charley in a loud voice.

"Very," said Mr. Haythorne, looking about for means of escape.

"Do you fumé?" asked Charley, tendering a fat Habana whose aroma was enough to floor an abstemious man, and standing exactly in front of his victim so he couldn't pass. "By thunder! you look weak this morning."

"Thanks. I never smoke in the street in daylight!" answered Francis with an annoyed wave of the hand.

"Plenty of pretty girls in Millville," suggested his tormentor, expanding his great chest and towering a head above the passers-by, a giant provoking, and like a giant, weak. "Deuce take it!" warming, and nettled too, as the fastidious Francis betrayed his disgust more and more plainly. "I'd like to kiss 'em."

"Why not ask permission?" said the Sybarite dryly, drawing away from this coarseness at the same time, as if he had been petitioned for the salute.

"By Jove, I will!" cried Charley, incensed at the gentleman's tone. "If you say so, I'll hoof it down Main Street, offer my jug-handle to every woman I meet, and see if she won't let me brush a trifle of lily-white off her damaged cheek. Hang it! I will anyway. Just go long 'tother side the road and watch."

Mr. Haythorne declined, and mentally searched his Sybarite vocabulary for a delicate phrase expressive of "confounded donkey, despicable jackass," and permitted his handsome features to curl with a sneer. But Squire Hitchcock, who was one of the little group Charley had contrived to collect about them, felt his old blood stirred

with youthful heat, and volunteered his services, adding :
" You'll have to be spryer than July hopper grass to ketch
some on 'em."

Francis Haythorne watched the precious pair with
contempt; but when they encountered Mrs. Dennis, with
a covered basket on her arm, and three full-blown yellow
roses and one pink one on her hat, his wrath got far
beyond even the memory of a consoling maxim.

" Suffer me," said Charley, trying to embrace the good
woman's stout figure, and imprint a salute upon her
mature cheek.

She shifted her basket just in time to send him stagger-
ing back, in the precise attitude of the starved apothe-
cary in Romeo and Juliette. "Do you think I'll have ye
to kiss me, ye slobberin' dirty jackanapes?" she cried
shrilly, her plump face crimson with wrath as she surveyed
the young harlequin. "Hugh, Hughey Dennis, come
quick, and smash his iley, moppy head for insultin' yer
mother! Bedad thin, I'll do it meself," as no Hugh
appeared; and she set down her basket, and unpinned
her plaid blanket shawl accordingly.

" Oh, dear! my good woman! I wouldn't," said Squire
Hitchcock in a deprecatory tone, rubbing his well-
developed abdominal region inquiringly as he spoke, for
Charley's elbow had come in violent contact therewith in
his precipitate retreat; "I wouldn't! I don't believe
he meant anything."

Mrs. Dennis turned on him, blazing with indignation.
"I've jest wan piece of advice fur the likes of you:
Have naught to do wid you graceless scamp; belike he'll
lead even your gray hairs asthray, wid his impedunt
thricks. An' wouldn't that be a sad day, think ye, for
the puir things housin' amidst 'em?" The vindictive-

ness of her tone brought the peace-maker's fingers to his
maligned locks involuntarily.

"By thunder! she had you then, Squire," shouted
Charley, delighted. "I was in earnest, madam. It
wouldn't hurt you any, you know."

He approached her, though she waved him back majestically; and something cried "wee! wee! wee!" in her
basket, but she heeded not the voice of the charmer.

"It's not me, the mother of seven sons, all in glory
but one,—heaven rest their souls,—as 'ud be doin' such a
thing," she went on, in a tone of impressive dignity, and
took a half-step back so as to give a grander sweep to her
voluminous skirts, whereby she trod on the tail of a cat
investigating the contents of her twig-woven casket.
"Saints be praised!" she continued, sublimely unconscious of the howling animal; "I've buried Dinnis this
five year; but"—("wee! wee!" vehemently from the
wicker-ware)—"I'm as thrue to his memory as the day I
laid him wid tears and heart-break beneath the church-
yard sod." At this point, the squeaks becoming very
audible, Mrs. Dennis imposed silence by a back kick.
"An' sence he died," she went on, without a pause,—
"sence he died I'm niver in the street, save to buy bread
for the childer, such as bees now in me basket, or," another kick, which tipped over the object of her solicitude,
followed by a jubilant squeal, "mayhap a small bit of
calico for meself, a dress, or shirts for Hugh, as is too in-
tyerly principled a boy to come before uptown folks in his
ragged cloes; or,—bedad, an' the pig's out! Run for
him, if ye'd have the name of gintlemin." Exit Mrs.
Dennis in hasty chase, followed by a crowd urging on
the knotty-tailed quadruped with shrieks and hoots.

The objects of her eloquence remained behind, stamping
and screaming with mirth, Charley being finally obliged

to lean against the fence to keep his balance, and the Squire slapped his big legs so hard in extremity of delight, that they must have been sore for a week after. "This is bully!" said the representative of the Pelicans, at last, and settled his attire by help of a reflecting shop-window.

"Yes," returned his companion, just then remembering his grievances; "yes; quite so. You haven't ground the pints to them elbows o' your'n lately, hev you? I didn't know but you was feelin' for my crop a short spurt ago."

At this point, Susie Jenkens' little sister Gracie came tripping down the street, in all the light-hearted gayety that belongs to girl-life. Poor maiden! Red Riding Hood was not more innocently amazed when the wicked wolf petitioned a salute, than she when this lupine marauder snatched a kiss. She stood quite still, her golden curls tossed all about her dainty head, the very image of bewildered fright, and put out her small hands to push him off, with a pretty, touching gesture, and gazed a long minute into the cruel fellow's face, which he contrived to make really earnest and beseeching. Then she gave a little cry, and darted up a side street, her feet keeping time to the hurried beating of her heart. Pity that the very tears of alarm she shed should be mingled with feelings of admiration and gentle sorrow for the handsome scapegrace! I fear she thought of him very often during the next few days, especially when she discovered he was Peace's brother, and I know she debated long if she had done as she ought, and experienced in murmuring her sweet prayers that night, how good it is to forgive our enemies, and them that do despitefully use us.

Even Squire Hitchcock felt mean at this adventure. "Bones of Aunt Tommy! this ain't nowise fair," he be-

gan, and then stopped, for old Miss Petingil appeared
on the scene. She was jogging her way up the street,
very complacently, inasmuch as she held under her arm
a paper of sage and half a pumpkin,—gifts of the Mc-
Crosses. It was a good hour since she started from Fir
Covert, so frequent had been her delays to relate her
story. Spying our amorous couple, she began at once.

"Now, Square, hev you heerd what a dreful prank—"

Here Charley nudged Mr. Hitchcock in the ribs, and
begged an introduction in a stage whisper.

Miss Petingil bridled and smiled. "Ain't you Peace
Pelican's brother?" she asked, with a simper forty years
out of date. Charley took the blue cap clear off, and
fairly tucked it under his arm in graceful acknowledgment
of the fact, and telegraphed "success" to his accomplice.
"Like to speak with me," said the spinster, cheerfully.
"I dus' say you want some tailorin' done. I ain't bad at
it;" drawing towards the fence for privacy. "Here's
a pair of pants I'm doin' now for Deacon McCross,—new
pattern;" and she proceeded then and there to exhibit it.
Charley vouchsafed a half glance, expressing too much
modesty to look at such articles in company. "No, no,"
said the ingenuous youth, blushing; "I'm ashamed to ask
you for what I want. But mother's away at Top Town
so long, and I'm homesick. She always comes and kisses
me before I go to sleep,—and you look so much like her."

"Dew tell!" said Miss Petingil, in sympathy, her love-
scrimped heart warming with motherly instinct. Our
Absalom *was* such a handsome boy, with his rich coloring, and lips now drawn into a sorrowful curve. She
couldn't help it. "Tain't likely you'll go home for a
week, mebbe?"

Charley shook his curly head as if heart-broken, and
drew out a white handkerchief, ready for application to

his eyes; but this was unnecessary. The old lady deposited her half pumpkin on the fence-rail, and wiped her withered mouth preparatory.

" There ! " said she, " take it. I hain't no boys nor nuthin'; but 'tain't no harm, no way."

The Squire, whose watery organs of sight had been some time glittering with rare enjoyment, could no longer contain himself, and now burst into a hoarse laugh. Mrs. Dennis, too, rushed by, still in pursuit of the pig. " Fools ain't all dead yit, be jabbers ! " quoth she, knocking the spinster's yellow treasure off the fence in her haste, and was gone like a dream. So was the pumpkin, for piggy doubled again, and spying, buried his nose in it. The sharp-cut wrinkles on the maiden's face all deepened, and the mother-look faded hopelessly. She craned up on the instant. " Almira Petingil is fit game for town loafers, p'raps ! " she cried, " but she's too much a woman to look at *you* twice." She picked up and wiped the remnant of pumpkin, abandoned with reluctance by piggy, and ambled forlornly away.

Next a tall, graceful figure, clad in sombre black, with a thick veil sweeping from her bonnet and hiding her face. The young man's heart sank as she approached. The modest unconsciousness of purity is a very wall of safety to its possessor. Charley's reflections resembled those of Le Docteur Faust in a similar situation :

> " No form like hers I can recall ;
> Virtue she hath, and modest heed ;
> Is piquant, too, and sharp withal."

He really hadn't courage to molest her, and, fairly vanquished, was about turning away, when, goaded on by a " haw ! haw ! " from the gentle Hitchcock, who had discreetly retired from the glances of wrath at betrayed confidence shot at him by Miss Petingil, he stopped the

lady with an apology, explained the case—a boyish frolic,
—would she excuse? and—permit?

She trembled a little, but heard with grave politeness.
He listened eagerly for the liquid melody of her voice in
answer. In vain, for she didn't speak. Her soft garments exhaled a rich, dreamy perfume. He was wild to
snatch aside the sweeping crêpe that hid her features.
He bashfully stretched out his hand to unveil her, but
she shrank back and shook her exquisite little glove defiantly, herself pulled away the wrinkled mask, and permitted him to press a kiss upon a cheek whose rich color
was beyond praise. Then she motioned him to go, with
dignity, though he thought he heard a faint gurgle of
laughter as she left him.

She stopped at the corner of the street to talk with
Louis Allwood. How merry they were! A horrible suspicion took hold of Charley's mind. Could it be, yes, it
was—Peace!—wicked, mirthful Peace; and she stood detailing the joke with nods and becks and wreathed smiles,
to a man whose quiet superiority he could never forgive.
O dii immortales! what should he do? How could he
ever have been so fooled! One thing was certain—they
should smart for it. This saucy clerk should know the
weight of his anger. Charley was fond of letting a horse
feel the curb, as he expressed it. Ah! here the fellow
came—smiling! villanously smiling!

"By George, man! you seem uncommon jolly to-day;
you have heard a joke, I see. Suppose you tell us about
it. I'll bet my head against your noddle the listener was
a darn sight worse than the story." Charley pushed his
victim toward the fence as he spoke, so as to make sure
of him.

"Je ne suis pas demoiselle, ni belle,
    Et je n'ai pas besoin qu'on m'amène,"

repeated Louis, with a quiet laugh at the other's discourteous touch. " As you say, the joke is excellent."

Though no French scholar, Mr. Pelican easily guessed that the quotation had some reference to his late misfortune. It added fuel to the flame. To be laughed at in an unknown language was beyond endurance. He tapped his boot with his cane angrily. " If you've got anything to say, don't mumble it in that gibberish; any fool can do that! Do ye hear?"

Now it was rumored about that Pelican was giving his clerk " a going-over," and people were collecting near, full of that vulgar curiosity which loves to see the humiliation of the superior and unfortunate. Louis writhed under it; there was an expression about his almost womanly delicate mouth, that promised ill to his antagonist. But his only reply was a graceful bow. He was one of those slender, evenly proportioned men, who bend as handsomely as a stalk of grain before the wind. It is their natural gesture. The act exasperated Charley from a sudden consciousness of this very fact. Anger irradiates its object as a torch while it consumes ourselves; and light in its nature must catch upon the salient points, be they beauties, or the reverse.

" You may think you're smart," pursued young Pelican, " but I'll have you to know I'm boss; and I won't submit to sass, either. It's bad policy to quarrel with one's bread and butter."

Louis bowed again. He was too angry to risk a word, and prepared to depart. I cannot picture the cool, polite scorn concentrated into that bow; but Charley felt it to the marrow of his bones. He shouted after the obeisant an oath, and an insinuation touching his manhood. Then Louis came back. The more my boy grew angry, the calmer he seemed. Even now, his voice was low, and every syllable distinct. He picked up and restored the cane Charley dropped, with the same courtesy he would have used toward Mollie. "Mr. Pelican, I do not desire to remain in your employment. A man who cannot conduct himself with propriety, cannot command others. Also you insult defenceless women." He walked away without another word, or even look at the object of his displeasure. A god sat in his eyes. He was master, and he knew it.

Unfortunately he strode into the arms of the village constable, and Mr. Cymbalinus Adolphus Brown, who came up at that instant.

"I have been looking everywhere for you, Mr. All-wood," said the official. "I want to bring you before Squire Hitchcock to answer fur last night's spree. It was drefful curless of you to do such a trick, but I hope you'll go agreeable, and not make no fuss." He was a short, red-haired, round-faced man, who looked rotund in his clothes, like a bran-stuffed pin-cushion; but Louis wasn't thinking of his circular dignity; his shame had come personified upon him. Pity Charley could not have seen his humiliation.

"On whose charge?" asked the arrested meekly. It was so opposite to his morning's repentance, he took it as a matter of course, and never thought of resistance.

"Deacon McCross's, Deacon Elizur McCross's," uttered the representative of law through a little round, purple mouth, like a half-open petunia, and speaking with emphatic deliberation, so that the prisoner might feel that justice was mighty, even enwrapped in fat. "Deacon E. McCross, and Mrs. Miranda McCross. 'Taint nowise likely you hain't heerd ov what they wanter see to, so please to come along."

"Did he, Mr. McCross, send you himself?" questioned

Louis, who could hardly believe it of the kind-hearted old man.

"He just did," said the constable, expanding his chest as he supposed, but really only bringing into relief a more prominent development, "an' he said he was goin' to have the law out of you too."

The young fellow shivered. To be brought up like a common drunkard! It was a shame he could never forget.

"Of course you'll plead guilty," said Cabby, button-holing him.

"I don't propose to deny facts," quoth Louis, annoyed at being spoken to. "I suppose a fine will satisfy the authorities."

"I should think so, certainly," said Mr. Brown. "When I travelled in Europe with a pahty, I recollect being awested as a Fenian spy. Had to have wecourse to the American consul. I assure you, it was vewy unpleasant—vewy!"

This was putting it in a less disgraceful light, or appeared to be. Louis' downcast face brightened like a tell-tale, as it was.

"Of cowose the less fuss you make about the matter, the less noise thaah will be in town," pursued the lawyer, who had a dog-like skill at countenance-reading. "I would like to be of sehvice to you, on account of my friendship with that pahticulah stah, Miss Mollie. The chahge, you know, is burglary, but it is all a fahce, gotten up through the madam's temper. Miss Petingil met me a few moments ago, and told me the circumstances of the case."

His guilelessness once laid the sharpest-sighted spirit in all heaven open to imposture, if Milton be correct; Louis had the same quality, and was consequently duped.

Besides, Mrs. McCross' tool played his part very well. They had not had their morning's consultation in vain.

"I am much obliged to you," cried the pure-hearted boy, warmly, wondering how he could ever have had such a thorough contempt for the insignificant dandy. "You are very kind."

"Not at all! not at all!" said Cabby, airily, with more truth than appeared.

They reached Squire Hitchcock's office, and that gentleman heard the evidence with as much decorum as if he had not been engaged in Charley's little game two hours before. Louis sat down and thought the matter over. Should he plead guilty and suffer, or bide his time and fight it out? For it presently appeared that it was no matter of fines and reproofs. In the one case, his name would be a hissing and reproach; in the other, Mollie's home rendered wretched, and her parents ridiculous. The brave reticence she had maintained in regard to her family discomforts could be no veil to Louis, and he knew that determined opposition would be then merged into active persecution; for it must be that the right would have way if he waited his trial. He reflected that his name would one day be his love's also—a fact now remembered afresh after years of forgetting. But profound emotion is a flood that tears away surface formations, regardless of the substrata revealed. Louis resolved to assert his innocence, and said, "Not guilty," firmly.

It appeared that on the date of the burglary Deacon McCross had lost some eighty dollars in bills, the same having been drawn the day before from the bank, in order to pay certain household expenses. Mrs. McCross accused Louis of breaking in and stealing the same, which charge she supported by several witnesses: the gardener, who had observed him about the place; the cook, who had overheard the angry interview; a tailor, to whom he had that morning paid the same amount; the clerk of the Millville House, who had seen him come in, pale and agitated, shortly after the supposed time of the robbery; and more to the same effect.

This sufficed for commitment. "Have you any friends, willing to give bail?" asked Squire Hitchcock, when the examination was concluded.

Louis walked over to the window,—a dirty window, full—he always remembered—of large, buzzing flies. He looked down on the bright little street, crowded with busy people hurrying about, on the tradesmen, and Gone-cussets, and gentlemen farmers, and rough workmen, and factory hands, all pushing, and jostling, and bargaining— every man with his heart full of his own cares.

Mrs. McCross had brought my boy up well; in all the noisy, happy town, he had few acquaintances—not one friend. So he came back to the ash-littered, fire-empty, tobacco-stained stove, where the men sat waiting. "I will not trouble any one," said he.

"Jest as well," responded the Squire. "Your case'll be up next week before Superior Court. It's about through the docket, so you don't have to wait long; an' your board won't cost you nuthin' meanwhile, you know. He, he!"

The magistrate, who hadn't given up hopes of getting rid of Euphemia, glared at Mr. Brown; and Mr. Brown, who wanted to borrow money of the magistrate, snickered, with his chin on his cane, and Louis drew himself up haughtily, and said he was ready to go.

So they took him to the jail; and, except that the cells were dirty, and the ventilation poor, he suffered in body less than might be expected.

He knew nothing of law; his dear piano, and dearer books, had absorbed far too much time to admit of great worldly experience. Even the Top Town life had been a surface gliding among treacherous marshes and bogs ; but, marsh-like, all had looked green and fair a-top. There were miasma and holes, and vermin in plenty ; but he had walked around on the made ground of wealth and position, —hadn't slipped in. He felt certain his innocence would be established. He knew the evidence against him was very slight, and had, besides, an instinctive idea that right would triumph because it was right. True, he couldn't tell upon what he founded his hopes, unless it was a general faith in human nature. But human na-ture, as Mr. and Mrs. Adam, No. 1 Paradise Row, dis-covered a long time since, is poor stuff. Louis' impres-sions were further strengthened by a visit from Mr. Brown, who assured him that he would certainly clear himself without difficulty, and, moreover, advised him to save his money and plead his own cause, assuring him that the case was too plain to make legal aid necessary.

Now Louis had nothing wherewith to pay a lawyer ; one ten-dollar bill at that moment comprising his whole finances. He therefore accepted the advice thankfully, and made up his mind to tell his honest story and await the issue.

Peace Pelican called the next day with Mollie McCross. She wore the charity uniform, whereby she had so vexed her unsuspecting brother, and looked as regal as ever. I have never seen a more strikingly handsome brunette than Peace. The superb coloring of her face, her large, lustrous eyes, but especially her finely moulded features, which could express the utmost merriment, hauteur, dig-nity, or compassion, almost at the same moment, made the pleasure of watching her amount to fascination. In her presence, one thought of odorous hot spices, of great tropical flowers whose breath is heavy with fragrance, of flamingoes, and stately palm-trees, and jer-falcons, and all manner of things that express beauty, courage, and intense life.

The friends found Louis studying criminal character, with a view to future practice at the bar; and upon his telling them so, sat down in front of his cell on two stools, which Mr. Marsh, the jailer, brought them, and straightway plunged contentedly into castle-building— which culminated in Louis' being Chief Justice of United States, and Mollie's appearance in black velvet and diamonds; simultaneously with Peace's buying three country houses for caravansaries, to be adorned with rows of orphan children in ruffled aprons, overlooked by herself, in cap and spectacles. It was so sweet to forget the horrible years of want now past, and once more go forth into dream-life, hand-in-hand with Louis; so passing sweet to realize that they could still build rainbow-castles together, that the actual speaking, doing, wearying, going up and down in the years, had not been a gradual drifting apart; that the, to them, better defined, more tangible thought-life, was not a severed, maimed existence to both. Mollie basked in the recovered joy, and grew gay, and playful, and girlish in her lover's presence.

By and by Peace became troubled. Charley, she said, had vowed vengeance against his former companion, and called on Mrs. McCross, in spite of all she could do and say to the contrary; had been seen drinking with the abstemious Mr. Brown; and was under the influence of liquor most of the time.

Whereupon Mollie changed into her every-day, care-burdened self, and begged Louis to be wary, for her father and mother seemed very sure of his conviction.

But he laughed at their fears, and kissed her hands through the bars, and added his entreaties to her parent's commands, that she should not appear as witness. There was no need to have their affairs made common property, he said. How could they prove a thing that wasn't so? And he playfully quoted poetry for her consolement, beginning with—

> "Desponding fear, of feeble fancies full,
> Weak and unmanly, loosens every power;"

and gently sliding into Wordsworth:

> "What are fears but voices airy, whispering harm where harm is not?"

Mollie smiled because she loved him, and, to her, all his ways were pleasantness; but the worry didn't get out of her truthful eyes, and when, as Peace put it, he had shot his last arrow, she still looked anxiously into his face.

"What! dearest of trouble-borrowers, are you still unconvinced? Don't you know—

> "Care to our coffin adds a nail, no doubt,
> And every grin so merry draws one out?"

She stood submitting to the light touch with which he drew mirthful lines about her fresh, sweet mouth, as if she loved it. "You *will* be cautious, Louis, won't you?" she urged, when he stepped back, and regarded his work with a serio-comic shake of the head. But he wouldn't promise, or do anything except enact the maniac by help of the bars of his cell; so the two women could only go home heavy-hearted, and talk about hope.

Leaving the prison they met Deacon McCross; but he slunk toward the wall, and wouldn't look at them. He had a milder, balder, more cowed-down air than ever, to

Peace's mind; but being one of those people who never bestow confidences with rough edges, she made no comment thereon to her friend.

Finally the day of the trial came. The jurymen were personally unknown to Louis; but the State's attorney, under Cabby's manipulations, had called on him, and advised him to plead guilty. The Judge, too, had been interviewed by the McCrosses in a friendly way; and before the prisoner came into court, every one's mind was made up against him.

It is odd that the very alleviations to real guilt, when that guilt is merely conjectural, are made to certify to it.

"Poor fellow! I suppose he needed the money."

"Yes, some folks think that, an' a good deal more of the McCross property, would change hands if justice had way. Likely he thought he had a right to it."

"How kinder peaked he looks. Don't seem stout enough to work. They dew say, Mrs. McCross wa'n't nun too good to him when he lived there; always shuttin' him up, an' snubbin' him; he wa'n't never let to set on the best chairs, nor nuthin'. When I got away I'd ha' had one good time ef I'd 'a ben be."

From these remarks it may be correctly concluded that the Millville ladies were out in force; less, however, from interest in Louis, than dislike of Mrs. McCross.

It struck the accused as strange, that Cabby, his openhearted champion, should appear for the prosecution; but he felt so hurt at Charley Pelican's conduct, that the outside treachery seemed nothing. His estranged companion, called as plaintiff's witness, testified hurriedly and noisily that defendant's past life had been open to suspicion; his habits expensive, his temper of late uncertain; that he was drunk the night of the burglary—they had been drinking together.

Deacon McCross said he had lost the money, and was sorry for the whole matter, and wished he hadn't got nothin' to do with it. The night of the trouble he had invited his ward to his house, but he didn't think he was layin' plans to rob him, the very time. He looked so bald and mild and miserable, that every one's heart steeled against Louis directly. All the moral half of the audience bethought them of serpents' eggs, dogs that bite the hand, and so on; while the immoral half said it was a darn mean trick for any one to play such a kind-hearted old chap.

Mrs. McCross' account was worthy of her genius. She had heard a noise in the night, and got up to examine the premises, and found a window open, and became aware at the same moment that some one was lurking close to the house. On perceiving himself observed, he had the impudence to begin a song, and when she ordered him off, insulted her and broke her windows. No one else had been about the house, and she found the prints of muddy boots on her floor next morning, clear up to the drawer where the money had been placed. She further spoke of missing tea-spoons during her ward's sojourn under her roof, and said, in conclusion, that she had prayed much that he might be plucked as a brand from the burning, yea, saved as by fire; but she feared her faith was vain.

At this juncture Miss Petingil, who had spared a day for the trial, remarked to her neighbors that it was peculiar of them Price gals to pray for folks they was a plaguin' on; and added, "How folks ken!" and took snuff on it in her snippiest way.

Then Bridget deposed that, returning home with her cousin, she stopped to do a bit of sparkin' by the gate, and so overheard the latter part of the quarrel. Yes;

she had swept up the foot-prints, and remarked at the time how small and slender they were.

Then they made Louis step out, and show his arched, haughty little foot, that part and parcel of his make-up was so perfectly formed; and the stamping cowhide-booted farmer-jury laughed sneeringly, and were glad in their secret hearts that they could count it down against him.

What between this testimony, and Pat's, which confirmed his mistress's, and the evidence of hangers-on at the Cereus, who corroborated Charley's deposition, the prosecution had things quite their own way.

All day long, Louis had held a half-formed resolution to send for Mollie, who most unwillingly yielded to his wish, and her parents' command, in staying away. He didn't know that she could help him, but he felt that he needed her presence. He hadn't given up hope; but his heart was growing very faint, and he could gain strength from her calm, earnest faith in him. When at length the Judge called for the defendant's witnesses, he rose to explain, and send for her, but at this moment the bent form of Deacon McCross presented itself beside him.

"Be you goin' to have Mollie on?" asked the old man in an anxious tone.

"Yes, sir," said Louis, "that is my intention."

"Don't," said the Deacon, earnestly. "I've always ben kind to you. I wouldn't ha' sworn what I did, ef Mirandy hadn't made me. Don't send for Mollie; think how Mirandy'll fly at her. She can't prove you didn't steal it, you know."

True, she couldn't prove that; Mrs. McCross knew better than any one else, better than Louis, what she could prove of intercepted letters, betrayed trusts, systematic plottings and deceptions; and the good lady watched the success of her little stratagem with no small anxiety. She had not to wait long. Her victim rose full of the generous impulse of youth, and answered firmly, " Except God, I have no witness of my innocence."

" Have you no defence," said the Judge, with pity in his professional voice.

And he answered, " I have nothing in these people's testimony to deny, except that I am a thief."

The evidence was slight, too slight it seems to me, though a lawyer of forty years' standing lately assured me that it was a very strong case. Any wise the jury had been industriously worked by Cabby, who was urged on by mean jealousy of an old rival, cupidity, and the hope of gaining a little practice by success, and made a willing tool in Mrs. McCross' hands. The defendant, poor—a mere stripling—estranged from the only friends on whom he could rely by right, had, we have seen, nothing to urge in denial. They brought in a hasty verdict of " guilty," and Judge Sistaire rose to pronounce the sentence, " Imprisonment for three years."

He was a man who " had been tender-hearted in this matter of punishment, but was used to it now." He felt many doubts about the matter; but there was no more light to be had, and the case had no contradictions; law was law, and this, after all, only business. Why! if he had every verdict to *his* satisfaction he wouldn't render a dozen decisions in a twelvemonth; he made fewer mistakes than any confrère in the State. But he said, afterward, that the mute agony in that young face was so terrible, that he would have given—well, the costs of the suit to reverse his decision. But it was too late.

When the words were spoken the court-room was very still. The whole mass of humanity turned toward the stripling justice condemned to suffer.

He put his hands before his face to shut out that terrible concentrated gaze. The air grew black and thick about him. He felt that he must shriek. In the effort to keep silence, the world receded from his grasp.

"Oh! Mollie! Mollie!" he cried, hoarsely, and then —and then they picked him up and brought him back to life with extremest care, to have opportunity to make good their sentence.

"'Tain't no use to send that feller to prison," remarked a rough-looking man to his companion. "Bless you, they hain't nothing for him to do; he can't never make shoes."

> "MILLVILLE JAIL, *September 30th.*
>
> "DEAR MOLLIE,—Our troubles are upon us, but we will not lose hope. I am sustained by your love. Don't visit me at Top Town. You would never forget me in thief's uniform, and my wife mustn't have such memories. Write as often as you can. *My* Mollie, I love you always, my faith, my hope, my wife.
>
> "LOUIS ALLWOOD."

She couldn't let him go so, and in spite of father and mother, came to the jail to see him before he was taken away. Poor children! They tried to console each other, but comfort died on their lips. There is no comfort, no mercy, for such as they.

CHAPTER XXI.

" Swim, swam, swum."

ILLVILLE was all excitement. There had been an overseer killed in the Penitentiary, and they had brought down the murderer to the county jail, and were going to hang him. Mrs. McCross and Mrs. and Mr. and Miss Hitchcock begged tickets for the show and got them; but Mrs. Williams bestirred herself too late, and had to buy her entrance like the rest of the jail-yard audience, while Payson took in the lesson from the crowded parapet of the neighboring bridge.

On the morning of the eventful day, Susy Jenkens— since Mrs. Hauxhurst, met Captain Slocum, and proceeded to unburden her heart touching the matter. He didn't seem to respond very freely, for a man of his known good-hearted, liberal views, and Squire Hitchcock joined the group.

" They abused the man; flogged him, kept him in solitary confinement till he was desperate. They maltreat the prisoners. The very brutes are kinder to each other than men," cried she, excitedly. " *They* never shut a fellow-animal up for the pleasure of deliberately torturing."

" I don't know about that," said the Captain, plunging his hands deep in his trouser pockets, and chewing a straw. " Our old cat had kittens the other day, and do you know, she ate one of 'em up."

" The fact is," seeing Susy look hurt at this application of natural history, " we mean to have prison-birds suffer. We put them there on purpose."

" But they don't try to make them better," said the

13

dear, simple girl; " they don't even teach them to read.
The men always grow worse.   It is a certainty."

She was actually shocked when Mr. Hitchcock rejoined,
" They ain't sent there to grow better.   You don't suppose
we honest folks mean to feed such truck on oyster soup
and mock-turtle?   We set out to have 'em wretched if we
can."

" And the system will never be altered, because it will
take time and money, and after-trouble; and honest
men won't be plagued when their enemies are so cheaply
and conveniently disposed of already," added Captain
Slocum, testily.   " Jerusalem crickets!   Why should
we?"

At this point both gentlemen looked uneasy and walked
away, and Mary McCross went by, meek and humble,
with her head down and her face averted.   The voices
had been loud; she must have heard every word.

.   .   .   .

A day or so afterward, Amos told his teacher that he
knew of two men that had died under the abuse at Top
Town, and two more made idiotic.   " Now, Miss Mollie,"
said he, " why don't they bring the warden down, and
hang him?"

.   .   .   .

The winter had been unexampled in severity.   The
frosts of November were followed by sleighing at Christmas; and the February snows piled themselves far above
fences and cow-sheds, from Maine to Massachusetts.
Now, in March, came a terrible storm, and then a sudden
thaw.   Down rushed the winter's accumulated drifts,
swelling brooks and rivers into flood, carrying away
bridges, and sweeping off cattle, and dams, and mills, in
one horrible destruction.   Of course no one had thought
it worth while to dyke Syllabub, though a scant rise of

Roaring River always laid it under water; and now pig-pens floated airily down stream, and people sailed out of their second-story windows if they could afford it, or starved quietly in garrets if they couldn't. The town hall was thrown open to those whose houses were quite untenable; and the Millville ladies gave blankets and clothing which were dutifully wasted; and the Goneeus-sets donated five hundred dollars' worth of soup to the sufferers—a fact publicly blazoned in the newspapers, and then assessed the sum privately on their workmen, which nobody knew anything about.

The whole town came out to admire the new Venice, and perhaps try a row through its submerged streets. The windows and stairways were crowded with women and children. Through the canals flashed the boat loads of excited inhabitants; carts piled with furniture and people ploughed their way laboriously about the shallower water; jests were thrown from skiff to skiff; and people, much fortified as to the inner man in consideration of the diluents without, abandoned themselves to hilarity. The saloons were crowded with drinkers, and every now and then rang forth a shout at the expense of some involuntary Baptist, or courageous swimmer and wader. Tired of waiting for help, young folk trusted themselves in extraordinary craft, and tubs, half barrels, and rafts floated wildly about. Half the young men emptied their pockets for flags, and the children continually stumbled into cellar-ways, and had to be fished out by their fond parents.

Amos, who wouldn't have been Amos if he hadn't owned a rickety boat, plied his oars all day for the penniless inhabitants, and took his pay out of Doppy's smiles, when after much urging she consented to be rowed over, "jest onct," for a bread-and-butter trip up-town, and a visit to Fir Covert.

Coming back with a singing, shouting load of work-men, his pleasant meditations were rudely interrupted, when, from a window above, Aleck Heffron turned a pan of cold water upon them. Aleck had grown into a slender, handsome fellow, rivalling Hugh in clog-dancing, and everywhere laughed at as the warm admirer of pretty faces, practical jokes, and—Aleck Heffron. He had rather worked away from the old place in the trio: pos-sessing neither Amos' steadiness, nor Hugh's unfailing good-humor; nor, perhaps, going on hand in hand in the upward-tending self-denials, that the boy puts on one by one as he matures into true manhood. Still he was one of "the fellows," and got well cursed for his prank accord-ingly.

"I was afeared ye might be forgettin' yer friends," was his tranquil reply.

"Ef I don't pay ye fur that, my name ain't Dennis," said Hugh, seizing a dipper floating by, and hastily de-taching a dead hen tied by a long string to the handle. "Leave me out, boys; I'm after him."

"It would even us wid 'em both, to row away," sug-gested the red-headed insurrectionist of Patience of Hope memory, who had now got half way through a black-smith's apprenticeship. Amos was not the man to refuse good advice.

As it happened, Mrs. Dennis had been visiting her friends, "a bit," and her son stood aghast to encounter her on the stairs. She instantly determined to save her quarter-passage money, and be carried home on Hugh's back. Accordingly she stayed only to tuck up her ample petticoats, and without waiting permission, precipitated herself on his shoulders. They were in the middle of the street before she remembered her bundle.

"The pertatees! Hughey Dinnis! left on the stairs, and not a sup of dinner can ye have without 'em."

But our good lady proved no light weight, and just then a mocking shout from the boat, with shrill whistles, and cries of "Crocodile," "Shoo-fly," "Hurrah for Woman's Rights," proved too much for equanimity.

"Stand still now, while I go back an' git 'em," said he, promptly dropping her to wade as she could, and rejoining his companions to receive a dozen offers of lodging on the spot.

With such jests, the light-hearted Hibernians beguiled the miseries of the situation; and Amos had for his next load the city missionary, who dispensed bread from Roaring River friends, and a new tract on Noah, written for the occasion by Mrs. Dr. Perfect, and published through the private subscription of her associates.

At night the scene became even more animated : lights flashed from the open windows of houses, in which every known instrument, from a jew's-harp to a bag-pipe, was put in requisition; and, without, tin horns and penny trumpets hooted in unison. The rum shops invested largely in cheap fire-works, and the street corners were hung with lanterns, to expose the otherwise unseen lamp-posts. The boats, no longer needed for business, carried parties of pleasure-seekers, who sang, or beat drums, or howled, as taste might incline; and their torches flared red upon the faces of the crew, and lit up the ripples of the black oily water, only to make succeeding darkness wilder, and every now and then, a party of gentlemen out to see the sport, or a policeman's barge, glided quietly onward.

The "Solomon Rodgers" stood a little apart from its neighboring houses, and though surrounded by water, was still habitable. Doppy, however, had accepted an invita-

tion to spend the night at Fir Covert; and Joe, after a
cruel beating with a rope's-end three days before, had
disappeared, no one knew where.

It was well on to twelve o'clock, but the two old men
still sat drinking in the dirty bar-room; less apparently
from enjoyment than lack of other occupation. The
dampness had soaked into the walls and air; the fire
smouldered in the stove; the smoky lamp on the counter
faintly discovered the sticky bottles and glasses, left from
the evening trade. Conversation flagged. Previously
drunk on whiskey, the pair had been sobering themselves
with lager, when Doppy's parent broke out:

"I'm an old man, Haverty, an' near the end. What
do you suppose will become of us when we die?"

"Whisth mon," said Joe's progenitor, taking a long
swig, and smacking his gray bushed lips thereafter.
"It's bad luck to 'mintion the thing."

"But I'm in airnest," persisted Mulligan, solemnly—
he was a little farther gone than his companion. "It's a
grraave question."

Thus pressed, Haverty said the "universal doctrine"
was good enough for him.

"No, no!" rejoined his friend with fervor. "Be you
willin' to go to heaven with Knox an' Brady, two d—n
scoundrels? I ain't."

"I'm willin' to take another pot o' beer," said Haverty,
waiving the subject.

"It's down on the stairs," responded Mulligan, rising.
"Come an' hold the light; we may's well make a night
on't."

The cellar was full of water, that ran in through its
open door, and all sorts of rotting débris had collected
there. The steps leading down were wet and slippery,
and the rays of Haverty's lamp feebly lit up the slimy

wall, and the horrible, noisome water beneath ; and you could hear the melancholy swish-swish of the waves against the building. "Come, hurry," said the man, yielding, in spite of his brutish obtuseness to impressions, to a compelling terror. "This hole is just right for murders. Look at those wandering glimmers a-top the current, and the black shapes floating like devils beyant. Hurry out o' here."

" Then take a holt," said Mulligan, below, selecting a cask from the half-dozen propped upon the stairs. " It's heavy enough to drag you to hell."

There be people who find prophecy and meaning in the utterances of the dying. Let such take note of these, for they were the last old Mulligan ever made. At that moment a gust of wind closed the door above, extinguishing the light, and his startled companion missed his footing, fell helplessly, striking first the wall, and then the man cumbered with his burden ; and both were precipitated into the flood.

.   .   .   .

A fortnight after, their blackened corpses were fished up from the cellar, as the flood subsided, and there being nothing left to bury them, Doppy's friends made up a subscription from their 'prentice earnings, and saw them decently interred with the unshriven in the corner Father O'Gorman allowed such at the cemetery,—and they had as fine a coverlid of thistles, in time, as the pious occupants of the Protestant establishment near by.

Amos comforted Doppy, saw to the funeral, and then hurried off to take counsel with Mollie. " It ain't no place to leave her in at the ' Rodgers ' alone," said he, after detailing the situation ; " and she won't go back on Joe, bad cess to her, and Joe's dcin' dreadful, and that makes it worse agin ; an', Miss McCross, I thought—" said he, in some embarrassment, "that is, I knew you wouldn't mind—" The anxiety he felt for success in his suit knotted up every muscle in his body.

"Well," said Mollie, encouragingly, as he clenched his large hands and turned his elbows inside out, and opened his mouth in gasps, "what would you advise me to do? I would be thankful to know your opinion. I want to provide for Doppy."

All Amos' contracted muscles relaxed, and his fine Irish gray eyes grew blue and alight with grateful feeling, as he straightened his tall form and answered, every whit manly:

"What I wish to say is, that I know of a respectable young couple as would move in and make it a dacent place, where Doppy could keep her old room, as she's set on; and would you speak to Mr. McCross to make the rint aisy for 'em, so they can afford it?"

The young lady's pale, weary face (it had grown sadly weary in the last few months) now brightened with pleasure. Amos' thoughtful care of his friend was a strength to her, who was forced everywhere to review the crooked, desolate, loathsome phases of life. "The 'Solomon Rodgers' is mine!" she cried, joyfully, "and the people can move in as soon as they like, and Joe shall have her garret as long as she needs it."

So Amos' new tenants, just six weeks married, took possession, and painted, and papered, and dressed the old-fashioned terraces with flowers, and hung the wainscoted, time-blackened bar-room with knick-knacks, making a sweet, pure home there. And Dorothea's "chances" widened and multiplied.

CHAPTER XXII.

" The north wind doth blow,
  And we shall have snow;
  What'll the robin do then?
    Poor thing!
  He'll sit in the barn,
  And keep himself warm,
  And hide his head under his wing,
    Poor thing."

AFTER all, winter could not forbear a final kick at Millville, and took advantage of the general wetness left by the freshet to bring on a parting storm. But this early May day the sun glanced mildly through the snow-laden firs that protected the Covert, and melted their white counterpane off the edge of the flower-beds in a quiet, determined way, that failed for once to rouse the pugnacious east wind.

Peace Pelican, equipped in high button-boots and ermines, hastily swung open the gate, and, without knocking, ran up to Mollie's room. She didn't find any one there, and so, leisurely pulled off her gloves and scarlet-plumed hat, laid them on the bed, unfastened her woolly jacket, drew an arm-chair near the cosey grate, took up the "Romance of a Mummy" lying open on the table, and settled herself to await her friend's coming.

This bed-room always seemed to me the ideal of a young lady's sanctum. Every detail partook of the individuality of its mistress. The parlors of a house must, perhaps, be sacrificed to family usage and French fashion. The once wide, hospitable hall, lined with settees and open-throated chimneys, hung with antlers, furs, and fowling-

13*

pieces, has assumed snaky proportions, and crawls dis-
mally through the house, deserted to hat-racks and foot-
men's chairs. The dining-room has fallen into the
clutches of servants and cut-glass decanters. But the
bed-room is the young lady's own. No alien hand should
dust its hundred knick-knacks, the invaluable accumula-
tion of years of friendship ; no flippant Abigail pry into
its old-fashioned albums and rose-scented boxes. The
dozen favorite volumes on the shelf,—Thomas à Kempis
or Colenso in the midst,—books gathered with great self-
denial and little pocket-money, how exactly they represent your intellectual life !

On the bureau stands the cut-glass vase, filled with the
one nicety of perfume your maidenly fancy prompts you
to set breathing from the folds of your garments, and
saluting the reader of your tinted billet-doux.

On the table is your orderly work-basket, furnished
with the pretty things mamma used when a girl. A few
pictures hang on the walls : some choice, some old-fashioned and faded,—grandmother's handiwork, perhaps ;
hunting-scenes, where plethoric squires in pinks pursue
long foxes, and bestride Suffolk Punches, neatly finished
with arched eyebrows and eyelashes.

The portfolio papa brought from Europe, the brackets
Cousin Dick carved when laid up with a sprain, the curious pebbles somebody picked up for you on the mountain the day you set the lunch-table, and he made so
many jokes you left the spoons behind, and had to go
back for them, and got wet in the shower ; the walking-
stick some one else carved with your name ; the pin-cush-
ions, mats, tidies, watch-pockets, and bits of water-color,
coming in Christmas after Christmas, have each a place in
this dear little sanctuary ; and so, in time, it comes to
pass that every familiar article has its own story written

all over it, and speaking lovingly to your memory, whenever your eyes fall thereon.

I never feel really acquainted with a woman till I have peeped into her bed-room. Says a certain man, who in his day, possessed a great reputation for wisdom: "Tell me with whom thou keepest company, and I will tell thee what thou art." But I have as good a dictum, "Let me glance into your sanctum, and I will tell you what you have been about all your life."

Mr. Haythorne, who dealt much in mystic lore, used to say that every room possessed an atmosphere, a spiritual influence, of its own. "For example," here he stroked his curling beard and glanced wickedly at Peace, "though I have never been in Miss Pelican's boudoir, I feel sure it is pervaded by a genius of uneasiness, a sense of things turned upside-down and inside-out; in short, a keen suggestiveness of the instability of human affairs."

"Hum," retorted Peace, pretending to finger thoughtfully her fluted apron, "I *have* been in your apartment; I found no manifest presence there except smoke."

Mollie's room was full of quiet restfulness, gentle repose. It was a place where one instinctively practised the amenities of social life, thought pleasant thoughts, felt kindly toward one's enemies, and arose strengthened for the battles of life It had a certain dignity, too, like Mollie's self, and rebellious spirits experienced a strong element of discord when they entered charged with a contrary animus.

Its furniture possessed so many histories that Peace once told its mistress she believed she had gotten everything in it out of her friends.

On the wall, in a dainty frame of Louis' workmanship, hung the butterflies the two had snared and studied together. There had been a pair of cases, but the other was

gone, and its place filled by a little crayon sketch of the
first Christmas Eve, with the initials " L. A." faintly
traced in the corner.

The half dozen volumes satisfying most young girls expanded into a well-chosen library, with a whole shelf of
controversial and meditative religious works, and sundry
leather-bound scrap-books, labelled " Egmont," " Hints
about the Aryan Race," "Genera and Local Species of
the Bombycidæ," " Herbarium of Local Ferns," and a
complete translation of " Count Monte Christo," sometimes in Louis' handwriting, sometimes Mollie's. All
the books were full of Louis. There were the German
Fairy Tales he delighted in ; the Merivale, and Froude,
and Lamartine they had conscientiously " done " together,
—the old poetry they had enjoyed—he always went for
a glass of water just before they reached the unpleasant
part, and so passed them by. Beside these, there stood
" John Halifax," that sweetest of life stories ; and another
tale or two of kindred worth : " Hypatia," " Barbara's
History," " Mary Barton," " Adam Bede," and certain
romances by a pleasant-tongued baroness of difficult name,
who makes Munich, Tyrol, and Innspruck history the
delightful property of such few Americans as nowadays
stay at home.

Mollie was no " amateur " musician, but she could sing
a simple ballad in a clear voice, and her dainty inlaid
guitar (Louis had taught her to play it) stood in one corner
of the room ; an aquarium and fernery rivalled each other
in the deep window-seat ; while on either side the casement
hung the cages of Poppy and a little Java sparrow Louis
had brought Mollie one day, because, he said, it made
him think of her ; its coat was so modest, and its bill as
red as her lips.

Peace sat some time refreshing her stately self before

she became conscious that her hostess had entered the room. In fact she did not find it out at all, until she heard a little cry, more a gasp than an articulate sound, from the sewing chair over by the garden window. She turned around enough to see her friend, white as the snow, with an open letter in her hand, and then wisely looked back to the fire, and said nothing. Half an hour passed—an hour—two hours—Mollie so intently thinking, that she did not hear the rustle of the leaves regularly turned by the reader in the arm-chair.

By and by she rose from her seat, put the epistle away among her papers quietly, and with care—Mollie never did untidy things; then seeing Peace for the first time, greeted her lovingly, and proceeded to make her welcome. If her cheeks were pale, and her eyes weary with secret tears, it was nothing new; whatever fresh trouble had befallen her, found no expression in word or manner. She drew towards her the basket wherein she kept the Patience of Hope sewing work, lit one of the wax candles held by the bronze griffins on the mantel-piece, selected Maggie O'Hara's dress, and began to rip out and hem down and baste together as if it was the only important thing to be done. She was right; for every accustomed anxiety has a certain thick atmosphere of its own, wherein all flame grows dim, no matter if the torch be fed with suffering or joy.

Conversation proceeded as usual between these friends. Peace usually talked, and Mollie listened; or else they argued like athletes, for pleasure of trying their strength: they were too good lovers to desire to convert each other. Peace, though often unhappy in these days, was always witty; but this afternoon her glee was genuine. Mrs. Pelican, whose comfort with Louis had been too great to forego willingly, had not long since given his place to

Francis Haythorne, and her daughter made it her chief good to torment him. That very morning he had been confronted with a curl of his own auburn hair, and his modest daintiness was annoyed beyond expression, the more that he couldn't tell how she came by it.

"Here it is," quoth the young lady, drawing a fiery ringlet, neatly tied with a blue ribbon, from her port-monnaie, "I have saved every hair I found on his coat for six months, and he thinks I must have cut it from his head behind, where he can't see it. I nearly died to watch him feel secretly for the place. I told him, if he hadn't left the ' Rape of the Lock ' in the parlor, I should never have thought of it.

"He said I had taken an ungenerous advantage of him, and wished, with Burns, people had gift to see themselves as others saw them. Then, to calm him, I repeated a little story I heard of him the other day. I said, ' Frankie, sweet, do you remember the prayer-meeting you led when an infant ? ' and seeing by his disgusted look he did, I went on in a soothing voice, ' And how, when all the good little boys were on their knees praying that the last-comer might have a new heart, and he laughed, you got mad and jumped up, and said, " Pitch him out of the window ? You were a darling innocent, but you should keep your little tempers better, Frankie ; ' " and this made him so indignant that he ran out of the room and banged the door."

Mollie could not forbear a smile at the maliciously beautiful face gleaming at her from the arm-chair, even if Francis Haythorne's flaunted metaphysics, and extreme fastidiousness in personals, had not rendered story and prank alike ridiculous.

"I make it my business to spread a Procustes' couch for him, I assure you," continued Miss Pelican. "I am going to present the curl to you ; I want to tell him that you have it in your Bible, the place where you keep your chief treasures. That will tease him more than anything else. I shall say I saw it put there myself."

Mollie did not answer ; she was gazing sadly off at some far-away thought or memory, and Peace, unforbidden, got down the large brown volume, much tattered from constant use, and carefully hid the stiff but perfumed ringlet among its leaves. She turned the pages a little to see the book-marks and pressed daisies that crowded the ancient mausoleum, and then laid it away with a satisfied sigh. "Come," said she, "the supper bell rang a long time ago."

Deacon McCross went softly and prayed long as usual, and his lady was not less tediously aggravating. She asked Peace if she had missed anything during Mr. Allwood's sojourn at her father's ; said she had lost two forks and a teaspoon, and for her part preferred silver that she had bought and paid for with her own money, to the same come back in poll parrots and what not : from whence we may rightly conclude that Poppy still flourished. Nothing but the look of acute torture on Mollie's face could have restrained Peace, who could despise a man in prosperous folly, for whom she would venture her life in impulsive championship five minutes after fate bowled him down. She instantly announced her intention of calling on the convict, as it was, and snippily asked if she could not bear him some message. Whereupon Mrs. McCross solemnly warned her to beware of evil companionship, and added that she had always regretted taking her husband's ward into the house, though she supposed it was charity—she thought he had tried to poison Mollie's mind. But even to this, her daughter said not one word.

Peace wondered how she could sit so marble-like and bear it—was almost ready to blame her as cold-hearted, when she herself thrilled in every nerve to her very finger tips with sympathetic pain. But she failed to consider that a life's training in such a school will teach calmness to the most ungoverned. Only once Mollie's heart got the better.

"Did I ever tell you about the raspberries?" said Mrs. McCross, looking over at Peace, who said "no," rather unwillingly.

"It was when he first came here," began she, rising, partly to cut the bread on the trencher, partly for greater freedom of gesticulation; "and I don't suppose the child knew much better. I spent all my time while he was under my care, trying to teach him manners. Mollie was so fond of raspberries, and one day she came running up to me, and said she was going to pick herself some for supper. She wa'n't bigger than a pint of cider, and she scratched her tender little arms, and burnt her face, but sure enough at tea-time she had her saucer heaping. What do you suppose the critter does but lick the whole of 'em up; never so much as said by your leave, ma'am; and Mollie, poor child, sat looking on with her red lips puckered ready to cry, and didn't dare say a word."

There can scarcely be anything more painful to a generous mind, than to hear one's self unjustly described as the victim of our loved.

Mrs. McCross had miscalculated her daughter's endurance. Mollie lifted her eyes from the tea-cup, in which she had been watching the floating cream, with every muscle contracted. "It is equally to your credit to remember and to tell of it," darted she, in those clear *white* tones that belong to the intensest anger.

Thereat Mrs. McCross lost not a moment in bursting

into tears, and refused to be comforted. She wasn't loved—wasn't even allowed to tell a harmless anecdote at her own table. She had better not live any longer. Her health was poor; she would soon be gone, and then she hoped they'd forgive a poor old woman, in that she liked a good story, and perhaps told it too often.

The Deacon, who had been eating potatoes with his knife, in an absently uncomfortable silence, the whole meal-time, now pushed back his chair, and hastily buried himself in the "Millville Universe."

Peace followed Mollie to the library, where she had hidden herself behind the dun curtains, and stood with heaving breast—for the moment beside herself; but she came out as her friend entered, her calmness regained by mighty effort.

Acceding to Peace's pacific request for cribbage, she brought candles, table, and the board—delicately painted by Louis—and sat down to play.

"Mother," said she, presently, "I was rude to you; I beg your pardon."

The weeping figure in the corner heaved a deep sigh. "You needn't say anything, my daughter," said she, in a plaintive little voice. "It's rather hard, I know; but only the treatment an old, sick woman must expect. Don't trouble yourself about it. I'll forget it by and by."

What was there to do, but beg her forgiveness over and over again, and kiss away her tears? In time patient quietude was restored, and the game begun. The Deacon laid down his paper, and eyed the players longingly, but dared not offer to join.

"Tantæne animis cœlestibus iræ?" Mrs. McCross was now a champion of morality. She sat back in her rocking-chair, and, consumed with pious horror, fired off pas-

sages of Holy Writ at the players, both pertinent and
pointed.

"It is sport for a fool to do mischief;" "As a jewel of
gold in a swine's snout, so is a fair woman without
discretion."

"Pooh! I know the original Greek," said Peace, resolved to keep sunny: "Inmudeelsis; inpinepitchis;
inclaynoneis."

"You would do well to bear in mind the translation,"
retorted Mrs. McCross, in a solemn voice. "And whoever
adds anything to this book, unto him shall be added all
the plagues that are written in this book."

"Exactly!" Peace rose as she spoke, and brushed
the cards together on the table. "I'm going up-stairs.
Good-night, Deacon McCross; I wish you a deep sleep."

The young girls had reached the upper hall, when
Mollie paused to adjust the candle in its socket. "I
knew your penchant for 'room enough to swing a cat in,'"
said she smiling; "so I have had the green chamber
warmed. I am sorry Tabby reposes under her bed of
catnip; but a few friends still keen for her at the favorite
spot; you can lie in wait for one, if you're particular."
She was still merry, and laughing with resolved cheerful-
ness, firm as fate, when she bade her friend a soft happy
dreams, and entered her own room.

Miss Pelican lay awake a long time, chafing over her
doubles' hardships, and, looking through her open door
(fear of being burned in her bed was her hobby), knew
by the shining crack of light opposite that Mollie had
not gone to rest. She thought her ear caught a noise at
intervals, as if some one was talking rapidly in a low
voice, and dozing off, heard the clock strike two, and
came to herself enough to notice again the same rapid
speech, a little louder, sharper, and more eager, now,

than before. Too nervous to lie still, she threw a shawl over her shoulders, and entered the familiar room. It's mistress sat quietly by her bed—her hat and cloak on, reading the afternoon's letter. "I'm married," said she with a meaningless laugh. "Here are the certificates; you'd better take them, to keep father from feeling bad."

"Mollie! What have you done? what do you mean?" cried Peace.

"My name isn't Mollie," said the girl; "corpses don't have names. They say the body of Mr. So-and-so. I'm a corpse; just stand me up in the corner of the room, and see what a nice-looking one I'll make. When they come to the funeral to-morrow, have me stood up; I don't think I should look so well laid out. And be sure you hide all mother's handkerchiefs but one. If you don't, she'll cry too much, and have no time for instructive sentiment. I think a great deal of correct sentiment, applied on a plaster. Mother always makes moral reflections at funerals, and eats too much at weddings. She always goes munch! munch! munch! She's eaten up Louis' dinner; but I don't care, for by and by he'll be a corpse and stand up in the corner like me, and then it won't make any difference. O, mother's crying! tears, idle tears, crocodile tears.

"' How doth the little crocodile improve his shining tail,
   And pour the waters of the Nile o'er every golden scale!'"

Now give me two nuts for infant piety, or you're scaley."

Mrs. McCross, attracted by Peace's call of alarm, was now fainting correctly on a chair, and her husband distractedly applied an asafœtida pill to her nose, but without result.

"Pooh!" said the girl with a scornful laugh; "she isn't going to revive, not she! She's up here to eat me, because I'm a corpse. She gnaws father and me every day; it makes his hair fall out."

And then came Peace with Dr. Jenkens, who nodded grimly, and talked of "long confinement, overtaxed nerves, brain-fever, insanity."

CHAPTER XXIII.

" Ding-dong bell,
    Pussy's in the well."

WHEN Louis first went into that stony benevolent institution, provided by Christian charity to the cure of diseased souls, he felt only two things,—the injustice of his sentence, and the loss of his good name. He was so swallowed up in these, that it was only by slow degrees he awoke to the present miseries of his situation. He kept saying over and over to himself, "I have a claim to my liberty. I am no thief; I am an honest man. They have no right to imprison me." But, as the warden observed when he entered, "Look a here: you say you're innocent; mebbe you be. They're all innocent in there." Then this philanthropist went on thus: "See that door? you're goin' in there now, and I tell you what, you'd better mind yourself. If you do as you're told, you'll get along. If you don't, we'll kill you. God Himself can't help that." After this he spat on the floor, flourished his cane, and the audience was ended. Being a sensitive, high-strung gentleman, Louis never forgot his salutatory, but added it to a fast increasing tale of realities that separated him from Mary.

" Mary," was the first and last thought haunting him. What would become of her? Would she pine for him? He hoped she would, but soon felt that this could not be. Mollie grieving over a thief? Impossible! His name was forever branded with the stain. Didn't Mrs. McCross insist him to be one? Wasn't she a pious woman? Didn't she have a voice in choosing the minister? Wasn't she strong on the doctrines, and the higher life? What was his—Louis Allwood's—rush-light, beside the brilliance of this wax-candle of the Lord? What if Mollie was faithful; he knew her true as truth. Wouldn't it be her duty to forget him? Mollie always tried to do her duty. That was something else to put down to the credit of religion. Having robbed him of his good name, it took his love also. He felt thankful he had always kept out of it.

After this came a reaction. Mollie was right. Wouldn't he do the same in her place? He pictured to himself a woman, false, vicious, drunken, and strove to invest her with his love's image, and loathed the hideous thing he fancied. " That's her feeling toward me," he said.

Now for her sake whom he loved, he analyzed his emotions toward the wretched creatures about him. His whole nature shrank from them. He abhorred their sly, sensual faces; observed with fear their animal, malformed jaws, bleared eyes, slouched forms, and told himself, " I'm one of them."

In due time he would have lost all shame, and learned to look with brazen face at the world; but one thing saved him, and that kept alive his misery—his love never died, though his self-respect fell away like shrivelled leaves from trees at autumn. For Mollie's sake, all the world stung him looking through her eyes. He hated mankind; but every stranger who came to view what,

in the bitterness of his heart, he called the human men-
agerie, caused him fresh torture. He never glanced up;
no need. He felt their cruel eyes blasting his soul.
"Some day Mary will look on me with just such
thoughts," was the ever present feeling.

Such brooding soon suggested an idea which he hesitated long ere putting in execution. His mind was made
up that his life was ruined, and he was not hasty in this
judgment. His friends had all deserted him. Not one
message had cheered his loneliness. The Pelicans he had
served so faithfully, the frequenters of the sample-room
his gentlemanly ways had rendered so popular, the Millville acquaintances—none came near him. "Mollie," he
continually said to himself, "must be either wishing and
afraid to ask a release, or else had begun to share misfortunes to which he saw no end. He knew the Deacon
and his wife well—didn't need to speculate about the poor
girl's sufferings. If the one belief caused pain, the other
awakened all the tender unselfishness that is the very
essential of love. He resolved to set her free. Then for
many noontimes and bits of evenings he sat down to the
sad task of cutting away the only interests misfortune
had not stripped from him, to arise again with the labor
unperformed. Sometimes misery ate up the cords of his
will, and he fell back into intense craving for her affection. Then, stung by thought of the sorrows in store for
whoever shared his fate, and shame for his own cowardice that would sacrifice her for his comfort, he tried to
write what would end all, and make him homeless and
alone forever.

Nerved to do this, new difficulties appeared. How
could he induce Mollie to grant his request? Would not
her love hold her to him? or if not her love, at least
her sympathy? His very troubles would only make her

the more his. His heart told him so. For a whole month he took refuge in, gloated over, the idea. She would not let him go; he had no right to ask it; it did not lie with him. He need not tear out his one life hope.

But conscience soon arose and shattered the delusion. Was he not charged with the care of the gentle girl who had confided herself to him? Was he not to cherish and protect? Should he permit her to sacrifice herself? Small love in that. No, he must accomplish the separation, force her to it. If she suffered it would only be to save from greater suffering.

So one day, his heart full of love and agony, he penned the letter, weighing every sentence that the pain might be the least possible, and yet the words of due effect. Since this one did not please, the next noon he wrote another, and then another, till he presently saw that he took comfort in thus putting off the dreadful day, and so finished the last in bitterness and haste, much more cold than the former ones, and, not trusting himself to read it over, lest he should draw back, he sent it.

No sooner was the missive gone, than he would have given worlds could it have been recalled.

Miss Mollie McCross:

My Dear Friend :—I have been thinking for a long time that our promises ought never to be fulfilled. My circumstances have altered, and much more my plans and views of life. Your family would never consent to our marriage, even if I asked it; but for many reasons I do not. Let me make you free, and for God's sake forgive the pain you have suffered at my hands.

Louis Allwood, convicted thief.
Top Town Penitentiary, *May 1st*, 18—

Louis waited his answer with a wish that may seem strange to us, people out of prison. Not only did he long to set his gnawing anxiety at rest, but he felt a childish longing to touch something that came from the world. He debated if the paper it would be written upon would turn out square or old-fashioned, pink or lavender; and hoped it would be thick and white. He would like the last missive from his vanishing love to be untinged with foreign color.

But no word reached him. Alternately he argued good and ill from this, and failed not to torture himself with the idea that she despised him, had cast him off out of her thoughts, was only insulted by that heartless letter. He felt that her respect was justly forfeit, but somehow failed to find comfort in the complete success of his note.

Then he got a new idea; he had wounded her too much, should have permitted her to wean herself gradually, and when strong enough demand her own dismissal; or if not, perhaps she was sick. At this all his love took a new channel. He forgot that she was nothing to him— only knew that he could not see, help, watch over her. Here, caged, immured alive, he could afford no aid, could not even beg forgiveness for what he had made her suffer. It seemed little enough once; most people would not have counted it anything; but now it piled mountains high. He wearied himself with frantic longings, desires, petitions, to a God he understood not.

To this was soon added a new pang. We hear of those old torture-chambers that contracted daily. Every morning the prisoner awoke to find the roof a little nearer his breast, every night lay down in a more straitened place, until at last the relentless pressure acted on a mass of broken flesh.

When Louis entered his cell, he possessed a mind limited only by the universe; and that mind was bound to a body exquisitely sensitive. What became irksome to some, was absolute misery to him. He used to long for a breath of free-meadow sunlight with such intensity, that the wish became a physical pang. He would stand by his grating at night and press upon it with a blind force that reacted against himself, and made him frantic. He was a prisoner. Oh, the untold misery of the thought! Without the sky smiled in one great happiness, the very reflex of God's face. One by one the well-remembered flowers came into bloom. Little by little the leaves took their fiery coloring, and the woods lived their familiar round of pleasant nature-story. Oh, for a single half-hour to feel the throb of nature's great heart in the woodlands, in the fields, anywhere, where he could forget his humanity, and be at rest. But no : day by day his soul horizon contracted ; he felt the narrow walls of his cell shutting off his mind's outlook. His thoughts no longer fled over the world. They all centred within the limits of the prison, the overseer's frown, the denied meal, the weary day's work, and worst of all himself.

In this God-ordained detenus there was chapel every Sunday morning. Once from among the representatives of Christ's law and mercy on the platform, a gentleman, high in the honors of the State, stood forth to address the convicts.

"Men," said he, playing with the massive chain that adorned his breast, and gazing from stainless broadcloth upon the purposely hideous garb of his audience—" Men, you're here, and I'm glad of it. You've done wrong, you are suffering for it. You ought to suffer." His voice, the living breath of the stony chapel, rang out harshly, his shaggy, gray-knotted eyebrows wore a frown.

14

Looking on the penniless, he fingered his golden ornaments. Respectability was come to reform humanity.
"Every man who suffers," said he, "earns his own suffering. If I have sent some of you here I count it a good
deed. If you don't want to suffer, don't do wrong."
The modern Christ sat down, and his listeners, under the
warden's eye, clapped applause. Among their sullen
faces were some flushed with powerless anger, but in such
the wound soon healed. Louis was not one of these.
"Every man earns his own suffering." He never forgot
that. He began to search his life for the causes of his
misfortunes, and finding sin in plenty, his heart to note
the origin of that sin. The more we know of a man's
soul, the more cordially we can despise, abhor him, upon
occasion. All Louis' abhorrence of his fellows never
began to equal his loathing for himself. Once commenced,
this self-laceration grew into a mania. His thoughts,
memories, sensations, were ransacked to add fuel to his
torment. His life seemed to him to have been only a
tissue of wasted opportunity, abused privilege, and petty
crime. He studied faithfully the prison Bible, to observe
that every leaf teemed with maledictions. He wished
to escape from his own existence, but he was shut in with
himself. Formerly, too, he had desired to die, but now
he feared the very thought. Prison life was doing its
work. Poor fellow, he seldom dreamed of Mollie any
more; her memory was the contrasted light to make his
darkness blacker. He hated, in the intervals of his self-
torture, his cell, his workshop. He knew every nook
and cranny in their bare walls. His artist-soul detested
their ugliness. He envied his neighbor's red and yellow
tissue paper, and began to calculate how it could be stolen.
Reflecting on the sin of this, he became convinced he was
losing all his principle. The unvarying routine of life,

made purposely of the utmost possible blankness, maddened him. He craved excitement. Once he found himself examining his tools to see if one of them could not
be made to plunge into the overseer's heart. He even
filed a little on the knife. Presently he saw two white
doves flitting about the prison-yard, and remembered
Mollie with her birds flying about her. As her face came
sorrowfully before him, the horrid thought passed out of
his heart. He went to the overseer and told him he
feared he was going mad, showed him the knife, and
begged for a few minutes' relief—only a little walk about
the garden—anything to take the leaden pressure from
his soul. The man laughed in his face. "You aren't
going mad, but I'll tell you where you are going—into
the dark cells, for injuring the prison property. I'd like
to know what you mean, filin' shoe-knives! I've got a
man a dozen for less 'n that."

Somehow this didn't mend matters. The prisoner's
mind grew heavy, his motions sluggish. He feared his
intellect was broken, and begged for books, but they
were useless. In the depth of his misfortunes, the fancied sorrows of fancied heroes, or the half-told woes of
real ones, seemed alike shallow.

Then began a race against time, a fight against idiocy.
He forced himself to perform difficult operations in mathematics, to invent stories, to remember history. But
how could added labor bring health to the weary brain?

He was a shadow in thinness. His pulse ran high and
unevenly; he couldn't sleep; every nerve was a separate
source of pain. The rough ways of the prison employés
jarred him, their profanity disgusted, their frequent exhibitions of brute power made him sick at soul. Louis
was, we say it again, in a model prison. You could
march a regiment through any of its workshops, and not

a man would look up. They made more money for the State, and enriched more contractors, than any similar number of convicts in the Union. And it was all accomplished neatly, too; with green peas, and strawberries, and the Dorsey (God bless it) dinner, every whit noticed in the Top Town papers. They neither poured gallons of ice-water over strangling men, as in Auburn, nor made their subjects idiotic by compression of the brain, as at Sing-Sing. They hung morality on the three tails of a cat, and reformed carnal vices by a diet of nothing.

Louis was too obedient to suffer unusually, but next to him worked a red-headed, red-eyed Irishman, whose face alone must have condemned him before an intelligent jury. On this young villain fell the weight of prison discipline. Sometimes, about once a year, a man killed himself in these retreats for soul elevation. Louis wished this fellow would; but no—it seemed he preferred to be killed.

But what is the use of thus chronicling his misery? Wasn't Louis sentenced for crime, and sent to the Top Town Penitentiary on purpose to suffer? and doesn't every other prisoner carry such a load? and isn't it according to one of God's own Bible precepts, that we should button up our pockets, and build the prisons in chills-and-fever marshes, where property is low? and sensible—humbly sensible, as we all announce ourselves at prayer-meeting —of our personal helplessness in the matter of any good work, hasten to get these souls back into the hands of their Maker with all speed?

Matters were just here, when Louis felt himself pointed out by a visitor. "That fellow is dying," said the gentleman. "He won't live two months."

His listener was glad. "Hell," said he, "is the life I lead, with this difference—ten-cent visitors are not admitted in hell."

CHAPTER XXIV.

" I'll give to you the key of my heart,
That we may love and never part."

ITH the first gleam of returning reason, came the thought of Louis; and as Mollie lay upon her bed, her mind laboring in the wearing treadmill of thought, she reasoned it all out again and again. Intense, sensitive, tenacious, she was essentially an out-going, not an in-gathering woman, and everywhere met by hurts, she had unconsciously learned to conceal herself from the world, in an outwardly calm, almost passionless, exterior. To no one, not even Louis, was she her real self; and Peace, who loved her best of all women, said she felt as if Mollie was in strata—every one different, and the temperature gradually increasing.

Accordingly, though she read Louis' letter backward to its cause, with unerring precision, she suffered the more for this very thing. To her, the bungling note spoke love, constancy, and misery unfathomable. There is a certain comfort in one's own pain. One can then always say, "Come, and behold how wretched I am." But Mollie never remembered herself at all. After she parted from Louis at the jail, that dreary day, her outward existence became a dream. Her actual life was all within, an imagined, and yet terribly real one, with him its centre. Nor had this very subtilty of pain a slight cause for being. Mollie had not taught in mission-school, and failed to learn the ways and abuses of our penal institutions, and a woman's imagination needs not the spur of affection to set it at work. She knew of shower-baths, iron-crowns, starving, balls and chains, beating with paddles, deprivation of light, practised in the soft retirement of American reformatories. She had heard sickening tales of cruelty on one side, and passive endurance on the other, from an old guard who had served in them. He boasted of prison brutality and his tender heart in the same breath. Let us do him justice—he was oftener an observer than an actor in such scenes. Mollie's ignorant and untaught boys had passed into the horrible arena, and she shuddered and suffered. Now her lover was the victim. By night she dreamed of tortures unendurable, and woke to set uncertainty at battle with fear. By day she panted in his stifling cell. She could not eat, because he might be starved. Her time divided itself into the prison hours. She shrank from human touch or speech, because he could not touch his fellow or speak. She loathed the world for his sake, who was cut off from it; obeyed the wishes of her friends without comment, and became more self-devouring within, but inert and deathlike without, every day. He had been growing into her life, ever since he came to her father's house, a gentle, silent child, given to lonely pleasures, absorbed in the books and music Mrs. McCross dared not deny her husband's ward. Mollie had shyly proffered companionship in his pursuits, and worshipped his idols afar off. He, in turn, found his butterflies gayer, his Mendelssohn more tender, with her to share. Louis interpreted other authors, but Seraphael was too twin-natured to him, to be anything but his voice. Later, he translated Homer into Scotch ballad meter, because she loved to listen, and read Plato into English a little too delicate to be earnest, to an absorbed critic. She pushed him into Euclid and higher mathematics, because he was ashamed to be beaten with a man's weapons, and yet admired her for his defeat.

So they had triumphed and suffered together, and grown into harmony of life, if not oneness of aim—Mollie, rich in her father's love, bestowing pity, admiration, and affection, all at once; Louis, finding his needs of companionship, satisfied to the uttermost in her.

As a child, he played with her. It is chronicled that the Deacon once saved her from an untimely end, having found her buried up to her neck in a pit, her yellow hair streaming over the ground, her calm eyes fixed on Louis with implicit confidence. Louis, who was in the act of putting the final shovelfuls of earth over her, *à la* some savage funeral rite which filled his imagination. As a boy, he worshipped her; as a man, he trusted her.

When the Deacon declared his ward's property lost by failure of investments, no one cared to question; and by and by Louis went to work to earn his bread, and a little over, if he could, for Mollie. For, as we know, it had become the great joy of this simple pair, alike unfellowed by the world, that they possessed each other.

Now, when one of these interwoven lives was full of agony, what marvel that the other reciprocated every pang?

About a month after this refinement of suffering had commenced, Mr. Growing brought religion to give Mollie strength to bear longer. He was going to call on Louis. Would she send a little token that he could turn over and over every day?

She thanked him. She would try to think of something. Would he want it to-morrow?

No! not so soon; but she could send it any time. He rose to go. She followed him to the door, mechanically, and stood leaning against the frame. Instead of going out, he turned and examined her wasted face. Its weary, pained expression wrung his heart. She looked unearthly in the twilight.

Fred Growing was a real pastor, who took up and carried every one's burden by instinct. He could not leave this sufferer without attempting aid.

"Mollie," he said in his pleading tones, "you were the first lamb God gave to my flock. Do you remember how you entered my study timidly, and told me you thought you could trust yourself in His hands?"

"Yes," she answered, wishing he would cease to speak of things whose meaning had become far off in her great sorrow.

"And you have forgotten how you came afterward, and said you began to understand the way God suffers daily for us?"

"No! Louis walked up with me that night, and stood outside playing with the lilac blossoms, while I talked to you. *My* Louis," she continued, with a passion in vivid contrast to her former lifeless expression—"my Louis, whom they have wickedly taken away from all the beautiful things he loved."

"This is Christian," said Mr. Growing, gently. "You trust your lover among the lilac blossoms, and are afraid to deliver him to Christ's keeping."

The quiet thrust went home, for Mollie was conscientious as earnest. She tried after this to believe more and grieve less, and so kept up till the letter arrived. But when she read that misery-begotten note, she felt that the worst had come to pass: he had given up hope. "They have murdered him," thought she; "God, let us die."

But she didn't die, and now as she lay feebly reflecting upon her lover's case, the thought entered her half-crazed brain, that they two had been marked out to suffer. Some people were. After they had borne enough, they would endure one more pang, and through it be rid of life, and all it was a name for.

She remembered a dreary saying, that in happier times she had laughed at with Louis : " Let this be my comfort, to be willing to lack all human comfort."

Sometimes she tried vaguely to make it her own, and sometimes strove to drive it from her. In either case it was ever-present—all-powerful. At last she gave up the struggle, and settled down to it as a fact. And religion came to proclaim patience under it a duty as God's will; and so, even in this bitter way, his right hand upheld her in the darkness.

She had scarcely become able to sit up a few minutes at a time, when she received a visit of importance from her father. Not that he seldom came; on the contrary, when she was delirious he would steal to her bedside, and pretend to scan the localisms of the " Universe," while his poor old eyes were filled with tears as he listened to her wandering talk. After her reason returned, he used to bring little bouquets, and lay them wistfully on her pillow; and when she grew stronger, he ransacked the town for poetry he fancied she liked, and read it in a high, cracked voice, whose gentle quaver spoke a world of love and sorrow not set down in the pages rendered.

Mollie, even when her heart was sorest, never blamed *him* for her troubles. She shut such a thought resolutely out of her mind. " He couldn't help it, poor father," was her excuse ; and she forgave and loved, and was gentler, sweeter, and more tender to him than ever.

But this time he entered with no cheerful alacrity,— rather as if impelled by some unseen, malevolent force. He sat down by her guiltily, and gave an uneasy glance around, especially at the tight-shut-door. Then he spread his red-silk handkerchief on the knees of his black pants, and, smoothing the thin gray hair over his bald crown, began deprecatingly :

14*

"I'm an old man, Mollie, and your mother is a trifle set, you know—"

The girl felt some new trouble coming. She was so learned in the ins and outs of his abused, weak heart, she had forgiven and pitied and grieved for him so long, she suffered with instinctive fear of his next words. Yet she strengthened herself to view the case from his standpoint, and to forget her own in his interest. So she laid her hand feebly on his tremulous fingers, because he loved the little caress. "Go on, father," said she, as brightly as she could.

"I know it's a hard thing to ask," he averred, protestingly; "but your mother's feelings are strong. She, —did you know she was quite sick?" said he, coming to a full stop, and giving an uneasy twist beneath his daughter's solemn gaze.

"Go on, papa, dear," said Mollie, blanching about the lips, but even then rallying a little more firmness. "Go on, please."

"I don't like to ask you, but I want to end my days in peace and quietness," reiterated he, beseechingly. He took up the red 'kerchief and wiped the beaded drops from his bald forehead. "I'm a peaceable man, daughter."

"I know it," said she, faintly as a whisper now—her heart sinking lower at every halt.

"You are a good girl, Mollie," he began again, gaining courage as hers fled. "You never said anything to me about the burglary, though I know it has fretted you sorely. It wasn't right, no way; but your mother and young Brown patched it up between them. I only swore truth, and paid the law bill. I only swore truth, Mollie."

She assented after a long pause, in which he watched her face wistfully. He was waiting, eager and agitated,

but she could not bring herself to speak. She had forgiven, but her heart was still sore. Her father felt her
thought, and got up, and wandered nervously about the
room, threw open the shutters and arranged the curtains,
looked at the garden, with his tremulous fingers crossed
behind him. A well-known step was audible below,—a
step whose vigor ill-health had never subdued, though it
sometimes dragged it a little. When the Deacon heard the
ominous sound, he came back to the bed, and took up the
hand Mollie had not moved since he laid it on the quilt.
But the caress was only the mute rendering of a petition,
not a motion of sympathy or love.

"I don't want you to give him up, my child; he is a
good lad enough. But could you promise not to meet
him, or have anything to do with him, while I am alive?
Your mother takes it to heart dreadfully; she talks by
day and night of it. You have a duty to your mother,
child."

Mollie was still silent; she had no words to reply. A
sense of unbearable wrong rose within her. Was all,
even to the very affection she felt for her father, to be
made her curse? for at the moment it seemed that everything that separated her from her lover was a curse.
She drew her fingers away from the hand that would
have held them, and pushed them aimlessly over the coverlid.

"I can't, father; don't ask me!" she cried, hoarsely.
The little gesture brought a look of pain to his wrinkled
face.

"I hadn't orter ask you; but I'm breakin' down purty
fast. I shouldn't keep you waitin' long. I've ben thinkin' I'd wish to get breath like this side the grave."

The woman watched him patiently. It was so. It
wouldn't be long. Lying there with every pulse-beat a

throb of pain, days, even years, or existence itself, seemed of little worth. Once she had dreaded suffering, as he did. But now, when her life was planned upon a chart chequered only by pain, should she let him suffer too? Once she had longed for rest. She and Louis were not to have any in this world, perhaps. What would be a little more trouble to bear? It was her duty. Her father should not be tormented for her; now he had no peace. The first sounds that greeted returning reason were those torturing pathetic tones rising higher and higher in endless argument and fault-finding. Poor father, she was stronger than he—to suffer. She and Louis must have faith in each other a little longer, that was all. She opened her weary eyes, and turned them lovingly upon the face held toward her with almost childish trust. Was it weakness or strength that made her whisper,

"Would it help you very much if I should do as you ask?"

Misery is selfishness made tangible. Deacon McCross was very miserable. He never knew the cost of her yielding, and he drew a long breath of satisfaction.

"It will quiet your mother. You can write or see him, Mollie, and tell him all about it; you know he is a kind boy—and say I always meant him well, though it wasn't fair about the burglary. But your mother did that."

I believe the old man's reason had begun to fail. For charity's sake let us hope so. Mollie answered, "I will do what you ask;" tried to look happy until he closed the door behind him, as he went half gladly, half guiltily from the room. Then she turned herself to the wall with an exceeding bitter cry.

CHAPTER XXV.

" I had a little hobby horse,
His name was Dapple Grey,
I lent him to a lady to ride a mile away :
She beat him, she lashed him, she rode him through the mire;
I'll never lend my beast again for any lady's hire."

RANCIS HAYTHORNE was hugely enjoying himself. The soft sunshine of Indian summer poured over all the land ; the parti-colored trees sighed and whispered under the wind, and all the charming, sad, and yet hopeful instincts of the day touched his sensitive soul. He had a large volume in his hand, and his face was composed to the decent gravity of unruffled content.

"Two hundred pages of 'Innocents Abroad,' and only been obliged to laugh once," he cried triumphantly to Peace, who entered broom in hand. "O, dear! you aren't going to sweep, when I'm having such a nice time?"

The young lady gave energetic assent, and proceeded to effect a commotion among the chairs and tables, which the ousted reader watched with lazy dissatisfaction. "Can't you put it off till next week?" he asked in a pathetic voice; "it's Friday already."

"Just a man's shiftless notion!" retorted Peace loftily, as she paused to adjust a scarlet and yellow bandanna over her jetty locks, so as to give the precise effect of a magnificent Egyptian-girl study exhibited at Goupil's last winter. "I should like to see your house."

"I hope you may," he responded. "I'll take care it's as well kept as yours!"

"I don't doubt that, if there's any duty for you to perform abroad."

"I had reference to the labors of a charming young person with a bewitching kerchief tied on askew."

"And he began to compliment, and I began to grin," rejoined Miss Pelican, with heightened color; "but it's no use; I shall sweep this minute: you must move your procrastinating bones elsewhere."

"On the contrary, I'll stay to assist," composedly settling himself in the open window. "There! that corner isn't half done; two—no, two and a quarter specks on the carpet. What makes you stir up so much dust? My mother never did. Why wouldn't something like a watering pot be good to quiet it, scented with rose-water or patchouli? You'll have to hurry, or one half the carpet will be worn out before you get to the other. I guess I'll open the door."

"You've blown every bit of the dirt back!" cried Peace, rapidly getting angry. "If you don't leave the room I shan't go on."

"Quite right; do stop," said he, sinking into an armchair and fanning himself with the cover of the "Innocents." "It makes me tired only to look at you. Come, sit down and tell me the origin of this sudden fit of industry."

"Because," said Peace with a tempting pout of ripe red lips, "you and Charley are so shiftless; I'm out of patience with you both. People who don't work, get to be worth just nothing at all. I lose all my respect for folks like you, who don't raise a finger for any one's help for the twelvemonth together. I shan't countenance you in it a day longer."

"If a man ought to accomplish all that is required of him, he must hold himself for more than he is," quoted Mr. Haythorne complacently; "I'm satisfied with myself; isn't that enough?"

"No," said Peace, "and it isn't true, either. You are ashamed of your inefficient, dawdling, dilly-dally, shilly-shally, small loss, fiddle-faddle existence: I know you are."

She was so animated that he couldn't resist saying: "Any more adjectives?" in his laziest drawl; but he wondered in his secret heart how she happened upon the discovery.

She paused while she drew in her full, free breath— Peace looked instinct with power when she breathed—and studied his face. Only a second, however: Miss Pelican never stopped long for anything.

"Why don't you energize?" cried she; "rush out and cure somebody. Dear me, if I was a man, there isn't much I wouldn't do."

Francis Haythorne said he had no doubt of it; to judge by women's habits in their own sphere, they'd sweep the world with the besom of destruction if they had a chance. By the way, if so emulous of notoriety, why didn't they distinguish themselves in dusting or washing matches? It would give them something to do at any rate.

"Women's lives don't lack work, but unity of purpose. With a central aim, and their tireless industry, what might they not accomplish?" returned Peace earnestly; and she was going to enlarge on her theme, when a mischievous curl at the corners of her hearer's auburn moustache quenched her eloquence.

"Now what is it?" said she, stopping short, with rising wrath.

"I was only thinking of Goethe's frogs," he replied in a mock apology of manner that only made his malice more exasperating.

"Go on," said Peace, tapping her foot impatiently;

"you may as well out with your meanness as keep it bottled up in your heart."

The tease caressed his flowing beard gently, and repeated the well-known lines with slow and emphatic diction:

"'A certain pond was frozen over;
The frogs beneath its shady cover
Could no more croak and leap;
They dreamed, however, half asleep,
That by the next return of spring
They all like nightingales would sing.
The south wind came, the ice it thawed,
And soon the frogs were all abroad;
And seated now around the shore,
They croaked away as heretofore.'

That's the woman question in a nut-shell!" said he dictatorily.

"Did you ever see a cherub on a tombstone?" asked Peace, punching her nose in with her forefinger and puffing out her checks, to no inaccurate representation.

"I'll never attempt to argue with you again!" he rejoined, nettled at her naughty settlement of his quotation, though she was only paying him back in his own coin; "I like people to use common-sense."

"Jacky wouldn't, cause he couldn't," sang she mockingly and bitter, as she rose and flourished her broom. "I am going to work. But since you would like an answer in kind, I'm willing.

"Froggy would a wooing go,
Whether his offer was wanted or no;
And thus this lovesick youth he bespoke her:
'Will you marry me, dear Ally Croaker?' To which she answered,
'Oh, what is life that we should fret, why make we such ado?
I'm ower young to marry yet: I canna—winna, buckle to."

"That lies quite within my capacity; I'm sorry I couldn't go any deeper, but then I don't live in froggy's well, you know. I've been happier since I had an ambition; probably you wouldn't. Ambition and self-complacency don't go nicely together. *I* never said I didn't belong in the bog, you know; it was reserved for the nobler patrician to deny his extraction and imitate the nightingale."

"Now, Miss Peace, don't!" he cried, rather startled at the genius he had evoked. "I didn't really mean it. I do think you've been more comfortable of late—that is for you. Won't you put down your arms, and tell a fellow? I'm interested—honor bright."

Peace, whose roses had deepened with roused pride, gave him a quick, sharp look to convince herself of his truth. He really was ashamed, and drawing a chintz-covered easy-chair toward the window seat, pointed to it entreatingly. He didn't quite like the idea of arraying the inferior feminine animus against himself, conscious perhaps of certain missing defences, such as one would expect to find in the ideal perfection at war with a deteriorated type. He hadn't his usual fluency of repartee in face of the situation, and Miss Pelican, finding him vanquished, pitied, and, woman-like, began patching up his tattered self-conceit with all possible expedition, and talked with a confiding air, becoming as infrequent.

Francis Haythorne refrained from smiling by a mighty effort, as she unfolded her heart; she was so simple, though it only added to her charms.

"Undo the harm of your father's trade! why, Miss Peace, how can you? You don't propose exhorting the well-dressed frequenters of the Circus, or drying the tears you suspect their families to shed. To clothe ragged drunkards is giving them exactly so much more whiskey.

No! no! what do you want of a wider sphere? You are too nice to waste your thoughts on such wretches. To brush away the cobwebs from our misty brains is the sum total we gentlemen ask of you."

Peace looked hurt. "That is all any one has to say to me," said she hastily. "There is no place in the world for women, except as a kind of intellectual parlor maids to their male acquaintance. I am planned for something better. Francis Haythorne, if you were any use in the world yourself, I should have more respect for your opinions."

"No," said he, with a bright look. "You think so, because you have never tried to be the mistress of the house."

But the same inspiration doesn't invariably shine upon two people at once, and she went on vehemently: "I've thought and suffered too much in these last three years, not to speak by experience. You can't tell how this God-cursed trade stands between me and the barest comfort. It is not too much to give my whole life to clearing myself of the stain. It is my torment—in church, in society, among my friends. If I enter my carriage, the very stones seem to cry out against me. It wasn't enough that my brother should be ruined, but every one who loves me must suffer; and now for weeks I've watched my best friend hovering between life and death, all because her foolish lover must pander his courage, ambition, earnestness, to the same detestable trade, and suffers the consequences. If she had died, we would have been murderers. I wish I was dead, everybody was dead!—at least I did, till I thought I saw a way to stem the tide just a little. Don't say you think it folly," continued she, lifting her eyes pleadingly to his face, as if the decision rested entirely on him.

The self-elected arbiter of her destiny was convinced that it was, but his reply savored of the usual masculine dissimulation toward women. " Poor thing," thought he ; " she seems quite worked up. She may as well amuse herself this way as any other, if it's a comfort. She hasn't the slightest idea of connected work, and so can't make any mischief ; and it's quite pretty and feminine of her to want to try to do something. Decidedly she should be encouraged."

So he said, " No, indeed ! I don't say it's useless, but I wouldn't let any one know I thought of it. It might— well, people might talk."

Poor Peace ! Charley could be notorious for folly, Louis for crime, Mollie's troubles town gossip, her own home turned inside out by tattlers ; it was all right. But she mustn't stir hand or foot to mend matters, because women weren't accustomed to do anything, and Mrs. Grundy would be astonished. Peace felt, as every earnest women has felt before her, that womanhood is hemmed in so as to be a curse ; or, to put it another way, that womanhood striving to rise from its praying and adoring knees, and stand upon its own God-given feet, is cursed of all *man*kind, and she said so then and there with a force that horrified her admirer. " I will *not* give up my life to no account trifles," cried she indignantly. " If I've anything in me that will give me a career, I'll develop it, and make my mark in the world."

Francis Haythorne hoped she wouldn't. It wasn't feminine business to be making marks ; he couldn't see why she should want to, when she could appear so advantageously at home, devoting herself to the everyday, planless prettinesses of a woman's life. He resolved to act a friendly part and keep her as quiet as possible.

Peace's energies were not exerted without due cause that

autumn morning. She had no less visitors than the Mc-Crosses in expectation, and she gave them the royal care of her own hands, busying herself with all those dainty love-suggested arrangements and rearrangements that sing welcome and joyful recognition at every turn.

Peace never received a guest without such care, but to-day Abigail was banished altogether, and under the mistress' skill the house presently bloomed with the last of the year's blossoms, and glowed with autumn leaves, and breathed with the subtile perfumes she loved. She was too nervous to sit still, blew imaginary dust out of bureau-drawers, rehung pictures, tipped over vases, and twitched the window curtains; then descending to the library, practised the Anvil Chorus on the grand piano, in a style peculiarly adapted to wrench Francis Haythorne's feelings.

" I guess they're all dead," said he, pathetically.

" Who ? " asked Peace, getting up, and coming over to the low grate-fire, where the gentleman sat reading and smoking.

" I thought you were doing it purposely, the devils, of course, scrunching their bones."

Peace was going to be horrified, when she glanced into the book in his hand, and mustering German enough to read M. M. Grimm on the cover, settled herself to hear the story. Francis Haythorne loved to take time, and work up a charming narration, and Peace was in no wise averse to listen. But in the excitement—the kissings and caressings—of Mollie's arrival, tale and teller were destined to be alike forgotten.

The Top Town people were hardly prepared for the new-comer's wasted appearance.

" Thin as a last year's mosquito," Miss Petingil averred, when she fitted her dresses, and so weak Mrs. McCross was very glad to send her out of her sight for a month or two. Not that she doubted the righteousness of her actions, but her daughter's pale face was a disagreeable object to her everyday vision.

Mollie sank into her friend's arms restfully. Poor child! she was glad enough to escape the wear and worry of Millville, and breathed more freely the instant she left it behind. She was come to that place when everything seemed fading out of her grasp; when all was gray in the fog of uncertainty and physical languor, and far-off fears loomed high, and near objects were indistinct.

Peace, who had been on a breezy, mirthful journey through the Catskills that summer, and come home fresh and strong for a long winter's work, with hearty resolves and rebellions, and hopeful outlooks, addressed herself to petting and spoiling with her usual energy. Her attentions seemed to Mollie equally delicious and unfitting. To busy people, who have been all their lives comforting others, these loving offices have a curious sense of novelty, just as if one were wearing one's friend's familiar overcoat for the first time.

Never were a more oddly assorted company brought together than now comprised the Pelican household. Charley Pelican, full of his gymnastic feats, and always keeping his mother in terror lest he should take a fancy to balance the parlor-tables on the end of his nose; Francis Haythorne, musician, connoisseur in painting, German student, always busy, never producing a practical result at anything; Peace, struggling with her old unrest, and maturing thoughts by and by to take shape in definite resolve; Mollie, weary and spent in her life battle; Mr. Pelican, deep as ever in orphan asylums; his wife, always wavering between her terror of the omnipotent Grundy, and her benevolence; and Deacon McCross, active in pursuit of knowledge during his short fortnight's vacation.

Mr. Abimelech Pelican seized on the inquiring old gentleman at once, and showed him every charitable institution in the place, inducing him to make speeches to the inmates, the first of which, according to Charley, ran thus:

"Dear children, I'm extremely glad to have you here. It always makes me happy to see so many little folks gathered at a festival [it was a festival]. I hope you—I hope,"—here the worthy orator scratched his head for a thought, which didn't come, and then exclaimed, wildly, "I hope none of these dear little boys throw stones, and above all be sure and not make yourselves sick eating ice-cream and candy."

Charley, too, had taken a violent fancy to the good Deacon, and showed him where the railroad-princes raced, and where the speculating saints talked up "corners," and coaxed him up to house-tops in elevators, and into basements to see low life, with the greatest zest; though the squeamish fear of mud, the rubbers and red muffler his charge invariably wore, and the tones of cheerful inquiry in which he was wont to suggest the price of everything he saw, rendered the reason of his young guide's enjoyment a little doubtful.

The Deacon, free from Miranda's restraining eye, was bent on taking all possibilities of liberty; and one night Mollie found him listening eagerly to a vivid description of monté as played at Coney Island, which Charley explained and illustrated, not without dexterity on his own part.

"Dew tell!" said the old man in his mild, high-keyed accents; "how dreadful smart, and they change the marked card quick as a wink! I never! I wish I could go once jest to look on."

"Do you," cried Charley, starting up delighted.

"There's a place in Top Town where they play. I'll show you; but don't you take your pocket-book: you'll lose it if you do."

Deacon McCross gave an inquiring glance at Mollie: she was beaming approval. He therefore surreptitiously abstracted *one* small bill from his purse before handing it over, and wiping his bald head, elevated his white hat, took his cane, and shuffled off benignantly, to return in high glee with *two* greenbacks.

"I tipped Knox, who was there, a wink to let him win," confessed Charley afterward, "and made it all right next day. Why, it was snab to see him teetering up and down on his toes, hat in hand, beaming innocently at those infernal scoundrels, and pocketing the plunder as pleased as if they'd given him a kitten. I wouldn't have missed it for a handful of Erie stock, you bet."

But Master Pelican's adventures with poor Mr. McCross were far surpassed by a scene with Miss Petingil, enjoyed that same week. The old lady, dressed in her best, came to town, partly to bring a parcel to Mollie, partly to shop; and of course invited herself to the Pelicans' to tea. There she made excuses to climb to the garret of the house, offered to descend on errands to the kitchen, felt stealthily of the pillow-cases, and detected a darn in the dining-room carpet. She also inquired of the family management in a familiar way of the cook, kicked up the hall mat to see if there was dirt under it, and rendered an unfavorable verdict of poor, gentle Mrs. Pelican. "I allow to say, if Almiry Petingil hadn't more snap in her, she'd never have grabbed her living out of the lap of a stingy world for forty years," thought she.

Her recognition of Charley was a trifle grim, the wrongs received in that quarter being ineffaceable; but he bore himself with sorrowful humility, and Absalom

could not long be out of favor. Willing to make good
his peace, he invited her to Lingard, and she accepted
at once. Notwithstanding Mollie's shawl, and Peace's
necktie, borrowed for the occasion, and the combined efforts of the young girls—offered with hearty good-will,—
from the scraggy cock's feathers on her bonnet, to the
toe of her congress gaiter, she never looked more lanky,
stiff, and angular, than when she hooked her lean arm into
Charley's, and tripped away in a flutter of expectation.

All went well the first half-hour, though she loudly told
her escort that it was contrary to Scripture for a man to
put on women-folks' things, when the "Widow" appeared.
She admired the songs, and the Lady-killer and after-
dinner speech were very favorably received. Notwithstanding that she took snuff in the pauses, she said the
morals inculcated by the show were not to be sneezed at
nor condemned.

Suddenly, half a dozen dancers pirouetted on to the
stage, their gauze skirts floating, their lank arms tossed
high above their painted faces. Miss Petingil glanced
at them sharply, to assure herself that she beheld the
often-heard-of abomination; and then, mindful of the unsophisticated youth in her train, hurried to place her
withered form before his wandering eyes, and screeched,
"Don't you look, Charley! don't you look!" in tones
too piercing not to be heard all over the house. Nor
would she remain a second to countenance the iniquity,
but stalked grimly from the hall, followed by her delighted host, to whom she called, "Come away this minute, Charley Pelican," over her shoulder.

The family were all gathered in the library one evening, for their usual desultory following each of his own
bent on a common ground. They had been indulging in
ice-cream and sponge-cake. Mr. Pelican highly disap-

proved of Mollie's partaking thereof, and had offered to
buy her a pound of ten-penny nails, as more susceptible
of digestion. But the repast was now some time ended,
and she sat playing with pencil and paper, and listening
dreamily to Francis Haythorne, who was amusing himself at the piano, rendering Clementi's sixty-first sonata.
She compared him inly with Louis, and supplied the well-
remembered boyish figure in the place of the handsome
Sybarite. How different they were! and most different
at the instrument they both loved! And her mind flew
back to the happy hours she had lived beside her lover,
watching his long, slender fingers, in a trance contoured
by the glorious melody of hope, sorrow, courage, he set
trembling about them. Ah! Francis Haythorne was
playing the andante. How perfect every note fell! a
cold, solid crystal. He could make his keys attune to
emotion, fascinating, stern, angry, coquettish, always
sprite-like, elfin; but he had no ability to render tenderness: while Louis' touch gave the very breath of modest
passion; sorrow, warm, living; love, chaste and divine.
Mollie might have gone on comparing the two with an
unsatisfactory pleasure in the broken, disjointed pictures
she called up, but Mr. Pelican rose from his easy-chair,
and produced a couple of decanters. "Deacon McCross,"
said he, seductively, "here is a chance to display your
Biblical knowledge. This," shaking up the smoky liquid,
"is Esau, and this, Jacob," exhibiting the paler fluid.
"Esau is too strong for me; but you can choose for yourself."

The Deacon, who was strictly temperate, declined; but
Charley accepted, and Francis Haythorne disappeared in
the dining-room with him, leaving Peace lowering as a
thunder-cloud. She now affected a maternal surveillance of
the red-haired, and regarded such doings as ravages of the

15

wolf in the fold. "How unkind of father!" she cried, angrily, "when he knows how I abhor this eternal tippling. If he must drink, why can't he go by himself, and not rush for every young man that comes within a mile of the house."

Her observation was quite loud enough to be heard, and Charley, himself freed from petticoat government long before, forgot to take his own decoction while he watched his companion, who didn't care to drink, and in his nonchalant desire to please all, was thus placed between two disagreeable alternatives.

"Why don't those lazy servants bring the ice-water?" cried his father, jerking the bell violently. "They never are on hand when they're wanted."

"Pooh, father! you know that tintinnabulator makes about as much noise as a lamb's tail in a felt hat," observed young Pelican. "You'll have to take it plain; you've incurred Peace's everlasting displeasure already. She's a regular hippopotamus vine—bless me! I mean parasite—when a fellow begins giving up to her," he suggested, in his usual genial disregard of precise verbal meanings.

"In that case I shan't tempt her wrath," answered Mr. Haythorne, putting down the decanter, not because he cared for the young lady's feeling, but from innate opposition to Charley.

Then the two Pelicans drained their goblets, and all three went back guiltily and sat down, fully conscious of the combined feminine disapprobation.

"You look as if you'd buried your last friend," remarked Mollie, mischievously. "What's the saying?— 'the dead to bier, the living to good-cheer.'"

"That is the root of bitterness; none of these dead

beats could get any beer," suggested Charley, relieved to have the silence broken.

"You ought to know by this time that beer is the only synonym of good-cheer in their vocabulary," flashed Peace.

"There! children!" interfered Mrs. Pelican, from over her knitting, bent on ameliorating the situation. "How ill-bred to wrangle before an invalid! Here is Mollie, who has mused all the evening, and no one tried to be agreeable."

"Why is Peace's opinion like a spirit?" persisted her brother, resolved to have the last word. "It's a conundrum; the answer is, 'Because it's immaterial.'"

"Miss Mollie does seem quite deeply engaged," said Mr. Haythorne, politely taking up Mrs. Pelican's cue. "Just watch her pencil hasten over the page! It's a shame for this Oberon and Titania to interrupt her with their broils. Mr. McCross and I are making arrangements to prance into the lily-cups and hide ourselves for fear."

"I am not so easily disturbed," replied she, laying down her paper with the true author-sigh at such emergencies. "You remember Goethe's old soldier pronounces writing 'only busy idleness.' I can comprehend the feeling."

"Could you ever understand poetry?" said Mr. Pelican to Deacon McCross, who was looking over a package of Prang's chromos. "Since I've been comparatively out of business, I am trying to learn. I used to have my wife select the hymns for my lay-sermons, and often gave out the wrong set for the service. My ear is poor, and the meaning is frequently enveloped, not to say smothered. Now I always take a dictionary and look out the words, but even then I find it eludes me."

Deacon McCross said he never had any difficulty. He was very fond of rhymes, for his part.

Mr. Pelican's aldermanic proportions expanded with satisfaction. He hastened to select a picture from the pile. "I was reading Rose Terry's 'To an Arbutus,' this morning," said he. "Here's the print, perhaps you can explain it. I find it misty, very."

Thereupon, while the two old gentlemen retired to a corner of the table and began a critical study of the text, Charley embraced his chance to collapse his mother's air-pillow. Of course the good lady's head went down with a plump; and her daughter was horrified to hear her snore audibly. "It's improper in public," said she, and woke her up without delay. Peace was Grundy-ridden also, in streaks.

To all appearance the students were successful. "I comprehend it so far," said Mr. Pelican stretching out his black-silk-stockinged legs, and looking fatter than ever, with the poetry in his hands, and a business-like glance bent through his glasses at the lean Deacon. "Do you?"

Mr. McCross nodded.

"But the next line *is* difficult," continued Mr. Pelican, ponderously. "'Tinged with color faintly like a morning cloud,'—what can that mean?"

"Why, what it says," remarked the Deacon; "didn't you ever see a cloud?"

"That's too easy!" said Mr. Pelican, "and clouds are dissimilar. We'll have to take the dictionary. Tinged —that means stained in a diluted dye; clouds—water; diluted. Ah! With color; that's right so far; faintly— that corresponds; morning—why morning cloud? There's the trouble! If it was mourning now, being black, one could get at it; or if she'd said "purple"—mourning is purple too; but morning! Mr. Pelican took refuge in his chromo. After a little careful study a light broke on him, and he exclaimed in a voice of perfect content : "I have it, McCross : it's a kind of a pink."

Peace chuckled audibly. "I began a poem awhile ago, father," said she. "Don't you want to hear the first verse ?

> " The day it blows,
> And blows and snows,
> And the frost it grows,
> Under the window pane."

"This is the second stanza," cut in Charley :—

> " The day it blowed,
> And blowed and snowed,
> And the frost it growed,
> Under the window-pane."

"And here's the third," said Mollie, laughing :—

> " The day it blew,
> And blew and snew,
> And the frost it grew,
> Under the window-pane."

"It has all the dignity of an epic."

"I can understand you so far, daughter," remarked Mr. Pelican thoughtfully; "what comes next?"

"That's all," said Peace; "I'm going to call it 'Le Jour, a Crystalline Incrustation of the Sybiline Leaves.'"

"I don't think modern poetry at all equals that of my youth," averred Mr. McCross, who had been plunged in meditation. "I remember a favorite hymn I learned once on my mother's birth-day, worth all I meet nowadays lumped."

"Do repeat it," urged Peace, brimming with mischief.

" It'll be good for Mr. Haythorne; and besides, I'm *so* much interested in old-fashioned psalmody! I've had one rendering much on my mind of late, and every day say :—

> " Come, my beloved, up and get;
> Don your blue breeches and sailor hat;
> Pluck up your heart, and take a row
> Over the lake for your little go."

Francis Haythorne looked solemn disapproval at this nautico-collegiate travesty; but Deacon McCross wore a bewildered air, as memory felt feebly for the lost lineaments of its life-time friend, beneath the horrid mask. He presently concluded it was all right, and rejoined with an old man's pleasure in her sparkling face: " Certainly, my dear; I'll do so with pleasure. We sing it to ' Mear.' The precentor always repeated it two lines at once :—

> " Give ear to me what time I call, *
> To answer me make haste,
> Like very dust my heart is dried,
> My bones like smoke do waste.
>
> My flesh within me smitten is,
> And it is withered
> Like very grass, so that I do
> Forget to eat my bread.
>
> By reason of my groaning voice
> My bones cleave to my skin ;
> Like pelican in wilderness,
> Forsaken I have been.
>
> I like an owl in desert am,
> That nightly there doth moan ;
> I watch, and like a sparrow am
> On the house-top alone."

* Old translation of Psalms.

The company had all been very quiet while the old
gentleman, who had pushed his spectacles up on his forehead, and shut his eyes, recited these verses in a slightly
quavering voice. When he pulled down his visual aids
and beamed mildly around, the applause was loud: and
Peace culminated five minutes' manœuvres by snatching
the coveted writing from Mollie's lap. "Here is different theology, I know," she cried, waving it above her
head in triumph. (Peace could do such difficult bits of
play with perfect grace and piquancy.) "You needn't
blush, Mollie; it's worth appropriating as common property, and I have possession, and make it over to the
company. Listen:

" Of all emotions of the human heart—
  Pride, hate, remorse or gratified desire—
  Nature responds in harmony to none,
  Except the pure simplicity of love.
  Go lay thy heart to hers, thou peevish child;
  And if the world, true to its falsity,
  Has played thee false, ask of her salves
  For disappointed hopes.
               She'll flout
  Thee to thy face: but come with love,
  And not a rock, or brook, or blade of grass,
  But seems a type framed justly for thy soul.
  Peace! calm thy weak complainings! she does well.
  There comes a time when all shall pass away
  But love.
  God made her like Himself, and in the fret
  Of narrow human life we lose the key
  She only keeps in tune.
  Herein is presage of the things to come.
  If nature answers to the voice of love,
  And will not hear to any other call
  (God setting thus His face in every flower);
  And we alone are out of heart with both
  (For all the instincts of God's being meet

In one great throbbing heart, whose name is love);
When love doth make us one in soul with God—
Then stars, and winds, and flames, and pain itself,
Shall be but as harmonious strings to one great harp,—
And we its players."

"Do you believe it?" said Francis Haythorne, eying its author with an odd mixture of dissent and tickled
intellect.

"Yes," said Mollie, simply. She was not anxious to
elaborate her statement. Theological ideals seemed to
her like shattered bell-glass nowadays—brilliant, pris-
matic, transparent, but broken bits after all, of what was
once a boasted protection. She dared not affirm the
truth that helped *her* in living, to be the great bell-glass
whose protection should foster to complete growth the
universal human cucumber.

"But where did you find it out?" persisted the student.

"Where *you* didn't," interfered Peace. "In the
sweat of her brow."

"Daughter," remarked Mr. Pelican, laying down the
pencilled word she had taken from her hand for thoughtful survey, "I know Mollie won't care for my saying
it—it's my opinion that your poetry was the best; one
could understand it in half the time."

"Here are some lines less difficult of comprehension,"
answered the thief, starting up, and laying a red-lettered
bill before him.

"Why, what's this, Peace? Forty dollars for eight
—no, sixteen quires of trash! You're enough to ruin
Crœsus. I won't endure it."

"Black and gilt is the most elegant style I've tried for
an age. I bought it more to support the credit of the
family than anything else!" quoth Peace, superbly.

"It's really ill-bred to write on plain paper nowadays. I thought of getting up the family arms. You know the shield bears a wivern gules rampant, quartered with three swans argent on sable; and the crest is a wivern gules rampant upon a wreath, with a dog in its claws— Motto, 'Mare et marte faventibus.'"

"Nothing but a race of thieves and pirates after all," suggested Mollie, smiling. Now, my family are going to have a turkey, rampant, with an angle-worm in its beak, when we quarter—Motto, 'Who grubs, eats.'"

"Father, I *am* as economical as possible," coaxed Peace, "I curtail my expenditures to a bare pittance;" while Mr. McCross asked Francis Haythorne why he didn't spread upon his pedigree.

"My ancestry and connections are just such as lead me to hear with pleasure of my friend's," replied the red-haired, smiling slightly.

"Humph!" said the good Deacon, feeling that he ought to be satisfied.

"Well, well!" exclaimed Mr. Pelican, overpowered by his daughter's eloquence. "I feel your economy to the bottom of my pocket. Things have changed since my day. Your mother and I wrote on blue fool's-cap with blue ink, folded our letters without envelopes, and sealed them with red wafers. We were glad enough to get them at that."

Peace gave an irate sniff at the Sybarite, who was repeating, in a tone specially directed to her ear, a certain poem, beginning, "Little I ask; my wants are few."

"Speak louder!" exclaimed Mr. Pelican, his poetic instincts instantly alive, as he caught the young man's musical, but slightly German intonation. "Good! good! I like that. Heavy silks are never dear. Mrs. Pelican, here's reason and sentiment combined; no figured spring cheats for him!"

15*

His wife looked up pleasantly beneath her shining gray curls. She was, we know, that kind of sweet which cultivates placidity as the great virtue. Peace did not share in the matter-of-course smile that went around the party; she was gloomily chewing up the original root of bitterness. Her father, whose paternal admonition had been a matter of general application, as he intended it, and who never refused her anything in his life, began to rally her. "My little Quakeress here never had a monogram, I'll wager," cried he, pinching Mollie's pale cheek. "On my word, it's right down skinflint, for you, Miss Spendthrift, to revel in these vanities. You ought to have one, too, my dear, and you shall. Peace, be sure she goes to order it to-morrow. Take advice, and have it fine. Haythorne, here, is one of those lily-fingered chaps, with nothing to do; get him to go."

Mr. Haythorne had been assaulted so frequently in this spot, that he began to be galled, and bit his lip—a habit he had when annoyed. But his customary gallantry conquered. "Anything for Peace," said he, easily. That young lady did not reciprocate, being in the mood when every touch came amiss, was vexed that he was open to her father's broad hit, and said to herself that his company would be detestable; so she replied, rudely, "Then take Thomas à Kempis' advice on the subject: 'But of the words or deeds of others judge nothing rashly, *neither do thou entangle* thyself with things not entrusted to thee; thus it may come to pass that thou mayest be little or seldom disturbed,'—exactly your notion of happiness."

Peace had frequent recourse to the old-fashioned moralist, for purposes of self-mortification; but she had no right to seize the weapon to jab at him, and she knew it.

"You do me but justice, most puissant mentor," returned he, bowing calmly:

> "Far from the madding crowd's ignoble strife
> My sober wishes ever learned to stray;
> Along the cool, sequestered vale of life,
> I keep the noiseless tenor of my way."

"That's plain," said Mr. Pelican, taking the browned meerschaum from his mouth to smile at his daughter's discomfiture. "I can understand that, if it does rhyme. You mean that Peace may look elsewhere for a beau, down-town, to-morrow; and I think you're right, my boy." Whereupon he attempted to insert the bowl of his almost dead pipe in his mouth, by mistake; and Charley merited the Sybarite's disgust, by flying him in the air with one hand by a grasp on the bottom round of his chair, and then deftly emptying him out upon the sofa, while Peace sailed off scornful and lofty.

Next day, true to his word, the generous Top Towner sent the two girls off in his dashing sleigh, gay with white-bear and seal-skin robes, and drawn by coal-black mustangs, to try the first snow of the season, and select the dainty toy.

Mollie looked very shyly at the well got-up individual, who descanted on styles of coloring, script, old English, and fancy capitals, in a way that dignified the matter into first-rate importance.

"Why not illuminate it?" cried he, his face glowing with enthusiasm. "We frequently do such work. See these samples."

Peace, who had heretofore waved down all suggestions in her stateliest style, now assented with benignant gravity. She abhorred familiarity with clerks.

The radiant enthusiast forthwith produced a sheet of

French designs, and skilfully sketched the monogram, with an air. "This," said he, in persuasive accents, "shall be gold ; this lake, or deep green ; this— "

"There is no proper flower here," interrupted Miss Pelican, with infinite decision. Those pansies might do for Chris. In fact, I think I saw something of the kind on her writing table. If Louis or Francis Haythorne were only near to consult. There he is now! " she cried, suddenly.

Mollie started up with a gasp, and caught at the table to steady herself. "Francis Haythorne, I mean," continued Peace, hastening toward the door to wave her glove at the coveted swain, with as much speed as was compatible with dignity, and a slight sweep of silk petticoat. She returned in a moment with her captive, who held three red-backed volumes, labelled, "Proceedings of Boston Medical Society," "Lancet," and "Medical Application of Anæsthetics," with a conscious blush. She hadn't time to review his tell-tale burden, but explained the case with impetuous rapidity. "We are at our wits' end," said she, earnestly.

"Happy thought ! " he returned, laying down his books with their backs away from her, and folding his delicate hands with thankful devotion : "I hope I appreciate the goods the gods vouchsafe. Indeed, Miss Mollie, I cannot well choose a flower for you. I only know it should be sweet and modest ; some such blossom as Bernard imagined near the celestial river :

> " Vpon whose bankes the sugar growes,
>   Enclosed in reedes of sinamon."

"And martyrdom hath roses, and fair and virgin lilies for virgin souls are found," said Peace in her heart, as she scanned the trembling frame of her friend, still unhinged by her sudden shock. Peace felt a sort of compassionate admiring pity for this love-absorbed life. "Poor thing!" was her invariable comment. "I couldn't be so noble."

But outwardly she began a rapid consultation with the clerk, which ended in his taking down an elaborate colored book of flowers; and pointing to a plate of exquisite pale blue clustering blossoms.

"Forget-me-nots, the darlings," cried Peace with ardor; "why didn't I think of it before?"

And while more sketching in and attitudinizing ensued, on the part of the sanguine clerk, and much comment and consultation between Peace and Mr. Haythorne, my dear Mollie sat dreaming with the volume in her lap, heedless of the others, gathering again the tangled threads of thought that held in their knotted meshes the well-remembered patient flower.

And by and by, when Peace came to take the book gently away, and bring her back to life and misery again, it was all settled about the monogram.

CHAPTER XXVI.

"When the pie was opened
The birds began to sing."

RED GROWING'S call on Mollie had been made in January, and he proposed to let few days pass over his head before the promised visit to Louis.

But Cannadasset was a busy parish, and four little Growings educated under his own eye were great con-

sumers of time. In the spring, too, his wife sickened
and died; and Ernest Laprise, his old college friend,
joined households with him. All this involved toil and
thought, the more lengthened because done in heaviness
and sorrow. So it grew to be August before he found
himself walking up the gravelled path that led to the
Top Town Penitentiary. He went slowly and thoughtfully, his open, impulsive, friendly countenance decidedly clouded, in view of impending difficulties. He
was *not* too solid a man to be up and down between
heaven and hell with sympathy; he *was* too true and
earnest to forget the crime in the criminal à priori;
he *was* a natural lover of men, and disinterested withal,
and a fine-grained student, if we would complete his
synthesis. He found himself in a specially hard case.
He had comforted widows and orphans in affliction;
heard dreary tales of woe and wickedness from bearded
lips, and sent the tellers away with better heart and purpose. He had led little dimpled feet along the path of
Christian experience, and held out blessed hands to those
fainting in the toils of life. But to-day he was to meet
one of his own acquaintance—one of his first flock, in
this saddest of all sad places. Being a man, he reflected
that if this youth had paid regular attendance to the
preached word, instead of roaming all Sunday among fragrant meadows, and dim hymn-intoning woods, he might
have kept out of the merited suffering. Being a priest
of the most lovely Jesus, he could not forget that he also
cared to wander in Nature's spicy thickets, and look
through her eyes to his Master's face. "God can certainly
teach himself through His own handiwork as well as I
show Him forth in mine," said he to injured pride; and
sweet charity having the better, entered the guard-room,
heart and face full of the Saviour's errand.

The officials were polite, with a sort of grim, tobaccoy politeness. They were willing to show him Mr. Allwood's cell; but he could see him where he was. Was he, Mr. Growing, a dominie? Nobody but sweethearts and wives and such ever came to visit the men. Then they laughed as if it was a joke, and one of them went out of doors, and up to the work-rooms, administering a kick and a curse to a big white prowling bull-dog on the way.

Meantime the reverend gentleman looked about him. There stood a case of guns at one end the long room; and two horrible pictures of darkeys, framed in old-fashioned, flat moulding, hung on the other side; in the middle of the floor stood a disgustingly filthy stove, with a bench behind it.

It seemed that other visitors were there on kindly errands; a pair of contrasting groups occupied the farther windows. A tone, a lady richly dressed, with a refined, suffering face, stood beside a stalwart man in prison uniform. Hanging frightened among his mother's skirts, their chubby two years' boy resisted his father's clumsy efforts at conciliation. "Jessie," the listener heard the man say, his deep voice quivering with emotion, "can this be our child?"

"An' Christie," screamed a voice, remarkable alike for good feeling and brogue, from the second window; "do ye iver see a priest?"

"No, Mrs. Dennis," quoth the stripling, whose boyish cheeks were equally wrinkled by pain and vice; "no, indade; sure the likes of a priest niver comes here."

The good woman spread the folds of her gorgeous red calico dress, and bestowed a glance of mingled suspicion and cunning on the complacently listening officials. "Here, Christie, take the chicken an' apples," she cried, shrilly; "I'll be bound they don't give you nothin' fit to eat;" then in a stage whisper, "An' lad, I'd see a priest if the devil himself stood in the doorway."

Presently the man brought in Louis, who sat down, sullen and haggard, near the stove, scarcely recognizing his visitor.

Mr. Growing might well be shocked at his appearance. He had come to administer comfort, but what comfort was there for this man who, crouching before him, seemed less a human being than a wild animal, wounded and surly, crept away to die.

Even the good-natured Irishwoman was struck by it. "Poor craythur, is he in for life?" whispered she. Her companion nodded abstractedly. "Belike, thin, he'll never live his sentence out," was her compassionate rejoinder.

The minister watching his friend's face, saw by the sly satisfaction playing over it that the comment had been heard.

"Poor boy! poor boy!" said he to himself; "has it come to this?"

Yes, it had come to that. Mollie would hardly have known her lover. He was too miserable to try to recognize himself.

Mr. Growing gathered his resources hastily, as he took a seat on the narrow bench. His task was more difficult, more momentous than he had anticipated. He hazarded a commonplace.

"You didn't expect me."

Louis on his side wished he would leave. What was the use of prolonging the agony.

"I don't see why any one should come here who can keep away," said he, without troubling himself to look up.

"Nor I either," retorted the visitor. "I couldn't

keep away, that was the matter. Why, every time I put the four little Growings to bed at night, and taught them to remember the fatherless, and those desolate and oppressed, I thought what a hypocrite I was, when you were shut up here and I hadn't fulfilled my promise to go and see you. I promised Miss Mollie, you know;" watching the man, he saw him tremble at the familiar name.

But the morose answer was unyielding: " I have no claim on anybody. Thieves don't have. The woman spoke the truth—I'll soon be dead and out of everybody's way. The sooner the better."

"Why, dear boy," said Fred, impulsively, his tones thrilling and pleading out of his earnest longing to help, "you talk as if God wasn't with a fellow everywhere, especially when he's in trouble."

"I mean it;" savagely. "God never came here; he don't know anything about Top Town States Prison (lingering over the words to suck the last dregs of bitterness from them); "he lives down at Millville Congregational Church, with them that fare daintily, and go in soft raiment."

The vulgar officials, listening, grinned at each other and spat enjoyingly on the floor, and leaned about the room on doors and wall, with their hands stuffed into their breeches' pockets, and their hats cocked on one side.

"Miss McCross has been sick—nearly dying all summer," said Mr. Growing, softly. "I saw her before she was taken ill, and she sent you this," bringing a stout brown-paper parcel from under his arm. "She said perhaps you wouldn't mind my coming. I was only a man, and a friend," stammered the kind-hearted gentleman, ready to cry with sympathy.

The convict turned toward him with studied deliberation. He said afterward it seemed as if the old soul muscles, once so elastic, were too stiff to move; his only motions, physical or mental, had so long been only such as shoe-making demanded, he feared to try any others.

"She is better; is coming to visit the Pelicans, when she is strong enough to travel. Haven't you heard? She's been delirious till within a week."

Louis didn't make any answer; he sat quite still. Mr. Growing's pity couldn't comprehend this persistent sullenness. He surveyed the young man closely, noticed the drawn bluish look at the corners of his mouth, and his glassy unseeing eyes sprang forward to raise him from the floor, senseless.

"He went pretty easy," said the guard, jumping off his high stool, and looking at him critically. "I heard the overseer in his room say he was falling off in his work, and I see he didn't take nothing to eat to his cell. Likely he's putting him through."

"Do you mean to say he's had no food to live on since early this morning?" exclaimed Mr. Growing, thoroughly shocked.

"Oh, that's nothing; there's always four or five docked every day. It's no account."

"My friend looks very ill," the sympathetic minister suggested to the warden, as he took his leave. "I'm afraid he won't live long."

"He'll get through his work a while yet," quoth that functionary. "He may need a little pushing. He don't stand very well, we'll have to give him something to sit on before long."

Mollie's gift was like herself and her love—a dozen gorgeous butterflies in a glass-case. If she had sought the world over, she could not have offered a more convincing message of her faith. Passion or instinct indeed

give the warp of love, but its woof is altogether made of
tender memories, and every frail insect brought Louis its
own recollection of happy days. There was the deceiving
May-fly he had incited Mollie to catch, with cunning
fables about its golden eyes. She worked a necktie
covered with silken May-flys for him, by way of a coal
of fire. Here was the great Cecropia they had fed
together; and here the tailed Luna and pink winged Io,
snared in the net with the contracting mouth, his own
invention. Way down in a corner, too, was the shadowy
Ajax he brought her one happy April morning when she
kept birth-day in the house, with a sprained wrist, and so
couldn't possibly help his putting his arm around her.
Only one Ajax, though, and he gave her a pair.

With the butterflies full of old-time memories, Mollie
sent him back the rights and claims of his free life, and
he dared to take them to himself, because they came from
her. A woman points her rejected lover to God, but she
prefers to have the man she loves think of herself. If
Mollie had stopped to remember this, she would have
altered the gift for conscience' sake. But God, being Himself the author of love, didn't let her. Having thus
regained self-acknowledgment of his title to manhood,
Louis found another help in the insects. They led him
forth into the outside world. Every night at close of
work, he used to seat himself with his treasure in his lap,
and begin his travels in a minute examination of the
beauties, when, lo! the plumy wings were buckled on his
own shoulders, each bright eyeball of the Sphinx once
more glowed luminous, to light him onward; and the
Ajax paraded his scarlet beauty spots, and yellow Troilus
wandered after a falser Cressid; Prometheus, in sable mantle and golden fringes, consoled his woes with blue-eyed
Io; and chaste Luna smiled and gigantic Polyphemus

strutted in the foreground of the fetterless world of fancy, memory and longing, of which they were the guardian spirits.

He hadn't held his new possession a week before the bitterness unconsciously melted out of his soul, Mollie's image nestling there unchallenged, and playing the sweet exorcist to his ghoulish broodings. His mind, no longer shut into the poisonous prison atmosphere, sought means of healthful action. He picked up the only book in his cell—a Bible, and began to look for verses about butterflies.

What is religion? Who is God? have been the world's questions since the day it was first peopled.

There is a difference between the Christian revelation of religion, and Christianity. Our churches are full of religious men but possess few Christians. Strip off half a dozen empty dogmas, and most disciples of Jesus of Nazareth do not differ materially in theory or practice from those of Confucius, Epicurus, Zoroaster, Moses or Mahomet. All say their prayers, all go to worship, all talk morality and violate it, all profess to love their wives and children. Creusa follows her dear Eneas through smoking Troy. Isis is a model spouse to Osiris. Madame Bazaine steals her husband away from prison. Berengaria, from her husband's wound,

> "—draws forth the poison with her balmy breath
> Sweet as new buds in spring."

And the wife of murdered Maximilian pays her tribute to her lord in a broken heart.

They all see visions, too; and the good priest sacrificing his hecatombs of cattle and provender was nearly as touching a spectacle of faith as Ezekiel wedding his good-natured, but not spotless wife—as he relates, at the command of Jehovah. What is the difference?

Christianity demands love, real human love, to the human chosen—the type of God. It is sufficient for religion to fear God and keep His commandments.

But those called by His name, recognizing the love-bond between the earthly disciple and the glorified Leader, cannot, it seems, agree in "points."

There is a sect with a litany so perfectly satisfying all wants, that other prayer seems needless; and so worship, religion, companionship with Jehovah or His chosen, have resolved themselves, among a majority of its adherents, into the morning and evening service; and they cannot understand how the schismatic sects say "Elder Brother," "Sweet Saviour," "Truest Friend," because the Prayer Book has it Almighty and Everlasting Father. They talk of humanity's resolution into the parent essence of God, as a drop of water falls into the sea. While, on the other hand, quite as respectable a body fail to comprehend how churches can exist without the tea meeting, the jocular pew auction, or the tear-moving excitements of missionary Sunday, and believe implicitly that the original devil taught dancing school.

In order to find the true essence of Christianity, we must cut away from every sect the peculiarity which is its greatest pride. Lop from the Catholic the pope, the real presence, confession, the saints; lop from the Presbyterian the saving grace of belief in dogma, and the delightful anticipation of seeing four-fifths of his immediate neighbors and the entire remainder of the world damned; lop from the Baptist his cistern, the Episcopalian his genealogies and prayer-book, the Universalist his speculations in Psychology, the Methodist his pride of Plebeianism, class-meeting, and the power, and keep the one common division of them all—for that is Christianity, and that only, be the residue healthy and good, or its reverse.

I have always observed two classes of sceptics—reformers and doubters. The reformers are animated by impatience of moral restrictions, and go forth of their own free-will; but the doubters are pushed out. Compelled, in their desire to explore their King's Palace, to pry away certain cracked and mossy stones at what they suppose the basis of the structure, so startled are they by the downfall of mouldy rubbish, that they fly terrified, never dreaming that it is one of time's old hostelries they meddled with, and not the God's temple at all.

Louis belonged to this latter class. Except the diffusive benevolence of the liquor-seller and the "Perfect" theology, he had scant ideals of Christianity in any shape. Dr. Perfect said it was blaspheming God to throw a die; and even good Mr. Growing, in a religious fog common to certain stages of the ministerial career, had been heard to declare from the pulpit, that Christ's abstruse and mysterious utterances were not equal to the reformation of mankind; only through the lucid explanations of Paul could they be properly understood and systematized into the Gospel of Salvation.

I have in mind three or four reasons why duty-loving people find it hard to embrace Christianity : the narrow-mindedness, religious egotism, and personal inconsistencies of its professed votaries ; the vast number of cant expressions which make the language of one sect perfectly unintelligible to members of another, and more obscure than heathen Greek to the unconverted ; the constant preaching of dogma instead of religion, and religion again and under the name of Christianity ; the constant cry to give up a vague all which nobody seems to have done, and catch if you can an equally vague something else in its place; the ecclesiastical command to be separate in peculiarity from a world to which the noisiest "Brethren" are evidently quite united in spirit.

It was a miserable truth which led Hawthorne to compare *popular Christianity* to the stained windows of European churches—from the outside, sombre, cold, forbidding; but within, warm with color and gorgeous in design. The true church is lighted from its centre, day and night, for the Lamb is the light of it; and having been commanded to shine, her patterned windows must needs be full of meaning to lookers-on.

At the end of the world, when the Book of Life is opened, it will be seen to be the roll of the members of the True Church; the united voice of that whole multitude will be found to have bound and loosed matters ecclesiastical and spiritual; Christ animating its members will have forgiven the trespasses of its people against each other; and the Christ who animates the whole will Himself have so forgiven sin, that they are beyond its power forever. There can be no schism in love; and if a rent appear in a theological robe, then it is plain that it is not *the* robe of the redeemed. Love is the dress of Christ's lovers. When Mary McCross was asked how to become a Christian, she always replied, "Fall in love with God,"—which sounds oddly, but is the root of the matter.

Dear Mrs. Pelican, who was an ardent Episcopalian, a devout believer in such adjectives as ineffable, transcendent, incomprehensible, illimitable, uncontainable, infinite, was painfully shocked by this way of putting things; told Mollie it wasn't refined, besides being irreverent; told Peace it must have arisen from association with those low people in Syllabub.

"You speak of Christ as if He was a man in the next street," she cried, summoning her religious sternness to the occasion. Mrs. Pelican, the most timid of gentlewomen, was as stiff as a last year's mullen-stalk in matters of faith.

"He is a man, not so far off," replied the young girl composedly. "I regard him as I might my shadow. When the sun is nearest overhead, I and my shadow are one. But as we turn away from that light, the shade stretches off farther and thinner every instant. So with Christ. Under the full warmth of the Sun of Righteousness, He is unit with me; but in the twilight of unbelief He grows less and less tangible. Like my shadow, too, He never quits my feet, and the minute I approach the light He appears."

"That's flowery and pretty," said Mrs. Pelican, disparagingly. "I'll have to tell mother about Mrs. Dennis," cut in Peace, illustrating her name, which, except in theology, she seldom did. "She followed us to the door the day we read the Douay Bible to her, and she found we weren't such dreadful heretics after all. 'Well, well,' said she, 'sure we're all servin' the same good gentleman—I mean God.'"

Louis was a most pious sceptic. It was because his ideas of Christianity were so elevated, that he couldn't accept as divine the ponderous machinery called by its name. He had read a few earnest books, every one set hard on the heels of religious folly, and concluded churches to be equally humbug and hypocrisy. He accompanied Mrs. McCross to the Millville prayer-meeting, to find its members feeding off husky formalities, with what he thought swinish delight and selfishness. He had dipped into a little Colenso, a little Swedenborg, a little Calvin; read half a page of Baxter's Call; had never seen the point to Pilgrim's Progress ; and since the structure of doctrines seemed to him like a card-house that a breath of doubt dissipates, concluded he was an infidel. Mrs. McCross fully agreed. Millville substituted the opprobrious title of atheist, and washed her hands of him. Thus left to himself, he perused Heine in the original, admired Goethe, tried to like Rousseau, flaunted his unbeliefs in every one's face, because they were like fire in his bones ; and he had an idea that he was somehow disgraced by them, and was too proud to sail under false pretences.

When I started on this digression, he was reading the prison Bible, and falling in love, as lovers will, quite unawares. Like most young men he had left it out of his Library of Useful Information in days of freedom, and for all his dreary studies of late, knew very little about it. Now, in this flood of joy, he was astonished to find what a delicious mingling it is of the human and divine. Its kinship with mother-earth was delightful to him— " like two roes that are twins," he said, being pure enough in heart and experience to see the chaste beauty of that song of marriage. He likewise read ecclesiastes with a shudder at its horrible pictures ; sighed with David, and revelled in Isaiah ; forgave the fairy stories for the facts ; and travelling on day by day, met a friend who had been long time awaiting him very patiently.

We do not give our hearts to the Christus Regnant, but Jesus, sad, rejected. We shrink from the martial prince whose right hand has taught him terrible things, who enters the city with his triumph of slaves, and captives, and spoil. Honors, which it is confessed only bruise the weary heart of their bearer, are no medicine whose beholding cures. *Our* chosen is he who steals slyly and delicately through the door we are too miserable to try to bar, and in his pure brotherhood of grief teaches us to bear our own. It was Christ's tenderness and simplicity and reposeful strength, his intense *naturalness* of perfection, that won Louis. He could not let His history alone, dreamed of Him while at his work-bench, lay contented on his prisoner's pallet while he mused about Him; pictured His journeys, threading the olive-groves, vineyards and hamlets of far-away Palestine; exulted in His simple fondness for flowers and birds; loved Him because He healed and comforted, and suffered willingly, and was satisfied with the rough adoration of a few coarse fishermen, rejecting the *world's* praises because He loved *it*, not them.

To Louis, unjustly condemned, the judgment-seat of Pilate was a frightfully vivid reality. Stripes, hunger, abuse, are tangible things to the prisoner. Himself the unwilling partaker, he knew the pain borne by Jesus, the voluntary sufferer. Not yet convinced of His divinity, the Nazarene became his hero. Little by little dawned on him the great purpose for which this man lived; the strange scheme by which, out of his own agony, he would distill healing, save every man by taking abode with him in the midst of his well-deserved wretchedness, conquer his visible Lordship by giving it up, prove his ownership of all men's hearts by breaking his own to mend them, deny to his comfort exercise of the very gifts he never refused to the most revolting suppliant, out of the niggardly gratitude of men build a kingdom whose only end would be to obtain their happiness.

In such a hero, who can point the difference from a god?

It was impossible for Louis to love any one without longing to share his burdens, enter into his life. The more he tried the homely rules of action set down by the carpenter's Son, the more he knew of their results upon the disciple, and through him upon his fellows ; the more deeply he felt that to pattern after his Master would as surely entail his Master's fate. The degenerate maxims of trade, politics, or popular religion have nothing in common with Christ's ideas.

"No," he said to himself, "to go after him would be to leave all." "Many," says old à Kempis, "are willing to follow Jesus to the breaking of bread, few to the drinking of the cup of his passion."

The battle waxed strong with Louis. He was astonished at his own cowardice, and yet he could not shake himself free from himself. "I have a right to my own life," said one nature.

"So had he," said the other.

"He was the son of a kind God," objected the first Adam.

"He called himself the son of ungrateful man," retorted the second.

"He wanted to suffer, and I don't," cried the first.

"Are you going to accept from any man what you won't do for him?" cried the second.

"No, no, no!" said Louis in a great hurry. "I hope I'm not mean enough to sneak. Besides, I want to help."

Then the sad-eyed man smiled right into his heart, such a thankful, satisfied smile, that his champion saw everything a thousand-fold given back in its wondrous peace and brightness. And this smile floating down to the bottom of the heart Louis had emptied of all, lay warm and sure beneath the burdens, hopes, and loves he piled above it in after life, and permeated them and the man himself so thoroughly, that its own beauty and sweetness became their beauty and sweetness, and its strength was the man's strength, and its trust his trust; and as time went on, it wrote itself all over his face and life, so that God saw in it himself, and his friends saw God.

Now, being thus far along his journey, a misfortune befell him. The peg whereon hung his precious butterflies had long been something unsteady; one evil morning it completed its treachery and gave way; the pretty insects lay upon the floor, a confused heap of broken wings.

The overseer's humor was villanous. A few years after, his men rose, felled him with a bench, and then sat quietly down to await their fate. To-day he was preparing.

"What are them things layin' there for,—you?" he demanded, seeing Louis' start of dismay at the cruel havoc. "Heave that ere trash out,—breedin' vermin an' lice. What are you waitin' for? I'll give you something to hurry about, if you ain't sharp."

A look of irrepressible misery came over the prisoner's face, as he exclaimed beseechingly: "Can't I have those that are whole? Indeed they aren't all spoiled. *Don't* make me throw them away."

"You'd better not give me any of your jaw," said the superior, stirring up the mass with his heavy boot. "Be lively! I'm in a hurry."

Louis swept them out with trembling hand, and ventured to pick up two green dandies from the wreck of his only treasure. "What have you got there?" demanded his jailer, enraged. "Didn't I tell you to heave all them things out? Sassy rascal! put them on the floor."

The convict drew the coveted beauties from his pocket and laid them lovingly on the staging; then threw back his head, a great lump in his throat only kept down by a mighty effort.

"Now you put your foot on them damn beetles, and think yourself lucky to get off without bein' reported for disobeyin' me this way. Impudent dog!"

And with that the "prisoner's friend" went to eat a vast dinner, with unruffled conscience, and the befriended threw himself down in a boyish heap, to mourn his irreparable loss. But the poor flutterers had done their work. Their master was not left empty.

CHAPTER XXVII.

"Thy life to mend
God's law attend."

HAT old fellow at the house opposite looks exactly like a grasshopper," said Peace, glancing malevolently from the window at the rainy prospect.

The only other person in the room made no reply, and the steady rattle of the leaves in her hand seemed to aggravate the unoccupied fault-finder. "There goes old Gizzard next door," pursued she; "always makes me think of a mud turtle on his hind legs. Mary McCross, I can't remember any habit more disagreeable than continually read—read—reading, when one's friends are cross. I invited you here to console me."

"'How can your griefs expect comfort
From him who knows not how
He can redress his own?'"

said Mollie, smiling, but not giving up her occupation.

"If you had your choice, what would you take to insure-your life-long happiness?" asked Peace, abandoning her pet and her window together, and drawing a low ottoman to Mollie's chair. "I've been trying to make up my mind all the afternoon, and it spoils my temper because I can't."

Her friend's eyes sought the bundle of yellow notes in her lap, superscribed in a childish hand. They were very few, remnants of Louis' attentions in their school-days, when he hid one each morning in her dinner-basket, because she confided to him, in the innocence of her heart, that she wanted what the other scholars had,—girls, whose beaux wrote billet-doux and smuggled them over the attic defendu regularly.

She read them every week now. It was cold consolation, but the best she found. Absently smoothing their confining bit of ribbon, she paused awhile to deliberate, and then said quietly, "I think, next to having the one I love best close by me, I could be happiest if there were some boys who liked to come and see me and tell me their troubles."

"Pooh!" said Peace, giving a decided head-toss; "I don't agree a bit. It's either ambition or a husband I want; but I won't be bothered with either."

"I believe in ambition for everybody," said Mollie, in a solid emphasis grown habitual to her, in her argumentative battles; "but," she added brightly, "the way to manage about a husband is to walk through life as one would through a field of burdocks. Before you reach to the other side, the stick tight is sure to get caught in your train."

"But suppose it isn't the right one," said Peace, intent, and pouting; "Men are such poor animals. There's Charley. How miserable the woman will be that gets him! I'm sick of living this way—in transitu—for years at a time! Nothing before, no end in life, no place in the world. Always headed off when I want to work."

Miss McCross didn't answer. She hadn't solved her own problems enough to be able to cope with other people's.

Peace was in her most winning mood this afternoon; not in the sense of yielding; but betraying an inimitable simplicity that underlay her whole character, and peeped out rarely, even with her trusted friends. "Do you know," said she, bestowing her honest confidence, "I'm miserable; I had to make some verses about it. If you won't laugh, I'll read them." Whereupon she drew the same from her pocket, and spread them on Mollie's knee for mutual consideration.

> "What the temptation to this weary world
>   That led us of our will to take it up,
>   Is matter for reflection. But once here
>   Our only end in living's plain enough:—
>   Just to fill life with cares, and so force down
>   Into the lowest deep of consciousness
>   Ourselves.
>   And here we stay, because the world is quit
>   In emptiness and silence; and, self at back,
>   We hate to try the trackless waste beyond,
>   For fear of murder."

Peace was all intensity, vehemence, storm, as she finished indicating the words to Mollie, with voice and finger, while the reader followed them with her own earnest eyes. "I feel it more and more!" cried the author, springing up impetuously, when she observed an uncontrollable smile cross the face of her sympathetic friend, and following her glance, observed Charley, who had squirmed his way thither unobserved, under cover of chairs and tables, and was now reposing at full length beneath the nearest sofa, with a wicked grin on his face.

"That sounds cheerful: I condole with you," cried he, emerging from his shelter, in a kind of elephantine walk on all fours, done with unbent knees, and equally difficult and ridiculous.

The girls experienced a disagreeable shock, such as one always has in discovering a long conversation overheard; and, after a rapid mental reduction, blushed with annoyance and vexation.

"Burrs! wives! happiness! and poetry!" proceeded the young man, counting on his fingers; "yes, absolutely, poetry!

> " 'When dearth of sense and rhyme you see,
>   Come make a poem out of me.' "

"Te he! te he! te he!" chimed Mollie.

"O give to me a cup of tea," tagged Charley.

"I'll think of it at night, D. V.," said Mollie.

"O Charley, what a—"

"Tease you be," interrupted the torment, as his sister, who was getting very angry, began an adjuration by no means flattering, to judge by the stamp accenting its beginning; and Mollie snatched the unfortunate verses just in time to save them from utter destruction. After a few interfering plunges and dives from Peace, well warded off by Charley, she found it needful to run away to her own room, and lock herself in, trophy and all. In a minute more, the voice of the abused author followed her through the keyhole: "Well! Mary McCross, it isn't often you can resist the devil when it 'll flee from you."

The Deacon stayed only a few days, but, as he told

Mollie at parting, they were the most comfortable of his life. The two were very happy together—went to prayer-meetings, orphan asylums, hospitals, poor-houses, public schools, insane retreats, newspaper offices, and insurance buildings, with amiable impartiality. She, modest, timid, and clinging to his arm; he, tall, gaunt, benevolent, and in search of wisdom, with a white stovepipe on his head, red yarn muffler about his neck, rubbers on his feet, an umbrella, and a memorandum book to set down the items, which should develop in course of their wanderings.

"We might just as well see the police court too," said he briskly, after every other spot of interest had been visited; "it's cheap knowledge, and we must improve each shining hour. I feel exactly like 'How doth the little busy bee.' I find it grows on me, too."

Peace, who ruled the house despotically, had a hand in his simple satisfaction. It was she who drew forth his rambling, old-fashioned stories, and she who invented missionary statistics to charm his eager thirst for mental acquisition, and to her complaisant ear he confided his horror of the present style of American dress, denouncing it as similar to the enormities of rings, ouches, crisping-pins, and round tires like the moon, and recited with sympathy sundry ballads from Cowper, relative to starved goldfinches, likewise fables with morals attached; and the reward seemed to her great, when he told Mollie in confidence that he felt his feet to have been set in a large place, which, poor man, was quite necessary—if they were in any.

The father and daughter stole about and made little donations to inconceivably absurd charities, and were patronized by rascally minister agents; and Charley beguiled them into Argentie's, where they presented each

16*

other with studs and cuff-buttons, and the Deacon paid the bill with childish glee. Finally they took an ancient history of Top Town, and hunted up all the places notable for Indian warfare, or the home of the oldest inhabitant; and he donated an immense package of French fruit to Peace, and, after much thought, filled Charley's bed with a pile of dumb-bells, clubs, and articles of gymnastic art, requiring very sly management to adjust, and at the same time preserve the important secrecy, on which account Peace commanded vacation of the premises by the household, and herself made aggravating little sallies at the conspirator, so that he had hard work to keep his plot undiscovered.

That night he sat in the dim twilight with his arm lovingly about Mollie's waist. He was to return to Millville next morning.

"You've never been so heavenly dear, daughter. When I'm away from you, I always think you were sweetest the time I saw you last," said he fondly. "Poor Mollie! you have such hard lines."

"No—not too hard to bear," said she, with a stout-hearted smile. Mollie never gave up before any one, least of all her father.

The old man patted her hand in a soft denial. "I know about it, dear. Don't think I don't. It will all be over some day. You mustn't come home this winter"— this with a smothered sigh. "You must stay here and grow strong. You've ben a good girl to me, daughter. I feel sometimes I hadn't orter ha' made you promise as you did; but I don't believe it'll be for long—I hope not, dear."

"Don't say so, papa, my own papa. Louis and I would rather have you stay," cried the girl, her heart swelling with the two loves and longings.

" Mebbe, mebbe, dear," said he, sadly. " Pelican got left on the train yesterday. My train won't leave me. You must gather up my papers and look them over when I go, with Louis—with Louis, mind. Have you written to him ? "

" No; I must see him before I leave for home." A little sigh escaped her as she thought how long it might be before they met again. She hoped he didn't hear it, and hastened to cover it up by saying, "I can tell him so much better. That was my promise."

" He is a good lad," said the Deacon, regretfully. "Let him know I think so. Do you remember how I used to hop like a kangaroo for you when you were a little girl ? " after a short silence.

Mollie nodded.

" And how we used to sharpen noses? "

She nodded again.

" We might do it once more ? " suggested he, doubtfully.

" Those were good days," he went on, after the childish action had been performed with the accuracy of a religious rite. " We have never been so happy since. Somehow, I've given up lolting much upon comfort here, any more. Life has long seemed to me only a journey from the cradle to the grave. But when we are dead it will be better. I don't believe we shall have to stand playing all the while. Probably God'll let us kneel down to pray between spells. We are all to be around the throne. Perhaps, as there must be a vast crowd there by this time, I won't be able to get near. But I can't help thinking that if I should even be three miles off, I shall be in the very midst of heaven; and if the Lord will only let me get a few years the start of your mother, I hope I can improve and do so well as to satisfy Him."

Mollie drew his gray head down to her shoulder with quick impulsive gesture. "Father," said she desper-·ately, "I will not let you die. I don't mind about my troubles. You *shall* be happy with Louis and me some day. We can all wait."

"No," said the old man, in sorrowful gentleness. "I have no time to wait. It was my blame that you have to; but you're good children, and won't lay it up, or anything, even when you find out—as you partly know—how bad it is. But it'll all come right by and by—I pray God very soon. I want to have it so, daughter, an' I don't like to have you pray the other way, for fear the Lord might rather listen to you."

So Deacon McCross went home. He looked a little pale and weary when he set off next morning, but that might be owing to Charley's having penetrated his room about two o'clock at night, for the pleasure of blowing a penny trumpet in his ear. "Well, well," said he, coming to at the first hoot, and bestowing a dazed but benevolent smile on the young fellow, "you an' Peace do play desput cunnin'." A commendation which the musician received with extreme gratification.

After her father's departure, Mollie settled into a quiet home-life. She studied, she visited, she darned stockings five German styles, to win Mrs. Pelican's heart. Old Mr. Pelican, who had of late taken a strong fancy for music, but possessed no ear, was charmed to find a soprano willing to help out his minstrelsy, though it *was* a disappointment to have her object to rising at half-past four in the morning, that being his time for practising in course the bass to each tune in the singing-book. When Deacon McCross had been there, they had held a few rehearsals together. But Mollie's father confided to her that friend Pelican's only successful tune proved to be,

"I was a wandering sheep," which exactly suited his style.

They played rubbers of whist in the long evenings, at which Charley concealed little less than the regulation twenty-four packs in his coat-sleeves, besides ornamenting the backs of the cards with mysterious scratches, and his father absently claimed every trick through the game without slightest reference to fourth-hand trumps, and partner's slaughtered aces. Peace revelled in afternoon toilettes and dainty fancy-work to match; and took Mollie on elegant shopping expeditions, where she met other beautiful ladies likewise attired with magnificence. She noticed on such occasions that they all bought in the ratio of four cents' worth of worsted to forty in bonbons, that they treated each other to ice-cream, talked of the musical glasses, and were every one reading the same novel; that the things each knew were identical, and they looked so precisely alike that she could not tell them apart.

Mollie's friendship for the son of the house was the oddest product of her visit. On her first arrival he used to sit in a corner of the room, with his chin propped on his palm, watching her, a look on his handsome face, half observing, half dogged ; and she on her side avoided him with morbid care. He was the family sorrow, and the author of Louis' misfortunes. Why should she not?

But she began presently to pity him. From the pet, he was fast becoming the scapegoat of the household. Never in her whole history had she found a fellow life in such case, without espousing its cause, and deliberating with careful tact upon unnumbered methods of reconciling it with itself. She could not help going through that course of thought, any more than she could help breathing. A deliciously sorrowful attraction drew her to the sufferer. Ordinarily shy, and reticent with strangers, she here became animated, witty, charming, in unplanned efforts to please. Utterly averse to formal society, she would instinctively exert her powers to the utmost to put herself *en rapport* with one of its outcasts. It had got to be a by-word with her friends, that Mary McCross was an icicle to a nice person, a nabob; and a Récamier, a De Staël, a Little Dot, to a man with a ticket-of-leave, a woman who had run away from home, or an " Irisher," of any rank, sex, or calling.

Originally drawn to Charley by this inevitable impulse she soon became attached to him for himself. With her, he developed an entirely new phase of character—treated her materially as one would a fragile toy or butterfly ; and spiritually with a humble, touching deference, as if she held the key to something he valued in himself, and only got at through her. Mollie possessed a stable, unobtrusive, sweet dignity, all her own, that was harmonious with her character ; though it sometimes repelled, it defended her from the faults of act or assaults of associates to which her complete forgetfulness of herself in the lives nearest would otherwise have constantly exposed her. It was this which made possible her numerous and warm friendships with what Mrs. Pelican called " out-of-the-way people " in a disparaging tone ; even enabled her to add the patrician Absalom to the list.

The relation began on this wise : He was sitting in the parlor, in the usual helpless forlornity of the masculine brotherhood, on a rainy day—nothing to plan, nothing to dream over, nothing to do but struggle in the gripings of Apollyon blues. Mollie found him reduced to that last refuge of vacuity—making cat's cradles by himself. She had some time grieved for him, watched with friendly pain his alternate lapses from excitement and folly to bitter, hopeless remorse, and back to reckless ill-doing again. His acquaintances were not ashamed or averse to show their contempt for him now; the more correct did not recognize him on the street. She could not bear to have things thus with Peace's brother. This afternoon, very timid, but resolved to comfort, she slipped into a seat in the corner of the sofa, and when he got the thread all arranged, leaned over and took it deftly on her own hands.

He gave a guilty side-look at this self-elected playmate. She was sitting graceful and dignified, with relaxed muscles—perfectly at ease—the pink and white thread on her extended fingers—her face bright with honest and kind intention.

He felt it a very simple thing to take back the string in the third position, and found the mountains of misery oppressing his boy's heart diminish as he did so.

" Hadn't we better be friends ? " said Mollie, resuming the first and original cradle shape, with satisfaction.

" I thought you hated me," said the man, meekly hiding his shame face, in side-wise study of the angles of the carpet.

" I expected to, but you're so miserable I can't," she answered, frank as usual. Charley looked up at her, intending to deny this imputation and assert his perfect —nay, brilliant happiness; but her glance was so pleasant and steady, and withal so clear, that he gave in directly.

" I may as well own it first as last," confessed he, with a free acting, impetuous impulse, like Peace. " I know I've done the scurvy thing by Alwood all along, and I wish from the bottom of my soul I hadn't. The fact is, my life has been a horrid mistake from the beginning. His ways made me feel it, though I helped to set him as wrong as myself, and went back on him afterward. He never was as bad as I am," said Charley, looking down with wholesome embarrassment. "There was something in him below the upper crust that wouldn't let him be. You and he are just alike, but somehow I feel differently toward you. Perhaps it's because you're a woman."

Mollie writhed from the sudden wrench at her heart-strings, and answered with manifest effort: "I don't blame you; I understand it all since I've been here. I've seen the Cereus, and the club-house, and all the spots he used to frequent. I have been putting myself in his place. One thing followed another. Louis would say, 'Be friends,' if he was with us;" whereupon she held out her hand, steady and true as of old, for all its wasted flesh and big, throbbing, blue veins, and they ratified the compact.

Deserted to each other's mercies that evening, they spent it talking—Mollie asking an occasional question, Charley relieving his mind by the first chat he had found a decent companion for in months. Next day they went out shopping together, and looked at pictures in Hazeltine's gallery. There was a large room filled with contadinas and marines, and daisies pied and ragged children, with all kinds of straw baskets, holding a great many varieties of very peculiar fruit; startling, pale-faced Io's bestowing tangible kisses on intangible Jupiters; and mild sheep with blue fleece, overshadowed by sky full of woolly clouds, well-curried oxen, and reflective fish-ponds.

Beyond, in the holy of holies, were pages; Venus just arisen from the Cytherean foam, in her shell drawn by turtle-doves; a couple of crucified Christs; some creamy-necked Madonnas, backed by gilt glories, and framed under glass. But in one corner hung a head of Jesus that made Mollie forget everything else.

The face was oval and narrow; the shading had long since faded into greenish, the thin nose gave an impression of utter flatness from its lack of profile; the hazel eyes were almost crossed in their intense, pleading, sorrowful gaze; and yet the picture contained an indefinable something that moved the observer even to tears. Charley stood watching Mollie, a thoroughly bewildered expression on his impulsive Absalom's visage, as she wiped the water from her lashes. The trouble so hopeless, and yet so patiently mastered, the hurt look of this friend of sinners, made her own woes yield an answering throb. Such a look Christ must have worn when He searched the multitude, in the judgment hall, for one familiar, loving face, in vain.

"Do you like it so much?" asked the young man, astonished. "It is ugly and meek. I don't see anything else in it."

"No, perfect," said Mollie, earnestly. "I wish it was mine. It is my exact conception of Jesus."

Its memory dwelt in her mind all that day, like the light of a star, so steady, gentle, quietly penetrating the darkness. Not even the afternoon's next adventure disturbed the peace it brought. The evening lamps were lighted before she quitted the gallery, her hand on Charley's arm. Ten paces from the door, a tall, roughly-clad fellow, with a scarlet silk handkerchief about his neck, came up, and putting his face almost under Mollie's bonnet, wished her good-evening.

Frightened and annoyed, she clung closer to her companion, who, however, only led her onward a few steps. "Now you're safe, and I'll go back and settle that," said he, and coolly returned, knocked the offender down, and, his mind free, escorted her home without more ado.

Mollie was shocked at this high-handed chastisement of her enemy; but she told Peace about it, and Peace highly approved, and deliberated upon his reward with sisterly pride—a resolve an hundredfold strengthened by the discovery of her friend in adoring contemplation of the Jesus-head which had found its way to the chimney-piece in her room. But the stately caresses tendered Charley by his sister were met with a marvellously ill grace. It was the peculiarity of this pair that they never could meet one another on common ground. Both had moods of intense desire for each other's sympathy, but neither had patience to wait for his mate to fall into his own mood, or to address himself to comprehension of his present mental state. Mollie used inly to compare them to the pith-ball illustrations of an electrical machine, which approach each other but to fly asunder with equal repulsion.

Francis Haythorne watched the friendship in progress with anything but satisfaction. He respected Mollie, and could not understand how she did right to find any pleasure in talking, riding, and walking with a man whom he despised for his irregularities. At the very best, she was belittling his idea of her. She ought to pick up her dainty garments and pass by on the other side.

A man's notion of a woman is always a clinging vine, his favorite type of the marriage relation a blasted pine-tree, rejuvenated and greened in the mantling embraces of an ivy. He rejects the notion that Baucis and Philemon became an oak and a linden whose interlaced branches formed one perfect shade.

> "Ostendit ad huc Tyaneius illic
> In cola de gemino vicinos corpore truncos."

It is a man's instinct to materialize every knowledge; but a woman's to idealize every sensation. He learns the world by knocks and bruises against sins and sinners, and she, by setting the tiny gauge of her own guilt-pangs against his faults, and having got the measure, immediately enlarging her own sufferings to fit. A man goes back to his childhood as his ideal of innocence; but a woman is purified by incessant vicarious pain every day of her life, and regards her first years with a sigh of regret, perhaps, but seldom fond regret.

In this way she knows all about him, and he exactly nothing about her.

He never understands the difference between paradise and heaven for any one but himself. When he hears of mental anguish, he thinks of remorse, not the infinite agony of pity. And because, poor blundering fellow, he loves the woman, he would deliberately take the matter out of God's hands, and lock her up in the garden, quite forgetful that she was the first to taste of the knowledge of good and evil, and so must always find his paradise only a fool's paradise, which to dwell in would be death.

How false this idea!—that no better thing could be said of a maid than that she had never left her mother's side. It means that life's smallest and greatest temptations are all before her, and every one of her weapons and defences still untried. What worse thing can be said of a girl than that her mother has never dared to trust her beyond sight? In short, the most subtle delicacy is that which is its own protection; the truest woman, she whose first training in life is to centre herself in herself, and then radiate what kindness and familiarity she please from the circumference of the perfect circle drawn about her by self-control, self-knowledge, and a purity resulting, not from ignorance of evil, but patient cultivation of good.

The world may be dangerous to the happiness of such an one; but never to her character. Her friendship is as safe to herself, as invaluable to its object; she makes it a part of her religion.

But Francis Haythorne being a man of larger theory than experience, could not know this; and a fresh instance of Charley's levity still more contributed to his disgust.

No woman ever yet took the slightest interest in an unmarried man, that she didn't urge him to go to church; and Peace and Mollie oddly enough fell into this folly at the same time. For you can sometimes improve burnt cake by frosting and paring; but an icing of religion is not leavening the lump; patience, kindness, day after day's quiet influence, and unconscious stimulating by example, are the human means to that end. And neither the Sybarite nor Absalom were in any condition to go to worship. Peace, however, rejected our theory, and held that in spiritual things boiling goes down, not up; and set her kettle under the stove, expecting ebullition.

The family were assembled in the library one Saturday night, when Miss Pelican produced a tiny prayer-book, with covers quarter of an inch thick, clasps, gold-crossed book-mark, and rubric, all nicely printed in its pristine color. "It's a philopœna present from Mr. Haythorne," said she, "and we are going to church to-morrow to christen it. I think it's so nice to have a church that dates back to the Twelve Apostles, where one can rest on authority, and one, too, so eminently aristocratic."

Now this was tantamount to throwing a fire-brand among the standing corn, in a family of Presbyterians, Episcopals, and Free-thinkers. Every one set himself firmly on his seat, prepared to maintain his cause or perish.

"I can't approve," said her father, drawing up his short, fat legs, and bracing for the struggle, "of any religious body that refuses to unite with any other, for Christian work or worship."

"But you and Mollie are schismatics," retorted Charley, devoutly crossing himself to aggravate Peace. "All schism is sin. Why don't you come over and have a bishop ?"

"Why don't I have a monkey and a hand-organ ?" remarked his sire, with disgust.

"Because you've got a poll parrot with a penny whistle," put in Peace, darting a wrathful look at the incorrigible.

Mr. Haythorne hereupon found himself in another scene, and began what he supposed, too fondly, to be an imperceptible glide from one chair to another toward the door. Of course Mrs. Pelican arrested his progress, by innocently inquiring if he didn't think written prayer far superior to extemporaneous.

"As near as I can make out," laughed Mollie, "Peace believes in a basket let down from heaven on a string of apostles, and scoops up whom she may; whereas her father erects an edifice over the pit, and hopes to ascend its winding steps of doctrine to bliss."

"I don't want any chuckle-headed fellow to prejudice the Deity against me, by his canting whines," was his instant reply. "My father was cheated by a Presbyterian deacon once, and I despise the whole brood."

"But you forget the force of the expression, 'Lead us in Prayer,'" said Mollie, reddening a little, for she still loved the forms of a church whose received extreme tenets she had long since left behind. "The speaker is the audible voice of the congregation. If you do not choose to join what the Methodist brothers call the

Amen Corner, you can offer your own petitions mentally."

"I prefer the regular service," answered Mr. Haythorne, shaking his head. "It is refined, and in absolutely perfect English, and taste."

"At least you like the system of Church letters," skirmished Mr. Pelican, the normal state of aggression on the part of the dissenters, and stately scorn among the genealogy elevated sect, being nicely preserved in these never-ending squabbles. "A young man goes away from home —is a member of the church—takes his certificate—and is thereby provided with companions and perhaps work."

"I don't think much of letters of introduction," quoth Mr. Haythorne, loftily. The Sybarite was a sceptic in pleasure excursions into metaphysics, but could not contradict his inborn love of refined, elegant, and æsthetical observances, if one was to observe religiously at all. "How do you know but designing persons might forge them? I had plenty of recommendations to officials in Europe, but I wouldn't use one."

A burst of laughter greeted this word of wisdom; and Peace turned to Mollie, saying, "I suppose you will hardly care to attend the same ministration that I do, to-morrow. The forms are scrupulously carried out, and I know how you dislike ritualism."

"Very true," acknowledged Mollie, composedly. "I do abhor any one that sets himself up in piety on an ancestry, but I bought a prayer-book myself, yesterday, and Charley and I are going to stay to communion."

His sister made a wry face. "He'll be just Presbyterian enough to sit through the Glorias, and stand in the prayers," cried she; "but never mind, try it if you like."

Charley made a slight facial contortion in reply to this.

"Did you say you had a cold and your nose was all stopped," said he, feelingly.

"Yes," said Peace, a little remorseful.

"Your tongue—I suppose nothing could stop that," in a still more concerned tone.

The young lady found the laugh against her, and being "touchy," in view of the family contempt for her victory in Francis Haythorne's religious training, retired soon after in gloom.

"There! I've snubbed Charley," said she, repentantly.

"Well," answered Mollie, who was darning stockings in her friend's room, absent-minded—as usual.

"But that's not the worst: I've snubbed father too, and I must go and make it right."

"Is it all fixed?" asked her friend, seeing her return radiant after a short absence.

Peace nodded, and replaced her scarlet morocco purse in her pocket.

"What did you say," inquired Mollie, curious to know how Lady Lofty would effect an apology.

"I asked him for fifty cents."

"Quem deus vult perdere prius dementat," might have been set down after the indignity Peace had offered her brother.

Next morning, Charley presented himself at Mollie's door, elegantly gotten up, with a view to accompanying her to worship.

The ringing bells and smiling day invited forth, and his companion was too deeply mindful of her recent study upon the preparation for confession, and the psalms, to mark the wicked look on his face, or the big horse-shoe magnet carried in a pious attitude under his arm.

The seat in church proved a matter for no small manœuvring; the young gentleman utterly refusing to

let Mollie pass in decorously with Peace, but thrusting
her with himself into the pew behind, after an ominous
glare at the occupying strangers.

Peace who was very devout, rose from her knees, and
disposed herself in a posture to give fixed attention to
the epistles and gospels.   Then Mollie, sitting too far off
to help, was horrified to perceive her escort produce his
instrument, and applying it gently to the back of his sister's head, draw forth, in triumph, an adhesive hair-
pin.

Off came the curl that imparted such a graceful air to
the neck, and the appendage was joyfully jammed into
Charley's pocket, while the sufferer looked behind her
uneasily.

" The glory of a woman is her long hair," read the
minister, just as Charley tackled an enormous bit of
iron that secured the whole coiffure.   Up to this time
all came easily from the loose twists of Peace's handsome
tresses, but the one in hand resisted.   The lady gave her
head an impatient toss, but the magnet wouldn't let go.
Charley determined to make or break—gave a fearful
pull that brought the tears to her eyes, and the whole
rippling abundance over her shoulders, while her jaunty
hat, deprived of its natural support, tilted over her nose,
and, after a futile clinging of perhaps a second, dropped
into her lap.   Mrs. Grundy saw the catastrophe, and
Peace found her misery complete.   She would fain have
concealed her tears of vexation in a handkerchief so fine
they leaked through; but Charley's vengeance was not yet
satisfied.   The last tune was given out—" Portugal;"
the congregation were to join.   Now it was Mr. Haythorne's turn to shudder.   His tormentor was a basso
profundo, and he dreaded, not without cause, for Mr.
Pelican was by no means backward in such preparations

as unbuttoning his vest, coughing preparatory, and expanding to the full his well-developed chest.

The organist gave the signal, the quartette piped up, the congregation joined like the guests at the Irishman's wedding, who came one in a gang, two in a gang, and three by themselves,—when suddenly Charley led in with a harmonic burst that shook the quavering soprano into fragments. And from that moment, organ, choir, people, priests—all faded away into that one central figure—head thrown back, foot keeping time, hands clenched, eyes devoutly rolled, Charley Pelican singing " Portugal."

If Francis Haythorne's horror needed a finishing touch, this gave it; and he lost no time in taking Mollie aside, and warning her not to associate with a young man whose reputation was so confirmed for recklessness and folly.

He came in an unfortunate hour. Miss McCross rose from the piano, at which she had been accompanying the scapegrace in an extravaganza upon the " Oysterman "— where the pathetic acting was perfectly laughable; coupled with a lesson in " Johnnie Smoker " equally amusing, and still red-cheeked and smiling, followed the remonstrating friend into the parlor, seated herself obediently, and prepared to give close attention to anything he might have to impart.

His conscience told him the task was ungracious, but what man can resist the opportunity to enact the harmless parental toward a charming woman. Without exactly analyzing the thought, the young physician had an idea of pleasant, steady eyes raised to his, dewy with gratitude, and a murmured " Thanks! how foolish I have been ! What have you saved me from ? Be my brother always," which should swell the aforesaid paternal interest

17

into delightful self-approval, and sense of difficult duty performed.   He accordingly waded in with boldness.

He referred to his respect for her, his long acquaintance; in short, her unprotected position and guileless nature animated him to his friendly task.   Forgive him, but if she allowed herself such unrestricted intercourse with young Pelican, people would talk.

Mollie's face during this little adjuration formed a study of discomfort, but it cleared as he proceeded, and when he finished, she asked with inimitable naïvete:

"What will they say?"

Mr. Haythorne was cornered.   In lieu of meek submission to the masculine judgment, she demanded explanations.   He wished he'd held his tongue, and remarked with freezing dignity, that no other young lady of his acquaintance would have entangled herself in so disadvantageous a connection, and he permitted his soul to hope she would dissolve it at once.

"You think, then, that I am not fit to be a friend to a man in involved circumstances?" asked Mollie, her innocent face precluding the belief that she comprehended his position.   "Thanks for your good opinion."

"I mean that a young lady has no right to any acquaintance except under her mother's immediate supervision," he exclaimed, thoroughly irritated, "and you prove it."

Miss McCross laughed softly.   His sense of politeness rose against him, he retracted, and became more enraged every instant.   The young lady was not a whit out of countenance.

"Admitting, then, that being a woman grown I have some shadow of guiding principle," said she in her calm, matter-of-fact way, "how am I to account to God for the friendship and respect with which he has inspired Mr. Pelican for me?"

Perploxed by this view, the gentleman suggested that he should think she ought to be smart enough to manage that herself.

"When I see Louis, how am I to explain my forgetfulness to do good to the one man who repented wronging him."

Mr. Haythorne said he didn't know; he was thinking about her reputation.

"Do you mean to say any one will attack my truth, my purity, or my faith to my lover, if I simply persist in rendering common kindness to a suffering man?"

"No, he didn't want to say he meant exactly that."

"But you think so," responded Mollie, quietly. "You have lived more years than I. Francis Haythorne, you have drifted easily down the current of a man's pleasantest experiences, but I have come face to face with life's realities. Forgive me if I, too, tell my opinion. Reputation in the slanderous tongue of gossip is not to be made the light-house by which an honest-purposed man can shape his course. It is not the light that will illuminate his success. If one will be true to principle, true to Christianity, he must not think of himself, must be satisfied to be, and let 'they say' prove what it will." She was in earnest, spoke out of her heart, full of the lesson her lover's pain had taught her, and the suffering whereby she learned it was still sharp. But the Sybarite could not understand; she saw that she was not comprehended, and condensed her answer. "In short, as long as Peace's brother honors me by his liking I shall do my best to be worthy of it, by promoting his happiness to the extent of my ability."

Mollie only meant to explain her position thoroughly, but her would-be protector rose stiffly, and said that he'd tried to do the kind thing, and should wash his hands of the whole business. Something about his self-satisfied disapproval suddenly fired the young lady's wrath, and she rejoined in a good deal of heat, " Quite a needless operation, Francis Haythorne. Those soft fingers have never been soiled in helping a single human being from the slough, be he never so wretched ; and let me tell you that to pass by continually on the other side, as is your way, will do for Levites and priests, perhaps, but is disgrace to a gentleman."

As Mr. Haythorne quitted the room thoroughly discomfited, and Charley, ensconced behind a window-curtain, had heard this whole interview, what more natural than for him to emerge thence all impulse, and, urged by shame and anger, pour out his woes to his declared friend.

" I haven't been drunk but twice since you've been here," said he, " and I shouldn't ever have turned out so, if father hadn't kept a horse-whip for me down cellar, and mother a hiding-place up garret, when she thought I'd get it. It isn't good for a fellow to be see-sawed that way," with a sudden laugh in the midst of his misery ; " I know my reputation isn't good ; it ought not to be."

" It might be bettered," suggested Mollie.

" But I don't love to behave," cried Charley energetically. " Be good and you will be happy, but you'll have an awful stupid time."

Mollie didn't answer, only looked down.

Her silence made Charley uneasy. " Did Haythorne surprise you to-night? " asked he.

" No," very unwillingly.

" Did you suppose it would cost you so much to make friends with me ? "

" Yes."

" Then it does cost ? " said Charley, half in interrogation, half regret.

"Yes," said Mollie, frankly, "it costs, but I'm willing."

He sprang to his feet and walked impetuously up and down the room.

Mollie sat quite still, and prayed for him in her heart.

"Why are you satisfied?" said he, throwing himself on the carpet beside her.

"Because I'm a Christian, and love Louis." This time the answer came with a struggle. It is hard to unveil our precious things to eyes that are alien. Mollie underwent a conflict with herself nowadays, whenever she named her affianced, and hating *cant* above all things—except to her Sunday-school scholars, she seldom mentioned her religious emotions at all.

Charley caught up the reply, and began a second race through the parlor. Pretty soon he came back, panting.

"No woman shall ever get a chance to bear this for me twice," cried he. "If I don't turn over a new leaf this minute, you needn't ever go down Main Street with me again. I promise—swear—anything you like. But you mustn't let Peace, or that doubled rose-leaf Haythorne, know, or I shan't have courage to keep resolution." Delighted with himself, he hereupon walked the elephant all round by the wall, and stood on his head, and looked at the acquiescent holder of his good resolves from between his knees.

Mollie went to bed happy that night, as who would not. But her feelings were destined to receive a slight check the very next day, when Peace took her favorite walk, past the bronze statue of Liberty. A pointing, snickering crowd had gathered thereabout, and no wonder! As soon as the girls came near enough to see, they found it adorned with a vast and magnificent bustle of newspapers; and Charley sitting complacently in the office opposite, watching the effect of his handiwork, and Francis Haythorne, pale with fury, in the act of being dispersed by a policeman, who thought he did it.

But for all this, the promise was kept, and Charley had a hard time, and so did Mollie.

Nursing that mercurial spirit back to hope, was no easy task of itself; but it entailed a host of outside troubles.

Mollie was separately warned by all her acquaintance, beginning with Miss Petingil, and, in the midst of the gossip and censure that every one felt it right to bring to her ears, she scarcely knew whether the tie that bound her to the reprobate was indelicate self-will, or solemn duty. Her griefs, forced upon her from without, had not a tithe of the stinging, maddening, soul exasperation brought by her pride and self-satisfaction, continually wounded through uncomprehending comment and rebuke. A thousand times she turned the key upon self and her troubles, half resolved to fly the struggle; but as surely, the fact that, respectable or the reverse, Charley was *trying* his best, and depended on her, made her duty plain. Then she would pray, remember Louis and his greater suffering, and peaceful and strong in sense of integrity, go down-stairs to endure and conquer.

She used to walk and ride with her care, when it seemed that every curious, doubtful glance bestowed on them was a brand laid on her soul; and she was thankful when her acquaintance crossed the street to avoid meeting her, the righteous disapproval in their faces made her so wretched.

And all this happened, not because Charley was vicious or criminal—other men did far worse than he every day of their lives—but simply because his follies were, little and big, all done in the face and eyes of society, in regardless opposition to its usages. And society frowned,

not because its morals were shocked, but because its hypo-
crisies were forgotten.

How much the origin of all this saw of his friend's discomfort, he never told; but the fact was he knew the
whole, and the sense that she was willing to suffer for
him was the gate that shut the old life out behind him,
and as truly the one source of courage to go on with the
new.

As long as a man stands face down-hill, he finds companionship in plenty, at every stage of descent. But let
him turn to climb back, and neither blood nor religion
give anything but kicks. Charley used to come home
frantic with the slights and insults he received, and rush
away to escape the annoyances that awaited him there.
The anxious, silent review his mother gave him at
every entrance; the matter-of-course counting out in
case of responsibility, by his father; Peace's invariable expectation of his wrong-doing where wrong-doing was possible; her lover's gentlemanly toleration of
him—were all merited, but none the less blows to the timid
and sensitive self-respect just beginning to spring out of
a new purpose of right living. The very guests at the
house would compliment Peace, be suave to Mollie, fawn
on the rich proprietor, admire Mr. Haythorne, and, with
bland purpose, forget Absalom's very existence.

It seemed to Mollie that the whole structure of society
was arranged to prevent a bad man's ever returning to good
behavior. Charley didn't talk much of his troubles, but
he'd sit brooding over them hour after hour, his handsome
face gray with misery; and she was forever on the rack,
lest in a moment of despair he'd give way to some piece of
folly, and roll down to the bottom of the Hill of Difficulty
without ado. At such times she used to bring her guitar,
and sing softly. It did no good to talk. Her old-fash-

ioned ballads, rendered with the perfect simplicity of feeling; her few quaint hymns, sung as if to please herself,
not her hearer, were a better, because more matter-of-
course, mode of consolation.

She used to begin with "Robin Grey," and then give
the "Rainy Day," and then "Kathleen O'Moore," or
"Captain O'Kane." By that time he'd be ready to have
her say, "Never mind, Charley; just keep on, and it'll all
come right," which was at once prophecy, advice, and
prayer. Sunday evenings she held to her custom of going off by herself to sing, "When marshalled on the
Nightly Plain," and "In the Cross of Christ I glory,"
and dream of Louis, who had loved to render them to
her in gone-by days. It often happened that Charley
stole thither, lonely and forlorn, to sit in a corner in the
dark, unnoticed, and listen; and Mrs. Pelican came with
equal silence to strengthen her soul by the Christian melody.
Peace, too, assumed the sofa, and Francis Haythorne
drifted without definite purpose to the other end of the
same piece of furniture; and by and by the brisk and
portly master of the house would appear, grumbling at the
neglectful servants, strike a light, dissolve the spell, and
reveal the astonished household to each other, soft-hearted,
off their guard, and ready to blend into the wholesome
family unity, so rudely shattered by misdoing and hurt
pride. But in spite of these swelling buds of promise,
the waiting time was dreary. Peace, who held far less
hope than Mollie, because she had more at stake, and
who blamed herself for bringing her guest into so hard a
place, was unnaturally mirthful, and belligerent, cross, and
exacting by turns. Old Mr. Pelican scolded Charley all
the time, because he neglected the business and took no
interest. His mother, with her usual quiet pertinacity,
resolved to have him make sure of his salvation, and go

into Holy Orders—which the poor fellow, whose new-sprung principles weren't any longer than cabbage sprouts, couldn't wish to do. Peace also presented him with an armful of nauseous sermons—never read by herself—and Francis Haythorne told her to advise him to culti-vate his sense of the æsthetic as a safeguard againt lapses from the ideal beautiful, and lent him Ruskin, and some treatises on art. Half wild among these well-meaning but diverse leadings, their subject had nearly gone under. Mollie fell into a panic lest the strain should be too great, and watched developments with increasing dismay. Just as he was on the point of loathing the honeycomb, she had an enlightening, and insisted that he should take her to Barnum's, Sam Sharpley's Minstrels, and the Man of Airlie. The family, who never hesitated on amusements for themselves, were in high dudgeon at this summary dragging to the slaughter of their recovered lamb. But it acted like soda on a disturbed stomach; and when she found her patient dyeing the poodle purple and yel-low, and subsequently hitching a tin dipper to his tail, in a renewed sense of the value of life in the paths of righteousness, she felt that it paid.

In the midst of all these disturbed waters, Francis Haythorne sailed serene. He was the only let-up in the house. Having freed his mind and swallowed his wrath at the result, he proceeded to oil the family points of fric-tion, fended off vexed questions, and made himself com-fortable in spite of all. He once or twice hinted to Mollie as obscurely possible some way of helping Charley, taking care at the same time to show that he disapproved utterly of her course. Otherwise, he left her altogether alone, devoting himself to Peace, who sadly needed aid; and he contrived withal to be imperturbably good-humored and at ease, so that a mere look at him as he strolled

17*

about the house, elegant and dainty and lazy, in the loveliest of purple velvet lounging caps, the furriest of dressing-gowns, the most beflowered of slippers, a brown meerschaum at mouth, and the literary sweets of the day in hand, the piano in dreamy contemplation—was refreshing.

——————

CHAPTER XXVIII.

"Chickeny, chickeny, craney-crow,
  I went to the well to wash my toe,
  When I came back my chickens were dead."

MOLLIE didn't lose the affection of Syllabub when she departed for Top Town. Few weeks passed without a letter or visit from some of the little group of friends her gentle kindness had gathered about her.

One day Peace entered the brown-and-gold bed-room, where her companion was wont to recreate herself with choice volumes of entomological lore, and all manner of curious needle-work. The damsel's eyes were flashing with mirth, and she sank upon a stuffed ottoman in a paroxysm of laughter.

"Amos Daley is down-stairs, and he's brought you something"—here she went off again,—"'something to keep ye from bein' lonely,' and he evidently expects you to bring it right up into your room for a pet."

"What do you mean, Peace?" cried Mollie, springing to her feet, pleasure quickening her pulse and breath; and she nervously smoothed her hair—always shining and dainty in arrangement—preparatory to descent.

"Oh, never mind! you'll find out," answered the cachinnating Juno, becoming apoplectic in her endeavors to obtain composure. "He has mounted guard over it as a soldier would over the stars and stripes.

> "'Win her with gifts, if she respect not words;
> Dumb jewels often, in their silent kind,
> More quick than words, do move a woman's mind.'"

Seeing her friend's emotions grown too strong for further utterance, Mollie sought Amos without delay.

Seated upon the extreme edge of a scarlet damask chair, his long limbs gathered under him, his hat tightly grasped as if prepared to run at the slightest alarm, our hero's sharp eyes had already photographed on his mind every item of the massive and completely appointed drawing-room. Somewhat embarrassed by the complication of pier-glasses, landscapes by Turner, velvet carpets, carved chairs and contadinas, sported by the Pelicans, the young man advanced, blushing but friendly, and deposited at Mollie's feet a covered basket, from which issued an ominous "cut-cut" that would not be stifled. "It's a small bit of a pet for ye from meself," he explained, with modest confidence.

"Sit down, please," cried Mary, and drew the enigma toward her.

"I must be goin'," said Amos, gazing wistfully at the door, but seated himself, notwithstanding, in a bolt-upright attitude, whose intense but persevered in discomfort did credit to his stoicism.

As Mollie peeped into the wickerware, an immense shanghai rooster suddenly straightened himself, and eyed his astonished recipient with a malevolent glance; then, coolly stepping to her lap, executed a clarion note that suggested to old Mr. Pelican, dozing off in his afternoon nap, a vision of war-painted Blackfeet uttering the fatal whoop, as he had seen them in his youth, and sent Peace away from the door crack in an audible giggle.

"How handsome he is!" exclaimed delighted Mollie, to whom any testimony of affection was sacredly precious, and whose valuing of a gift sometimes bore an inverse ratio to its fitness. The pleasure in her face was reflected on Amos' freckled countenance, as he exclaimed proudly:

"Jest hear him! I teached him to do that," and enticed the tall biped to his own knee with a low "Zack-Zack."

"This is a most majestic vision, and harmonious charmingly. May I be bold to think these spirits?" said Peace looking in.

"No, ma'am, it's a chicken," answered Amos, rising to make an angular bow; "and excuge me sayin' his name's Zack."

"Can't you have him sing again?" inquired the young lady, bent on aggravating the shy, proud visitor. "I can suck melancholy out of a song, as a weasel sucks eggs."

"Sure it's small politeness the cock owes the weasel," retorted Amos, "except the weight of his too futs just, which he'll show you ef you meddle with him, I'll be bound. Doppy an' me got him for you last fall, Miss Mollie; but he didn't take to no thricks easy, an' you fell sick before we had him larnt. I sez to Mr. Vedder, 'Mr. Jan,' sez I, 'there's a lady in Millville as I tought lots on, cause she'd ben kind to me, an' I wanted to give something to, an' them long-legged fellows was a fine sort of fowl;' au' 'Amos,' sez he, 'the perty white leghorns is better fur a lady—but you're welcome to anything ye see runnin' around the place,' meanin' the poultry yard, 'the place,' sez he—'at all, at all.' 'But sure it's the biggest I'd give, if any,' thinks I, an' Doppy an' me have brought up the chick from a little feller, and we thought"—here Amos glanced sidewise at Peace, who was brimming with mischievous fun, and came to a dead halt.

"Go on," said she, bestowing a look of studied tenderness on the strutting fowl, "there is much music in his fitful hymn heard in the drowsy watches of the night, I suppose?"

The angry blood rushed into the young Irishman's face, and, with one vicious swoop, he pounced on his rooster and started for the door.

Mollie, whose annoyance at Peace's jokes had been the chief incentive to their progress, was beforehand. Seizing the would-be tormentor by the arms, she forcibly turned her, laughing and resisting, from the room.

Intent on studying the ways of the big folks, Amos loosed his clutch on the pet, which made the first use of its liberty to fly at Mrs. Pelican, who had come timidly in to view the wonder. Away skipped the old lady, gray curls bobbing, and the red slippers, that caught Zack's fancy, in full display; Zack himself following with deep shaking wattles and outspread wings, round the parlor and out to the hall, through the parlor again, now fairly cornered, now skipping forth triumphant, the eyes of the fowl red with fury, the lips of his prey white with fear. "O Mollie, Mollie," she gasped, as, fairly penned behind the stairs, she strove to elude her enemy by a series of tremendous leaps, "would you mind asking the young man to call his chicken away? I mean no disrespect to the bird— but indeed—I am a little—" here she executed a spring prodigious, "out of practice with poultry."

"Of coorse," said Amos, concisely. "Bless ye! he was only playin' wid ye. Me an' Doppy larnt him that —Sakes, you hain't see half his thricks. Here, Zack, do the spread-eagle; bow to your missus." But Zack was too much interested in the red slippers, whereupon Amos quietly picked him up and stuffed him into the basket. "There," said he, deeply disgusted. "Doppy told me not to try to show him off in a strange place, cause it's the nature of us chaps to be bushful."

The awkward, self-conscious Irishman, vainly attempting to quench the eager, scarlet-eyed cock in the basket, on one side; Mrs. Pelican, exhausted and disarranged beyond parallel, in costume on the other; Peace executing cuts behind the dining-room door, in feeble imitation of her mother's and her own mental perplexity at extricating them from the curious complication in good-humor, were too much for Mollie's gravity; she sat down on the floor to have her laugh out, whereupon dear, gentle Mrs. Pelican, finding her terror temporarily suppressed, came from her hiding-place in the closet, among the brooms and dusters, with a few green and purple feathers rampant among her curls, perhaps as trophies; but she joined so heartily in the mirth, that Mr. Daley got over his mortification, and in lieu of instant departure, fowl and all, gave up the biped to the footman's care, with beaming face.

"Tell me about little Doppy," said Mary, when, their friends disposed of, they were cosily seated in two green easy-chairs in the library.

A cloud passed over Amos' open countenance. "I don't know," responded he, uneasily. "I hain't see her fur a week."

"Why not?" persisted Mollie, suspecting something wrong from his manner.

"Me an' Doppy ain't friends no longer," responded Amos, tracing out the pattern of fern leaves on the carpet with the toe of his boot. "I hain't nothing to say agin little Doppy. We've stood by each other for years and years; but she's contrairy beyond anything ever I see, and won't listen to nuthin,' howsomever you put it."

"What's she done?" cried Mollie, aghast.

"Me an' Doppy made it up together, an' Doppy left it fur me, she knowin' I like to do anything fur her; an' when I'd done it, she flies right up an' sez, 'Amos Dalcy,' sez she, 'it's a mean trick you've ben puttin' on the likes of me,' sez she, 'an' ye needn't be hangin' agin my door-posts, seein' you've served me so,' sez she, 'fur I hate the sight of ye; an' of coorse I wint."

"But what did you do that was wrong?" pursued Mollie, rather mystified by this recital.

"I hain't done nuthin'," insisted Amos, stoutly. "I minded jest what she said,—as how Aleck Heffron's sister was lonesome, an' had no partners at the social dances; and 'Amos,' sez she, 'it's no more'n right ov you to dance wid her an' be polite.' An' I done as she said. When the evenin' was past, seein' Aleck went off with the other young lady he had brought, an' the poor thing had none to see her home, I asked if I mightn't, though I didn't care too much, an' I thought Doppy'd come along widg us. But she wouldn't do no such thing; an' ran off as fast as she could. She hain't spoke civil sence, though it's most two weeks now."

His face of sleepless misery, when he concluded this dismal tale, was fairly heart-rending. Now too that the color raised by the excitement of Zack's performances had abated, Mollie noticed how tired and worn he looked.

"Are you very unhappy?" she asked by way of a feeler.

"Yes, I am," he answered earnestly; "I hain't had the spirit to work or nothin', sence; I lay awake the hull of last night thinkin' about it; you see it ain't the same between me an' Doppy, as it is between other folks.

Doppy an' me has ben friends from the time we was dirty an' swearin' an' miserable. An' I've helped Doppy, an' she's ben good to me, an' I've took care of her in ways her mother might ha done, if so be as she'd had a mother, lookin' after her in the matter of Joe. Though we're respectable, we can't forget how it was when we could call no man's good word ourn, that is, I can't."

"But you have plenty of other friends now," suggested Mollie, her soul giving ready homage to his faithfulness, but womanlike, wanting to try him further.

"Not like Doppy," with his whole soul in the denial; "takin' 'em all together, they ain't worth her little finger. From the day I shied the kitten at her, straight out, she's ben more to me, than any other feller in Millville. When she sez, 'Amos, you had orter go to work,' I went to work. She knows all my secrets, an' I know all hers. There isn't a day in the year but what I've see her; I split wood for her, an' set the glass in her windows, and liked to, and to do lots of things I wouldn't for any one livin'. An'—an' now it's all up!" Poor Amos choked down a sob.

> "'If love were what the rose is,
>   And I were like the leaf,'"

quoted Peace, who rather enjoyed such complications. "The trouble is, that Amos don't know the difference between Daphne and Amyrillis. Is Miss Heffron as handsome as Aleck?"

"No, she ain't," positively, and exchanging the expression of half-intelligent perplexity, with which he usually followed the ladies' side conversations, for one of certain disgust. "She sets her eyes on a feller as if she wanted to eat him for table sass, an' when you're dancin' with her, she mighty nigh puts her head on your shoulder.

I've heard Doppy say many a time it warn't no right thing for a girl to do. Doppy, she always carries herself like a queen; an' though she's a real beauty, no feller ever laid a finger on her arm, even. As for the Heffron, I never want to set eyes on her agin, an' I wouldn't then, if it hadn't ben for Doppy."

"Oh, well, there are better fish in the sea than ever were caught; get another friend if she's so disagreeable," advised Peace with an eye to possible aggravation. Such feeling in men looked like a myth to the coquette.

"I don't want no other," cried he passionately; "I won't have nobody but her. She's the only one I care anything about in Syllabub. I dare trust my life with Doppy, but now she's so mean I hate her."

"You must have had an encounter when you went for Zack this morning," suggested Mollie, who was pretty well decided to seek an early interview with Miss Mulligan.

The remembrance apparently added fresh fuel to the fire. "Yis, I did," cried Amos, clutching his basket vindictively, "an' small loss if I hadn't. 'Here,' sez she, puttin' her head through the window, 'hadn't ye better carry yer old rid, cluckin', paddy hin, to Miss Mollie?' an' I tuck it. Now I understand that for an out and out insult," cried Amos, getting on his dignity. "I'll not let her nor nobody else, be it who they may, say to me, as has had the care of Mr. Vedder's fancy poultry for up'ards of two years, that I don't know a fine shanghai with a dash of fighting blood in him, from one of those miserable animiles runnin' around Syllabub; I'll never forgive her; I'll never speak to her again—not if she stands weepin' afore my eyes for a hundred years." Moved by the pathetic thought of Doppy in tears, Amos looked as if he would gladly have forgiven her then and there; a shudder of terror ran through Mollie's sincere sympathy. She could take a fowl of low degree into her affections. But a game cock!

"Will he fight, Amos?" she asked, bestowing a terrified glance at Peace.

"Without doubt," interrupted that young lady joyfully; "Amos would never have brought him at all this trouble, if he couldn't. How I shall enjoy setting him at Francis Haythorne! I haven't been able to think up anything to plague him, since I let off the alarm clock to flirt with medical students in the next block, and he turned out to have been there and heard it."

"Dade, an' ye tell the truth," cried Amos, flattered. "With his size, 'n the fightin' blood in him, I'll lay him agin any rooster not trained in all Millville. Why, Doppy an' me had to keep him shut up, on account of him pickin' the eyes out of all the chickens that comed into the yard. If I was you, I wouldn't let him loose when strangers bes around. It's a trick of hisn' to run at old gentlemen, specially if they wear low shoes."

His listener shuddered, remembering that such was Mr. Pelican's invariable custom.

"He don't eat more corn than most roosters, an' he is good for one thing—to wake you up. Doppy sez he'll never let her sleep after five o'clock in the morning, even in winter, he makes so much noise. I've heard him myself where I live; that's two blocks off. He's better'n a whistle for that. But what's the use? Doppy's mad, an' takes on so, I don't care for him, nor nothing else, any longer."

"Can't you prevail on her to listen to reason, Amos?"

"No," returned he, sorrowfully, "I don't expect to be friends with her no more. I didn't think it would ever come to this; but it has—so— Well," said he, getting up and grabbing his cap, "I may's well be goin'. You wouldn't do nuthin' about it, would you? I allus thought lots of Doppy, but the style she's ben goin' on these two weeks is awful, lookin' the other way when you meet her, an' callin' you a hypocrite, an' then sayin' that about Zack: it's too much to stand!"

"She only did it to plague."

"More shame to her," he answered. "She had a right to know different by now. When she'll want to hurt a feller as has never gone back on her, she's got a bad heart. Now she's respectable, she thinks she can't do better than rid her of a great awkward lout, as was friends with her afore, an' it's a new boy, with a beaver hat an' cane, that sings a rowdy song out of tune, she's takin' up with. Good-by, Zack; I don't want to stay in Millville, nor nowhere near. Good-by, miss."

Poor Amos!

CHAPTER XXIX.

" Had a little Hobby-Horse,
　　His name was Dapple Grey,
　　His head was made of pea-straw,
　　His tail was made of hay."

"COME," said Mr. Pelican, senior; "come, Mollie and Peace. Let's all go and hear Wendell Phillips to-night. He is to talk on 'Temperance, Labor, and Women.' The Temperance Society— Good Samaritans—bring him here, and I've bought course tickets to help them along." So the rich liquor-dealer's family, with Mr. Haythorne in close attendance, in due time settled themselves into the most prominent seats in the hall, and addressed their minds to a characteristic talk from the veteran agitator.

Quiet—a fine-cut gentleman—absorbed so much in the grandeur of his subject as to identify himself with it, the very simplicity of his silver tongue carried conviction to his audience. Old Mr. Pelican writhed under the stabs of a huge pin Peace brought with her as a punctuation point; and Francis Haythorne sniffed in all the critical parts, but his sniffs were those of a man convinced against his will. The orator spoke of the home, not as a spot to be brutalized by coarse influx of masculine error, but as a heavenly centre, whence light should issue to all the world; the temple of the Lord, from beneath whose threshold shall flow the waters of healing and purification. The family, he said, was God's type of government, and should be carried out. It was not because women were good that they should vote; but because God made man and woman one flesh, and in their every separation we possess but half a thing; and so a maimed politics, maimed religion, maimed civilization.

Mollie sat perfectly quiet, weighing, and feeding off every word. We often go on living for long months, with every day, as it seems to us, just like every other day; and then suddenly some half hour's talk, some book, some well-sung opera, some sermon, some chance word, sets fire to the trains thus unconsciously laid, and we experience a mental explosion, and are never the same to ourselves again. Thus it happened with her. Years of work in Patience of Hope, unwittingly doing just what men say women cannot do; years of agony for one and another friend snared in the pitfalls of life, about which, women, they say, can possibly know nothing;

years of patient reading on all the questions that perplex political economists; years of self-dissatisfaction, because, in all these things that she cared for, she could have no part, for she was "only a girl"; and now the door was all at once opened, and she stood outside of tradition, and knew that what God put in her to love, God set her to do. In the joyful new consciousness of her birthright, she felt her eyes again and again fill with tears. Her heart throbbed with longing to find her clew, and begin at once the work for which she had thirsted so long. Just then she was startled at seeing Charley drag his immense silk-handkerchief ostentatiously from his pocket, and duck his head as if to sneeze.

Now if they had walked through the snow instead of riding in state; or if the audience had been rough, and smelled of beer and dish-water, rather than ylang-ylang and bouquet; or if the atmosphere had been chilly, not tempered to the utmost nicety of steam horizontal pipe-heating—it might have been necessary to sneeze; but under the circumstances it struck her as singularly out of taste.

"I'm some on sternutation," whispered he confidentially.

"O Charley, don't!" she implored, catching hold of him, "for pity's sake don't."

This attracted Peace's attention. "Have the kindness to behave yourself if you know how," said she, sharply.

"I wish I hadn't come," complained Francis Haythorne, miserably sure that something wicked had called up the innocent expression adorning the face of the handsome scapegrace.

Charley overheard, and catching the gentleman's anxious eye, laid his finger under his nose in marked attempt at suppressing the intruder—alas! without avail. Out

it came; not one, but two, three, four,—each like a
thunder clap—the sufferer bowing himself to the work,
and apparently feeling intense mortification.

If there was anything Mrs. Pelican feared, it was
taking cold. She said it always located in the back of her
neck, and injured her comfort for weeks; and she whispered to Peace that she knew she felt a draft on her
left cheek, and immediately began coughing and sneezing
herself, each effort being extremely violent, and the
accompanying noise ludicrously small.

Aroused by these demonstrations, a woman in the seat
behind observed that if she had supposed the night so
damp she should not have brought Freddy—a delicate-
looking child with black circles around its eyes—and
soon after, becoming alarmed, she rose and left with him,
he holding back and wailing feebly the whole way out.

This was the signal for the audience to commence
shivering and coughing, led off by a little black-and-tan
terrier dog, who emerged from concealment under the
petticoats of two extremely pretty girls. The young
ladies looked daggers at our party, and the orator, who
could not avoid noticing the disturbance, finally became
a victim to the epidemic, and sniffed in concert.

Meanwhile, the originator of the trouble sat serenely
chuckling, till a forbidding person in black—the exact
illustration of the popular notion of woman's rights—
turned round, and offered him three nicked pepper loz-
enges, with the sour remark that they were good for
gripes in the throat; whereupon, after a parting effort,
Charley enveloped his face in his handkerchief, and went
humbly down to the billiard-room below. . . .

In spite of this little episode, Mollie and the household kept the run of the argument in the charming talk,

and even Mrs. Pelican resumed her furs, and sat melted as in a furnace for the pleasure of hearing the whole.

After the lecture the party went behind the scenes, and were introduced to Silver Tongue, whom they found surrounded by a bevy of admirers.

"I never wanted to vote before, but now I do," said Mrs. Pelican, the omnipotent Grundy forgotten in enthusiasm.

"Haw! haw! haw!" snorted an individual fresh from the Cereus' hospitable doors, with added sense of the weight of the masculine dignity as manifested by difficulty in keeping its lodging house off from the floor. "I s'pose you'll ave-to—angels oughth do er (hic) do as they pleash." Charley's eyes were fixed on Mr. Gizzard, with an expression too ominous for even his befuddled brains to ignore, and Francis Haythorne carried Peace off directly.

"I don't know as I'm right," said Mr. Phillips, careful and gentle in assisting Mrs. Pelican down the slippery stairs; then pausing a moment in the street to finish his sentence—"I may not be, but it will set you thinking."

Is there any better mission in this world than to set people's minds at work? No doubt but what he'd accomplished it here. That night the dispute waxed hot in the family mansion—the gentlemen making common cause against their indefatigable adversaries, old Mr. Pelican intrenching himself in the high ground of conjugal obedience, and his wife pursuing a kind of feminine buccaneerism, wherein she demolished whichever side she found open to attack.

They began very grandly, Francis Haythorne remarking that it was folly to talk about things so exactly contrary to the process of nature. Men came to maturity five years later than women, and lived that much longer.

Supposing, then, that they kept up with each other till the feminine possibilities of growth were exhausted in that added golden five years, the male mind would incontestably prove its superiority.

Mollie asked, dryly, when that invaluable period began.

"When the young lady leaves school, she stops growing," said her antagonist.

"That's the very time when she makes first acquaintance with young men," said Peace, pointedly.

"Then boys are sowing their wild oats; they begin to improve again by and by," retorted Charley, drawing on experience. "Who ever heard of a woman's improving?"

"You mean that as long as they are under the same circumstances they do the same thing, and that altering the conditions, the results differ," put in Mollie.

"Why should women want to don breeks and leave the humble sphere where God placed them? Now, when ladies run the country post-offices, the men can do nothing but lounge in liquor dens and be ruined," said Mr. Haythorne. "It impoverishes the country."

"Poor things," retorted Peace, sneeringly, "why don't they leave their natural sphere and go to work, driving engines and doing the hard labor they were made for. The fact is, they accuse women of being *quite* inefficient in order that they may take their places, and be as nearly so themselves as bread and butter getting will admit."

"How absurd for a male political economist to talk about reducing the number of unproductive consumers, and making *all* producers, rendering a people poor!" remarked Mollie.

"You wouldn't vote, would you?" said Mr. Pelican, surveying her with parental anxiety.

"Yes, indeed she will," interfered Peace, forced out of her inborn conservatism by inward fret. "If women would only listen to the stump speeches, their perpetrators wouldn't have to be held upon the balcony by their coat tails, too drunk to stand alone; nor would courts of justice be such ill-spoken holes, if women were there."

"Hush," said Charley, "let Mollie speak."

"Do you want to know?" said she, quietly. "If the time ever comes when I can go as a woman with papa, and vote for them that have rule over me, I shall be very glad; and I am even disposed to push the matter a little, and clamor for room to exercise that duty."

"Pshaw!" said the young man, disappointed; and then noticing the rising color in Mollie's face, "I mean—I hoped—"

"You needn't say," interrupted his mother; "you know very well how angry you were when I heard how you kept open shop last election, and I haven't forgotten that Peace cried all night because three of Mollie's Sunday-school scholars went to that horrible jail, every one drunk on your liquor, served out at the corner grocery. Now if you'd known Mollie'd be on hand you wouldn't have done it."

"What do you want to accomplish, Mollie? Haven't you rights enough?" asked Mr. Pelican.

"I want to have the world's permission to follow out the instincts toward labor I feel in myself. I want to work for my race."

"You'll never get that to do anything," said Peace, bitterly; "nobody has a right to do an act not stereotyped, till after it has been successfully accomplished, and after that one is not allowed to stop. _I_ have no element of success," she added, restless and self-depreciating as always.

"It is absurd to think we study, investigate, or create for the world," said Francis Haythorne. "At best we labor for the trifling coterie whose proximity is immedi-

18

ate, and whose tastes run with our own. To every one else our work, if known at all, is foolishness; and our beacon-light a bubble of marsh gas."

" It's a stumbling-block to the Jews, too, isn't it ? " suggested Mollie.

"That's why you refrain from embarking in any, I suppose," said Charley, pseudo thoughtfully; " heretofore my principle has been the same."

" Well," exclaimed Mr. Haythorne, out of temper, "I hope there'll be some place left to men, where women won't come tagging after them, a perfect nuisance —everywhere a restraint."

" Go on," cried Peace, scintillating with delight at his discomfiture, "go on; you want one spot at least where you can be as indecorous as you like."

"I do," retorted he. "I think it's a shame women will be in every dish. Men don't want to be compelled into eternal effeminacy by their presence; made so pure and sweet, they are good enough to sit in the parlor all the time."

"That's true," agreed Mr. Pelican. " Men must be men; they've a right to be."

" Do you propose to carry your smoking-car and electioneering habits into heaven, as the essence of the masculine prerogative ? " asked Peace, looking provokingly beautiful. " I supposed a gentleman to be a gentleman everywhere. A new light breaks on me when I find the germs of your superior strength, intellect and manhood in the dirty talk, gambling, and drinking in which you admit you indulge, as a class, in your chosen retreats."

" I don't admit it! I never do an ungentlemanly thing anywhere; but I don't want it fixed so I can't if I like; " this in increasing heat.

" I wonder," put in Mollie, " if Christ, whose superiority I am content to acknowledge, would have been the prime favorite of political suppers, clubs and bar-rooms. I supposed the truest man was the most like Him. If the sexes are of so different a nature I am perplexed that He didn't live twice,—once for our pattern, once for yours."

"Pretty opinions for a church member, Mr. Pelican," said his wife, taking off her glasses and wiping them, the better to look him out of countenance.

"No such thing," he returned; "what women think indelicate isn't. Women's standards and men's differ."

"Mine is John the Baptist," remarked Peace. "I don't call to mind any of his acquaintance who objected to his ideas, except Herod."

Mollie interrupted a retort to this piece of insolence by saying, haughtily, "You are much mistaken, Mr. Pelican, if you think I or any true woman would wish to thrust herself unbidden into your company. We have a right to follow to perfection any gift God has endowed us with, and if He don't give us any talents for your favorite professions, then we have no right there. As for hard work, no one has ever denied woman that. If anything more fatiguing than washing, and house cleaning, and cooking can be invented, mention it. It is not harder to tend engine than kitchen range, or to run a telegraph machine than to polish windows, or to keep books than to carry on a laundry. *I* never heard that women desired to be conductors of cars, or sailors, or soldiers, or even artisans in metals and heavy manufactures. That they are already represented in every possible employment, has been the unnoticed result of agitation; and let the men produce something else and give us two sources of wealth instead of one. No! you are angry that genteel employment is now pronounced feminine, and your soft womanish muscles must ache in your necessitated use of your vaunted strength.   For the rest woman should be sought, not seeking—("Long Branch and Saratoga," interpolated Charley,) "in matters of society; and if there is a difference of necessity in the moral elevation of the sexes, clergymen's seminaries, medical schools, courts of justice, and the elections of our rulers, are not places to give play to those passions which all condemn, however they may yield to them.   These are sacred spots, and to confess yourselves sinners against right, is only acknowledging incapacity."   She rose and swept away, earnest, and battling inwardly with her theme.   The party broke up at her exit, to unite next day at precisely the point of separation.

The breakfast-table is the axle about which every well-regulated family revolves.   There it is that the doings of yesterday and the labors of to-day are brought under discussion.   The family life is concentrated about its tea-pots and coffee-urns.   Mines as sprung from behind its toast racks.   Calamities are first made tangible and blessings appreciated in the household reveillé it sounds.

This must be our apology for making mention of so common an episode as eating, with such frequency.   It seems to me that if the story-teller should attempt to give his adventures unconnected with this natural rallying point, his hero would inevitably be a Monte Christo or Jack Shepherd, and his heroine a Mathilde or Becky Sharp.

It was at the breakfast-table, then, that Charley propounded a question which he stated as the "Elevation of women and niggers,"—a possibility which his father denied so vehemently, that he forgot himself, and emptied his cup into the sugar-bowl, under the idea that he was sweetening his tea.   Adjourned to the library for prayers, they began to say their verses.

"God made man pure, but he sought out many strange inventions," began the old gentleman, with a severe look at Peace, who had been very unmanageable.

"Green basswood," suggested Charley, recalling a speculation of his father's.

"The man is the head of the woman," continued Francis Haythorne, likewise glancing at the young lady.

"The fool is wiser in his own eyes than seven men that can render a reason," said Mrs. Pelican, by way of general application.

"Speak not in the ears of a fool, for he shall despise the wisdom of thy words," retorted Peace.

"What have you got to say, Mollie?" asked Charley, seeing her hesitate.

"A blessing," responded she, wearily: "and last of all, the woman died also."

After that Mrs. Pelican began, "Here I'll raise my Ebenezer," as a last effort toward restoring sobriety to her household. And Mr. Pelican, worsted in the conflict, took his revenge by praying that God would open the blind eyes, and give to all wholesome submission to them that He had appointed to have rule over them.

But Peace squared this by quoting, in airy but audible aside to Mollie, as they rose from their knees, "If a wise man contend with a fool, whether he rage or laugh, there is no rest,"—which being delivered in an impersonal way, stung without possibility of answer.

The household were no sooner scattered to the day's occupations, than Charley and his sister, left alone together, had another passage of arms. The excitement of the evening before had somewhat unsettled the family temper, and Peace was doing worsted work of a very jerky pattern in an appropriate style.

"It's not true that women have the hardest time,"

cried Charley, sourly. "They always live the longest. Top Town's half full of widows this minute."

"You've done your share in killing their husbands," was his sister's tart reply; "you'd best say as little as possible about that."

Then ensued a pause, during which one whistled, and the other angrily pulled her worsted from the ball on the floor. "I thought father was talking about giving up Dives' Water Casks," recommenced Peace.

' I don't see why you should be so mean to a feller," said Charley, lifting the mahogany rocking-chair to the ceiling by the extreme end of its left rocker, and balancing it there a minute or two to soothe his feelings. "You spend the money; what's the dif so long as you get it? If father hadn't gone into distilling, we should have shinned it all our lives, instead of riding in state." The brother and sister had not been growing in concord during the last few weeks. Peace, who having once taken hope of Absalom, directly administered reproof, advice, and moral sentiments in bushels, met with irritated denial and jeers at every trial. Charley seemed to have become a sort of unbelieving porcupine, with quills out. He flaunted every sort of law-subverting doctrine in the faces of his family; and, while pursuing strictly his newly entered path of rectitude, tried to make himself out a sort of budding Don Juan, Bonnet Rouge, Aaron Burr, Ketchem. As a sample of his doings, he bought a picture of Ben Butler, whom he announced to be his ideal statesman, which he carried in his vest pocket, and frequently ogled with an amorous air when Peace was in seeing distance.

"I wish we did go afoot," cried Peace passionately; "we should at least be honest."

"Honesty *is* the best of policies," said Charley nonchalantly. "That's what I told the fire insurance, when I applied father's premium to my own private necessities. You aren't sensible to quarrel with your bread and butter. It's all very well to talk cold-water nonsense, but liquor buys every one of the rags you flaunt in; even the money you waste on your unwashed savages at Patience of Hope, comes from the till of the Night Blooming Cereus."

"Seems as if every cent of it was a curse to them," flashed Peace.

"Very likely," said Charley, bearing on as men will; "that only proves the fact. Why, the money father gave you this morning is what young Gizzard's mother paid with tears in her eyes the week before he hung himself, and his father's going the same way. We were fools to let them run on so. They'll never be good for another dollar." He gave the information with gusto, and smiled as the spider might smile on the fly. At least Peace thought so.

"Then I won't touch a cent of it," she cried indignantly. "The girls were getting up a subscription for the Gizzards last week. They asked Mollie to contribute, but never said a word to me. If the rum-seller's daughter can't be charitable, she can at least be just. I'll pay every penny back to Mrs. Gizzard to-morrow."

"Do," said Charley, sardonically, "you couldn't offer a better advertisement for the Cereus. The generous gambler that befriends his dupe, always gets double the money out of his reputation."

It was so. She was hedged in, cursed in her basket, cursed in her store; cursed in outgoing, cursed in incoming; and cursed most of all, as she felt to her heart's core, in this her brother. She sprang to her feet, hot and defiant. "I hate you," she exclaimed. "I wish I was

dead—I wish you—everybody was dead! I'll leave the
house, teach school, set type, be a dress-maker! I've
borne this long enough. If I can't live honestly, I'll
starve."

Instead of replying in kind, Charley straightened himself, and looked down at her with sympathetic admiration.
"You're a good girl," said he approvingly, and continued
to feast his eyes on her indignant face. Then, as she in
turn stood surveying him in something like terror at this
sudden reversal of tactics, he came over and took her
in his arms, and kissed her. "My poor sister!" said he,
tender, and suddenly manifesting a gentle, strong phase of
soul, new in the unstable pleasure lover. "How cruel to
torture you only to torment myself! No! Peace, you
are not to go away—at least not yet. I have taken my
resolution. It is I who am to leave Top Town—very
soon."

A woman adores manhood, strength. She humbles herself before it instinctively. She will render up every
prerogative joyfully, if only to teach her dear ones to
manifest, prize, their power. Charley was never so noble
in his sister's eyes, as when he asserted claim to his man's
right to a self-denial as costly as needful. She laid her
hand on his broad shoulder with pride, and waited
silently to hear him out.

"All you've said is true, dear. If you can think it,
I ought at least to act on it. I am going out West to
start again, to make a new life for myself,—to be clear of
the liquor trade, and work for my bread. I didn't think
I could make up my mind, but I'm quite settled now.
And when I'm successful, just a little successful, I'll
bring you to live with me, and we'll have a happy time.
I don't know exactly what I shall do for a living,—you
remember 'non palma sine pulvere,' which being inter-

preted is, no hand not dirty," he added with a rueful
smile.

"I've been dreadfully mean to you, Charley," sobbed
Peace, taking refuge in the window-curtains. "I wish I
hadn't. You wouldn't have acted so if I had done my
duty, and pitied your little failings; and now you're good,
and I wasn't in it."

Her brother was full of emotion too, but he couldn't
help walking the elephant toward her, and then she made
a little airy kick at him, as she wiped away her tears;
and he caught the liliputian weapon, and gallantly
kissed the toe of its embroidered slipper; and now at last
they were very happy together in this first union of heart
and purpose.

And so, just as Peace gained her brother, she parted
from him, not that moment exactly, but a few weeks after,
when, almost against his father's direct prohibition, he
started for the frontier.

Old Mr. Pelican couldn't see why, as long as Charley
had reformed, he wouldn't stay home, and take charge
of the Cereus; and his mother cried most of the time at
the thought of the temptations to which he would be exposed away from the paternal roof, forgetful of the follies
against which it had been no protection.

But Peace and Mollie made common cause, and fought
it through, and the sister came out in her new rôle
gloriously, and was so delightful, so sweet, so tender, that
the poor fellow wondered why they had never found each
other out before, and, in his desolate foreshadowing
of friendlessness and hardship, most of all regretted that
he must leave her affection behind.

18*

CHAPTER XXX.

"This is the man all tattered and torn,
That loved the maiden all forlorn."

OLLIE was sitting alone, thinking.

In this story of her inner life, dealing with her almost always in times of misfortune and misery, it may have seemed as if she was one of those melancholy people who have a subdued and piteous appearance, like half-dried tear-blots. But this is not so. Whatever might be her burdens, they were so little obtruded on her friends that the latter had the habit of considering her a singularly happy person, and bringing all their trials to her sympathy. It is true, except when roused to combat for some oppressed class or darling theory, she talked little, and even that little was too thoughtful to be reckoned brilliant. But she had her delicate soul-feelers, always alert to cognize the moods, passions, principles, of her acquaintance; and a kind heart moulded the knowledge into that subtle, inestimable tact that is better than wit, wisdom, or beauty to its possessor. Moreover she loved and sought goodness steadfastly through all, and so had whereupon to be always cheery, and a wholesome companion. In her suffering days she locked herself up, and waged battle alone and unflinching.

On this occasion she had plenty to muse over. Charley had just gone. He had held his own bravely to the end. The evening before his departure he spent with his family at a church festival, where he beguiled the time by presenting the girls with gum shellac as candy, lifting his male acquaintance with one hand, and placard-

ing his father "Beware of Pickpockets,"—in which guise
the unconscious old gentleman strutted about with extraordinary dignity. Then, finding that it rained, he slipped
into the dressing-room, and opened every single umbrella,
placing them extended in battalions, and thus producing
a singular effect on the owners at going-home time, when
the chosen young ladies stood indignantly waiting the arrival of their perplexed escorts.

Lastly, he hung his Ben Butler photograph, neatly
framed, and lettered, "St. Benjamin," in the Sunday-
school room, side by side with the remainder of the holy
pictures calculated to instruct the youthful mind.

And next morning the household saw him off on the
cars, and retiring thereafter to their respective bedrooms,
appeared no more during the day. With all their faults
the Pelicans were a *family*, and joyed and loved and
suffered with generous heartiness. Mollie was glad to
have it so. It comforted her to be able to be sorry with
them. She had received her first letter from her mother
a few minutes before. She skimmed it through once, re-
read, and then crumpled and threw it down with a sigh,
as if she would willingly have crushed the thoughts it
called up, with their cause. Ye lovers of precious home
epistles, who have known "mother's words" God's best
help in your trials, see what Mollie was feeding on—

"MY DEAR CHILD :—I have at last found courage to
clean up after you, and am now sick in consequence.
Your father, however, don't seem to care for that any
more than other folks. I don't see why you should have
bamboozled him into buying those sleeve-buttons. He
works day and night to earn money for you to fool away.
Mr. Brown hasn't been here since you left, but once, when
he leaned against the garden gate, and admired my Vesu-

vius colored jacket, and hat with the Paree brulay and
Paree on sond roses. You ought to be ashamed to have
lost such a man. You'll go all through the wood, and take
up with a crooked stick at last. But you were born to be
a bill of expense, and your own perversity will prevent
any one's bearing it but your parents. I hope I shan't
die in the poor-house through your selfishness.

"Be very careful of your complexion, and always wear a
veil when you go out. Don't put on your black silk if
you can help it,—it is too good. Be sure and attend
prayer-meeting regularly; there are some fine young men
in the Top Town Congregational Church. Three cents is
quite enough to offer in the contribution box at a time.
'And seek ye first the kingdom of heaven, and all these
things shall be added unto you.'

"Your suffering mother,
"MIRANDA McCROSS."

But besides these excellent subjects for cogitation,
Mollie had another nearer, and deeper still. She was
going to the prison to see Louis. Would she find him
sick, or dying, or crazed? Could she comfort him? or
had she waited too long, and was he beyond all comfort?
Had she wronged him by that promise to her father?
She could not tell. It was a long time since they had
parted in the bitterness of their affliction. It would be
longer yet before they could claim each other for the
forever. Mollie did not look ahead. One day, and then
another, not all at once, or she would lie down and die.
She didn't want to lose her life, and so her chance of
helping him.

She took some dresses from the closet, and spreading
them on the bed, sat down, chin in hand, to contemplate
them. She had lost the plump beauty of early woman-

hood, and seemed almost too fragile for humanity. But her face, glorified in its sweetness and strength, colorless and pure, looked akin to the cherished Christ over the mantel. She might not have been beautiful to a stranger, but she was beautiful to me, who held her dear.

She was thinking that in all their years of coming separation she would fain be lovely in Louis' eyes.

These dresses were like Mollie: a blue merino, with dainty black velvet vest; the silk over which her mother mourned; a white muslin evening costume, with satin bodice; and last of all a cashmere of rosy dove color, that shaded dark and rich in its graceful folds—not very many or striking, but every one characteristic of its wearer, and perfect in conception.

She looked them over thoughtfully. Of course they weren't all appropriate, but she would bring the best out for choice; she only liked them because he would have admired her in them. Her thoughts were all for him.

The little Java sparrow chirped with melancholy interest from his Chinese pagoda, carved long before with his donor's jack-knife. Some flitting memory made the young girl smile, and she selected the gray robe without more reflection, and arrayed therein, with the scarlet velvet ribbons hanging from her neck, stood the very counterpart of her little pet.

She knelt a moment before the quaint cage as a sort of shrine. Her Bible opened to its old place : "They that wait on the Lord shall renew their strength." The page was worn and faded with continual touch. Mollie bent over it silently a few moments, and then closed it upon her doubts and fears, and putting on her dove-colored hat, and cloak, and gray furs, took up a well-filled basket, and knocked at Peace's door.

Peace regarded this expedition in the light of a peni-

tential pilgrimage. As she told Mr. Haythorne confidentially, she had rather be hung than go, though go she
would; and she had been banging doors, and anathema-
tizing pins, and stamping at her cuffs and hat—which
little indications of a mind at variance with itself worried
Mollie to desperation. The truth was, Miss Pelican
ought to have seen Louis before. During the whole twelve
months and more of his incarceration, she had been about
to perform that duty next week. In fact, this was the intention of all his friends—to the end of the first year—
when they concluded that if he'd stood it without them
so long, he certainly could the rest of the time, and set
conscience at rest without longer delay.

During their whole acquaintance Francis Haythorne
had never addressed a remark to Mollie about Louis.
But Peace had learned, in her brother's dreary struggle
for hope, to seek a confidant, who, out of his unruffled
placidity, was always ready to supplement her needs by
quiet, easily rendered helps, or willing burden-bearing.
In that short three months she had almost forgotten to
ask sympathy of Mollie, and went by instinct (and instinct is always the impulse toward pleasure) to repose
cares, griefs, joys, and experiences, with a child's simplicity, in his consciousness.

He was, therefore, well advised of the impending trip;
and quite as much to please Peace as Mollie (whose
character for common-sense had declined daily in his es-
teem), waited for the prisoner's fiancée as she passed
through the hall.

Her complete possession by this ill-starred love seemed
poorly judged, in the light of certain late possibilities relating to the wealthy and still juvenile choleric neighbor
—whom Mollie refused even to see in his frequent visits.
Having lost her chance of winning himself, the probability

of eternal singleness or wretched degradation seemed plain; and with a sincere interest in her welfare, it irked him that she should throw by an opportunity to marry a fortune, a good home, and the incumbrance not unpleasant either, for a woman who has missed her one golden opening, and of whom *erit æstas non semper* was dismal certainty.

But as she descended the stairs in her sadness, forgetting of all in the soon approaching meeting with her outcast beloved, her eyelids swelled and faintly rosy, as the Beatrice Cenci's whom she looked not unlike, perhaps, her graceful form steadied through nervous concentration, her beauty wrought upon this Sybarite as her sorrow could not; and it was with sincere sympathy that he pressed into her hands the bouquet of hot-house flowers, and the note he waited to deliver.

The emotion illuminated his clear-cut features as Peace joined them, and her smile reflected the radiance in a fervor of gratitude. She never approved of him so thoroughly as when he placed her beside her friend in the sleigh; she even turned to watch him, as he stood leaning against the door a moment, and watching their departing vehicle.

They drove silently over the crisp snow, and arriving, went timidly through the bare hall into the guard-room, where the ugly darkeys leered at them from the wall, and certain photographs of wardens killed in the prison hung between the windows, and where the coarse-voiced superintendents were making tough jokes for the five minutes between dinner and duty.

Francis Haythorne's letter was addressed to the warden of Top Town Penitentiary, and announced that, as friends of the shoe contractors wished to visit the prison, any politeness shown them would be to the undersigned firm. The reigning chief was not in, but Mollie delivered the precious sesame to his deputy, a fat man with a red head, and cruel, passionate face. He said he would willingly show them about, but he had a tremendous big job on hand; and, as he went into the yard directly and kicked the white bull-dogs, the waiting women concluded that must be it.

Then they looked through the grating and saw the long lines of pallid men marching to their shops, with faces averted, and stamped with misery and pain; and after following with the joking, laughing visitors, peeped into the comfortless cells, into the spotless workshops, where are made rulers and silver-plated wares, into the weaving department, into the grimy machine-rooms, where rogues learn exactly the best knowledge to apply to lock-picking; and then they came to the shoemaking, and, going in, Mollie stood still and looked straight before her at a man pegging boots. Through the window you could see the dry sticks of the garden plants rising desolately above the December snow; within, were the hopeless, wicked men, plodding heartlessly through their tasks, and four stone walls shut him and them together in a world which had neither outlet nor refreshing, and he all she had. She trembled lest he should hear her panting breath and look up;—no fear of that. Every glance cost a blow, and work must be done. He hurried on with it in feverish energy, but once, as he laid down a finished boot, he sighed—a long, tired sigh. When the guard called them to move on, it seemed to Mollie as if she had been standing there a lifetime, her perceptions of her lover's pain were so strangely wonted and old. Back in the guard-room, one of the officers said he would go and bring the prisoner; and Peace, haughty and defiant, some of the people having pointed out thieves and murderers to her, and then inquired if she was any relation, betook herself to absorbed study of certain antiquated firearms, in a case near the prison keys.

Mollie, too much agitated to be seated, stood by the window, trying to master herself. She had forgotten that they must pass by; could that be he? ill clad, with eyes on the ground, bent to the regulation slouch—hers!

Their steps sounded on the flagstones of the dormitory. The door opened. He came forward hesitating, uncertain of his reception. They sat down on the bench together—he, shivering from his sudden plunge into the freezing court; she, warm and lovely, and throbbing from head to foot with emotion. She forgot the lookers-on, and snatching both his thin hands in hers, held them fast in her electric clasp, whispering,

" My own Louis."

" My Mollie ! " answered the convict, looking hungrily into her eyes; and then they sat silent, all the multitude of things that must be said crowded quite out of their minds in the joy of meeting. It was only after concentrated study of the floor and each other, that Louis ventured to remark, with his old flickering blush, " that he'd got a pair of new shoes." But this was so inapposite to the weighty matters that pressed on their hearts, that they both smiled; and the ice being broken, all the hoarded necessities of their confidence rushed out pell-mell. But when Mollie told of her illness after his letter came, and her promise, and her father's message, Louis' glance sought the floor.

" That may be a long time, Mollie. It is very hard."

She had known it always, but never so bitterly as now.

" Is he very feeble ? " Louis made his questions after miserable pauses.

" Yes," Mollie said, and thought at the bottom of her

heart that even feebleness was no excuse for such cruel demands upon her love ; and waited passively to hear if her betrayed would pardon—not him—but her.

Her suspense was short. "Tell Deacon McCross," said he, throwing back his head, masterful and earnest, "that I forgive him all,—even this worst thing,—all : from the first day till this moment. Tell him I shall prove a man yet."

But the woman's head drooped lower, as his was raised, her dilating eyes fixed with piteous intensity on his face, that worked with emotion.

"O Louis, how can we, how can I, live so?" she broke down all at once. "How could I promise? How could I help promising? What virtue is there in life to make us live?"

He drew her hot face to his shoulder, covered by the coarse harlequin prisoner's jacket. Its touch recalled her to their surroundings, but she would not move : she was so tired—so tired ; and she wiped from her eyes the scalding tears, welling with long gasps from her deepest soul, but kept her place—her own dear place.

How strong Louis felt himself grow beneath that help-less weight. It is so passing sweet to be sought for shelter of our dear! No caress given in their free glad wooing had half the delicious, heart-swelling power of this tearful pleading cry, and sinking upon his help, here in the prison.

"Darling," said he, bringing his new precious experi-ence to comfort her, too eager to remember how he was half afraid to realize it to his own soul in his lonely cell: "God that we both love will help us. There is no sorrow like unto his sorrow."

Then Mollie, nestling in her place, knew exultant what she had been finding out through all this hour of sore

agony. Hers was a nobler prop than the old boyish affection; her Damascene sword had been tempered in the
fire; her woman's soul, given so freely to suffering, should
no longer bear the whole burden. It was supplemented
by a manhood, noble, deep, entire as her love.

"One thinks a great many thoughts in penitentiary,"
said Louis, gently, as she sat up still circled by his arm,
and tried to control her sobs. "I have learned the meaning of life, here. It has been a painful year, but it was
necessary: God knew best. Was I harsh about your
father?" making abrupt stop. "I often remember how
he tried to be kind. Once he stood on an empty ash
hogshead behind the barn, to steal his own grapes for me,
and, as he reached up to pick them, we heard your mother
coming, and the head fell in, and he with it. He doubled
his length once or twice, and curled down, thinking he
was hidden; but just as she was going to pour in her
pail of coal, he rose and confronted her like an amiable
ghost. I shall never forget how mild and bald and funny
he looked, neatly powdered with cinders, the tell-tale
fruit in his hand, and half a dozen bunches hid in my
apron."

Little enough of happy memory can be strung on the
thread of home-worry; but Mollie smiled gratefully, and
was comforted—as what woman will not be, if it please
the man she loves to attempt her consolation?

And now Peace, who had been trying on handcuffs at
the other end of the room, attended by the jailer, whose
heart would soften in spite of himself, came over to end
the interview, and lighten their feeling by a pound of
candy, presented with a set speech.

But she had hardly begun, "On this occasion, unaccustomed as I am," when she fell to crying for sympathy
with these poor children, who were so patient in their

misery.   A second time, it was Louis whose strength
sufficed to soothe.

" Miss Peace," said he, in voice tremulous, but manner
calm, " your sorrow is like a divine light, but you mustn't
feel bad for Mollie and me: God is taking care of us.
' Whom He has joined together, no man can sunder.'
Mollie is my wife, and I am her husband forever."   Then
he went bravely away, though the kiss he threw them as
he passed the window was almost a sob, and the answering smile from Mollie near broke her heart.

CHAPTER XXXI.

" What are little girls made of ?
          Sugar and spice
          And all that's nice,
That's what little girls are made of."

THE family were sitting in the library when Mollie
came back.   Francis Haythorne, in particular,
lay stretched out in a great green easy-chair,
with the leaves of a half-cut " Eclectic " between his fingers, the picture of mannish comfort.

Miss Pelican sailed up to him at once, her eyes blazing,
her movements lithe with excitement, her short upper lip
curled to its last extent.   " You needn't tell me they
don't abuse the prisoners," cried she; " I know better!
they could every one of them stand for models in the
court of death."

The gentleman opened his red hazel eyes into a glance
of unmoved inquiry, and replaced on the ottoman the
slippered foot her abrupt attack had startled to the floor.

" It will be a wonder if Louis Allwood lives till spring.
I don't see how Mollie endures it," she went on vehemently. " I know that human bull-dog of a warden is
cruel. If I was a prisoner I'd cut my throat."

" Indeed ? " said Mr. Haythorne, instantly shutting
his oyster-shell dislike of useless agitation over his sympa-
thies, and languidly fluttering his magazine leaves; " I
suppose the knaves deserve all they get. To tell the
truth, they're too coarsely unpleasant to be interesting.
Will you have the heavenly kindness to excuse my laziness, and close the window, as you're standing near it. I
feel that the single white hair in my head is catching cold.
This is a capital article on Punch and Judy."

In Mollie's wretchedness she came to one inevitable
experience, bitterer than all. It wasn't that she and
Louis suffered. They were set to suffer. She never re-
belled against necessities. But nobody cared. If Louis
had died, or been crippled, or robbed of property, if any
misfortune had overtaken him that entailed no responsibility on the community, every one would have overflowed
with sympathy. As it was, when anything brought their
misery to people's minds, they felt uneasy and made haste
to forget. *No one wanted to alter the pressure that crushed
them.* The replies in Peace's dialogue, prefaced by a window bang, sampled every one's mind. .

" But Louis is a gentleman, and suffers unjustly."

" Oh, you think so."

" I know it ; so would you, if you weren't too snippy."

" Ah ! well ! he must have done something to get into
the fix. Justice must be satisfied. You don't look into
the social necessity of punishment."

Though not at all interested in the point at issue, the
Sybarite was by no means blind to the magnificent soul-
impulses and facial expressions the beautiful woman

before him unconsciously developed. He, in his turn, approved of her with all his heart. He loved to watch her, and continued with a little more animation: " As for working them, you can't expect us to pay for their living; and if we can get anything extra, we've a right to it to make up for the trouble they've caused."

(N.B. Our justice to people under our thumb is usually rapacity; but we call it political economy, and its exigencies afford favorite opportunities for Christians to get very rich.)

" But brutality and want assault every prisoner," urged Peace.

" I don't know anything about that."

" You could, if you pleased."

" I don't want to ; why should I ? "

Why should they, indeed? Outside the pricks of self-interest or the gad-fly of necessity, what excites anybody to do anything? Why should they even open their eyes, when if they did a duty would lie straight under them? This whole world is a huge press whereto selfishness is the screw, turned by avarice and revenge to squeeze out the life-blood of the unfortunate. If misery be a gridiron, respectability oils the blistering limbs with pious regret, and cupidity furnishes coals.

If it takes form in the guillotine, Christianity looks the other way while Christian expediency lets falls the axe. If it be a subtilly twisted cord of disgrace, acquaintanceship kicks away the scaffold, while revenge on high moral grounds rifles our pockets and adjusts the rope around our necks.

There is no evil in which individual or people can be placed, where all the spiritual virtues do not furnish men good reasons for refusing aid ; and yet, among the endless frauds and peculations that rot all business honor, to wrong one's fellows seems no great crime, unless the fraud

be badly planned : then indeed nineteenth-century rectitude achieves a parabola, and ends at hell gate.

"A man's a man for a' that," said Peace, who had
been saying in many words what I have set down in few.

"I'd like to know what you're going to do about it?"
quoth her auditor, stroking his curling beard with a hand
snow-white and dimpled. He was thinking inly how
noble a help, a champion, she was showing herself, and
delicately enjoying every unconscious revelation of her
turns of thought and emotion. Peace had a habit of
talking to people at large on the rim of herself, which
proved aggravating to similarly customed masculines.
Even the red-haired had never explored the centre of this
delightful volcano. She held his answer as insult, boiled
down, double-distilled. "A Daniel come to judgment,"
said she, seating herself in desperation, as if effort was
no use. A woman is worth nothing when there is any
good to be done. If I was only a man! If you were
half a man!"

The unpleasant person sitting in the great arm-chair
began to laugh, conscious that the kitten had claws.

"Be calm, good Mrs. Fry," said he.

"Keep thy heart at seventy throbs a minute; from all
sick people, maimed wretches, afflicted people, turn away
thine eyes, and depart elsewhere," she hurled at him
scornfully.

This time she touched him. He straightened up flushed
and angry, exclaiming, "If you mean to call me a selfish
puppy, do it in plain English!" when Mollie stole in and
sat down meekly, in a corner.

"You are very unfair, daughter," said Mr. Pelican,
breaking the pause following the dialogue. "It's the
contractors' business to see that their men are cared for,
not ours. The system does, has always done, well; change

would be expensive. If there are abuses let the Legislature remedy them. It's not our affair."

If you want to know the aggregate resisting weight of all the people in the world, propose a reform, and take only one step in it.

"By 'doing well' you probably mean that once immured you hear no more of a convict," said Peace.

"About that," confessed her father, "the point is to save honest men from annoyance. Any way you fix it, imprisonment is better than the old plan of hanging a man for stealing a loaf of bread."

"That wasn't theft under the Jewish law," said Mollie abruptly. "It ought never to be under any. But nine times out of ten it would be more Christian to kill a man than to send him to State's prison."

"No! no!" cried Mrs. Pelican, shocked. "We have no right to take life."

"When you shut up a life away from activity in the world in a prison, don't you take it and put it there? When you cut five years out of a man's existence, and make them empty years, only marked by pulse-beats of suffering, don't you take so much life! When you gradually transform a man from a sinning, suffering human being, into a brute or a devil, by subjecting him to circumstances known to rob him of morality and affection, don't you take his life? When, being innocent, you slowly break his heart, and so kill him, don't you take his life? When, having warped his soul out of all possibility of rectitude, he dies in the ditch, or by suicide, or by the hangman, and goes to hell, haven't you taken his life, and put it there? Which is the worst—to give him at once to the mercy of his Maker, or serve him so? And for every soul thus damned, aren't you, who have power to help it and don't, murderers?"

The whole family were horrified at this way of putting it, and when Mollie, frightened by her own outburst, hastened from the room, with face deadly pale, and form shaking like an aspen under sway of passionate sense of wrong, they stared blankly in each other's faces.

"She speaks the truth," said old Mr. Pelican at last, thoughtfully. "It is murder. But I'm sure," rallying, "I haven't time to attend to it. What with the Congregational Sunday-school, and the missionary fund for China, I have neither interest nor money to give."

"Yes," said Francis Haythorne, looking very uneasy. "I might, I suppose, get up a petition, investigate, compare, write a pamphlet, do something of the sort. But then it would make one so conspicuous—so—take so much time, have to talk to so many people. It's non-·ense to speak of it."

"Besides," added Mr. Pelican comfortably, "if I meddled in the business to get that young Allwood out, Mollie'd be certain to have him. And he's spoilt for life, and she's a fine girl with money. I don't think it would be right to stir in it."

"And I," cried Peace, bitterly, "am a rich man's daughter, of high breeding and all the feminine virtues. It would be bad taste to put myself forward. *I* can't do anything." With that she banged the door defiantly, and went to comfort Mollie.

But Mollie's self-mastery was regained outwardly. She had summoned her terrible will to her help. She would not show emotion now, not if Louis and she both died at their rack. And her steady eyes looked out with their every-day quietude from their black, suffering, chiselled caverns. Poor Peace was miserable, too; and it was partly her fault. She was wrong to speak out. Silence was her only safety. She was folding the pretty gray

19

robe, and humming " Robin Adair," when Miss Pelican, absolutely frightened by the even ripple of that sweet voice at such a time, paused at her door.

Mollie heard her, and called her in, still busy with the creases of the cashmere.

"From little matters let us pass to less, and lightly scan the mysteries of dress," said she, easily. " What are you going to wear to-night ? "

" Mollie ! povera mia ! have they broken your heart ? " cried Peace, brushing past her remark.

" No," returned Mollie in a clear, decisive tone, " nor can't. I never felt such capacity for endurance as I do at this moment. I can and will bear to the end. Now, let us talk of more agreeable things. Your father, this morning, bade us all to see the Ticket-of-Leave Man. With what shall we adorn ourselves ? "

" You are not going to that play ! " exclaimed Peace, more and more terrified. " What was father thinking of to propose such a thing ? The miserable sequence to kindred misfortune will half kill you after this morning's experience."

" You are mistaken. I know the story, and, rather than hurt your father's feelings, would sit out twenty such performances. As we are to have a box, it will be necessary to go without bonnets. I have about settled on blue merino, with white in my hair. Have I hurt you by my heartless talk ? " said she, stopping at the aghast look on Peace's face. " Do you know I frequently doubt if I have any real affection for any one,—even Louis—

" ' Love, like a waxen image 'gainst the fire,
Bears no impression of the thing it was.' "

" No, it isn't that exactly ; it's a stolid incapacity for emotion of any kind."

" I'm sorry," said Peace, with a great sigh. " Comfort Mollie ? Where should she find it to give ? " She was going sadly out of the room, when her friend called her back.

" Dear girl," said Mary, putting her love-thrilling hands on Peace's shoulders, and giving her one of those rare glances of tenderness, and willing self-unveiling, that were equal charm and reward. " It *is* true that Louis and I have a hard time. I don't know but it is as wrong to be false and deny it, as it would be to deny our blessings. But God is with us, and we shall not fail utterly. Don't fear. We will be happy yet. And your sympathy is my greatest comfort on earth." That was the longest confidence Mollie ever made about her troubles. . . .

" I would give a good deal to know what those round white things are that you have circling your throat," said Francis Haythorne, lazily inspecting Peace, as she put finishing touches to her toilet that night, in the up-stairs sitting-room.

" What, my wax beads ? " returned the beauty, making a half pirouette before the long mirror, and pausing in an attitude. She had mourned over her friend all the afternoon, but even misery itself cannot prevent some women from being coquettes before a looking glass.

" They aren't wax ; they break like mica," said he, in a scientific manner.

Peace sat down in mock despair. " You haven't been destroying those beads ? Francis Haythorne, how old are you ? "

" A sage in understanding, and a babe in iniquity. Years are no account. I only crushed a broken bubble," said the young man, innocent as the cat after banquet on canary. " I wanted to know what made them so white and shiny. You don't care, I suppose."

"No," answered she, in that plaintive tone which, used by a pretty woman, is very fascinating. "Did you melt it?"

"I didn't think to," replied the investigator, intent in pursuit of knowledge, and forthwith held the rounded bauble in the gas-jet, his face demure and grave.

"Oh!" said Peace, suddenly. "You burned me. That horrid wax melted on my hand."

"Give it to me, and I'll cure it."

"Well," she replied, stretching it out to his grasp, carelessly. "There! you promised me a great deal; what is it?"

"I'll give you myself;" his cultured musical voice earnest and tender. The afternoon's study had been working in his mind, and the possibility his fancy had often suggested had now taken form as resolve.

"Poh!" exclaimed Peace, jerking her hand away, and putting it behind her. "I want something worth having —candy for instance."

"Is that all the value I have to you?" said he, hurt; "any fool can give you that."

"True," retorted she, reddening; "but I only ask it of the biggest."

"Then I will complete my folly, and entreat you to be my wife. O Peace, you surely must have known my love for you—you cannot have called me to be your very shadow for months, have glittered and coquetted before my eyes, and all for me, and not felt that you held my soul in your fingers. You cannot mean to turn me away empty." When this man once let go of his Sybarite inertia, he was as impetuous and precipitate as Niagara. It was not lack of power, but motive, that made him what he appeared.

This Peace felt; she recognized him as an equal, but

she had by no means forgotten how she had returned with Mollie from the prison; and, for the bitter sorrow they brought back, no one cared. She had hated them all ever since, and, with the inky record of his selfishness not dry in heaven, he presumed to think she would love him.

"Oh, but I do!" she exclaimed, angrily. "How was I to know I was ensnaring your heart?"

"You took pains enough;" resentful and astonished.

"You are mistaken. I was only exercising what you have often called woman's sole vocation—the artistic. I never did anything worthy of love any more than you. I made fancy-work in the library, and you played the piano, and talked German moonshine. Was there anything of value enough to call forth affection, self-abnegation in that? I mourned over poverty and crime, and did nothing to help the sufferers, as is appropriate and becoming to women;—and you, you didn't even mourn. You were too selfish; you would still rather play the piano, and diddle around art, and dangle about me. I detest myself—I despise *you*. Marry you! I would, if only to show you what a worthless thing I am, if you were not so much more contemptible. You are a trifler, and nothing more. Any other handsome face will captivate you as thoroughly as mine. You pretend to love your profession, and are alarmed at the exertion of giving eau sucré to an infant with hiccoughs; that is the worth of your devotion. Plenty of women will give frittery hearts for paltry attentions. What did you ask me for? I wish I was dead—you—everybody! Get out of my sight!"

Francis Haythorne, as I have intimated, possessed a head of extremely auburn hair, and if Peace had a gift, it was capacity for stirring people up from the bottom of their souls.

The young man was too indignant at the first part of her speech to notice the pain she betrayed at its close. He rose incensed and insulted. " I won't," said he, stamping his handsome foot. " I won't! I won't! you must go out with me this very evening. You're a heartless flirt. I *will* see you every day, here under your father's roof; you can't prevent the dear delight of witnessing your beauty, and suffering from your temper."

" I can, and will! " retorted Peace. " I'll accept my invitation to Cragenfels, and start to-morrow! How sheepish you look, stamping like a pet lamb! Do you know ? " she added deliberately, gazing straight at him from her immense malicious black eyes, " if I had ever thought you had any heart, I might have been careful; but I didn't suppose you *could* love any one but yourself."

" You'll find out that I do," exclaimed he, his voice husky with rage. " I'll make you care for me, and marry me too, in spite of your airs."

" That you never can ! " Peace had lost the last vestige of her self-command by this. " If you want to hear, I would have adored you long ago, if you had been good for anything. But you weren't, and I'm glad to have a chance of telling you my opinion."

Instead of flaming up still more under this, her worst stab, the dismissed suitor took a seat and began to laugh.

" Of a truth," said he, " thou hast spoken many words ; but there is no harm done, for the speaker is one, and the listener is another."

And before the incensed object of his passion had time to retort, the door opened to admit Mary McCross, who come forward quicker than was usual; and they noticed, as she stood in the reflected blaze of light from the pier glass, that the muscles about her mouth were set in deep, pain-marked lines, from the effort she made to hold them composed. She hurriedly laid a telegram before the combatants.

"My father has had a stroke of paralysis," she said. "Mr. Haythorne, I must trouble you to get me an express wagon. I shall leave on the midnight train."

"And I too," said Peace, defiant and sympathetic at once.

CHAPTER XXXII.

"Old Trot's Dead."

MOLLIE was glad to find matters at home no worse. True the Deacon's left side was entirely paralyzed, but he wasn't to go yet—not for many months; and his daughter dismissed both the spinster and Peace to their merry-making, and set herself to patient care of her dying.

It was a piteous thing to see the old man completely crippled, and the girl clinging to him, holding him back from death by sheer force of will. She wheeled him about in his arm-chair, into the sun, into the shade, into the sitting-room, back to the parlor; for the poor invalid was never at ease. She fed him, read to him, watched his slightest want from morning till night; and, except to care for her Syllabub friends, never left him an hour.

The news of his illness thronged the house with applicants for missionary charity and widow's relief funds. Men came clear from Top Town in search of bequests; lank ministers, in seedy black, were forever ringing the door-bell; and a legion of needy Prices and McCrosses, forgotten years before, started up suddenly, and came in at the kitchen door, Brussels carpet-bags in hand, and asked anxiously after dear cousin Elizur,—of the cook. Mrs. McCross' immense energy was fully occupied in heading off these pertinacious condolers. But Dr. Perfect, mindful of duty, one day called while she was off guard, to find Mollie and her father together, as usual.

His ponderous black form filled up the sea-green sitting-room, and the pair put away the hymn-book they had been perusing, with a sense of crime.

"Good-morning, Deacon McCross," said he, in grating bass, folding his black cashmere scarf and laying it formally across his knees—"I hope to find you resigned to your affliction. We should say in sickness, *Deus nobis hæc ostia fecit.* I have this moment returned from a visit to Mrs. Starbird. Very rebellious at the loss of her babe. Terribly rebellious."

"Of course you comforted her?" said Mary. *She* was ordinarily dumb in the presence of affliction, and sorely felt her deficiency.

"*Bonis nocit, quisquis pepercerit malis,*" said the Doctor, smoothing the scarf over his lap, and looking at her severely. "I told her, ma'am, that we must hope for the best; but we cannot tell about these unregenerate infants. In my opinion there are children in hell not a span long."

The sick man's face grew pained and weary under this enunciation of a creed he could never shake off; but he made no remark. It was a foolhardy thing to oppose Dr. Perfect.

"I have come! *ut prosim,* this morning, to lay before you a much more interesting subject," said the worthy pastor, majestically waiving the question. "It is a frequent practice of people excepting speedy dissolution to make a bequest of their earthly possessions to the Lord; in brief, to the erection of churches or the endowment of collegiate institutions. It is my mission here, as a man to whom you have delegated the care of your spiritual part, and therefore the one most fitted to advise in such case, to state that there is no ecclesiastical building in Millville of our denomination, the one across the river being, I regret to say, almost wholly in the possession of the Moabites. Knowing you to be instant in every good work, I would recommend you to endow a church,—the McCross Memorial Church of Millville, which I will myself undertake to see ædificated; and I will make it the recipient of my pastoral care. In fact, with due regard, *jurem humanum*, it would be well to have this a stated condition of the gift."

Mollie looked curiously at her father, wondering if he would rise to the tempting bait, or follow his new rule, and class the great Dr. Perfect in the long line of disappointed legacy-hunters. She didn't care what became of the family wealth. It had brought her nothing but sorrow. She half wished it was to be transformed into bricks and mortar, and so got out of her way; but she felt very sure the heavy walls of such a structure could never be hospice to any on the road to Jerusalem.

The Deacon did not seem surprised at the coolness of the proposal, or flattered at the prospect. He closed his eyes, and lay back with weary face among his pillows, thinking painfully, and (shall it be chronicled?) Dr. Perfect, D.D., LL.D., was obliged to wait. It seemed to Mollie, as she sat on her low stool, fondling her father's hand, and watching, that the good gentleman had more at stake than appeared. Drops of sweat stood thick upon his knotted forehead, and the ponderous ministerial hand trembled visibly.

" The fact is," said he, breaking in on his parishioner's reverie, " I speak it in confidence, Mrs. Perfect and my-

19*

self would be loath to leave Millville; but the spiritual atmosphere of Roaring River, *graviora manent*, is lamentably uncongenial to the doctrines of holiness. *Sic itur ad astra.*"

"Tell me," said Mr. McCross, opening his eyes to bestow a keenly business-like glance on his would-be adviser, "will God thank me to leave a sin unrepented of, provided I will Him property enough to build a church?"

"*Rem acu tetigisti,*" quoth the Doctor, making a rapid calculation under cover of the Latin, of the advantages in Honesty the best Policy. "Almsdeeds are taught to be an expression of penitence. What better thing can a sinning man do than trust unlawful riches to the retributive hands of his Maker. *Spes tutissima cœlis.*"

"He can give them back, Dr. Perfect, and do his duty. I suppose you came here by my wife's advice?"

"Well—no," said the applicant unwillingly. "Mrs. McCross is so notoriously *nunquam non paratus* in deeds of charity, that I doubt not she would readily acquiesce in any disposition to the Lord you choose to make of your goods."

"Then I'll answer for her," said Deacon McCross. "She wouldn't let you have a penny, and you know it. I'll give you a hundred dollars, because I'm as wicked as you are; but my property is all disposed of. Daughter, hand me my cheque-book."

The ponderous dignity of the pastor brooked acceptance of the money. It went into his purse like a fly into a frog's mouth, and he departed with stately stride.

"Now Mollie," said her father gleefully, as she returned from seeing their visitor to the door, "I calculate that unless Pelican tackles me for his orphan asylum, I've said 'no' to the last one. Go and bring me my tin box and keys. Is your mother come home? Look and see."

She got them without a word, and watched him open and fumble among the tape-tied contents. He was thinking again,—over some effort that ought to be made; —hesitating, always hesitating.

Mollie wondered if he would have the strength to go on with it. She would not push him; it might make some little difference in human affairs. She didn't believe it would in divine pity.

No, the cost is too great. Big tears gather in the old man's eyes, and fall among the deeds and mortgages. "I meant to tell you, Mollie, but I can't," he said, brokenly. "Lock 'em up, and keep them yourself; and read them over and understand them with Louis, when I'm gone. He is a good boy. And daughter," bringing out the enforced cunning of a life's training, "fasten the drawer where you got them, so your mother can't get in—and stay! take them to-day to Squire Hitchcock. That is safest."

After the first shock of her husband's illness, his wife came and went irrespective of him, as before. She headed a colored prayer-meeting, and occupied herself collecting funds in aid of freedmen in Arkansas. She was too busy, far too busy, to bestow much thought or any care on the broken-hearted man slowly drifting into eternity.

This was, indeed, as Dr. Perfect said, a season of refreshing to the dying man and his devoted nurse. They created a little ideal world for themselves, and lived therein. He liked to wear an old-fashioned flowered dressing-gown and black velvet skull-cap, that his daughter made him after a description of some owned by an antiquated artist, seen in his youth. Thus arrayed he received Peace in her occasional calls from Cragenfels, where she was trying by systematic merry-making to drive away or grind out the unrest at her heart. Poor Peace! the packet of Johnnie Hauxhurst's friendly letters, results of the Kanterskill expedition, Chandy's jokes, and Sabrina's pleasant high bred companionship, had no power to make life seem worth while, or anything but a desolate, useless traversing of earth space. She herself did not know why she suffered; why the family disgraces were so bitter and life so profitless. But all the more she laid pitfalls for the "Widower," exasperated Charley, and turned them all to frolic. " Go to, now, I will prove thee with mirth; but this also is vanity."

Something of her unconfessed restlessness seemed to affect the paralytic, who, fond as he was of her bright face and flippant tongue, always breathed a sigh of relief at her departure. He thought over all the possible feminine wants that had come within his observation, and asked Mollie if she supposed money would be any comfort to her friend. Upon an affirmative he gave her enough to set up ten poor families in housekeeping, and more (Peace was at such work now); but the result did not justify his hopes.

It would have been a comfort to Mollie and her father if Francis Haythorne, who had returned to Millville, could have stayed at Fir Covert; but Mrs. McCross, conceiving that this might make her extra trouble, peremptorily refused her husband's meek request, and went on with her holiness meetings and spiritual work, with as much eagerness as ever.

As the spring deepened into summer, it became more and more plain that the sufferer's hours were numbered. He grew gradually too weak to bear removal from his bed, and spent his time singing hymns in a cracked voice, and looking at the blossoms he and Mollie had nursed so tenderly for years. There were certain plants old as his nurse herself—he had them stand in a row on the window-ledge, where he could see them every day. Two geraniums he selected from among them, which he said must be planted above his grave; and on the sticks that marked them, she found in faded writing the names "Louis and Mollie."

He used to make her read " A charge to keep I have," as a sort of penance, always pronouncing the last lines himself in his old-fashioned articulation :

> " Assoored if I my trust betray
> I shall forever die; "

and then the Psalm, " Blessed is the man whose transgression is forgiven, and whose sin is covered;" and, " Say unto Jerusalem that she hath received at the Lord's hand double for all her sins."

Sometimes they perused long stories together, Mollie selecting from her favorite shelf. She found her calculation of fitness oddly astray. Villette grated, and Hawthorne's reveries became trite on the ear of the fast fading spirit; not so John Halifax, always noble, sweet, and strong; he could not bear to wait for its end, and as his daughter read on, the wholesome trusting spirit of the book seemed to exorcise all the tangles in the skein of memory and anticipation. Mrs. McCross made no objections to the occupation beyond a disparaging glance, being otherwise intent. But her husband was more heedful of her occupations; and used regularly to inquire where she was, with every indication of anxiety, though he never wanted her near him. One day she brought Cabby home in attendance, and proceeded with vivacious enjoyment to feed him with cake and wine in the adjoining sitting-room.

The Deacon heard his thin affected vocables through the open door, and the old man's emaciated features flushed. "Tell him, Mollie—tell him that I—Elizur McCross, am a dying man, and don't want my last hours disturbed by him. Tell him when I'm dead he can come often as he likes, but not while I'm alive."

The old man's high-keyed, fretful wail sounded distinct in one room as the other, and Cabby, muttering something about going to be measured for boots, rose to depart; but this Mrs. McCross would not permit.

"Stay where you are and never mind him; I won't have him hen-huzzying around," she muttered, angrily; and Cabby required little urging to resume his seat.

The Deacon didn't reiterate his request. "They that dwell in mine house count me as a stranger; I am as an alien in their sight," said he, sadly. "You are all the comfort I have, daughter."

As the struggle between matter and spirit waxed fiercer, he grew querulous at times; and the fit past, counted his little personal possessions again and again to bestow them on the object of his harmless outbreaks; but the hymns and Bible readings proved unfailing source of rest.

It was not very long after the completion of Mrs. Craik's wonderful history, that the Deacon called his wife to his side, and stretched out his poor shaking hand for hers. "Mirandy," said he, feebly, "you and I did a great wrong once; since then our barns and storehouses have run over with fatness, but leanness has entered our souls. Cursed be he that perverteth the judgment of the fatherless; the Lord shall plead their cause."

Mrs. McCross returned no answer, but her small, thin features looked more tallowy than ever in the twilight.

"Mirandy," said her husband again, pleadingly, "there is still time to make it partly right. The money matter must all come out when I'm dead. I've put a memorandum of his property in the will, but the other—wife, I don't want to leave the world so, the burden is too heavy to bear—it was a cruel thing to send that boy to prison when we knew the real thief. It's not too late, if you'll consent to help that—think of Mollie."

Still no reply.

"My dear," his voice was almost a whisper now "won't you give up to ease a dying man?"

"Deacon McCross, I've always considered that money as fairly earned. Gold wouldn't pay for the trouble I took with him, and what little we've got I mean to keep. As for confessing any other nonsense—if you choose to, go to the jail and condone the faults of them two burglars and get 'em to leave your own ward to go where they belonged; you did it yourself; you've no right to mix up my good name with your double-dealing, in any way, shape or manner."

She stood glaring at him out of her faded eyes, that could only light up with one expression—malice.

The Deacon didn't entreat any longer. He turned his head away from this woman, the evil genius of his life, and a few minutes after said, still more feebly, "Will you call Mollie?"

Something, perhaps, in the lingering tenderness with which he dwelt on the name aroused the mother's ire.

"No, I won't," said she, peevish and self-asserting; "it's nothing but 'my daughter, my daughter,' from morning till night, I wonder if I'm no account in my own house! If you want medicines I'll give them."

A minute after a light footstep sounded in the doorway. "Mollie, Mollie," he called, "come quick, darling;" and then in a glad, free tone, "Oh, boys, school's out."

But hasten as she might, one was there before her, who brought him forth to his long holiday.

CHAPTER XXXIII.

"Mary, Mary, quite contrairy,
How does your garden grow?"

IT may chance that some people, who have hearts to take interest in the lower classes, are wondering about little Doppy. But it happened very naturally. Mollie had not been back from Top Town a week when the aggrieved damsel made her appearance. She had cried herself sick, looked thin and yellow; entering, her lip quivered at Mollie's greeting. She jerked off her bonnet, dropped sidewise into the first chair, and began without preface or explanation:

"An' have you seen Amos?"

"Not since I left Top Town—when he brought Zack."

"Oh, to bring Zack! with a toss of her head, an' much good it may do him. I'll be bound all his talk didn't run on the rooster."

"No, it ran on his tongue. The rooster had enough to do to carry himself," said Mollie, with a smile.

"Whitcht!" cried Doppy, aggrieved at the triviality. "I know what he talked about. Amos! Amos Daley, if I do say it, is too mean to live. He's selfish and he's cowardly and he's underhanded. Pooh! I know him. Haven't we tramped together these years?"

This being unanswerable, Mollie assumed the offensive.

Indeed, to tell the truth, at the bottom of her feminine soul, Miss McCross was a trifle out of patience with her charge. To her whose whole life was a sacrifice to love, it seemed so strange that Doppy, a woman with a heart as leal and warm as her own, should torture herself and the man she cared for in this way. How could she know what love was! argued Mollie, and not in all these years have learned that its very essence is self-abnegation.

"I must hear the story," said she, taking the firm little Irish hands in hers, and diving down into the depths of the open Irish soul with a friendly glance; "Amos always seemed a good boy."

"Yes, seemed!" Dorothea's voice took its highest key. "When you know him, same as I do, you'll tell another story; you're too easy imposed upon by half." But all the time the girl was yielding to Mollie's gentle tranquillity, and the last word died away in a sob. "It aint—anything—worth talking—on—only—only—sob—sob—I'm so miserable." She hid her face in her friend's lap, and cried convulsively, every tear washed cleaner her mental picture of the situation. It ain't much to tell," said she, sitting up at last and drying her eyes with her little cotton handkerchief, "but it's awful hard to bear. To have Amos, as I've tramped with sence we were no size, jilt me and take up with Mary Ellen Heffron, that don't care any more for him'n Jack—no, nor half so much." At this dreadful disclosure Doppy again betook herself to tears. "No, I ain't mistaken," seeing denial in Mollie's eyes; "it was this way : I sez to Amos, that Mary Ellen Heffron was without even wan partner, bad luck to her for a black flirt as she is, and I thought it would be nought but kind to show her some small attention, meanin' perhaps wan dance, and him to go on that and invite her for foor quadrilles—yes *foor*—leavin' me settin' by the wall the hull time, only I didn't; and then to ask to see her home! Suppose he tought me the lass to take up wid some of the lazy-bones he left; but that's not my way. 'I toold 'em to take care of themselves and let me lone; I didn't need them if Amos *had* got a simperin' miss to think of, and cut me."

"You did!" said Mollie severely, conscious of a certain picnic when Louis carried Peace rowing, and left her to set table.

Doppy's angry blushes paled to reappear shame-bidden; but she wouldn't give up.

"You must have treated Amos very ill. Tell me if you haven't been just as mean as you could be ever since that night?"

"Of course," said Doppy stoutly, "and I had a right. I always set out to treat every one just as they treat me."

"It's a poor rule that don't work both ways. What do you suppose Amos thinks of you?"

No woman wants to lose her lover's good opinion; its desire in such matters is her greatest power over herself. Doppy grew uneasy. "He's no business to act so. I meant to teach him better. Sure" (with a rueful smile) "you've often said I've the care of his edication."

"If you haven't taught him several things this time, it's not your fault." Mollie had the art of dealing in generalities. On occasions like the present, she made a few observations, not inapplicable, and left conscience to do the rest. This saved trouble to all parties. People who really are fit for advice, must have already taken considerable moral emetic. A trifle more will usually set matters right. There is another thing that born advisers—some are—do. With a hand touch their electric force puts them *en rapport* with the sufferer, and their mere will-power compels resolve. It isn't the best way. Its too frequent use exhausts the one, and destroys the soul poise of the other. Mollie was so afraid of disturbing Doppy's identity, that she loosened her warm hand clasp, and sat waiting. She wanted her protégée's decision to be one of principle, not result of her own overpowering influence.

"Mary Ellen Heffron looked mighty handsome leaning on his arm," was the audible conclusion of that damsel's mental struggle.

Nothing from Mollie.

"But I'm sorry I was so mean about dancing with Hugh Croslow, just to plague Amos. P'raps he couldn't help payin' her attention, bad luck to that same for makin' him."

"Mary Ellen Heffron sometimes takes in sewing—I bought Amos a dozen handkerchiefs in Top Town, but father's illness—"

"Miss Mollie," cried Doppy, starting to her feet, and setting her arms akimbo, energetic as hurt; "if you give them things to her, I'll just hate you, so there!"

The sequel is easily told. Amos, in a tumbled and seedy condition, but quite unable to keep away, must needs shamble by the "Solomon Rodgers," whistling very loud and looking into dim distance.

Doppy ironing the last of the set in the "dacent young couple's kitchen," glanced out of the window, and saw him. She had stitched all her anger into the hems, and made up her mind that to do his sewing was quite as much happiness as she deserved. At least it would make life a barely endurable burden. It wasn't Amos's fault that, being so perfectly desirable, the "black coquette" would entrap him. She must learn to live without own-

ing him, it seemed; but he should own her, anyway.
That was better than nothing.   She would mend his
clothes, and learn to exult in his conquests.

Her face reflected her changed feeling.   Meanwhile
Master Daley was past the middle of the opposite house.
Would he be always angry?   Would he refuse the handkerchiefs?   Would he say "I liked to take your work
because I cared for you, but I hate jealous people and
won't give up Mary Ellen."   But she was willing to have
him like Mary Ellen.   He'd see it if he looked that way.
But he didn't mean to—he should.

"Amos!"

Amos just in the midst of his careless tune, thought,
"I hate her just as much as I did, but I'll go over to the
other side, and hear what she has to say."   It couldn't
make any difference.   He would stare the other direction
to show his unconcern, and tie up his shoe by accident.

Doppy's courage all came back as he turned toward the
house.   It fell a little when he seemed so sullen.   There
was something dangerous about this quiet, determined,
albeit miserable, mien.   He had let her pull him about as
she pleased so far.   She had never seen him in this guise
before, so white and grim at once.

"Amos," faintly, "come in, I've got something for
you from Miss McCross."

"I'll take it through the window," with studied stolid-
ity, inside thought, "I won't have it patched up.   I ain't
a man to be jiggled all the time—seein' she don't care for
me."

"No, you won't," said Doppy, flashing out at the
idea that it was another woman's influence that thus
metamorphosed "her boy."   "If you have taken up with
that contemptuous Heffron girl, an' so thrown me over-
board that you can't pay attention enough to enter my

doors, you shan't have 'em." Whereupon she did them small in a grab, threw the bundle at his head, and slammed the window.

Before Amos knew it, he had reached the kitchen, handkerchiefs in hand, and, setting his back against the inside of the door, exclaimed : " Dorothea Mulligan, I can't take them things wid your work on 'em, an' you feelin' as you do."

It wasn't the anger, though he was angry, it was the sorrowful dignity of his words that awed her. His voice, deep, and earnest, thrilled her. He didn't act—well, as she had fancied and feared. She wished he would show passion, and so put them on even terms. But there he stood quiet, unyielding, resolved.

" Amos, I don't feel no way," said she, nervously.

" *I* didn't at first, but I do now," firm as a rock in sense of wrong.

Doppy couldn't let it go on so. " I ain't mad, Amos," imploring him with tone and gesture. " If you like Mary Ellen best, I ain't goin' to stand between."

" I don't care nothin' for her," he answered in his slow way, "but I think of my manhood. I can't be drawed off an' on like a glove, Doppy, or mayhap an old shoe. Though there's no weariness I've not been proud to save your feet. I must have my place all the time. I'm awkward and ugly, but if I've any value to you, I must hold it for always, lettin' none push between."

" If Amos was a fool, Doppy wasn't. Plainly there was a mistake somewhere. " I hain't let nobody between. You danced wid Mary Ellen, an' oh, Amos, you looked as if you liked it."

Master Daley seeing the wicked deceiver growing rosy, and gazing modestly at the floor, was conscience-stricken, but he wouldn't give up; he had suffered too much.

"Do you like me best?" said he, coldly.

"That depends altogether on the depth of your affection for the Heffron," said provoking beauty.

But Amos wasn't versed in the ways of women or flirts. He was refused an answer to a plain question. He would go—forever; the sooner the better. He dropped the handkerchiefs unconsciously, and opened the door. "I despise *her*, and I *hate*—"

"Not me," cried Doppy, rushing at him, dragging him back, and jamming the latch fast, all in a breath. "Now sit down, Amos. Was there ever such a man! Of course you're first. I thought you knew it."

THE END.

1875. 1875.

NEW BOOKS

AND NEW EDITIONS,

RECENTLY ISSUED BY

G. W. CARLETON & Co., Publishers,

Madison Square, New York.

The Publishers, upon receipt of the price in advance, will send any book on this Catalogue by mail, *postage free*, to any part of the United States.

All books in this list [unless otherwise specified] are handsomely bound in cloth board binding, with gilt backs, suitable for libraries.

Mary J. Holmes' Works.

Tempest and Sunshine	$1 50	Darkness and Daylight	$1 50
English Orphans	1 50	Hugh Worthington	1 50
Homestead on the Hillside	1 50	Cameron Pride	1 50
'Lena Rivers	1 50	Rose Mather	1 50
Meadow Brook	1 50	Ethelyn's Mistake	1 50
Dora Deane	1 50	Millbank	1 50
Cousin Maude	1 50	Edna Browning	1 50
Marian Gray	1 50	West Lawn..........(new)	1 50

Marion Harland's Works.

Alone	$1 50	Sunnybank	$1 50
Hidden Path	1 50	Husbands and Homes	1 50
Moss Side	1 50	Ruby's Husband	1 50
Nemesis	1 50	Phemie's Temptation	1 50
Miriam	1 50	The Empty Heart	1 50
At Last	1 50	Jessamine	1 50
Helen Gardner	1 50	From My Youth Up (new)	1 50
True as Steel.....(new)	1 50		

Charles Dickens' Works.

The Pickwick Papers	$1 50	Martin Chuzzlewit	$1 50
Oliver Twist	1 50	Our Mutual Friend	1 50
David Copperfield	1 50	Tale of Two Cities	1 50
Great Expectations	1 50	Christmas Books	1 50
Dombey and Son	1 50	Sketches by " Boz."	1 50
Barnaby Rudge	1 50	Hard Times, etc	1 50
Nicholas Nickleby	1 50	Pictures of Italy, etc	1 50
Old Curiosity Shop	1 50	Uncommercial Traveller, etc	1 50
Bleak House	1 50	Edwin Drood, etc	1 50
Little Dorrit	1 50	Child's England, and Catalogue	1 50

Augusta J. Evans' Novels.

Beulah	$1 75	St. Elmo	$2 00
Macaria	1 75	Vashti.....(new)	2 00
Inez	1 75		

Miriam Coles Harris.

Rutledge	$1 50	The Sutherlands	$1 50
Frank Warrington	1 50	St. Philip's	1 50
Louie's Last Term, etc	1 50	Round Hearts, for Children	1 50
Richard Vandermarck	1 50	A Perfect Adonis.—(New)	1 50

May Agnes Fleming's Novels.

Guy Earlscourt's Wife	$1 75	A Wonderful Woman	$1 75
A Terrible Secret (new)	1 75		

Julie P. Smith's Novels.

Widow Goldsmith's Daughter	$1 75	The Widower	$1 75
Chris and Otho	1 75	The Married Belle	1 75
Ten Old Maids (new)	1 75	Courting and Farming. (In press)	1 75

Captain Mayne Reid—Illustrated.

Scalp Hunters	$1 50	White Chief	$1 50
War Trail	1 50	Headless Horseman	1 50
Hunter's Feast	1 50	Lost Lenore	1 50
Tiger Hunter	1 50	Wood Rangers	1 50
Osceola, the Seminole	1 50	Wild Huntress	1 50
The Quadroon	1 50	The Maroon	1 50
Rangers and Regulators	1 50	Rifle Rangers	1 50
White Gauntlet	1 50	Wild Life	1 50

A. S. Roe's Works.

A Long Look Ahead	$1 50	True to the Last	$1 50
To Love and to be Loved	1 50	Like and Unlike	1 50
Time and Tide	1 50	Looking Around	1 50
I've Been Thinking	1 50	Woman Our Angel	1 50
The Star and the Cloud	1 50	The Cloud on the Heart	1 50
How Could He Help It	1 50	Resolution (new)	1 50

Hand-Books of Society.

Habits of Good Society.—The nice points of taste and good manners	$1 50
Art of Conversation.—For those who wish to be agreeable talkers or listeners	1 50
Arts of Writing, Reading and Speaking.—For self-instruction	1 50
New Diamond Edition.—Small size, elegantly bound, 3 volumes in a box	3 00

Mrs. Hill's Cook Book.

Mrs. A. P. Hill's New Cookery Book, and family domestic receipts	$2 00

Famous Books—"Star Edition."

Robinson Crusoe.—Elegant new edition, illustrated by Gustave Doré	$1 50
Swiss Family Robinson.	Do.	Do.	Do.	1 50
The Arabian Nights.	Do.	Do.	Do.	1 50

Don Quixote.

A Beautiful New 12mo Edition.—With illustrations by Gustave Doré	$1 50

Victor Hugo.

Les Miserables.—English translation from the French. Octavo	$2 50
Les Miserables.—In the Spanish language. Two volumes, cloth bound	5 00

Popular Italian Novels.

Doctor Antonio.—A love story of Italy. By Ruffini	$1 75
Beatrice Cenci.—By Guerrazzi. With a steel engraving from Guido's picture	1 75
Battle of Benevento.—By the Author of "Beatrice Cenci." (new)	1 75

M. Michelet's Remarkable Works.

Love (L'amour).—English translation from the original French	$1 50
Woman (La Femme). Do. Do. Do.	1 50

Popular Novels, from the French.

She Loved Him Madly.—Borys	$1 75	So Fair Yet False.—By Chavette	$1 75
A Fatal Passion —By Bernard.	1 75	Through Thick and Thin.—Mery	1 75
Led Astray.—Octave Feuillet	1 75		

www.ingramcontent.com/pod-product-compliance
Lightning Source LLC
Chambersburg PA
CBHW022028110726
47901CB00006B/1685